P9-DSY-215

What the critics are saying…

"…a wonderful story of a young woman coming of age and finding herself in spite of horrendous circumstances…It is a story of second chances, love, laughter, and romance complete with a historic setting." ~ *Ansley Velarde for The Road to Romance*

"This isn't a typical romantic story. The pain and torment Colette must endure is so tragic. She is a very strong heroine…and Philippe is a compassionate hero. *Seduction of Colette* is a sad and thought-provoking story of the journey to true love." ~ *Renee Sizzling Romance*

"Ms. Thompson has penned a wonderful story of survival and love that all women should read. I found myself crying about what happened to Colette but in the end I was cheering. Bravo Ms. Thompson!" ~ *Angela Black Sensual Romance*

"This story gives you all the heart and soul a story can give… brings the reader to the brink and then draws them back from the edge. The characters captivate the reader from the beginning…highly recommended…if you like dark erotic stories." ~ *Dawn Love Romances*

"Dark and erotic, the SEDUCTION OF COLETTE is an excellent addition to Ms. Thompson's repertoire." ~ *Liz Ragland-Thompson Romance Reviews Today*

CLAIRE THOMPSON
LEDA SWANN

LESSONS
IN
Seduction

ELLORA'S CAVE
ROMANTICA PUBLISHING

An Ellora's Cave Romantica Publication

www.ellorascave.com

Lessons in Seduction

ISBN # 1419952609
ALL RIGHTS RESERVED.
School for Virgins Copyright© 2004 Leda Swann
Seduction of Colette Copyright© 2004 Claire Thompson
Edited by: Briana St. James
Cover art by: Syneca

Electronic book Publication:
School for Virgins August, 2004
Seduction of Colette March, 2004
Trade paperback Publication: November, 2005

Excerpt from *Sunlit* Copyright © Leda Swann, 2004

With the exception of quotes used in reviews, this book may not be reproduced or used in whole or in part by any means existing without written permission from the publisher, Ellora's Cave Publishing, Inc.® 1056 Home Avenue, Akron OH 44310-3502.

This book is a work of fiction and any resemblance to persons, living or dead, or places, events or locales is purely coincidental. The characters are productions of the authors' imagination and used fictitiously.

Warning:

The following material contains graphic sexual content meant for mature readers. *Lessons in Seduction* has been rated *S-ensuous* by a minimum of three independent reviewers.

Ellora's Cave Publishing offers three levels of Romantica™ reading entertainment: S (S-ensuous), E (E-rotic), and X (X-treme).

S-*ensuous* love scenes are explicit and leave nothing to the imagination.

E-*rotic* love scenes are explicit, leave nothing to the imagination, and are high in volume per the overall word count. In addition, some E-rated titles might contain fantasy material that some readers find objectionable, such as bondage, submission, same sex encounters, forced seductions, etc. E-rated titles are the most graphic titles we carry; it is common, for instance, for an author to use words such as "fucking", "cock", "pussy", etc., within their work of literature.

X-*treme* titles differ from E-rated titles only in plot premise and storyline execution. Unlike E-rated titles, stories designated with the letter X tend to contain controversial subject matter not for the faint of heart.

Contents

School for Virgins

Leda Swann

Chapter One

Jack Langton unbuttoned his breeches to allow his rampant cock to break free. He stepped out of them with a sigh of relief and let them fall carelessly to the rug. Ah, that felt better. He'd had an erection ever since he walked in the door of his mistress's small but tastefully furnished apartment in St John's Wood and it was starting to get uncomfortably pressing. He'd had a frustrating day, a day in which none of his deals had come to anything, and he was more than ready for a good, hard fuck. The fact that he intended this to be the last visit he ever paid here only added a certain piquancy to the situation, and made him more eager even than usual to get to the point.

His mistress, Marie, was already on hands and knees in front of him on the bed, her smooth, white rump raised invitingly into the air. The glimpse of her pussy, its bush neatly trimmed, and the little round pink pucker of her asshole nestled in the cleft between her buttocks, made him hot enough to shrug off his jacket and pull open his cravat in record time.

Shirttails flapping around his privates, he climbed up on to the bed behind her and ran one exploratory hand between her legs. She shook herself enticingly and gave an encouraging moan as his fingers rubbed gently at the lips of her cleft. "Mmmm, zat feels delicious."

The husky timbre of her voice turned him on even more, as the little witch knew it did. Marie was by no means a spectacular beauty, but she had other compensations. Her sexy French accent, for one, which never failed to make his cock stand to attention. And the expert way she used her mouth, for another. He felt his cock grow as hard as steel. The sight of her naked bottom, waiting for his cock, combined with the thought of the

11

inventive ways she had with her tongue, was almost enough to make him come before he had hardly even touched her.

He obliged her by letting his hand explore a little more, inserting his fingers gently into her cunt, and pumping them back and forth until she moaned again. God, but she was wet in there. She felt as randy and as ready to be fucked as he was to fuck her. He liked that in a woman.

Without any more fuss, he settled himself between her legs and thrust his cock deeply into her. A woman's cunt, he thought to himself, as he pumped furiously in and out of her with an avid desperation, must be as close to Heaven as any man could get in this world.

She urged him on, grabbing a bedpost with both hands for support and bucking under him enthusiastically.

He held on to her by the shoulders and pulled her toward him, making sure that he thrust into her as hard and as deep as he could possibly go. A wild ride was just what he needed to chase the cares of the day away. He wanted only to lose himself for a few moments inside her soft, warm body.

In just a few minutes of frenzied pumping, he was ready to come. He urged himself on harder and faster until, with a hoarse cry of satisfaction, he spilled his seed deep into her.

Replete for the moment, he rolled off her and lay on his back on the bed to let his breathing settle back down to its normal rate.

Marie rolled over and lay on her back next to him, her face as calm and serene as ever. In comparison to his labored breaths, her lungs seemed hardly affected at all.

He reached over and patted her thigh affectionately. As usual, she had completely satisfied him. "That was good. I needed that."

She gave a slight laugh. "I could tell zat much. You are not usually in such a rush. You came inside me in such a hurry zat I hardly had time to enjoy myself before, pouf, you were gone again."

He shrugged, not really caring. She was well-paid, and besides, he kept her for *his* enjoyment, not for her own. If she received physical pleasure from their liaison, that was a bonus for her as far as he was concerned, not part of their agreement. Their arrangement was simple enough—he furnished her with a house to live in and paid her bills, and she gave him access to her body whenever and however it pleased him. It had suited him well over the past five years, though it was now time to draw it to a close.

She pouted at his lack of conversation and drew one hand idly across his stomach. "You are serious tonight. Serious and silent." She hesitated for a moment before continuing. "Somezing is weighing on your mind?"

"Maybe," he grunted. Considering he had committed himself elsewhere, or rather promised to commit himself elsewhere, he had to tell her that her services were no longer necessary. Now that he was side by side with her, however, it was not as easy to get the words out as he had imagined it would be.

The tone of his voice evidently aroused her suspicions. She sat up, gathering the sheets around her breasts as if to protect herself from the blow that she could see coming. "Are you planning to leave me?" Her voice shook just a little as she spoke.

He stayed lying flat on his back. This way he didn't have to look at her and see the hurt or disappointment in her eyes. "Yes. As a matter of fact, I am."

There was silence for a moment before she gave a shaky laugh. "Ah, I see. I knew it would happen eventually. Have you tired of me at last?"

He'd not consciously asked himself that question before, but now he thought about it, he discovered he *was* tired of her. The sex this evening had been good, as it always was, but that was all he would miss about her. They shared nothing more intimate than those few frenzied moments of passion as they fucked, and a slightly uncomfortable aftermath when he really only wanted to summon the energy to get out of bed and escape.

Still, he had no wish to hurt her feelings. "You've been a good mistress to me these five years," he prevaricated. "I will be sorry to lose you."

"Then you are planning to get married?" she asked matter-of-factly. "And you need to uninstall your mistress before you install your wife?"

He raised his eyebrows. He'd thought that few people knew about his plans to take a wife. Gossip evidently traveled fast in this part of London. St John's Wood was notorious as a haven for the kept women of wealthy men. "Have you heard my news already?"

She shook her head. "That is always the way of it. Men leave their mistresses for a bright young wife, and then return to them a year later when the newness of their new plaything has worn off."

He objected to being put in the same class as every other man. His situation was quite different. "I have promised that I will wed the daughter of a friend of mine. Considering my promise, it would be in bad taste to continue our liaison."

"You are no different from other men. You will be back," she predicted confidently.

It was his turn to shake his head. He wouldn't be back. Even if his new wife turned out to be a disappointment in the marriage bed, he would stay true to her. "No. I am truly not going to return." One thing he knew for certain, if he were ever to take leave of his senses and stray from his marriage bed, it would not be with Marie.

She stayed silent, wrapped in the bedclothes and in her own thoughts. "The house?" she prompted eventually.

"It's yours." He had seen his lawyer that morning and arranged it. He owed her that much.

His words brought a genuine smile to her face that nothing else had done. "Thank you. You are very generous."

He shrugged. The expense was little enough and she had been a faithful mistress, keeping him entertained and well-satisfied whenever he had need of her. "You're welcome."

She let the sheets drift down her body, exposing the pink tips of her breasts. "I have enjoyed our time together. You have been good to me."

He felt unaccountably pleased that she had enjoyed their lovemaking. "You liked having me in your bed?"

She shrugged. "It was not so bad. But you have never beaten me or shouted at me or wanted to share me with your friends—and I liked that. I can't persuade you to stay?"

Her lack of enthusiasm reinforced his decision to go. "No."

She lowered her head to his chest, until she was resting against him. "You're sure you won't be back?"

"I'm sure."

She lowered her head further, until her breath was hot against his flaccid cock. Though he was utterly satiated, he still felt himself stir at the nearness of her. "Then I will have to say goodbye to you in style," she said, and she took him into her mouth.

There was no reason he couldn't enjoy her one last time, he decided, as his cock sprang to life once more under the expert sucking she was giving him. No reason at all.

* * * * *

Helen Fairchild surveyed the trio of anxious mothers perched like sparrows in a nervous row on the ottoman in front of her. Somehow or other she needed to soothe their fears. They were the roof over her head and every morsel of food she ate.

"You'll teach my Clarissa everything she needs to know?" the eldest of the three, a nervous-looking woman with a tic that rhythmically creased the corner of her mouth, asked her with an anxious air. "Her intended is not the man I would have chosen for her—his past is rather shady and he has a wild reputation,

15

you know—but my husband insists that she must accept him and she seems happy enough with the arrangement."

Helen clasped the older woman's hand tightly in hers. "I'll teach her everything I know—everything that your dear aunt ever taught me and more besides. I guarantee she'll learn her lessons so well that her husband will never stray from her side."

"And you won't ever let Mr. Harbottoms know what you teach our daughter in your classes?" asked a stout lady in a bright blue gown cinched tightly in at the waist. "My dear husband is a sainted man, but he would never forgive me for it if he were ever to find out. He thinks Hermione is coming to you for deportment lessons."

"I will be as discreet as always," Helen promised. "And enjoin on your daughters the need to keep what they learn a secret from everyone. Until, of course," she said with a small smile, "they have daughters of their own to carry on the tradition."

"Naturally you will ensure that they are not encouraged in lewdness and debauchery?" the third woman asked, pushing her thin-rimmed glasses up on her nose with a bony finger. Though she was the youngest of the three, her narrow, stooped shoulders, gray hair, and the look of permanent disapproval etched into her face, made her look a generation older than her companions. "I would have Annabelle well-educated in all matters she might need to know, but as a spinster I am ill-placed to teach her myself. I must insist, however, that she comes into contact with nothing but lessons with a good moral, Christian bent."

"I assure you that my lessons are free from all lewdness." Helen composed her face to the look of moral piety she had practiced for so many hours in front of the looking-glass. She knew this type of woman only too well, but she had to win them over if she was to have any hope of increasing her business as she wanted to. "I teach your girls only how they may best please their husbands—with due respect for piety and sobriety."

The third lady gave a small harrumph. "My friends assure me that you have the highest moral character and that your reputation is beyond reproach, or I would never have entertained the idea of sending my niece to you. I would not have Annabelle bring a bad name on her family. And with a mother like hers, I cannot be too careful of the development of her moral fiber."

Annabelle's mother had become pregnant by her husband's seventeen-year-old footman and had run off with him to the continent, leaving behind her grieving husband with their young daughter. At the time, it had been the scandal of the Season. Helen would venture to guess that she wasn't the only person who still remembered it as clearly as if it had been yesterday. "I will take care of your niece as carefully as if she were my own daughter."

The spinster gave a nod of acknowledgement. "Twenty guineas, then?" she said, as she drew a small bag out of her reticule.

Helen gave a sigh of relief. Another customer won over. Another few pounds to be paid off her loan. Another few steps on her road to an independent living. "Twenty guineas in advance, and another five at the completion of the lessons," she confirmed.

The women, their fears laid to rest and their deposits paid, soon took their leave.

Once they had been safely escorted out of the door, Helen clutched the gold with delight. Sixty guineas felt heavy when they all lay in her hand at once.

She took five of the heavy gold coins out of one of the bags and laid them on the mantel shelf, looked at them for a minute with her head on one side, and then reluctantly returned one to the bag again.

Four guineas would be enough for her to live on until the next batch of girls started. Four guineas meant no coal for any fire but the one in the schoolroom and no meat from the butcher, but they were luxuries she could do without. If she only spent four guineas, that left fifty-six guineas for her debt.

Those fifty-six guineas that had seemed so heavy in her hand when she had earned them made a very small pile of shining gold on the desk of her banker the next morning.

He looked at the paltry stack of coins on his desk with a sniff. "Fifty-five guineas, did you say?" His voice was dry and dusty, like a book that had sat too long unread on a bookshelf.

"Fifty-six," Helen corrected him.

He raised an eyebrow as if the last guinea, that represented no small sacrifice on Helen's part to do without, was of supreme unimportance to a man such as himself. "Fifty-six then."

He wrote it down in a column, totted up the figures, and then sat back and looked at her with a glint in his eye that made Helen squirm in her seat. "That leaves you just three hundred and twenty pound, seven shilling and sixpence remaining on your account. A large sum of money for a single young woman to owe to her bankers."

"A sum of money that I am paying back as I was required to do when you agreed to lend me the money to set up my school," Helen reminded him, not liking the tone of his last comment. "I have not missed a single payment."

He steepled his fingers together. "True."

"And I continue to repay you faster even than you demanded. You were due only fifty guineas this quarter."

"Remarkable for such a young woman. I never would have thought it possible. Still, circumstances being as they are…"

Her uneasiness was growing by the second. "What circumstances?"

"The bank has made some losses lately." He shrugged his shoulders noncommittally. "An aggressive loan here and there, unwise investments in a series of South Seas schemes. All in all, the balance sheet does not look as healthy as it should." He paused, waiting for the import of his words to sink in. "As manager of the bank, it is my duty to retrench, to reevaluate, and to call in all the loans that, although they were acceptable at the time they were made, now represent an unacceptable risk of loss to the bank."

Helen felt a cold shiver run down her spine. "You would not call in my loan?"

He gave a dry cough. "Your loan is among those that I have identified for termination. I regret to say that I must insist on a speedy repayment of all monies we have advanced to you."

All her worst fears were suddenly realized. She hardly had the strength to speak. "When?"

"By four o'clock this afternoon."

Helen's soul collapsed into a puddle of despair. "That's impossible," she whispered, more to herself than to him. "I can't do it."

He let out a satisfied sigh. "I'm too kindhearted for my own good, but I can't bear to see a lady in distress. I shall let you have until ten o'clock tomorrow morning. It's the best I can do."

She raised her head and looked into his eyes, but saw no mercy in them. "And if I can't pay you? What then?"

A smile curled his lip, but didn't reach his eyes. "Then you must go to the place where all people who can't pay their debts go. Debtor's prison."

She shuddered with horror, already feeling the cold, thin fingers of prison scrabbling toward her. She would not go back there, into that slimy pit of filth and corruption, where every good human instinct was buried under the need to survive. Her soul would not survive such torture. Her only hope would be to die before she lost all her reason. "No." Her breath caught in her throat so she could barely get out the words. "Not that."

The banker leaned over his desk and took hold of Helen's hand in his clammy fingers. "A beautiful woman such as yourself need never find herself in that hellhole," he rasped. "You have options."

A glimmer of hope, mixed with suspicion, broke through her despair. "I do? Will you give me more time to pay?" She didn't think she would like any of the options he might present to her, but they had to be better than debtor's prison. Any would be better than that. Anything at all.

He paddled the palm of her hand with his fingers, his raggedly cut fingernails catching on her skin. "You have a good payment record. I could be persuaded to be lenient." The tone of his voice made it only too clear what he meant.

She closed her eyes with distaste, but that only made her feel the oppression of debtor's prison lie more heavily on her. With a supreme effort of will, she opened them again. Whatever happened, she would face it head on, with her eyes open. "How?"

Her banker grinned, showing a line of uneven, yellow teeth. "You would have to be nice to me."

She felt a familiar deadness cramp her insides. She'd hoped never to have to revisit this part of her life again. "How nice?"

He licked his lips, leaving a slimy tidemark of saliva on his chin. "Undoing your buttons for me would be a pleasant start."

With a deliberate movement, she started to undo the buttons of her bodice. She would not show her fear or distaste. She knew from bitter experience that any sign of weakness would be exploited by her tormentor for his own gain.

His eyes were glinting with a greedy lust as she opened her buttons one by one. "Take your bodice off." A trickle of saliva ran out of the corner of his mouth and dropped onto his shirtfront.

She pushed her bodice off her shoulders, letting her breasts swing free, and making her nipples pucker up in the cool morning air.

"God, how I've dreamed about this. Your boobies are so pretty." His breathing had quickened, and his knuckles were white with tension. "Touch yourself for me."

She took the weight of her full breasts in her hands, mechanically caressing the bare skin, and lightly pinching the nipples between her finger and thumb to make them stand to attention. She'd worked out his game all right. His tactics were only too transparent, but effective nonetheless. He had her caught.

If she refused to play along with his game, he would likely call in her loan and force her into debtor's prison. She could not afford to call his bluff. She would not survive going to prison again.

If she agreed to be his mistress, he would not call in her loan. At least not yet. Of course, there was no guarantee that he wouldn't call in her loan in the future, when he was tired of her. And if there was even the slightest whisper that she was not as good as she should be, her reputation would be ruined, her customers would desert her faster than if she had the plague, and her school would tumble around her ears faster than a house of cards in a draught. There was no security in going down that road.

She had thrown off her old life so completely that nothing of it had remained. She was now Helen Fairchild, respectable widow, and headmistress of a small finishing school that catered to London's aristocracy and the wealthiest of the merchant classes. She had fought bitterly hard and sacrificed more than she cared to remember to attain this much. Was this how she was to lose her reputation, her school, and everything she had worked so desperately for? At the hands of a grubby old man, blackmailing her into his bed?

No, she was a fighter. She wasn't going to play his game if she could help it. She would give in to him now — but only to win herself the time she needed to defeat him.

He was breathing harder now, his lungs sounding like an old pair of bellows as they forced air through his windpipe. The legs of his chair grated against the wooden floor as he pushed out from behind the desk for a better view of his victim.

"Pull your skirt up," he ordered in a voice cracked with delight, "and let me have a look at your legs."

Helen pulled her skirt up to her thighs and spread her knees wide apart. She knew what he wanted to see, and knew also that the knowledge of the power he had over her was a potent aphrodisiac to a man like him. She would forestall his orders where she could, and deprive him of the pleasure of giving them to her.

"Touch yourself. Play with yourself. I want to see you pleasure yourself."

Helen brought her hand to her mound and began to stroke herself, but she was too tense for her juices to start flowing. She was dry and barren. Her fingers rasped her delicate skin, and there was no pleasure in it for her.

He'd undone the buttons on his breeches and freed his engorged cock to wave in the breeze. "Moan a bit, my sweet little cherry. I want to hear as well as see you pleasure yourself."

Helen obliged with a perfunctory moan as she continued to stroke herself. Despite her tension and the mechanical nature of her caresses, she was starting to enjoy herself. It had been too long since she had pleasured herself in this way, and even longer since she had had a man to pleasure her. Without being asked, she picked up the pace of her caresses, lightly pinching her nipples, teasing her sensitive bud with featherlight touches, and delving into the wetness of her cunt with a growing enthusiasm.

She hardly noticed the movement of the banker's hands as he stroked his cock up and down, its huge purple head glistening with drops of his excitement. All her attention was focused on the growing demands of her own body.

Her hand was slick with wetness now, soothing the heat of the friction of her questing hands. Her heart was pounding in her breast and her breath felt labored. The sound of her breathing and her small gasps of enjoyment were all she could hear.

The tension in the pit of her belly built to an unbearable pitch, until with a quick gasp of achievement she surrendered to the little pulses of relief that released her.

She'd beaten the banker to enjoyment. His face was still contorted with a desperate desire as he rubbed his cock frantically up and down, grunting to himself with the pleasure of it.

Just as she let her skirts down to cover her naked belly and mound and thighs, his breathing stopped for a moment and his white seed splattered out between his legs to soak into the wooden floor at his feet.

"You were born to be a whore." His voice was thick with repletion, and he grinned with sated delight as he tucked his limp, dripping member back into his breeches again. "Most young ladies like you need a stint in debtor's prison before they satisfy me as well as that."

Helen felt ill at the sight of the sordid satisfaction he had obtained at her expense. One way or another, she would make him pay for calling her a whore.

He gave a dry chuckle. "I've been waiting for this moment ever since I first saw you. I agreed to lend you money because I was sure you would never be able to pay it back again. I was wrong. I thought you would be begging me for more time to pay after the end of a week, but you forced me to take drastic measures. You are such a luscious little morsel that I couldn't wait any longer for you."

Helen felt sicker than ever. How cleverly he with his twisted little mind had managed to manipulate her, first getting her into his power, and then using her for his pleasure.

"I shall look forward to our little meetings to discuss your debt. Come to me again next Tuesday at the same time. Since I am in a generous mood, I shall give you a whole week's grace for your delightful performance today, though I don't know how I will do without seeing you again before then."

She walked home with a determined step. She had a week's grace. Surely she would be able to find a financier to take a chance on her within that time. The sum she needed was so paltry, her expenses were as low as she could make them, and the earnings from her school were good. She would not go to debtor's prison, but neither would she prostitute herself to that disgusting little man again.

If she could not raise the money, she would run. She would have to reinvent herself once more: take a new name, invent a new family tree, dye her hair, change her accent, take to wearing spectacles, and open a new school. Bath or York would be good places—they both possessed a good society of people with money who would pay handsomely to have their girls suitably "finished". The thought of starting over again was too daunting to dwell on for long, but if she had to, she would be prepared.

By the end of the fifth day of grace, Bath or York were looking more and more attractive.

Her three new pupils were no trouble—they were amenable enough to her teaching, though slow to learn. She doubted they would ever fascinate their new husbands with their gymnastic abilities in the bedroom, but they ought to be satisfying enough.

More worryingly, she had not located a single banker who would hear her out, let alone agree to lending her the money she needed. They all gave her the exact same answer—they did not lend money to young, single women. If she had a husband to stand behind her, then maybe, just maybe, they would be able to consider her proposal. But as it was, their hands were tied. Every bank policy was that no loans were to be made to single women.

By late on Monday, she was growing desperate. She mounted the steps to the last financier on her list with a determined air. If she had no success here, she would go straight to buy a ticket on the train for early the next morning. If she could not pay her debts, she would run from them.

"I am here to see Mr. Langton on important business," she announced to the young clerk in the outer office.

He lifted his head from the huge ledger in front of him and looked at her with a short-sighted frown. "Is he expecting you?"

"On important, urgent business. I need to see him now."

The clerk rose to his feet. "I will see if he is free to see you, Mrs...?" He waited for her to supply her name.

She remained silent, crossing her arms in front of her and tapping the toe of her boot on the ground to indicate her impatience.

Cowed by her manner, the clerk scuttled off into an inner office, only to return a moment later with a chastened look on his face. "Mr. Langton is otherwise occupied this afternoon, but he will make an appointment to see you later in the week if that would suit you."

She ignored his words. With a determined step, she marched past him to the inner office, walked smartly in, and shut the door behind her with a bang.

The man behind the desk looked up with a scowl on his face. "I'm busy. Come back and see me on Friday if you must."

She assessed him with a rapid, but calculating, gaze. He was quite handsome, despite his scowl. He wore his thick, dark hair longer than was fashionable and his shoulders were broad and muscular. Powerful, and not too concerned with what the rest of the world thought about him, she would guess. "I said I have urgent business. Friday will be too late."

She had his attention now. He tossed aside his pen, drew his watch out of his fob pocket and laid it down on the table in front of him. "You have five minutes. Use them well."

He was evidently in no mood for pleasantries. She might as well just get down to business. "I need to borrow three hundred and twenty pound, seven shilling and sixpence. Tonight."

She considered herself an expert on reading body language, but she could make nothing of his. Even his voice was dispassionate as he asked, "On what security?"

At least he hadn't refused her outright simply because she was a woman. Maybe, just maybe, she would not have to decamp to Bath in the morning after all. "The ten-year lease of a house in Belgrave Square."

He drummed his fingers on the desk. "How long do you need the money for?"

She made a quick mental calculation. "I will repay you over the next five years in quarterly payments."

Still his face was impassive, unreadable. "What interest rate are you prepared to offer?"

She named a generous, but not overly generous, rate. "Six percent."

"Why do you need the money?"

She thought of the banker's dry hands and shuddered. "I had borrowed it from another institution. They are calling in my loan."

A look of distaste swept briefly over his face. "I presumed as much. What do you need the money for? To pay off your gambling debts?"

The patronizing tone of his last comment grated on her nerves. "I run a finishing school for young ladies of good birth and education who are about to be married. I needed to borrow money to set up the school, and so far it has given me—and my previous banker—an excellent return." She pushed a thick ledger across the desk toward him. "Here are the accounts for the last two years that you may check for yourself."

He leafed through the pages, a frown of intense concentration on his face. Helen waited in an agony of impatience for him to finish. Her school was highly profitable, and could be made more so. She hoped that he could read the story of hard work that lay behind the bald figures in the rows of ledgers.

Finally he closed the book and sat back in his chair. "Three hundred and thirty odd pounds over five years at six percent to run a fashionable finishing school?" He shook his head. "You may have fallen right out of favor by next season. The odds aren't worth it."

She'd prepared herself for this reaction and had allowed herself room to maneuver. "You are in no danger of losing your money—the lease on the house is worth more than double the loan I'm asking for."

"What use is a ten-year lease on a house to me? I already have a house."

"Seven percent then, if you insist."

He lounged back in his chair and put his hands behind his head. "I'm a financier, not a banker. The odd percent or two interest on a loan makes little difference to me."

He was bargaining with her, not turning her down. That in itself made her hope they would reach an agreement. "What would make the difference?"

His answer was immediate. "A half-share in your school."

She had not been expecting this and the shock of it startled her into rudeness. "A half-share in my school? That is worth ten times more than the paltry sum I need to borrow."

He opened a drawer of his desk and counted out a gleaming heap of gold coins which he stacked just within reach of her fingertips. "I'll advance you four hundred pound immediately as a down payment on a half-share in your school."

She narrowed her eyes. He had better not think she would sell half her precious school for a song just because she needed the money so badly. "How much are you offering for your half-share?"

He picked up his pen and scribbled a few notes to himself before coming up with a figure that made her gasp.

Still she hesitated before answering him. She hated to give up control of her school, but the money he was offering would be a real boon. With the extra capital, she could pay herself a decent living allowance and even afford to hire assistants and expand her services without falling once more into the power of lecherous bastards like her banker. If he would be content to be a sleeping partner in the school, this might just work.

"Take it or leave it — those are my terms."

She temporized to gain herself a little extra breathing space. "How involved would you want to be in the running of the school?"

He gave a bark of laughter. "I'm a financier, not a dancing master. You will continue to run the school — and be paid a respectable salary to do so. I will put up half the money and reap half the profits each quarter. I must warn you straight away that I demand well-kept accounts. You would be more foolish than I take you for if you were to try to cheat me."

What choice did she have? "I agree."

He counted out a pile of gold coins and pushed them over the desk toward her. "Leave the accounts with me. I shall have a clerk copy them and return them to you within the week."

She tucked the precious coins away in her reticule. She would spit on each and every one of them before flinging them in her banker's face the next morning. "That is all?"

"What more do you want from me?"

She could not believe it had been so easy. Nothing was ever that easy. "Nothing."

Chapter Two

Helen Fairchild was an astute woman, Jack thought to himself, as he tossed his greatcoat over his shoulder and headed back to his bachelor apartments for the evening. Her school certainly earned a significant amount more than he would have expected from such a modest establishment. At least, he was assuming it was modest. Judging by the lack of capital she had invested in it and the tiny sum she needed to continue, despite its excellent returns it could hardly be schooling on a grand scale.

She must offer high quality education as well as having a fashionable reputation. No school could last very long with just an empty reputation to trade on; it also had to offer something special that people were prepared to pay a premium for. A school for young virgins about to be married, he supposed, was that something special. He liked the idea of a school that taught young women the more solid skills necessary to run a household and keep their husbands happy. He could only presume that she taught her charges how to manage servants and keep linen smelling sweet and other useful tricks that women needed to know. The school certainly sounded more practical than the usual finishing school rubbish of dancing and drawing and other fashionable fripperies. She had a captive market of young women and their parents, wanting to make sure the girls made a good fist of their marriage. An unhappy marriage was a particular burden to the woman involved, and divorce was difficult to obtain and too expensive for any but the very wealthy. Was it any wonder that responsible mothers felt it was their duty to help their daughters through this important change in their life, and equip them as well as they could for their future?

He chuckled quietly to himself as he let himself into his empty apartments, tossed his coat on to the hall stand, and poured himself a slug of brandy. It was smart of Helen to see this need and to charge a hefty sum for her services. She was a woman after his own heart — a self-made woman with an eye for the main chance. She had spunk, too, walking into his office as if she owned the place and demanding that he loan her money. She'd been well-prepared and had argued her case well, with all the facts and figures at her fingertips, and come ready to negotiate a deal. For all that she was an attractive young woman, she'd been a more convincing businessman than most of the men he'd dealt with recently.

Women like her didn't come two a penny. If Marie had had one tenth of Helen's attitude, he might not have been able to leave her quite so easily. Indeed, if he'd ever found a woman like her who would have him, he would have gotten himself married years ago.

Which reminded him he had a duty to perform that he really must not put off any longer. The latest rumor on the street was that old Mr. Harlow was so close to bankruptcy that a single bad move would tip him over the edge. He couldn't let that ultimate disgrace befall his old mentor. It was past time that he put himself in a position from which he could help the old man — the position of son-in-law.

He eyed the rest of the brandy in his glass with a sigh. If he stayed to finish it, he would feel even less like paying a social call than he felt at present. Still, he was a man of his word, and he had given his word in this matter. It was too late to retract his promise to marry the girl if she would have him. The timing was a bitch, that was for sure. Now that he had met Helen, the duty that had seemed only mildly onerous before now struck him as positively unpleasant.

With a grimace of distaste for the necessity that forced this move on him, he clapped his hat back on his head and strode off to repay his own debts.

By the time he reached Russell Street, the brightness of the day was fading into a gloomy twilight. He rapped loudly on the door with his cane, suddenly in a hurry to get his business settled.

The old, stooped butler who answered his knocking showed him into a large sitting room chock full of ponderous mahogany furniture and gilt chandeliers. "I'll tell Mr. Maurice that you're here," he wheezed as he shuffled off in his broken-heeled slippers.

Jack stood, his back to the empty grate, surveying the room. A casual observer would have thought the owners of the house to be as prosperous as they still pretended to be to the outside world. A casual visitor would not have noticed the threadbare corners of the old-fashioned sofas, and the way the light shone through the thinning fabrics of the heavy drapes at the window. To Jack's practiced eye, however, the room screamed of encroaching poverty, and fairly stank with the effort it was taking the inhabitants to maintain the appearance of normality.

The man who came in just a few moments later gave off the same air of shabbiness and dilapidation that was just short of desperation. He was a large, portly man, with a red face that spoke of good living, but his waistcoat was missing a button and his slippers, though not as broken as those of the butler, were still decidedly down at heel. He greeted Jack warmly, but warily. "Ah, Jack, my lad. You've been too much of a stranger to us lately."

Jack shrugged uneasily. He knew he had been putting off this moment, and he wasn't particularly proud of himself for it. He was a grown man—and nervousness about this meeting could be no excuse. "I've come to see Clarissa." He could feel his face growing hot. It wasn't every day that he plucked up his courage to propose marriage to a young woman he had known most of his life, and yet whom he barely knew. "On that matter we mentioned a week or two ago."

At his words, Maurice stood straighter upright as if a huge weight had dropped off his shoulders. A huge smile spread over his face and he clasped Jack heartily by both shoulders. "Ah, Jack, you're a fine man. I knew you wouldn't let me down. I don't mind telling you that the missus has been worrying her head for the last few days, wondering if you'd ever come, but I told her, now, Mrs. Harlow, don't you worry about a thing. Jack's a good lad, and he won't go back on his word. And here you are," he said, his voice trembling just a little, "just as you said you would be."

Was it his imagination or could he feel the cravat around his throat constrict until it was as tight as a noose around his neck? He could barely breathe. "Yes. I'm here." He pulled at the knot in his cravat, trying in vain to loosen it and let some air into his lungs.

"Let me just fetch Clarissa down so you can get it all fixed between the pair of you." The older man's voice was plainly tremulous now. "And I can fetch out the old bottle of port, the one I've been saving for this very occasion, and we can toast your engagement in fine style." He wiped a tear away from his eye. "I may be temporarily down on my luck, but I've saved that bottle through thick and thin and I'm going to enjoy it to the last drop."

Jack had finally managed to wrench his cravat open a little and take a deep breath. He only hoped that Clarissa was as delighted about their marriage as his future father-in-law clearly was. "She knows about...she knows that—" He didn't know what his old friend Mr. Harlow would do if Clarissa had decided against accepting him after all.

Mr. Harlow cut him off with a carefree wave of his hand. "You needn't worry on that score, my boy. Clarissa won't be turning you down. I've had a talk with her, just as Mrs. Harlow has, and we've both told her what a fine match it is for her. She's a sensible lass, that one is, and she won't be refusing you."

He wasn't sure if Clarissa's matter-of-fact decision to accept him before he'd even asked her to marry him made the whole affair seem better or worse, but it hardly mattered in the end. For her father's sake, for the sake of the helping hand that Mr.

Harlow had extended to him when he was just a boy, he was bound to marry her. That was all that mattered. Her feelings hardly entered the equation, and his didn't figure at all.

Mr. Harlow strode to the door. "Clarry, my dear," he bellowed up the stairs. "Come down into the sitting room. You have a visitor." He turned back to Jack and gave him a wide wink. "Go to it, Jack. I'll be waiting in the next room with the open bottle until I can drink to the happy news."

Jack paced up and down nervously after Mr. Harlow had left the room. He didn't have long to wait in suspense. In just a few moments, Clarissa glided in noiselessly, like a white ghost.

He was struck anew by her ethereal manner. Everything about her was pale, from the paleness of her face, to the pale white-gold of her hair, to the pale sprigged muslin of her dress. Even her eyes, the watery blue of an early morning sky, lacked color and vibrancy. She moved gracefully and without a sound as well—her movements as colorless as the rest of her.

She was a pretty young woman, he supposed, if one looked at her dispassionately. Her figure was well enough, as far as he could tell. Her features were regular and her face not unattractive. Still, he couldn't summon up more than the slightest spark of sexual interest in her. He couldn't imagine her lying back on the bed, her legs opening for him, her body welcoming his, her eyes alive with desire for him. In fact, he couldn't imagine her desiring *anyone*. She was too virginal. Too pure. The thought of fucking her seemed almost sacrilegious. She was too childlike, too unworldly to be the object of his desire.

She bowed her head to him as she entered the room. "Mr. Langton," she murmured. Even her voice seemed somehow lacking in color.

"Miss Harlow." He took her hand and bent his head over it, just grazing the back of her hand with his lips. "It's a pleasure to see you again." Unlike Mrs. Fairchild that afternoon, who had smelled of soap and sex, Clarissa didn't have a distinctive scent of her own. If anything, he could detect a faint smell of lavender in her clothing—pale, uninteresting flower that it was, with an equally pale, uninteresting scent. It was a smell he associated with clean linen from the linen press, more suitable for a pillowcase than for his wife.

"Likewise." She was not one to waste her words, economical with them as she was with everything else.

He didn't relinquish her hand until he had led her over to the sofa and sat down next to her on it, feeling like he was an actor in a rather silly sentimental drama. "Miss Harlow. Or may I call you Clarissa?"

She nodded. A faint touch of color briefly came and went on her pale cheeks. "If you please, Mr. Langton." She was sitting primly on the edge of the seat, her hands folded in her lap, the very picture of untouchable virginity.

"And you must call me Jack."

"Yes, Mr…yes, Jack."

His name sounded odd coming from her lips. He shrugged. He'd get used to it, just like he'd get used to being married to this odd, fey creature. "I wanted to see you tonight. I had a question to ask you."

He had made his meaning as plain as he could, thinking to spare her maidenly blushes, but her composure was quite unruffled at his words. "Yes, Father told me he'd suggested a marriage between us, and you had agreed to the plan."

There was a short silence as Jack looked at his boots for inspiration and found none.

Clarissa continued to stare straight ahead, quite unembarrassed at the turn the conversation was taking. "I presume that *is* the question you were planning to ask me? Whether I would marry you?"

"Ah, yes," he managed at last, rather discombobulated at the extreme common sense and matter-of-factness that she was showing. "I wanted to ask you whether you would do me the great honor of becoming my wife."

Her lips twitched in an almost smile. "Yes, I am quite prepared to marry you. Though I believe the honor on this occasion is all mine."

"You are a beautiful woman," he protested uneasily, wishing he could feel some measure of happiness at the prospect of being married to her.

Sitting there beside her, he couldn't manage to summon any feeling other than a faint dread at the thought of having her as his wife. He felt barely even the faintest spark of sexual interest in her. Sure, she was a virgin, and wasn't a young, unsullied virgin supposed to be every man's wet dream? But bedding her, he suspected, would be about as exciting as bedding a blancmange. Did she never get excited about anything? Ever? Was she really as placid and as cow-like in her docility as she seemed? "Any man would be pleased to have the right to call you wife."

"I am also quite poor," she said calmly. "For all that Father has tried to hide the ruin of his affairs from Mother and I, I am not ignorant of our situation. I may only be nineteen, but I am not naïve. We have not two farthings to rub together anymore. I will bring you no dowry—not in money or in land or even in jewels." She touched the necklace that lay around her throat with a rueful grimace. "The only ones I have left are fakes and not worth the effort of selling or they would have been sold long ago. If you take me, you will be marrying a pauper."

He knew only too well how true her words were. The Harlows had been all but ruined in the recent collapse of the financial markets, brought on by too much speculation by the masses and the greed of a few. Had it not been for the money he had lent them over the last few months with no expectation of repayment, their ruin would already be complete. Their financial straits were the reason, after all, for his promise to wed her. "I already owe your father a debt I will never be able to repay. He saved my life when I was barely a boy and gave me my start in the world. If it had not been for his kindness, I would have been hanged as a thief and a pickpocket before I was even full grown.

Looking after and protecting his beloved daughter is a small price to pay in return. And I promise you that I will keep my word to both him and to you. Once you are my wife, you will never lack for anything that I am able to provide for you."

Again that slight smile that made her look faintly amused and superior at the same time. "Even your love?"

His love? He felt an icy coldness blossom in his chest. She did not seem the romantic type, but she was young. Did she really expect him to play the part of a romantic young fool, swept away by his emotions?

He could not do it. Not even for the sake of his mentor, to whom he owed so much. But for Clarissa's sake, he could not tell her outright that he found the thought of bedding her about as unappetizing as having a slab of raw meat dumped on his dinner plate and being expected to eat it with a good grace, even a show of hungry enthusiasm. "I've known you since you were a baby in petticoats, and I'm fond of you," he began. "As man and wife, we'll rub along well enough together. I'm sure that in time our liking for each other may well be nurtured into something stronger."

"You don't fancy yourself in love with me, then?" She seemed curious rather than hurt or disappointed in any way.

To such a bluntly honest question, he had to give an equally blunt answer. "No, I don't. Not yet. But I like you well enough and I think we would suit fine. If we are lucky, perhaps love will come later."

To his surprise, she nodded, satisfied at his honesty. "I'm glad of it. I, too, like you well enough, as a girl likes a favorite uncle, or a sister likes her brother. I have no desire for you to make yourself into a mooning puppy dog over me. I would cease to like you at all in that case." She gave another rare twitch of her lips which passed as a smile. "Which would not be a good start for our marriage."

He barked a quick laugh. So, she wanted no embarrassing emotional displays or declarations of love from him? That suited him just fine. He had always preferred honesty himself, however uncomfortable the truth was or however beguiling a pleasant lie may seem. "Agreed. I shall make no fine speeches and you shan't expect them, and we shall both be happy. But I need your agreement to one thing."

She raised her eyebrows, silently waiting for him to continue.

He cleared his throat, slightly uncomfortable at broaching the sensitive subject with a young virgin. "This will be a proper marriage. You will share my bed and be my wife in every way." If he was going to marry her, then by God he would fuck her as well, and see if a good pounding wouldn't break through that damned composure of hers and turn her into a real woman.

Again a calm acceptance of his terms. "I had expected that," was all she said.

Little as he particularly wanted to fuck her himself, he didn't want her welcoming every man in London into her bed, either. It would be better for them both if they had a clear understanding on that score, as well. "You will invite no other man into your bed. I do not want to breed up a cuckoo in my nest."

"I had expected that, as well." Her voice was as calm as if they had been talking about the weather and the likelihood of rain.

"Once we are married, I will be faithful to you," he said, in justification of his demands, "and I expect faithfulness in return." He would not add hypocrisy to his list of sins and condemn her for taking a lover if he had one of his own.

She did not look the least offended by the bluntness of his language. "I have no desire to invite any other man into my bed. I may safely guarantee that I will not betray you with another man." She shuddered slightly at the very thought. "I can assure you, I will never ever so much as wish to do so."

He shook his head in disbelief. Was she really as unfeeling as she made out, or did her indifference stretch to him alone?

Did she have no spark of desire at all, or did it simply not light for him? "You may not love me, but do you love another man?"

She gave her head a slight shake. "You need have no fears on that score. I like you quite as well as any other man I know. I am certainly not secretly pining for a different husband."

It was hardly a declaration of love, but he supposed it would have to do. He should be relieved that she did not actually dislike him. Many a marriage had started off worse than theirs would. There was at least no active dislike on either side in their case. "Then we are agreed?"

She nodded, as calm and pale as ever. "We are agreed."

They sat there in silence for a few moments. Rather to his discomfort, Jack found he had nothing else to say to her. Small talk seemed out of place at such a time, but what other conversation could they have? He knew nothing of what she liked, nothing about what interested her.

Their situation, in the best parlor in her father's house, was hardly amenable for seduction either, even if he had been inclined to try. He gave the possibility a moment of serious consideration, before dismissing it again with the uncomfortable thought that he was decidedly *not* inclined. She had made her indifference to the whole subject of love and making love quite clear, and he wasn't in the mood to be rebuffed by his new fiancée.

Finally he hit upon a safe topic. "I see little point in a long engagement. We may as well wed sooner rather than later." The sooner they were out of the no-man's-land of this odd engagement and into the everyday reality of a conveniently loveless, though amicable, marriage, the more comfortable he would feel.

She lifted her white shoulders a fraction and dropped them again. "September?" she suggested, as if the matter was of supreme indifference to her.

That was only a matter of eight weeks away. He felt his insides begin to churn. Was he to give away his freedom so soon? He loosened his cravat a little more before it began to choke him once again. "September," he agreed.

At that she rose, her hands still folded in front of her. "Shall we go and tell Father? He will be vastly relieved at the prospect of getting me settled in life."

He rose to stand beside her. She was now his affianced bride and he had barely touched her. One brief touch of his naked hand on hers, and the most fleeting touch of his lips to her fingers was all he could boast of. "Come, kiss me to celebrate our engagement."

She stood obediently, her face raised to his as he brushed a kiss on her pale, unmoving lips. It was like kissing a porcelain doll for all the feeling that she put into their brief embrace. Her lack of response quenched any ardor he might have felt for her as surely as if she had doused him with a bucket of cold water.

He trusted he would be able to work up more enthusiasm for their wedding night or she would have a very poor impression of the man she had married. He had always been a lover of willing women—the lustier and more enthusiastic they were at being roundly fucked, and the wetter and hotter their cunts were as he thrust into them, the better he liked it. If his wife responded to him only with such uninterested coldness, he doubted he'd be roused to much of a showing. Poking a virgin's dry, unwelcoming cunt wasn't his idea of a good time.

He trusted *she* would be able to work up a little more warmth and enthusiasm for their marital bed as well, or he would be doomed to a life devoid of heat and passion and everything that made life worth the living. Not to mention that fucking her would put his cock in serious danger of getting frostbite.

Chapter Three

With a little persuasion and the promise of a significant financial reward, Jack Langton's clerk had finished copying Mrs. Fairchild's ledgers within twenty-four hours.

Jack grabbed the originals and stepped out into the sunshine. Time to personally inspect his latest acquisition.

At least attending to his business would take his mind off the scene with Clarissa and her family last night. Mr. and Mrs. Harlow's enthusiasm for the match had only been exceeded by Clarissa's polite indifference. He'd begun to wonder whether he should not just have bailed old Mr. Harlow out of his latest financial mess, settled a decent annuity on the old fellow out of hand, and dropped the subject of a wedding with his daughter.

He knew why he hadn't, of course. Old Mr. Harlow had too much pride to accept what he saw as charity from an old friend and former protégé. A generous financial settlement from a wealthy son-in-law, however, would be perfectly acceptable. Once he was part of the family by marriage, it would be not only his privilege, but also his duty, to help support his indigent parents-in-law.

He gave an impatient shrug and shook off the thoughts of his marriage. His personal life would have to wait. It was time to turn his attention to his business affairs. On paper, Mrs. Fairchild's school had looked to be an excellent proposition. It wouldn't make anyone fabulously rich in a hurry, but considering its small size and the small number of pupils it catered for, it turned a handsome profit.

He didn't usually invest in such small change propositions. A fleet of ships to the West Indies, a new railroad development, or the opening of a coal mine in Wales were closer to the scale he dealt in.

He'd been fascinated by Helen Fairchild though. Her confidence most of all. She'd swept into his office and demanded that he lend her money, as if she had no thought that he would dare refuse. He had to admire her determination and spirit. She was so alive with color and spirit. Where Clarissa Harlow was pale and white, Helen Fairchild was every color of the rainbow and a few more besides.

And now with the excuse of returning her ledgers, here he had the opportunity to cast an eye over her facilities, and perhaps even eavesdrop on one of her classes to examine her teaching techniques. He rather hoped the class would be something slightly interesting, like keeping house, which he admitted to himself was a bit like running a small business.

As long as it wasn't dancing. He detested dancing.

The building that housed the school had a pleasant aspect. The front courtyard was clean and tidy, and the door itself was painted a gleaming white. His first impressions were favorable so far.

The door was unlocked. He let himself in. As half-owner in the school, he was entitled to come and go as he pleased — a privilege that he intended to make good of. The knowledge that he might visit them unannounced at any time of the day or night for an informal inspection helped to keep his business partners honest. With Mrs. Fairchild's school, too, he would start off as he meant to go on.

From the back of the ground floor apartment he heard the sound of muffled voices. Mrs. Fairchild must be engaged in teaching her pupils. He made his way to the room next to it to see if he could hear the lesson.

"Now girls, gather round." Helen's voice came clearly through a crack in the wall, and he moved closer so he could hear better. "Today we are going to introduce ourselves to oral techniques."

What was that? wondered Jack. Perhaps how to correctly instruct staff, or to deal with deliverymen.

"As usual, we will use George to practice on," she continued. "First, to ensure proper hygiene, we'll give him a wash off."

That piqued Jack's interest, and he moved until his ear was plastered up against the wall. He heard the sound of water being poured from a jug into a basin, and the swish of a washcloth being rinsed. Next, he heard something he was sure was not correct. What had Helen actually said? It sounded like "Be sure to wash most carefully around the testicles and penis." But of course that was ridiculous. Clearly he misheard over the sound of the splashing water.

Burning with curiosity, Jack edged himself noiselessly around to peer through the crack in the wall.

Helen and three girls were clustered around something that looked from his vantage point like a person lying down. One of the girls moved around, jockeying for position, and he saw more clearly. It looked like a life-sized mannequin, reclining prone on a long, waist-high table.

To his utter astonishment Jack saw the mannequin was naked—very naked—in every anatomically correct detail. In fact, so correct was this "George" that he sported a very respectable, highly polished, leather erection.

The girls finished washing around the groin area of the mannequin and moved to one side of the table, while Helen remained on the other. Jack could see Helen's back as she talked, and the girls faced his direction. Two of them looked slightly disengaged, while the third wore a look of intense concentration as Helen began talking.

Jack gave a start and bit back an exclamation of surprise as he realized that one of the girls was Clarissa Harlow, his own intended. She was here, in Mrs. Fairchild's house, learning whatever Mrs. Fairchild could teach her about the married state.

He turned his ear with a greater degree of attention to what Mrs. Fairchild was saying…

"You will recall from our earlier classes that some areas of the man's private parts are more sensitive than others. Some can be handled reasonably roughly, which your husband will enjoy, while others are more delicate and require a light touch. Your mouth and tongue, combined with your hand, can provide this variation of sensation.

"You will also remember that men are visual creatures, and the art of giving oral pleasure to your husband is best performed when there is some light so he can watch."

By this time Jack was in a very confused state. His head told him that he had just made a huge mistake by buying a half-share in a house of moral disrepute. On the other hand, another part of him, a lower part, he thought to himself, as he felt the growing hardness in his trousers, found the thought of teaching girls how to suck a man's cock hugely arousing. Especially when one of those girls was to be his own wife in a few short weeks.

Maybe he had underestimated Clarissa. Maybe there was a passionate woman hiding under her exterior, just waiting for the right man to come along and wake her up. Maybe she was just waiting for their wedding night to try out her skill at cock sucking.

As he peered through the crack he imagined Clarissa sucking on his cock. Not just Clarissa, but all the girls sucking on his cock, one after the other. Their tongues licking his balls, up his shaft and around the large purplish head of his cock. Perhaps all three of them could please him at the same time, taking it in turns to suck and lick on him until he couldn't hold out any longer and came right into their open, eager mouths. He felt the blood rush to his own cock, swelling it up to twice its usual size and more, at the mere thought.

Jack's fantasies were interrupted as Helen's voice once more penetrated through the wall. "The first thing you must learn, girls, is to control your husband's thrusting in order that you do not gag. Place your hand around the base of his penis like this. Now you can place your husband's penis in your mouth and control his thrusting without fear of discomfort."

As she finished speaking, Jack could see Helen lean over the waist area of the mannequin. She was silent now, and he imagined her mouth engulfing George's large cock, her tongue moving in rhythmic circles around its knob.

He moved as close as he could to the crack in the wall, his eye pressed hard against the wood. He reached down, unbuttoned his trousers and released his own hard cock from its confining prison. He stroked it with mounting pleasure as Helen continued her lesson.

"Remember, I said men are visual creatures. If you place yourself near his feet while pleasuring him with your mouth he can look down at you, and you up to him. He can see his penis as you lick and suck it. You can look into his eyes. This position is also good if your husband is standing while you kneel at his feet. He feels powerful, in control, although of course he is not— you are. He will be dough in your hands, completely under your spell. Alternatively if your man is lying down you can kneel at his feet with his legs apart. His testicles are very accessible in this position. And once again you can achieve that eye contact. Watch now as I demonstrate."

Jack watched as Helen moved from her position at the mannequin's waist to its feet. She got up on the table, spread its legs and moved closer to the large erection jutting proudly up into the air. Jack had a fine profile view as Helen proceeded to demonstrate what she had just explained.

He gripped his own cock harder and increased the rhythm of his strokes as he saw Helen lean over and take the oversized phallus completely into her mouth, her lips touching its base.

His eye was pressed so close against the crack that he could see almost as well as if he were in the same room as her. He groaned silently with desire as she took the penis in her hand and started an alternating motion with her mouth and hand, her hand making small reciprocating motions near the base as her tongue rasped the glans on the underside of the head. Still he stroked himself, imagining that she was sucking and stroking not a model of a man, but his own living, throbbing, pulsating cock.

He was sweating with need when she took the whole penis into her mouth. He could almost feel on his own body the delicious way she bobbed her head up and down while maintaining a tantalizing suction with her mouth. Her lips slid up and down the cock until Jack nearly came into his hand with the thought of it.

Helen pulled her head away just in time, but his torment wasn't over just yet. "The penis is not all that is available to you from this position. While stroking his penis with your hand you may also lick his scrotum, suck on his testicles, and even lick around your man's very sensitive rear passage."

After a brief demonstration Helen looked up at her class. "Be sure to use a variety of techniques, learn your man's body language, feel the tension in his muscles and listen to his moans. You will soon learn what he likes most. Keep him on the edge, and you will find him most agreeable to your every suggestion. He may be the man of the house, but the power will be yours."

Jack was getting very uncomfortable in his place of hiding, his body twisted to enable him to peer through the wall while he stroked his cock.

Helen resumed her demonstration, her tongue licking at the very base of the mannequin's scrotum.

The thought of her taking each of his balls in her mouth in turn, licking his shaft and then taking it in her mouth was too much for him to bear. Involuntarily he let out a soft moan of pleasure and agony. Helen ceased her ministrations on George and looked up in Jack's direction, a look of puzzlement on her face.

She had heard him for sure. How could he possibly announce his presence now or inspect his latest acquisition with any sort of coherence? He had never felt less ready to conduct financial business in his life.

He had to leave—and quickly, before he was discovered. What would Mrs. Fairchild think if she caught him spying on her lessons and playing with himself as he did so? What would Clarissa think if she found him there? She would despise him as the worst sort of Peeping Tom, and rightly so. With indecent haste, he forced his tumescent cock back into his trousers and fled down the hallway and out into the street.

Fucking. That's what she taught her innocent young students, he thought to himself in wonder, as he strode through the streets to his bachelor apartments, his balls still aching with unrelieved tension. She was teaching his own future wife how best to suck him and fuck him to keep him satisfied.

He wondered how many of their fathers knew exactly what their virginal daughters were being taught in the prim and proper Mrs. Fairchild's school for young ladies of good quality about to be married. Few, if any, he supposed.

So then who paid the delectable Helen's steep bills?

The answer came to him in a blinding flash. It had to be the girls' mothers—many of them married to unfaithful husbands themselves, he would wager—teaching their daughters how to keep their new husbands occupied in the best way they knew how—in the bedroom. She was teaching proper young girls of good breeding and family to be as entertaining and as exciting as any professional courtesan, born and bred to the trade.

He chuckled to himself as he strode into his apartments and bolted the door behind him. Mrs. Fairchild had hit upon a gem of an idea. His investment would be more than safe in her highly capable hands.

Still, he ought to make her pay for misleading him as to the nature of her school he decided, as he reached the sanctuary of his bedchamber and could finally unbutton his trousers and take his still half-swollen cock back into his hands once more. The shrewd little hussy deserved nothing less for the torment she had put him through.

He stroked himself with increasing fervor as he thought about her and her school for young virgins about to be married. She was far more delectable than any of the young virgins she was teaching, his own Clarissa included. He would rather have *her* hands on his body than any young virgin's. He would rather have *her* mouth taking in all of his cock, sliding it in and out of her wetness, licking him and sucking on him until he came right into her mouth.

He ought to insist that she take him on as her newest pupil—and tutor him in the ways to please a woman. After all, when he took Clarissa as his wife, he would not want her to stray any more than Helen's young pupils wanted their husbands to seek the company of other women. Indeed, if he wanted to make sure his heirs were his own, he would be wise to keep Clarissa as content in his bed as he ever hoped to be in hers.

He grinned painfully to himself at the thought of Helen teaching him how to fuck a woman, to have her writhe with pleasure under the touch of his hands and mouth and cock. He liked that thought. So did his body. He was so ready to orgasm now it hurt to prolong the anticipation for even another second. He'd been ready ever since he first heard her voice this afternoon.

He wondered if she would be so bold with him as she was with her female pupils, or if she would stammer with embarrassment and blush as she demonstrated each position in the graphic detail that he would demand.

He barely had time to picture to himself the first lesson he would demand, when his passion overcame his self-control. He groaned with solitary pleasure as his seed spurted out with force onto his bed hangings. God, yes, he would make her teach him, and he would test what he had learned on her.

She would be bold, he decided, as he poured some water from the pitcher into the basin on his dresser and washed himself down again. Bold and confident. Somehow he did not think she was the blushing type.

* * * * *

Helen sat behind her desk, holding a pose of distance and respectability she deliberately cultivated for the fathers of her students. "Mr. Langton, I'm pleased to see you."

Jack lounged on the sofa, looking impossibly large and male. "I've come to inspect my investment. If you have no objection, I'd like to sit in on one of your lessons."

Helen didn't bat an eyelid. She was always prepared for this eventuality. "The first lesson of the day starts momentarily," she said, her voice smooth and welcoming. "Please, join us."

She led the way to the room at the end—the main classroom. Near the leather couch at the rear of the room stood Helen's three pupils. She introduced Jack to them all. "Miss Harlow, Miss Harbottoms, Miss Musgrave, this is Mr. Langton, the new part owner of my school."

He bowed politely. "Miss Harlow, Miss Harbottoms, Miss Musgrave."

Clarissa nodded back, as did Annabelle Musgrave, whom he also knew slightly, but didn't see fit to acknowledge their relationship in any other way. She was not, he admitted wryly to himself, the most effusive of fiancées.

Indeed, Clarissa and Annabelle, her bosom buddy, were dressed perfectly correctly and behaving quite properly, but something about them disconcerted Jack. He hadn't seen them together for some time, though he knew from Mr. Harlow they seldom spent more than a day out of each other's company. They stood close together, facing each other, wrapped up in each other's presence to such an extent that it was as if the rest of the world did not exist for them.

A wild thought entered Jack's head. It was something about their body posture, the tilt of their heads, the way their bodies seemed to be touching, and yet not. They somehow gave, he thought, the appearance of being more than close friends. They looked, he thought, just like lovers do.

Ridiculous, he told himself firmly. He should know better than most how relentlessly asexual Clarissa was. She had never shown the least bit of interest in him. Even when he had kissed her to seal their engagement, her reaction had been disinterested acceptance at best. The overcharged atmosphere in the room was simply making him see sex everywhere—even in the virginal Clarissa.

"To your seats, ladies," Helen called. "Today we shall have a lesson on wording invitations."

The girls moved as one to their seats, where they sat down close to each another, their heads in a row. As Clarissa and Anna walked past him Jack could have sworn he smelled a musky smell, that intimate scent of a woman that made his cock jump with the thought of it. Surely these girls…

The thought remained unfinished as Helen began her lesson.

The next hour was interminably dull. Jack fidgeted with boredom on the leather sofa as Helen talked at length about the proper way to address an invitation, and the subtleties of meaning in whether it was delivered by hand or entrusted to a delivery boy.

He was thankful when she stood up at length to take a break, ushering the girls outside into the air.

"I'm afraid you do not find my lessons particularly enthralling," she said as soon as they were alone together.

Jack was amused by her coolness. What an accomplished dissembler she was. "They are not exactly what I had expected, I must admit."

"Lessons for women," she said with a deprecating smile as she joined him on the leather couch. "Do not let me keep you from more important business. You may be assured that I will send you my accounts religiously every quarter."

He grinned at her not so subtle attempt to dismiss him. "I had thought to hear about something more exciting than how to address invitations."

She raised an eyebrow, as cool as ever. "Such as?"

He leaned toward her so that he could whisper in her ear. "Such as how to suck a man's cock to give him ultimate pleasure."

She drew back, a haughty expression pasted on her face. "You, sir, are no gentleman, as well as being grievously misinformed."

Her confidence amused and aroused him in equal measure. "I do not think so. I enjoyed yesterday's lesson far more than this morning's."

Her back became more rigid than before and her face paled slightly. "So my secret is out. Yes, I teach young women how best to please their husbands. Are you shocked at the idea that I teach young women about sex? Disgusted at my immorality for talking openly of such matters? Are you going to give me back the half-share you have just bought and call in your loan?"

He shook his head. "Not at all. You have hit upon a brilliant idea and I applaud you for it."

The rigidity of her body relaxed slightly. "Then what do you want?"

"I want to be your pupil."

She looked startled for a moment. "You want to take on the part of a girl and learn how to please men?"

He grinned, sure that he had her now. "You teach women how to please men so their husbands are faithful to them. I want you to teach me how to please a woman so she has no thought but to be faithful to me. As, like most men, I have a natural aversion to bringing up any other man's child as my own, the knowledge will be useful to me when I take a wife."

She sat still for some moments, staring blankly out of the window, thinking over his unusual request.

So Jack thought to intimidate her with his maleness, did he? He would soon find out that she was no delicate hothouse flower, but a girl of the streets who had no qualms about fighting dirty.

Did he expect her to refuse him with indignation and shock? Agree out of fear that he would withdraw his money or expose the real purpose of her school to a legion of irate fathers?

She doubted he would be so foolish as to expose her. He owned half the school now—it was in his interests to keep it running at a profit. He was too astute not to know that if he ruined her reputation, he ruined his investment in her business along with it.

"You are to be married soon?" she asked, to buy herself a little more time to think.

He gave her an assessing look. "Does it matter?"

"No, I suppose not," she conceded. "The lessons you need to learn will be the same regardless of whether you want to please your wife or your mistress."

She taught young women about pleasing men every day. She could equally well teach a man how to please a woman. It was about time at least one man thought to learn.

He wanted to put her in her place—make her feel exposed and vulnerable in his company. She would turn the tables on him and strip his soul bare instead.

She knew her opponent well, and every canny woman's weapon of choice against such a man was her body. She would use her body shamelessly, as she taught her pupils to do. Before his lessons were finished, she would have him on his knees before her.

She held out her hand to shake on the deal. "Agreed. I will teach you as you desire, as long as you promise you will be a painstaking and obedient pupil."

A triumphant smile spread over his face. "Most assuredly. I will be the most attentive pupil you have ever taught, I can assure you."

Helen narrowed her eyes as she watched him strut away, as cocky as if he was king of the barnyard. Foolish man. So, he thought he had won this round, did he? He had a lot to learn for sure—and his first lesson would show him that she was not a woman to be manipulated. Oh yes, she would well and truly make him pay for his boldness in asking her to teach him. She was no woman if she did not make him regret the day she had first walked into his life.

* * * * *

Helen greeted him at the door and ushered him into the classroom. "You are punctual, Mr. Langton."

He bowed over her hand. "I am looking forward to what you can teach me."

She removed her hand from his and took a step back. "First of all, we need good light. Please take a seat on the sofa while I light some lamps."

Jack looked around. It was already quite bright in the room, with the afternoon sun just sneaking in the window to make a bright patch on the floor and wall. Still, he did as he was bid and sat down.

Helen returned to her desk and lit the two lamps that rested on either corner. She stood in between the lamps, directly in front of Jack. "Have you ever looked at a woman, Mr. Langton?"

He opened his mouth to protest that of course he had, he looked at women all the time, but she waved at him to be quiet.

"I mean really looked? Have you studied every part of a woman's body? Can you recall clearly what the last woman you made love to looked like? Did she have any scars or moles? Was her pubic hair thick and bushy, or fine and thin? How big were her nipples?"

He was silent. He doubted that she really wanted an answer to her questions. Besides, even though it was only a week or so since he had dispensed with Marie's services, he couldn't remember exactly what she had looked like naked anyway. Her cunt had been warm and wet and she'd satisfied him well enough, and that was all he'd cared about.

"I am to teach you the art of pleasing a woman. Today you will start by observing closely the body, you will see closely what you must pleasure. Today you will learn that above all else a woman, young or old, whatever her shape or size, loves to be looked at and admired in her nakedness."

Jack looked at Helen as if seeing another person, a tantalizingly erotic stranger that had magically taken the place of the businesswoman he knew. Fantasizing about Helen teaching him was one thing, but it was another matter all together to sit down in front of her and talk matter-of-factly about the details of a woman's body. He didn't know how to answer such questions, as the color came to his cheeks and a swelling burgeoned in his groin.

"For your first lesson you will do nothing but look. You may not touch me, not at any time. You may make no objection, and not speak unless you are directly addressed—in all things you will be an obedient pupil. You will sit on that couch and not move—for this is not about your own pleasure, but about learning. If you do not agree to this, I will not teach you."

He nodded his agreement, his heart beating a little faster at the thought of what would be coming next. He would be a statue for her, if that was what she desired.

She smiled her acceptance. "Good. Then we shall start."

She was wearing a long black coat, fully buttoned, and her usual boots. She moved her hands to the button at the bottom and moving slowly upwards she undid her coat, button by glorious button. As she lingered over the last button, the coat fell open to reveal her completely naked body underneath.

His breath caught in his throat as his eyes moved from her throat, past her breasts and lingered over her honey-colored pubic bush. He looked at her, really looked, and he liked what he saw. He would not forget the sight of her naked body as easily as he had forgotten others. It was seared on his memory.

She turned her back to him and slowly removed the coat, sliding it over each shoulder before letting it fall to the floor. She kept her back to him as she spoke. "Look carefully at my legs, Mr. Langton. See how the high heels of the boots shape my calves. Look how my buttocks are firm as I stand this way. See the curve of my back."

Jack leaned forward on the couch for a better view. Helen stood before him, barely three feet away. He longed for a peek at her cunt, nestled at the top of her long legs. His desire was growing, making his trousers uncomfortable. He resisted the temptation to reach out and touch her.

Helen turned sideways to him. "Look at my breasts, Mr. Langton. See the fullness of the shape, how it flows smoothly to my nipple."

She traced a line from her neck to the apex of her breast with a fingernail as she spoke. "Look how my nipple enlarges, becomes sharp and hard when I touch it."

He was looking so hard that his eyes watered. Her breasts were heavy and round and made for the touch of a man's hand. He wanted to be that man, to take them in his hands and suck greedily on their pink tips.

She lightly flicked at her breast, then pinching and pulling at both her nipples, which had become quite long and hard indeed. As she massaged her full bosom she turned to face him, legs slightly apart. She cupped her breasts with her hands. "Look how soft they are, Mr. Langton."

Her hands flowed to her belly, and his eyes followed her every move. "See the smooth white skin, how it goes forever from my breasts to my navel. See the depression of my navel, a secret place. Does it contain hidden treasure?"

She brushed her hands over the hair at the top of her legs. "Behind here is hidden treasure, a marvel for the eye."

Helen's words and actions were tormenting Jack. He'd had enough of looking by now. He needed action. Urgently. He squirmed around on the couch to provide some friction to his hard cock, trapped in its prison of layered clothing. He longed for Helen to touch it, to free it and slide her hands over his engorged knob, and to place her mouth over it as she had to the mannequin, to suck his balls and to lick his large and sensitive sac.

She sat on the edge of the desk, her legs dangling momentarily off the floor as she slid backward and lifted her boots up onto the desk.

He thought his torment could get no worse as he looked at Helen before him. Her legs were spread wide apart as her ass and feet formed a triangle on the desk.

She leaned back, her elbows supporting her, and all Jack could see of her was her boots, her thighs, and her cunt, open and glistening at eye level. As he watched, a trickle of liquid leaked from her pink opening and formed a small puddle on the desk.

"Look at my wet cunt. See my lips open. Some women have large lips that can be held, framing the entrance to pleasure, some woman have almost no lips, keeping their secret hidden for as long as possible."

Oh, God, she was actually pleasuring herself in front of him, and asking him to watch her as she did so. Before this day, he'd always concentrated so hard on his own needs that the woman who was fulfilling them was merely incidental to his pleasure. He'd never ever considered that a woman's arousal could be so erotic, and that her wants and desires could fuel his own in such a way.

Helen supported herself on one elbow as her free hand moved to open her vagina wider. She inserted one finger into her wet cunt and then placed her finger in her mouth, licking her juices. He licked his lips in his turn, almost tasting her on his own mouth.

She returned her hand to her mound and rubbed around the top of her slit, then plunged two fingers into her cunt as deep as they would go.

"Look at my moisture, Mr. Langton," she said, as she slid her dripping fingers out again. "See how it sticks to my fingers. Look at how it makes me slick, ready to receive whatever I may wish to use to give me pleasure. Sometimes I use a man, sometimes not."

Jack's breathing had become so heavy he could hardly drag in enough air to fill his lungs, and his cock was an iron rod, needing attention with a painful urgency. Never had he seen a woman in so much detail, or heard her speak in such a way. He had not thought a woman *could* act like this. The sight, smell, and the sound of Helen's arousal were unbearable. He desperately needed some pleasure of his own. Damn Clarissa and damn his impending marriage. He wanted to fuck Helen and he wanted to fuck her *now*.

Helen had to be aware of his need, but she continued without mercy. Her hands moved once again to her cunt, and using both hands pulled her lips up and open, displaying her clit in its full glory. "See how I can reveal my center of pleasure to you, Mr. Langton. Look how it looks like a tiny penis. It's very sensitive, exposed like this. The slightest touch with a tongue or feather can send me to heaven."

He had no more control over himself. She had brought him to a state of mindless lust and still she continued to torment him. He started to surreptitiously rub his iron-hard cock with his hand, moving it around to a more comfortable position beneath his trousers, and continuing to quietly massage it, top to bottom. He had no more control over himself than a schoolboy.

She sat up, and glanced sharply at him. He guiltily moved his hands away from the front of his trousers, though it hurt him to do so.

"Have you seen my most intimate parts, Mr. Langton?" As she spoke, she stroked her cunt with long, languid strokes, starting at her asshole, and sliding her finger up to the bright pink entrance of her dripping cunt. She momentarily delved with two fingers to cover them with her juices, before finishing the stroke at her engorged clitoris. She repeated the stroke again and again whilst staring into Jack's eyes.

"Yes, er, yes," he replied, his voice failing him at first, his throat was so dry with desire.

Helen stopped stroking and got down off the desk. She turned her back to him, placed her feet wide apart and reached around with both hands to pull her ass wide apart. She bent over slightly and Jack found his eyes were no more than twelve inches from Helen's asshole. "Have you ever had a woman here, Jack?" she asked, as her fingers lightly touched her tightest of holes.

Jack's voice failed him completely as he stared at the sight before him.

Keeping her back to him, Helen climbed onto her desk once more. With her knees and head on the desk and her backside high in the air, her cunt and ass were completely open to Jack's mesmerized gaze. She reached behind her once more and inserted two fingers into her cunt, withdrew the now sopping fingers and slowly slid them into her ass.

While her back was to him, Jack had resumed touching his cock. As Helen's fingers penetrated her ass he suddenly came, his body rigid as he involuntarily cried out with spasms of release.

Helen removed her fingers from her ass, gave one last long stroke to her cunt and got quickly off the desk. She stood before him hands on hips, boots wide apart. "This lesson was not intended for your pleasure, Mr. Langton."

He looked down miserably at his lap where his cum soaked through his trousers. He had never felt so excited and humiliated together. Despite his release, he was still desperate to fuck his teacher, to have his fingers, tongue and cock where her fingers had just been. He could feel his cock growing engorged again at the very thought.

"If you want to learn how to please a woman, you must learn some self-control. Maybe, Mr. Langton, we should make that the subject of your next lesson."

Helen stood at the side of the window, her coat draped over her shoulders, furtively watching Jack as he walked along the street. She ran her hands over her naked breasts and stomach, fantasizing that they were Jack's hands intimately exploring her body.

She liked the way his body moved. She liked the lean hardness of his torso and the tightness of his ass that his unfashionably loose clothes couldn't quite hide.

Her hands moved to caress her thighs and ass. She was looking forward to touching his naked backside, running her hands over his smooth buttocks and sliding her fingers into the tantalizing crevice between them.

He wasn't like some men, who used their clothes to conceal the imperfections of their body. She was reasonably sure that Mr. Jack Langton's body was a prime specimen. Of course, she'd have to see him quite unclothed before she would be able to tell for sure. That, she was quite sure, would be easy to arrange.

She'd enjoyed the lesson today more than she had expected. Just the remembrance of him sitting in her classroom, his legs apart, stroking his cock until he came in his pants, was enough to make her cunt tingle with excitement all over again. She had almost come in front of him, right as he was watching her touch herself, but she hadn't wanted to give him even that much power over her. Hearing him cry out in his own orgasm had nearly sent her over the edge herself. She'd restrained herself only with a huge effort. Her hands moved down to her cunt, now so wet that the juices were starting to run down the inside of her leg. Now that he was gone, she didn't need to restrain herself any longer.

She wanted him panting and unfulfilled—just as she was now. As a businesswoman, she was only too aware that a man never stayed satisfied for long. Men always wanted what was just out of their reach, and soon became bored with what was too easily attainable. If she were ever to completely satisfy Jack, he would lose interest in her and in her school. She could not afford for him to lose interest in the school—not until she had saved enough money to buy him out of their hasty partnership.

Besides, as a woman, she found the thought of keeping him on the edge deliciously arousing. She liked the thought of the control she would wield over him. She would keep him at her mercy—never quite satisfied, always wanting far more than she ever allowed him. By the end of their lessons, he would be on his knees in front of her, begging to be her sexual slave.

The thought had her rubbing her clit harder and faster, every so often dipping her fingers in and out of the wetness of her cunt, as she imagined Jack in every submissive posture that she could dream up, ready and willing to fulfill her every desire. Before he had even turned the corner and disappeared from sight, she was arching her back in ecstasy as the irresistible waves of her own orgasm rolled over and over her.

When her breathing had returned to normal and her heartbeat had quieted down once more, she withdrew her fingers from her sopping cunt and moved away from the window with a rueful grimace. Just fantasizing about Jack had made her come more powerfully than she had in years. What would she do if he had been inside her, driving into her with his powerful member until he came in her cunt, filling it with his hot, wet seed? It disturbed her how much she liked that thought.

She would just have to make sure that she didn't start enjoying the lessons a little too much herself. She needed him to be *her* slave, not the other way around.

She brought her hand to her mouth, smiling as she licked off a taste of her juices from her wet fingers. Indeed, the thought of Jack being her slave gave her a good idea for his next lesson.

Chapter Four

Jack, suffering through an interminable afternoon visit to his fiancée, was struck with a suddenly overwhelming urge to escape from the claustrophobic surrounds of the Harlow parlor. He stood up abruptly and held out his hand in invitation. "Walk with me, Clarissa." Maybe their conversation would be less painfully stilted out in the open air.

"I will fetch my maid."

He shook his head. "No. Just you and me." She hesitated. "After all, we *are* engaged," he reminded her. "There is no harm in spending some time alone together."

She raised her eyebrows at the unusual nature of his request, but then, ever the obedient fiancée, silently nodded and went to fetch her cape and bonnet.

The park in the middle of the square was almost deserted. He took her arm and placed it in his. Arm in arm they strolled along the perimeter of the park, Clarissa picking her way carefully through the damp grass in her dainty slippers. She did not use his arm as support, he noticed, or lean on him in any way. Her fingertips lay gently on his coat sleeve, her touch light and quite impersonal.

She did not need him or even want him at all, he thought, not even as a support in case she were to stumble. She did not need him for anything but the respectability he could give her by walking at her side—the respectability of marriage to a wealthy man.

He wondered what had impelled her into accepting such a bargain as they had made between them. Was it just the fear of poverty and the desire to please her parents that had made her accept his offer? Or was there a deeper reason for her decision?

He would never know, he supposed, lapsing again into gloomy contemplation of his bride-to-be. She was not exactly forthcoming in sharing her thoughts or desires.

Of course, he was presupposing she *had* desires—which her coldness was starting to make him doubt more and more with each passing day.

When he couldn't bear his own thoughts any longer, he finally broke the silence between them. "September is not so many weeks away now. Are you looking forward to getting married?"

There was a short silence before she answered. "In many ways, yes."

He was genuinely curious to know more about his wife-to-be. After all, they would be sharing a house and a home for the rest of their natural lives and they needed to know enough about each other's likes and dislikes to rub along well enough together. "What are you looking forward to most of all?"

"My independence, I suppose," she said, as she picked her way over a muddy patch in the path. "Married women have far more freedom than single girls do. I am looking forward to taking full advantage of my status as a married woman."

Her answer came as a surprise to him. "Your parents hardly keep you cloistered away from the world."

"Not on purpose, no," she replied, her attention on her feet still, rather than on him. "But they are careful of their only daughter. And besides, there is little enough money in our household budget for the necessities of life, let alone for small luxuries like hiring a hansom cab to go any place, or for paying for any entertainment when we get there. So I stay mostly at home."

"You would like us to keep a carriage?" He had never thought much about the question before, having little need of one himself.

"Yes, I would," she replied equably. "But only if you have no objections, and are well able to withstand the expense. I am not marrying you for the sake of a carriage to ride in."

Which still begged the question as to exactly why she *was* marrying him. "I think I could arrange matters satisfactorily." A new carriage would be a handsome wedding gift for his new bride. He would order it on the morrow.

"Thank you," she said simply, her eyes still on her feet.

Suddenly tired of sharing her attention with nothing more exciting than a muddy path through the grass, he stopped in a secluded part of the park where they were screened from the eyes of casual passersby. "Doesn't the offer of a new carriage deserve more than a simple word of thanks?" he murmured, wishing he was here with Helen rather than with Clarissa. "Shouldn't you thank me properly?" Helen would know how to thank a man properly. If he were with Helen now, he would have his hands up her skirt and deeply embedded in her hot, wet pussy and she would be writhing with pleasure and moaning her thanks into his open mouth.

A flicker of unease passed across Clarissa's face — more expression than she usually showed in a fortnight. "What more do you want from me?"

He leaned back against a sturdy tree trunk, his legs apart, and pulled her in between them, into his embrace. "A proper wife would thank her husband with a kiss." Maybe with some encouragement she would be more forthcoming about physical contact with him.

"We are not yet married," she demurred, pulling away from his embrace.

"But we will be soon." He held her there, trapped between his hard thighs, her body barely a heartbeat away from his own. "In just a few weeks you will be my wife and I will be your husband and I will expect to be kissed with great enthusiasm. Come, Clarissa, come and kiss me properly."

She assented with a small sigh, turning her face up to his and accepting his kiss, but her shoulders were still as stiff as a board and her entire body was tense and unwelcoming.

He was a complete novice at this virgin-taming business. The sight of the resigned expression on her face was enough to dampen his enthusiasm and wonder why he had ever started. She was not Helen and never would be. "Relax, I'm not about to bite you."

"I never thought you were," she said, her voice tight. "A kiss is quite bad enough."

Even the thought of kissing him was repugnant to her? Instead of kissing her, he wrapped his arms around her unyielding body and hugged her close to him. It was a long time since he had had a desirable woman in his arms, and, despite her coldness and lack of reaction to his caresses, his cock responded almost instantaneously to the feeling of her slim frame pressed against his. She was slighter than Helen was, and shorter, but she was still a woman. His woman. He'd been celibate ever since he'd said goodbye to Marie, and the strain was starting to tell on him.

He pushed his hardening cock against her soft belly, keeping his arms wrapped around her so she couldn't back away. "Feel that," he whispered. "That's the part of me that is looking forward to getting married the most."

She gave a small whimper and tried to shake off the arms that were holding her. "Please, don't."

He didn't let her go—just held her there against his body. "Don't worry, Clarissa, I'm not going to hurt you. I'm not going to touch you. I'm not going to do anything to you at all that you don't want me to do. I'm just going to hold you here and talk you to."

"I do not want to be held like this," she said. "Let me go."

"At least I won't touch you today," he added, still not releasing her. "But once we are married..." He let his voice trail off into a meaningful silence.

She took the bait, just as he had intended. "As soon as we are married? Then what?"

"As soon as we are married," he repeated, bending his head down to nuzzle gently at the white softness of her neck and nudging his erection against her belly. "As soon as we are married I am going to delight in touching every inch of you — with every inch of me. And I am going to teach you how to touch me back again."

She didn't seem terribly impressed with his offer, but remained ramrod straight in his arms.

"I'm looking forward to touching you all over." With a great effort of will he managed to keep his hands still on the small of her back as he spoke. "I'm going to strip you naked in the bedroom and just walk around you, admiring your body." Just as Helen had taught him to do to please a woman. "Then my hands will admire your body in their turn, touching and stroking your thighs, your belly, your breasts, your ass. My fingers are itching to get acquainted with your cunt lips and to delve into the wetness of your cunt."

He could feel his cock getting harder and harder as he spoke. His own words were starting to turn him on, even more than the feeling of Clarissa's body pressed against his, her small, virginal breasts pressed against his chest, her slim frame between his legs and his cock pressing into her belly.

He thought back to the lesson he had inadvertently overheard where Clarissa had been taught how to suck a man's cock and he got even harder. "I'm looking forward to you touching me in your turn." He nudged her with his cock, which was almost painfully hard now, rubbing it up and down against her belly. "I want your hands on my cock. I want your mouth on it, sucking me. I want you licking my balls, licking my ass, loving every inch of me with your tongue."

She shivered in his arms and gave a little whimper, whether from pleasure or trepidation, he didn't know. He hoped that Helen's lessons had borne fruit already, and she whimpered from pleasure.

He thought of Helen now, displaying herself to him in all her naked glory, touching herself for him. He would have Clarissa do exactly that for him and then he would fuck her, pretending that she was Helen. "I want you naked in front of me, spread-eagled with your legs apart, holding open your cunt lips for me. And I want my cock inside you, right up to the hilt, touching your womb. And I want you riding my cock like you would ride your favorite horse — hard and fast — until you get to the place you want to go."

He was breathing hard now, thinking about doing just that to Helen. "I want to fuck you, Clarissa. I want to fuck you hard and fast. As soon as we are married, I will keep you in bed with me for days on end, just fucking you and fucking you until I can fuck you no more." He was rubbing up against her hard now, impatient with the clothes they were both wearing. His straining cock was desperate to touch her bare skin. For the first time since he had known her, he was turned on by the thought of having her in his bed. He wanted to fuck her now. He *really* wanted to fuck her. "That's why I agreed to marry you."

With a sudden wrench, she broke away from his loosening hold. She stood there for a moment just looking at him, big tears starting to leak out of the corner of her eyes. "I am not sure that I can do this after all," she whispered, more to herself than to him, before turning on her heel and hurrying out of the park.

He stood and watched after her, amazed, his cock still hard and throbbing with desire. He'd never seen her move so fast in her life before. It seemed he had managed to break through her composure with his whispered words of lust, but they hadn't had exactly the reaction he had been hoping for. He'd been hoping to make her just a little bit hot and bothered, a little bit excited, a little bit interested and curious to experience the pleasure of fucking with him, but instead he had frightened her away.

He gave a rueful shrug of his shoulders. Damn this virgin-taming business. At least he had proven to himself that he could get turned on by her if he tried. But she clearly wanted him far less than he wanted her. As far as he could tell, she didn't want him at all. He was a fool to be marrying her. He was a fool ever to have thought it could work between them.

Especially, a little voice of temptation whispered in his ear, when the delectable and eminently lusty Helen was still unwed.

* * * * *

He'd wanted to stay away from Helen. He'd wanted to tell her that he didn't care for her lessons or for her method of teaching. He'd wanted to show her that he was not a man to be humiliated in such a fashion. But most of all he wanted to prove to Helen that he wasn't a randy schoolboy who came in his pants at the mere sight of a sexy and desirable woman touching herself. He wanted to show her that he was a real man with as much self-control as any woman, even his hardhearted tease of a teacher, could ever want or need. But after Clarissa had run from him in such haste, disgusted and appalled by his sudden enthusiastic lust for her, he'd needed Helen's warmth to take away the coldness. He needed Helen. That was all there was to it.

Which is why he found himself once more standing before Helen's desk in her empty office, taming his rampant desires as best he could while he waited for her to come and give him his next lesson in how to please a woman. He clearly hadn't learned enough yet, given the way that Clarissa had run from him the previous day. He'd started these lessons to give him an excuse to see Helen again, to get hot as he talked about sex with her, but it turned out that he needed them more than he really liked to admit.

Moreover, however much he tried to control himself, he still could not stop thinking about his previous lesson, about how he had inspected every part of her, and had been unable to enjoy any of the delights that had been spread before him. The thought made him more ready than ever for his next lesson, but still Helen did not appear.

He stood in the center of the room impatient at the delay, shifting his weight from one foot to the other, as his semi-hard cock pressed uncomfortably against the fabric of his trousers.

A rustle of silk outside the door had him standing to attention. The handle finally turned, the door opened, and Helen stepped into her office.

She was fully clothed this time, looking as prim and proper as if she hadn't displayed every inch of her naked body to him, in the most wanton poses he could ever imagine, just a few days before. His cock throbbed with his desire for her to take them all off again, but mindful of her previous disdain at his lack of self-control, he said nothing beyond the barest of polite greetings. He was sure she would take all her clothes off in her own good time. The whole evening lay stretched out before them. He was in no hurry—he could afford to wait.

She, however, was evidently not in the mood for waiting. "Your clothes." Her voice was brusque, without even the hint of a welcome in it. "Take them off."

He raised his eyebrows at her in a silent challenge. He wasn't sure he liked this new side of Helen. "Was that a request or an order?" he said in a dangerously quiet voice. He was a wealthy businessman, master of himself and slave to no man. No one, but no one, was allowed to speak to him like that. Had she been a man, he would have horsewhipped her for her temerity.

"I am the teacher and you are the pupil," she reminded him with a vicious sweetness in her tone. "If you refuse to follow my instructions, I shall refuse to teach you. Now, will you take your clothes off?"

He hesitated, his hand over the fastenings of his coat. He knew that he was her pupil, but God, it galled him that she should speak to him like that. Who was she to order him around?

"Or shall I show you to the door?"

The memory of her body, splayed naked in front of him, her fingers thrust up to the hilt in her wet pussy, undid him. He wanted a taste of that cunt. He wanted to feel his own fingers inside her, and to taste the juices that her body made for him.

He unfastened his coat and tossed it casually on the back of a chair before turning his attention to his boots. Damn her, but he needed the lesson more than he disliked being ordered around.

He could feel her eyes on him as he shrugged out of his jacket and peeled his trousers over his hips. He turned his head and snuck a glance at her out of the corner of his eye. Her eyes were fixed on his hands as they slowly undid the buttons of his shirt. As he slid out of the sleeves and let his shirt slip to the floor, the tip of her tongue sneaked out and licked her bottom lip

The knowledge that she was watching his every move with such avidity gave him the confidence to step out of his linen underwear with a flourish, unashamed of the desire that he was showing for her.

By the flushed look on her face, he would lay money on it that his teacher was not made out of stone, either. In fact, he would wager that she was just as hot for him as he was for her. The thought of her soft pussy growing wet for him brought a smile of anticipation to his lips. Bossy little tart that she was, she would enjoy teaching him tonight. He would make sure of that.

She nodded with approval when he stood before her, as naked as the day he was born, his cock jutting up proudly in front of him. She walked around him, looking at him from every vantage point. He could feel her gaze on his chest, on his straining cock, on his hips, his back, his legs, his buttocks. The heat of her gaze almost flayed him in its intensity, tracking a burning path of fire everywhere it landed. "Good," was all she said.

"You seem somewhat overdressed in comparison," he ventured, as she made no moves to disrobe in her turn.

She looked at him repressively and said nothing.

He winced slightly as he recalled how she had so quietly and disdainfully instructed that he must learn self control. *Fuck the idea of self-control. I will not sit meekly in a chair today, a passive watcher in this lesson.*

He looked challengingly at her. "Today's lesson will be different from the last one," he warned her. "Very different."

She gave him that confident smile of hers, the one that conveyed a promise of exotic delights and more than a hint of mystery. "You are quite right. You have so much to learn and in so little time that no lesson will be a repeat of the one before it."

Had she not picked up the warning in his voice? Did she not catch what he was trying to tell her? "I am not in a mood to sit meekly on my chair today as you tantalize me into madness."

Again that mysterious smile. "I would be disappointed if you did. Come, give me your hands."

He held out his hands to her, palms up.

From one of her capacious pockets she drew out a handful of narrow strips of black leather with small brass buckles on the end. She stepped up close to him, her womanly scent filling his nostrils with a sensual promise, and before he realized what she was about, she had fastened one of them around his neck.

"What the—" he began, his hands reaching up to unfasten it again. He was no stray dog, to be collared in such a fashion.

She hushed him with a finger over his mouth. "Don't be so touchy. There is no harm in it and it sets off your nakedness quite beautifully. You are quite a fabulous specimen of manhood. Come, give me your hands."

He hesitated, suddenly unsure as to the direction that this lesson was taking.

"Your hands," she commanded imperiously. "If you take such an age about every small request I make of you, we will have no time left for the lesson."

He held out his hands, grudgingly this time, and she fastened a leather chain around each wrist. She was right, he supposed. There was no harm in a small piece of leather fastened loosely around each of his wrists. If that was what his teacher wanted, he would play along. For now.

"And to finish with," she said, dropping to her knees in front of him and doing to same to each ankle.

He didn't even feel the restraints as she buckled them around his lower leg. All his attention was focused on the closeness of her soft, wet mouth to his jutting cock.

Her lips were parted slightly and he could feel her breath on his shaft as she concentrated on fastening the buckles. Did she know what she was doing to him?

He jutted his hips forward slightly so that his cock came to rest against her open mouth, the tip just pushing in between her lips.

That took her attention away from her task. She moved her head back a little, looked up at him and frowned. "Mr. Langton," she said in a repressive tone. "I am not here to pleasure you, but to teach you. I would thank you to remember that."

God, the touch of her tongue on his cock had been so arousing that with just a few licks and sucks, he would have come right in her mouth. *That* would have been a fine way to show her he had plenty of self-control. "Yes, ma'am." He couldn't quite manage to sound contrite.

She rose to her feet once more and dusted off her hands. "Follow me, and we will begin."

He followed her out of her office and down the hall to a small door at the end that opened on to a narrow staircase.

"Mind the stairs. They are quite steep."

He followed her down the spiral staircase, picking his way carefully in the dim light.

Helen had negotiated the stairs nimbly, and was quickly lost to view. All Jack could hear was his own footsteps. They seemed to echo on forever. He wondered if he would ever reach the bottom.

He thought of calling out to her to ask how far down the staircase went, but his pride stopped him. He was a man, and she had had the upper hand too often lately. He was just keyed up because of the situation he was in—naked except for the leather straps, in the dark, in a strange house, with a woman who seemed intent on tormenting rather than on teaching him.

After two or three spirals the stairwell became completely black. He placed each foot after the first, feeling with his toe to ensure a step was actually there. His arms were out on each side as his hands steadied him on the handrails.

As he came to the bottom of the stairs, his eyes still not fully adjusted to the dim light, he heard a muffled clanking and felt a light touch on each wrist and ankle.

The dim shape he could make out in the middle of the room must be Helen. He picked his way over to her and went to reach out to touch her, but found that he could not. The leather bands were now restraining him, holding his arms up and out away from his body. Jack fell forward as he struggled.

"Hey!" he called out angrily, as he regained his footing. "What's the game?"

"It's no game." Helen's voice was full of amusement. "It's your second lesson. The lesson in self-control."

Suddenly his arms were drawn over his head, spread wide, and he found himself immobilized. Now he could not even move his feet. It was as if he were glued to the floor.

He struggled violently against his bonds, but it was no use. He could not undo the buckles or slip the leather bands over his wrists and ankles. Nor could he break the chains he was tied with. He was trussed like a beast for slaughter, limbs pulled wide apart, totally exposed to the night and the darkness all around him.

He didn't want to think what might be happening to him, finding relief instead in fury. "What the hell is going on?"

"Do not forget the object of this lesson is your temper, Mr. Langton. Self-control."

He took a deep breath, willing himself to settle down enough to speak to her with some semblance of calm. Who was she to think she could truss him like a Christmas goose? "Release me this instant or you will be sorry." He smiled a grim smile to himself. The instant she let him go, he would have her in those restraints herself, and let her see how she liked it.

She laughed—a low, melodious sound that made him see red. "It's too late to back down now. The lesson has begun."

If her pretty, white neck had been within reach at that moment, he would've wrung it without a second thought. "I no longer want any more of your damned lessons. Take off the bands."

"All in good time."

And despite all his ranting and cursing and swearing that she would regret it, she would not untie him.

Helen lit a directional gas lamp that illuminated her subject, but left her in the shadow. This lesson was not to be about her, but about him.

She was glad that she had put the heavier chains on the leather bands to bind her pupil with—her instinct had been right that the lighter chains would never have held him. Jack Langton in a naked fury was an awesome sight. Particularly bound as he was now—his wrists chained to a hook in the ceiling, his legs wide apart and his ankles bound to a pair of manacles on the floor. He was spread-eagled in the middle of the room just for her. She felt a hotness in the pit of her belly start to grow at the sight of him, helpless before her, vulnerable and hating the weakness she had tricked him into. She had all the power over him that a woman could want—and she intended to make him feel it. Tonight he was her slave. He would learn how to please a woman not by dominating her, as was the usual way of men, but by submitting to her every whim, her every desire.

And her first desire was to look at him, as he had looked at her in the previous lesson. She wanted to see all of him, as he had seen all of her.

She looked at him critically, his broad shoulders, the firm muscles of his chest, his legs well-formed and muscular. He looked strong and powerful, as if he had spent his life laboring on a farm or loading and unloading goods on and off the barges that lined the river Thames. He didn't look like a wealthy financier who spent all his day behind a desk—he looked more like a highwayman or a brigand than that.

But not all of him looked proud and strong at this particular moment. His poor cock, she noted with a smile, was suffering from anger and cold, seemingly trying to withdraw into his body. How different it was from the proud, jutting member it had been in her office. Really, women had the advantage over men when it came to hiding their feelings. A woman, even a naked woman, gave few clear signs that spelled out how aroused she was. Whereas a man's feelings—or lack of them—were evident even when they were fully clothed. Poor Jack. She would have to remedy his lack of eagerness if this lesson was to be a success.

He noted the direction of her glance and his swearing grew louder and more vociferous.

She ignored his bad temper. Men were such predictable creatures—she had never met a single one who could bear to lose control when they least expected it. He would get over his pique soon enough once the lesson had properly started. "Are you cold?"

Her only answer was more swearing.

Really, she thought, his language was more colorful than any other gentleman she knew. He must have had a particularly misspent youth to know such colorful words as were spewing forth out of him like a torrent. But for all the heat of his fury, his skin was prickled all over with goose bumps. He would start to feel cold once his temper cooled.

She walked over to the grate and touched a match to the fire that was laid there. Although the cellar room was chilly, even in the heat of summer, she had not wanted to light the fire before now. The light that it gave out would have given Jack some warning of his fate, and may have allowed him to escape being chained and manacled to the floor. Far better that she should get him safely tied, though it meant he would suffer just a little from a chill.

The leaping flames put out an eerie glow that danced and flickered over the walls and the thick rugs that lay scattered on the stone floor. Helen moved a painted fireguard in front of the flames. She had no intention of roasting poor Jack like a pig on a spit.

His swearing had died down now into a muted grumble.

"You have a nice body," she opened, conversationally, as the fire danced merrily in the grate behind her. "Strong, firm, and very manly."

He grunted something unintelligible back at her. It sounded suspiciously like more swearing.

She held up the gas light so that it shone on his chest. "Not very many hairs on your chest. I like that in a man. So many men are covered all over in fur like a bear, but your skin is smooth. Smooth is so much nicer." She reached out and touched his chest with one fingertip, running it down the hollow in the middle of his chest.

He flinched at the touch of her finger and growled at her, but didn't start cursing again.

"Soft and smooth. Just as a man's chest should be. But with nice, broad shoulders. Strong shoulders and arms that look like you could pick me up with no effort at all. Strength is good in a man, too. No woman wants an undersized weakling in her bed."

That certainly got his attention. "I am no undersized weakling. Not anywhere." His aggrieved tone showed his outrage at the very thought.

"I never said you were." She reached up and touched one of his nipples, brushing it lightly with her forefinger until it lost its softness. "You are hard in all the right places."

A shudder coursed through his body at her touch, and his cock in its nest of curls started to stir. Excellent. He was responding to her lesson in just the way she had planned on.

She carried her light around to the other side of him to admire his buttocks. "Beautiful," she said, running her hand over his taut cheeks. "A woman likes a man with a nice, tight ass. We like to watch men as they walk away from us, their asses moving with each step."

Jack made a choked noise in the back of his throat. "Is this turning you on? Looking at me, touching me, while I'm tied up here like an animal, unable to respond?"

She brought one hand around to his front, feeling rather than seeing. His cock had more than tripled in size while she had been admiring his buttocks. "I would have to differ with your assessment of the situation," she said primly. "I think you are responding quite nicely to your situation. Altogether as expected, in fact."

He made an exasperated noise. "You know perfectly well what I mean. Don't pretend that you do not."

"This is a lesson in self-control, Mr. Langton. You are being restrained for your own good. It is necessary at times to have self-control forced on you, to make sure that you learn your lesson properly."

"Being tied up in chains and shackled to the floor?" He barked a harsh laugh. "Forgive me if I seem unimpressed with your lesson so far."

She came around to face him again, and set the lantern down on the floor so that the light fell on his well-built torso. Judging by the size of his erection, he did not seem to be overly upset at being tied up. He was, she suspected, complaining merely for the affront to his dignity, and not because he found the sensation unpleasant in any way. "Men are so used to having what they want, taking what pleases them. They seldom stop to think about what a woman would really like."

He didn't look impressed. "Isn't that why I have come to you for lessons at all? If I didn't care what women thought of me, I would never have wasted my time with you. And I would never have ended up here, tied up naked in a cellar with a madwoman wielding the chains."

"Men like to look at women. I proved that last week," she said pointedly, making his color rise just a trifle. "But have you ever stopped to think that women might like to look at men as well? Have you ever thought that we might find it exciting to look on a man's naked body, to gaze at it as we please, without the fear that he will overpower us with his strength? Have you never thought that women, too, may want to take a turn at being the dominant partner?"

"Only a man-woman like you would ever think of such a perversion," he grumbled. "Men were born to be in charge while women were born to be subservient to their masters. You have reversed the natural order of things."

She came closer to him and laid one hand on his chest, tracing the lines of his ribs with gentle strokes. "Maybe so. But in that case, I like the natural order of things to be reversed once in a while."

"So what do you plan to do with me, now that you have me at your mercy?" He was starting to sound interested now, rather than aggrieved. That was definitely a good sign.

She stepped back, her hands on her hips, and looked at him for a moment, consideringly. "As I said, first of all I want to look at you."

"Just look?" There was a note of disappointment in his voice.

"Just look," she confirmed.

"Please, be my guest," he said wryly. "Look at me to your heart's content."

She hadn't stopped looking at him the whole time. Her cunt was already getting hot and wet with the sight of him, tied in chains with a huge erection just for her pleasure. She wanted to lift her skirts, wrap her legs around his waist and ride his cock hard and fast, but it wasn't the right time or place to indulge her erotic fantasies. "Thank you. I will."

"As it is, I can hardly stop you."

She moved in closer to him, kneeling down so that his cock was at eye level. She could see it all now—the ridges along the shaft, huge, purple head engorged with passion, the twin sacs that hung underneath. "And that bothers you?"

He swallowed convulsively as she inspected him. "Less and less."

"I'm glad. I would hate to have my pupil go shy and embarrassed on me all of a sudden. Shyness has no place in the bedroom."

That made him laugh out loud, though his voice was rather strained. "Believe me, I had already noticed your lack of shyness. You touched yourself in front of me. You put your fingers in your cunt while I was watching you. And then in your ass." He groaned audibly.

She was sure his cock had grown another inch as he was speaking. "You didn't like watching me?"

He groaned again. "You know damn well I liked it. I liked it so damn much that practically the only thing I've thought about ever since is getting my hands on you, getting my own fingers inside your cunt and inside your ass, thrusting my cock hard into you again and again until I come deep inside you. And here I am tied up like a lamb, unable to move, unable to touch you." She could hear the pain and frustration in his voice. "Do you have any idea how angry that makes me feel?"

"A little," she confessed, getting to her feet again. "Which is why I took the liberty of tying you up. I knew you would never have consented to keeping still and obedient and letting me have control over this lesson if I did not."

"And when you have finished looking at me? What then?" He still sounded truculent.

She looked him right in the eye. "I shall do whatever I please to you. And you will learn the pleasure that comes from letting me have my way with you."

He gave a frustrated wriggle of his shoulders—the only part of him he could easily move. "And just what will please you to do to me today?"

The only answer she gave him was to reach around him and spank his naked buttocks—hard.

He let out a gasp that was partway between pleasure and pain as the flat of her hand connected with his bare skin.

"I think I want to discipline you today," she murmured softly, as she spanked his buttocks again with a firm hand. "I think you have been a naughty boy and need to be punished. You need to be shown who's the boss. What do you say to that, Mr. Langton?"

His only answer was a strangled, "Oh, Christ, Helen."

She took that as permission to keep going. She kept on spanking him, with first the palm of one hand and then the other, until both her hands were sore.

His buttocks were bright pink and she knew that they must tingle almost unbearably. This time when she brought her hand to his buttocks, her touch was gentle. Slowly she stroked his cheeks, and the cleft in between.

His breathing was now harsh and heavy, rasping in the silence of the cellar with an unnatural loudness.

She sank down to her knees and replaced her hands with her mouth and tongue. Slowly she soothed his pink, punished flesh with her tongue, licking away the pleasure-pain she had caused him.

Then, ever so gently, she nudged apart his buttocks, and began to lick the cleft between them.

As her tongue touched his ass, his whole body convulsed. "Christ, Helen, what are you doing to me?" he forced out from between his gritted teeth.

She reluctantly raised her head for a moment. "Exploring you." To her surprise, she was enjoying this lesson at least as much as her pupil was. It had been far too long since she had had such a gorgeous male body to explore like this. Or any male body at all, come to think of it.

She turned her attention again to his ass, licking him there greedily. With each stroke of her tongue, he gave a groan of pleasure. "God, Helen, I don't think I can take much more of this." His voice sounded as though he was in severe pain. "I need to come so badly I'm going to explode."

She ignored his plea. Her tongue had found his balls now, and she was too engaged in licking them, taking them into her mouth and sucking on them, to answer him. Besides, she knew just how aroused he was. Instead of hanging down loosely like a couple of small sacs, his balls were hard and tight, driven up into his body by the force of his need. She sucked on them, pulling them toward her, massaging them with her tongue, reveling in the salty taste of his skin. Every so often she licked right up to his ass again, and each time his body jerked and spasmed as if he was having a mini-orgasm.

"Suck my cock." The words burst forth from him with the force of a swollen river bursting its banks.

Helen licked up around his balls to the base of his cock. "You're hardly in the position to order me around," she said mildly. "Ask me nicely and I might consider it."

"Suck my cock—please." It was still an order, dressed in a veneer of politeness this time.

She teased him with her tongue just a little higher on the base of his shaft. "Still not good enough."

"For God's sake, Helen, please take my cock in your mouth and suck on it."

That was rather more like it. "Are you begging me?"

"If I beg you, will you suck it?"

She wanted her mouth on his cock almost as much as he wanted it. She was wet with the thought of sucking on him. "I can never resist a man who begs me."

"Then yeah, I'm begging you. I'm begging you with everything I have." He shook the chains that were holding him captive with frustration. "I will do anything you like, be as submissive as I know how to be, if you will only stop tormenting me and just suck the damn thing."

Ah, how she liked to hear the wealthy and arrogant Jack Langton begging her like that, even though his words held just as much anger as true desperation. Sex gave women more power over men than anything else in the world, and oh, how men hated women to find out this little secret of theirs. How men hated women to know that they could be led around by the nose by a woman who controlled their desires.

"Please." This time the begging in his voice was genuine. It was the voice of a man who had almost reached the limit of his endurance.

"Since you asked me so nicely," she said, almost purring with expectation as she moved into position. She slowly licked all the way up the length of his shaft, moving her tongue around the swollen, purple head of his huge cock. An impatient dribble of moisture was already starting to leak out from the tip. She touched it with the tip of her tongue, savoring its salty flavor. Ahh, she hadn't tasted the juices from a man's cock for longer than she cared to remember. She had forgotten just how good they could taste, how delicious it was to have that flavor of a man on her tongue. Finally, she moved her mouth over him to take him all into her mouth.

He let out a long groan of absolute pleasure as her mouth engulfed him, and bucked his hips so that as much of him as possible would fit into her greedy mouth.

He was so engorged that she could hardly fit her mouth over his head, and she knew that he was close to coming. After just a few long sucks, she raised her head. "Remember, the object of this lesson is about self-control."

Jack's face was contorted in to a grimace. "I am trying my best to remember that," he gritted out between clenched teeth.

She bent to his cock again, unwilling to stop sucking on it and licking it just yet. She liked having him quivering on the edge for her, she loved the control she had on him when his cock was in her mouth and he was hard just for her. She could've sucked him and sucked him until he had run dry.

After only a few moments, Jack spoke again, his voice strained to breaking point. "I'm not sure if I can remember the object of this lesson for much longer."

Reluctantly Helen ceased her ministrations and stood up. It wasn't part of her plan to have him come in her mouth. She was his teacher, not his whore. However much she was enjoying herself during their lesson time, she had to remember her real function. She must not allow herself to feel anything for him. He was her pupil and her financier — and the terms of their contract did not specify anything about allowing him anything else.

Jack was standing in his chains, a look of pained outrage on his face. "You can't stop now."

She raised one eyebrow as she looked back at him. "I can't?"

"Christ, Helen, I was so close to coming you could just about have tasted me — and then you stop? You're trying to drive me insane. You're trying to drive me absolutely and utterly barking mad."

She could tell by the tenseness in his body that a couple of sucks, a couple of strokes and he would orgasm.

She would like to suck on him until he came in her mouth. She surprised herself by the strength of her wanting. She had never wanted to do that to a man before. Still, she must remember to keep the lesson impersonal. She must remain his teacher and feel nothing more than a professional interest in her pupil, however handsome and well-built he may be.

With a sigh, she reached up behind him and unshackled one of his hands, letting it fall to his side. "Make yourself come for me," she instructed him.

He lifted his hand and stared at it as if he had never seen it before, as if it wasn't a part of his body. "You're not going to keep on sucking me, are you?"

It was a statement, rather than a question. She repeated her earlier command. "Make yourself come for me. I want to watch you spill your seed on the floor."

With a muffled curse he gave in and started to stroke his cock, the chain still attached to his wrist rattling at every movement.

Harder and faster he stroked, until his body stilled and then shook with spasms, and his seed shot out of his body with the force of a bullet from a gun.

With one final groan he let his hand fall to the side, at once both satisfied and defeated.

Helen unfastened the shackles that kept him immobile, trying to ignore the insistent desire in the pit of her belly, trying not to feel the way the fabric of her bodice rubbed so enticingly over her nipples. He may be satisfied now, but she was not.

How she had wanted to raise her skirts up to her waist and bend over in front of him, so he could thrust that cock of his into her hungry pussy. She'd wanted him to fuck her and fuck her until she melted into a pool of desire at his feet.

Instead, she had left him to satisfy himself while she had watched, hungry and wanting.

He took that moment to turn and look at her with those green-brown eyes of his—the eyes of an alley cat on the prowl. His eyes told her that he hadn't forgiven her for making him satisfy himself—and that he wasn't likely to forget it in a hurry. His eyes promised retribution.

She shivered under his gaze. His eyes promised her that one day soon he would fuck her until she was screaming with pleasure.

Hang the fact that he was her pupil and he owned half her school. Hang the fact that she wanted him to be like clay in her hands so she could retain control over her investment in the school—and over her life. His eyes told her that he was a man and she was a woman and they wanted each other.

In that moment she decided that one day soon she would give in to his wishes and fuck him all day and all night long, and to hell with the consequences.

Chapter Five

Jack stretched his arms and legs, stiff from being shackled during the lesson. Christ, but Helen was a tease, tormenting him until he was on the edge of an orgasm, and then withdrawing and forcing him once again to satisfy himself like any schoolboy.

All he'd wanted was for her to turn around and lift her skirts for him so he could sink into her cunt, thrusting in and out of her warm wetness until he shot his seed into her womb. Failing that, he'd wanted her to keep on licking his balls and sucking his cock so he could come into her eager mouth. At the very least she could have stroked him herself, so he could have come into her soft hands. But no, not Helen. She couldn't even do that much for him.

Instead, she had stood there, all her clothes on, just watching him as he stroked himself to a desperate conclusion.

If he'd been less excited, he'd have been embarrassed for a woman to see him shoot his own seed out with such force, such need. Helen had left him no room for embarrassment. She had left him no room for anything but a fierce desire, and a desperate need to bring himself to orgasm in whatever way he could.

Now that he was out of his bonds, however, he would take charge again. He had had enough of being ordered around and played with as if he were no more than a plaything for her pleasure. He was stronger than she was, and more determined. She would be in his power, and he would make her feel his dominion over her in every fiber of her being.

He unclasped the chains from his wrists and ankles, and dropped them on the floor. Then, without even stopping to unbuckle the bands that clasped him around each wrist and ankle, he advanced on her.

She paled as she caught sight of the look in his eye, but she didn't flinch or run from him, as he had half expected her to do. She simply stood her ground, her arms folded across her chest, one boot tapping impatiently on the stone floor, as he stalked toward her.

"You tied me up," he said accusingly, as he stopped in front of her, towering over her in his nakedness. "You stripped me, you tied me up and you spanked me. That was not smart of you."

She gave him a satisfied smile and touched one fingertip to the band that still remained on his wrist. "I did."

He was trying to intimidate her and failing miserably. "You're not even sorry, are you?"

She shivered all over with pleasure. "No, I'm not. Are you?"

He ignored the impertinent question. It was time that Helen Fairchild took some of her own medicine—and he was just the man to give it to her. "You didn't ask my permission before tying me up. That was most remiss of you. You will have to be punished for it."

She was undaunted by his threats, standing her ground in front of him as if he wasn't twice her size and strength. "I will?"

"You spanked me, too, until my backside was burning." He stared at her for a moment, trying to decipher what her game was now. Her face was unreadable, a blank. "Did your mother never tell you it was dangerous to play with fire?"

They could have been discussing the weather for all the emotion she showed. "Not recently."

He unbuckled the clasps from his wrists. "Did she never warn you that if you played with fire, you were liable to be burned?"

"No, she never warned me."

He reached out, took hold of her arm and buckled one leather strap firmly around her fine-boned wrist. "Then I think it is time I taught you in her place."

"You're planning to tie me up?" she asked, her voice not quite as steady as it was.

Ha, so she *wasn't* as cool and collected as she was pretending to be. "I am," he confirmed, as he buckled the other strap around her wrist.

She shrugged as if it didn't matter to her, but he could tell by the spark in her eye and the willingness that she gave herself over to the leather straps that the thought excited her. "I was going to allow you to tie me up and teach you how best to touch me for our next lesson," she said calmly. "But if you would like to bring the lesson forward and complete it this afternoon, then I am willing."

He liked the sound of that. "Good. I always prefer my women willing."

"But there are some rules around this lesson," she continued, as if he hadn't spoken.

"Rules?" He shook his head with no small amount of satisfaction. He was agreeing to no rules. "By the time I have finished with you, you will be in no place to dictate rules to me."

"Which is why we have to agree on them now," she said firmly, her arms crossed militantly in front of her.

He didn't like the sound of these rules. He didn't trust her, not at all. "And if I do not agree? What then?"

Without warning, her hand shot out and grabbed his naked testicles firmly enough to make him wince.

"All right, you have my attention," he said with some haste, feeling slightly queasy in the stomach at the thought of what she might do if he didn't agree quickly. "Dictate your terms, and if they are reasonable enough, I will agree."

She loosened her hold slightly. "You will dress yourself right away and keep your clothes on at all times during this next lesson—just as I did during the previous one."

He was about to open his mouth in protest but she forestalled him. "You may take off all my clothes and explore my body as intimately as I explored yours," she offered. "Indeed, I will help you to explore my body by suggesting where and how you may touch me and telling you what feels good to me. You will not, however, touch me with anything other than with your hands or your tongue—just as I did not touch you with anything other than my hands or my tongue—unless I give you express and explicit permission to do so. Do you agree to this?"

He nodded reluctantly. He would at least get to taste her, even if he did not get the chance to bury his cock in her cunt as deep as it would go. Not unless she begged him to do so. And he would do his level best to make her beg him to. "I agree."

"I must warn you," she said with a slight smile, "that I am *not* going to beg you to fuck me, so you can get that idea out of your head right now."

That was easy for her to say, but not so easy for him to do. He liked the thought of her tied up to the shackles as he had been, begging him to fuck her, to let her have an orgasm, to put her out of her misery. Tied up as he had been, he would've given anything to have been able to fuck her. He could only hope that she would prove more susceptible than she thought herself. "I am willing to take the chance that you will change your mind." She only had to weaken for a second, and his cock would be inside her. Then it would be too late for her to change her mind.

"And the last condition. If I tell you to stop, you stop. No questions asked, no hesitation. You simply stop whatever you are doing on the instant and wait for further instructions."

He hesitated. Was she deliberately going to tease him again? Tantalize him with the promise of exploring her body and then refuse to allow him to do what he wanted to do?

"I must have your agreement to this or I will not agree to be tied," she said, the warning pressure on his testicles increasing slightly. "But in return I promise you that I will not ask you to stop idly or on a whim. Only if I need you to."

He had no choice. He had to agree. "I swear that I will stop if you ask me to." He grinned at her wryly. "I can only hope that you don't ask."

"Then we are agreed. Come, get your clothes so we can begin."

Jack followed her up the spiral staircase and into the study again with reluctant feet. He had no wish to get dressed again, but the thought that Helen's clothes would come off her delectable body as soon as his were on again hurried his steps.

He had never dressed himself so fast, even ripping off one of his shirt buttons in his haste to clothe himself. When both his boots were finally pulled on, he turned to face her.

The tables were turned on them now, and he was going to enjoy every moment of his dominance. "Take your clothes off," he ordered her, as he flung himself onto the armchair.

She pouted at him, not moving. "Don't you want to help me?"

He shook his head. "No—I want to watch you. I want to tell you what to do and how fast to do it. I want to see you strip for me and I want you to do it just as I tell you to. Now, take off your slippers."

She began to crouch down to take off her slippers, but he stopped her with a word. "Don't crouch. Bend over. I want to see your ass."

She bent over, her backside facing him, and fumbled with her slippers.

He wanted to see her ass, not just her skirts, as she bent over. "Pull your skirts up around your waist. Let me get a proper look at you."

She pulled her skirts up, revealing a pair of white pantaloons. Full of pleasurable anticipation, he contented himself with just looking at their lacy softness until she had finished taking off both slippers.

Suddenly it wasn't enough for him. He wanted to see her naked skin. He wanted to see the pinkness of her flesh, the cleft of her buttocks, and the tight little hole hidden between them. "Take off your pantaloons."

She reached under her skirt to unknot the strings that kept her pantaloons about her waist. The frothy lace fell to the ground, and she stepped out of them in her stockinged feet. If she were to bend over now, he thought with delicious anticipation, he would see not linen and lace, but her naked ass. "Bend over."

She bent over for him, pulling her skirts up around her waist, knowing what he wanted without him having to tell her.

He could see the rounded globes of her bottom and the tantalizing cleft between them. How he would like to slide his cock up and down in that cleft. "Pull your buttocks apart. Let me see your asshole."

She obeyed him without any hesitation, pulling her buttocks apart so he could gaze at her secret rosebud. His fingers itched to touch her there, but he contained himself. Right now he was just going to look at her. Touching would come later. "Now your stockings."

She stood up again, dropping her skirts so they covered her legs again. One foot up on a chair, she pulled her skirts up over her knee, and undid first one and then the other garter that rode high on her thighs.

Her thighs were milky white and the way she was standing gave him just a glimpse of the nest of curls that hid her cunt from him. She was the most sensual woman he had ever met, deliberately tantalizing him with her body. He could feel his cock stirring again with the desire to fuck her every way he could—in her mouth, between her breasts, in her pussy, and up her ass.

Her breasts. He wanted to see her breasts again before he was too distracted by the promise of her seat of pleasure. Her breasts, so high and full, were worth gazing at for hours together. "Undo your bodice for me."

She made a moue at him. "You'll have to help me. I can't reach all the buttons by myself."

He crooked his finger at her, salivating at the thought of having an excuse to touch her at last without her complaining of his lack of control. "Come over here, then, and I shall help you."

She came to stand obediently in front of him so he could reach her buttons. Instead of helping her right away, he could not resist pulling her down on to his lap before starting on her buttons.

She wriggled her hips, lifting her skirt until it was bunched around her waist and her naked bottom was pressed against his trousers. "You're hard again."

Why on earth did women have so many tiny buttons on their bodices? It must take them an age to get undressed each night. He concentrated on each tiny button one by one, until at last the entire row of them had been undone and her bodice gaped open at the back. "You're one layer of fabric away from sitting on my cock. What else would you expect?"

She sighed theatrically as she wriggled around on his lap, making him harder still. "Did you not learn your lesson well this afternoon? Do you need to be tied up again until you get it right?"

God, it felt good to have her sitting in his lap. It felt too good. "I learned my lesson perfectly well, thank you all the same. And the only tying up that's going to be done from now on is *me* tying *you* up." He slapped her on her rump. "Now get off my lap, hussy, and take off your bodice."

She stood up between his legs and shimmied out of her bodice. Her pink-tipped breasts swung free of their confinement, barely an inch from his nose. She was as beautiful as he remembered her being. Her breasts were high and firm and her belly as flat as a girl's.

He cleared his throat. Looking at her breasts for hours on end would have to wait for another day. He was suddenly impatient to see her naked as the day she was born. "And your skirts. Take them off, too."

She unfastened the ties around her waist and stepped out of them, leaving them to pool on the floor at her feet. She stood there in front of him, proudly naked—not overtly flaunting her body, but not attempting to hide any part of it, either.

He feasted his eyes on her nakedness, looking at every inch of her, really looking at her and appreciating every part of her body, as she herself had taught him to.

"Turn around," he ordered her. "Slowly."

She held out her arms and turned around so that he could see her from every angle.

He almost groaned with pleasure as he gazed at her. From top to toe, from the crown of her blonde hair to the pink of her toes, she was nothing short of perfection. He would give all he owned in the world just then to have the right to look at her naked body every day for the rest of his life.

For the rest of the evening, however, she was his to do with as he pleased—within the limits she had prescribed, of course. He would make the most of the time he had with her.

He retrieved the remaining two leather bands from the floor and tied them around her ankles, his hands shaking slightly at the knowledge that he was preparing to immobilize her for his pleasure. "Downstairs with you." He could hardly wait to have her tied up for him, as unable to move as he himself had been. She would be his to feast on until he was so satiated he could feast no longer.

She walked primly along the hallway and down the spiral staircase in front of him, quite unselfconscious of her nakedness.

He wished he could feel as calm as she looked. Despite the tremendously powerful orgasm he had experienced not so long ago, the need for her was building up in him like a disease. The heat he felt for her was worse than any fever.

The chains were still on the floor as he had dropped them. Helen walked over to the shackles and held her arms out to him. "Come, chain me up as I chained you," she said, her voice husky. "Then you can explore my body, every crack and every crevice of it, as I explored yours earlier. I will tell you how to please a woman, where to touch her to make her cry out with the joy of it, and you will prove to me, on my own body, how well you have learned your lesson."

She was as eager as he was for this lesson. The knowledge that she wanted him to chain her up and use her body as he pleased, to touch her and taste her all over every part of her, made his own eagerness increase tenfold.

He clipped the chains on her arms and shackled them to the ceiling of the cellar, and then chained her legs, wide apart, to the floor. She was his now—all his. He gloried in the possession of her.

"What do you want me to do to you first?" he asked, as he walked around her, admiring the curve of her buttocks, the swell of her breasts, and the strong shape of her thighs in the dim glow of the firelight.

"Touch me all over," she murmured, throwing her head back so that her long, blonde hair streamed down her back. "Just touch me."

He stretched out one hand to touch her shoulder. He had seen her naked before—all of her—as she played with herself, but he had never touched her. He suddenly found that he was burning to touch her all over.

His greedy hands smoothed over her shoulders, her neck, and then her breasts. They were heavy in his hands, womanly and round.

She gave a soft sigh at the caress. "Play with my nipples," she whispered. "I like it when you touch them."

He took her nipples between his thumb and forefinger, rolling them until they were hard as tiny rocks in his hands. "Do you like that?" he murmured into her ear.

She moaned with pleasure at his attentions.

He was suddenly greedy to hear more than moans. He wanted to hear her voice. "Moaning isn't good enough. Tell me with words how you feel."

"I feel good." Her voice was husky with desire.

"How good?"

She moaned again. "I feel like I want you to keep touching my breasts. Like I want you to suckle on them with your mouth and lick at them as if they were your favorite treat. Like I want you to keep on doing that forever."

He bent his head to her breasts and touched the tip of one of them with his tongue. "Like this?"

She arched her back so that more of her breast was pushed into his mouth. "No, not tickling like that. Harder and stronger."

He took her whole nipple and as much of her breast into his mouth as he could manage.

"Suckle on me," she said, writhing under his touch as if it burned her.

He began to suckle on her breasts, first one, then the other. Her nipples were tight and hard under his tongue. She writhed under him with every suck, trying to get closer to him and rub her naked body against his clothed one.

He moved back a little so she could not get any relief that way. She had not let him touch her when he was tied up. He would play the same game as she had, and, now that he had her tied up, he would not let her touch him. Besides, even clothed as he was, the touch of her body against his might just cause him to lose control and fall on her like a ravening animal. He couldn't very well do that. He had to show her that he was enough of a man to keep control of himself, whatever provocation she dished out to him.

He sank to his knees in front of her, eager to touch and taste the rest of her.

Her thighs were creamy white and smooth under his fingertips. He stroked them with greedy hands, noting each little freckle, and even one tiny mole high up on her leg, on the inside of her right thigh.

He bent his head and brought his lips close to that tiny blemish. Her skin smelled of soap, lavender soap, and of the essence of womanhood. He shut his eyes and breathed deeply of her scent, as if he could inhale the very essence of her along with his breath. Only when he had breathed so deeply of her that he knew her scent would remain with him forever, did he touch his lips to her mole.

She gave a start when his lips touched her warm skin, and he heard her take a sharp breath, but he forgot her surprise in the delights of tasting her at last. Her skin was slightly salty under his tongue. He licked her mole, her thigh, and then higher and higher.

She was pressing her thighs together, so he could not get to her cunt as he wanted to do, as he needed to do. She was in his control, under his power. That would have to stop.

He slid one hand in between her thighs and spread them apart. "Open your legs for me," he ordered. "Open them wide."

She shuddered as she opened her legs at his order.

Ah—that was just as he had imagined her for days, standing in front of him, as naked as the day she was born, every part of her exposed to his view.

He brought his fingers up and touched her between her legs, exulting in the gasp that he wrung from her at the touch. Slowly he ran one finger over the surface of her folds, touching her intimately for the first time. She was as soft as satin, and twice as inviting.

He could not resist any longer the temptation to slide the tip of his finger into her. "God, you're wet," he rasped out, at the feeling of his finger being engulfed in her dripping flesh. He'd never felt any woman wetter than she was now. She was enough to drown a man. His cock was no longer half-alive again—it was fully alive, and more than ready to do his lady service. A cunt as wet as hers was begging to be entered, and by more than a single finger.

"Spanking you turned me on," she said, wriggling her hips to introduce more of his finger inside her. "Spanking you made me so hot for you that I nearly came. Even with all my clothes on, even with you not even touching me, I was so hot I was ready to burst."

"Instead I was the one who finally burst," he said, as he thrust his finger deep inside her, as far as it would go. He had not quite forgiven her for making him fondle himself to orgasm. He hadn't quite decided yet if he would try the same tactics out on her.

He didn't think so, he decided. He wanted to see the look in her eyes and hear the cries she made as he gave her pleasure. For his own sake, he couldn't bear to hold off her gratification. He wanted to have her melt in his arms and to know that every bit of pleasure she was experiencing was due to him.

Besides, she was a contrary woman. Once she was out of his power, if he dared her to touch herself, she would probably refuse. She was a hardhearted wench with a will of iron, and she would no doubt refuse to do as he ordered her to do, simply because he had ordered her to do it. And then she would taunt him with his lack of skills in the bedroom and claim that he lacked the means to properly satisfy a woman.

No, he couldn't have that. He wouldn't stand for her mocking him. He wouldn't untie the delectable Helen until she had had at least one orgasm at his hands.

He bent his head to taste her, his tongue searching out her sensitive bud of flesh. First he teased it with the lightest of touches and then he began to suck on it with all his might. She tasted just as he imagined she would—of honey and summer and sweetness. She tasted of the essence of femininity, of womanhood. He sucked at her greedily, wanting to taste all of her that he could.

Another finger joined the first in her cunt, the two digits pumping in and out rhythmically as he licked and sucked on her.

She opened her body to his ministrations, begging him to keep on going, thrusting her hips to meet his fingers, urging herself onwards to the peak. Her breathing was harsh and labored now, as if she were in the throes of a nightmare. Even the skin of her thighs was flushed and red.

His fingers thrust deep into her cunt again and he felt the first tentative tremors of her pleasure start. When he withdrew his hand, she made a sigh of protest, only to have it turn into a scream of pleasure as he thrust three fingers deep into her and held them there as her body convulsed around them.

Watching Helen orgasm was almost as good as coming himself. Almost. He adjusted his breeches, which had grown decidedly too tight for him again. He would have to buy himself a looser pair of pants if Helen insisted on him keeping his clothes on during their lessons. He was sure this pair would be permanently stretched out of shape by the time he finished.

Because he wasn't finished yet. Not by a long shot. She had been so hot and wet for him that he'd barely had to touch her before she ignited into an explosion. That hardly showed his skill as a lover—it just showed that it was far too long since she had had a real man in her bed. Her first orgasm would have taken the edge off her hunger for a man, and by her cries of delight, she had certainly enjoyed it. Her second one, though, he intended to make a work of art. He would be so attentive to her needs, so accommodating to her desires that he'd be damned if he didn't do his best to ruin her for any other man. By the time he finished with her, she wouldn't want to look at any other man. She would belong to him, and to him alone, and she would know it.

Her tremors had died down now to just the occasional twitch. Slowly he drew his fingers out of her dripping cunt and wiped the wetness over her thighs and belly. "You liked that," he said, as he massaged her own juices into her soft skin.

"Mmmmm." She was too exhausted and sated to talk.

He liked that in a woman. Once he had untied her, he would do his best to keep her that way — too sated to be able to give voice to her annoying demands. "You liked that a lot."

"You passed your first practical lesson in how to please a woman with honors," she murmured. "So, will you untie me now?"

He shook his head. "No."

"You like me tied up?"

He didn't bother to answer her. Instead, he bent his head to her and thrust his tongue right up inside her open cunt, lapping at the last of her juices as if he were a thirsty cat drinking a saucer of cream.

She gave her torpid body a surprised shake. "I gather that means yes."

"I haven't finished with you, you know," he said, when he had finally satisfied himself with her cream. "I'm going to make you come again and again and again until you beg for mercy. I'm going to give you so much pleasure that you won't be able to bear it."

A sleepy smile spread across her face. "I can hardly wait for the torture to start."

It already had started, he thought, trying to ignore the insistent ache in his loins, and the demands of his insatiable body. Only mere minutes had gone by since he had pleasured himself in this room. The stain of his seed still lay on the ground at his feet, and yet his body was begging for release again.

"I have some tools over in the chest," Helen suggested delicately, indicating with her head an unobtrusive wooden box that stood in the far corner of the room. "If you are really intent on making my life a torment, you may find them useful."

With mounting excitement he knelt over by the wooden chest to inspect their contents. There were several contraptions he didn't recognize at all, and was at a loss to think of a use for them in the bedroom, but among them were some more familiar items; a leather whip, just what the wench deserved for spanking him, and a couple of dildos, one large, one small.

He hefted the whip in his hand and gave it an exploratory swish and a flick against the stone wall of the cellar. The leather tip made a satisfyingly loud crack as it snapped against the stone. "You deserve a few lashes with this, don't you?"

She shook her head. "No whipping today. I'll save that for when you have been very bad indeed and need stricter chastisement than a spanking."

He didn't want to hurt her unduly, but he wasn't averse to seeing her white skin tinged with the warm pinkness of a light lashing. With some disappointment, he tossed it on to the floor by the fire. He wouldn't forget about it just yet.

"Bring over the dildo."

He brought out both of them. "The large one or the small one?"

"The small one."

Again, he was disappointed, and he hesitated before he dropped the larger one back. The small one really was very thin — she would hardly feel it inside her cunt. He'd like to see the large one inside her, see her cunt lips stretching apart to take all of it into her body.

She seemed to read his thoughts and give in to his desires. "No, bring both of them."

Both of them? This was suddenly starting to sound most promising.

"And the string of balls. Bring those out, too."

He rummaged around in the chest until he found a chain of small wooden balls, strung on a piece of smooth twine. He held them up to her. "These ones?"

"Yes, those ones are good. Now bring them all here to me."

He flipped the lid of the chest down again and carried his booty over to Helen, laying the two dildos and the string of balls down at her feet.

Her eyes were flushed with excitement again and her nipples were perked up into hard buds. He touched first one tight pink nipple and then the other with the tip of his tongue. "So, can I touch you with all three of these?" he asked, kicking the pile with the toe of his boot. "Wherever I want to?"

"You can use them on me when I give you the word. The small one, first."

He bent down and swiftly retrieved the thin dildo. "At your service, Ma'am."

"Women like to have things in their cunts," she whispered. "They like to feel filled up with a long, hard, thick male member. But when there's no hard male member around, we don't despair. There are other toys we can use to approximate the same sensation. Toys like a nice leather dildo like this one. We can rub it between our legs, tease our clit with it, push it up into our cunts, and pretend that it is a male member in every way. That way we can accustom ourselves quite nicely to our lack of the real thing."

He took her words as an invitation to do that very thing, rubbing the small dildo between her legs until she shivered with delight, and then thrusting it up into her cunt with a fluid motion. The tiny toy almost disappeared right up inside her. When he withdrew it again, it was dripping with her juices. "This can hardly be much of a substitute for a man," he murmured, as he thrust it in and drew it out of her again several times. "It is hardly bigger than a finger. Nothing like the size of a real man."

"You're right," she admitted with a smile, "the bigger one is better for some purposes. Come, pleasure me with the big one, now."

He drew out the baby toy with alacrity and took hold of the man-sized phallus instead, hefting it in his hand with pleasure. This one rivaled him at his biggest and hardest in size. This was definitely the sort of toy that Helen deserved to play with.

He rubbed it between her legs to start with, backward and forward, first with a touch so soft it was barely the tickle of a feather and then grinding it demandingly into her pelvis, wetting it all over on her juices, until she was squirming in her restraints.

"Put it inside me now," she finally begged him, as he showed no signs of wanting to pleasure her fully with it.

"All in good time," he answered, rubbing it gently between her legs a few more times for good measure, just to fully savor the tormented look on her face. How he liked to see her writhing with lust under his hands. He would like to keep her tied there, ready and available for him to play with, for a month together. She had teased him for so long that it was time he took his revenge on her and teased her back again, taking her to the brink of orgasm as she had done to him, but never quite pushing her over the edge—at least not until she was begging and crying and pleading for the release he was denying her.

"Please," she begged, opening her legs even wider than the restraints forced her to do and jutting out her hips at him. "I'm so ready to take it inside me. Fuck me with it now. Fuck me with it hard and fast."

Her cunt lips were red and swollen with desire. He parted them gently with two fingers, dabbling the tip of the dildo in the rich cream that leaked out of her. Slowly he pushed the rod inside her, watching her delicious cunt stretch to accommodate its thickness.

She shivered all over as he slowly thrust it inside her as far as it would go, and moaned her appreciation to the cellar's stone walls.

He withdrew it a little way and then thrust it back into her again. "You like it like that?" he asked.

He didn't need to ask. Her wordless cries and the action of her hips, urging him on, told him everything he needed to know.

In and out he thrust the dildo, until the tenseness of her muscles and the way she began to hold her breath in anticipation told him that she was close to orgasm again. He slowed his stroke and slid the dildo out of her cunt again, dropping it on the stone floor at her feet.

Ignoring her cries of protest at being robbed of her pleasure, he picked up the string of balls that she had asked him to get out of the chest. "And what do I do with these?" he asked, dangling them from one finger.

She pouted at him, her eyelids heavy with unslaked desire. "You're teasing me."

"Of course I am." He slanted a wicked grin at her. "Just as you teased me. Now, are you going to answer my question, or will I have to experiment?"

Her pout grew more pronounced than before. "You put them inside me," she said, offering up her wide open cunt to him again. "You put them all inside me, one by one, until my cunt is so full it can't take any more, then you lick and rub my clit until I'm ready to come, and just as I'm starting to come, you pull them all out again in a rush and give me a taste of what heaven must feel like."

He liked the sound of that. He liked it a lot. But he wasn't ready to make her come again. Not quite yet.

He knelt down in front of her with the string of balls in one hand. Starting with the smallest first, he pushed them one by one into her wet cunt. Helen moaned and arched her back with pleasure as ball after ball was thrust into her throbbing tunnel. Finally, when every single ball had disappeared and it was utterly full, and only the tail of the string was left hanging out, he stopped for a moment to let her regain her breath and to fully savor the feeling of the entire string of balls inside her.

He couldn't bear to wait for too long before he started on the next adventure—his poor cock felt as though it had been in a permanent state of erection for hours and he was dying for another release. He barely gave her enough time to accustom her body to this strange invasion, before he started to push the bottom-most and largest ball gently up and down with one fingertip, causing the whole string to shift and move inside her.

"Oh, goodness," she whispered in surprise as a shudder swept over her entire body. "Do that again."

He could do that again. He could do more than that, too. Her cunt might be full to bursting, but she had another orifice still to fill. And he knew just the tool that could fill it for her.

He reached over and grabbed hold of the thin dildo, still wet from her cream. "Let me put this inside you, too," he said, before swiping his tongue over her swollen cunt lips and sucking gently on her clit.

She shook her head. "It won't fit," she gasped. "I have too many balls inside me for anything else to fit at all. Not even your little finger could get inside me now."

"I wasn't going to put it in your cunt," he explained, reaching around behind her and tickling her between her buttocks with the blunt tip. "I want to put it in your ass. Now that I've filled your cunt with balls, I want to suck your clit and fuck you in the ass with this little toy until you come."

She stiffened for a moment, holding her breath, and he thought she was going to refuse him. But then she let out a gusty sigh and relaxed again. "Put it in my ass, Jack."

He didn't wait to be asked twice. Slowly he slipped the tip of it inside her tightest hole, making her gasp for breath all over again.

Then slowly, ever so slowly, he pushed more and more of it into her, until her ass, too, was filled completely. "Do you like that?" he murmured into her stomach, as one hand thrust the dildo gently in and out of her ass and the other tickled the balls into massaging her cunt from the opening to her womb on down to the very entrance.

Her head was thrown back and her body arched into his, shaking and shivering under his touch. But still he wouldn't let her come. Every time he sensed she was near the brink, he slowed down a little, until she had retreated away from the edge and was once again out of the danger zone.

When he had drawn back for the fifth or sixth time, and her whole body was quivering with need, she was finally reduced to begging him. "Please, I can't take much more of this." Her words were full of pleading frustration. "Please, let me come."

He would take pity on her. Much as he would like to see her pleasure herself, he wouldn't be as cruel to her as she had been to him. He bent down to his task in earnest, licking around her cunt and over her clit with light feather touches of his tongue, his hands still busy with ass and cunt.

The touch of his tongue drew cries of delight from her. He was going to make her come now, and she knew it, and was looking forward to it with greedy anticipation.

A long suck on her clit, and he felt her tense up her muscles again, ready to explode.

He drew his tongue over her clit one last time, and he pushed her over the edge. As her convulsions started to shake her body, he thrust the dildo hard up her ass and with a sharp tug pulled the string of balls out of her cunt in a rush.

Her neck and chest were flushed red with passion, her back was arched, her eyes were shut, and a look of intense wonderment was spread over her face. She held herself there, motionless, her mouth open in a wordless scream, for what seemed like five minutes or more, before slumping back into her restraints, her whole body screaming out its perfect satisfaction.

He could hold out no longer himself. With shaking hands, he stood up, unbuttoned his trousers and took his throbbing cock into his hands. His eyes glued to her naked body, still oozing complete sexual satisfaction from every pore, he stroked himself with wild urgency.

Before she had even recovered enough from her orgasm to open her eyes, he had joined her in satisfaction, spraying out his seed on to her breasts and belly with such force it was as if it had been shot from a gun.

His second pleasure once achieved, he sank back down to his knees, exhausted from their lengthy sexual games.

The silence was broken at length by her soft whisper. "Untie me."

He looked up at her face, still wearing the repose of utterly satiety. "You think you deserved to be untied now, do you?"

She gave him a sleepy smile. "I do. Now untie me."

He reached down and unbuckled the ties around her ankles before standing up to free her wrists as well.

She shook her wrists to get the blood flowing freely in them, before taking hold of his hand and pulling him over toward the bearskin rug laid out in front of the fire.

"Come and lie down beside me," she said, stretching herself out on the rug and basking in the warmth of the fire just like a contented cat. "I need a nap. You've worn me out." A wide yawn attested to the truth of her statement.

Now that the edge had been taken off his hunger and need for her, he wanted nothing more than to lie in her arms. He hunkered down next to her and curled up on the rug by her side and listened to her fevered breathing gradually attain the regularity of sleep.

The silence and the warmth and the peace worked their magic on him. Within minutes, he too was fast asleep.

He was woken some time later by a tickle on his jaw. A sleepy protest and a half-hearted swat brought forth only a trickle of laughter. Reluctantly, he opened his eyes, blinking at the light from the glowing coals on the fire in the grate.

Helen was leaning on her elbows, tickling him with a strand of her beautiful golden hair. When she saw him open his eyes and look sleepily at her, she gave him a saucy wink. "What do you think about lesbians, Jack?"

Chapter Six

He'd thought he was exhausted nearly unto death, but at her words his ears pricked up and he felt a new surge of energy run through his body. "What do you mean?" he asked cautiously, as he stretched out full length on the rug beneath him, his hands behind his head. Was she really meaning what he thought she was meaning?

"You know quite well what I mean, Jack," she said, in a tone of rebuke. "You heard what I said. I'm talking about women who prefer the touch of other women to the touch of men. Women who like to kiss each other full on the mouth and to fondle each other's breasts. Women who like to stroke each other's naked bodies, who like to rub up against each other, mouth to mouth and breast to breast and cunt to cunt. Women who like to touch each other in the most intimate way, who like to pleasure other women and be pleasured by a woman in their turn." She suited her actions to her words, pressing her naked body against his clothed one and rubbing up against him like a hungry pussy cat wanting a saucer of cream.

Before she had even finished speaking, Jack's cock was rock-hard again. He'd always supposed there were such women, just as he had always supposed there were men who preferred other men to women, otherwise why were their laws forbidding sodomy as an unnatural practice? Still, he hadn't wasted much time on thinking of such women. All they needed, he was sure, was a man to fuck them, and they would turn from their unnatural desires quick enough.

"Would you like to see such women?" she asked, as she twined herself around him. "Would you like to see women making love to each other?"

His mouth fell open in astonishment. She never ceased to surprise him. "You know such women?"

She gave him an amused look. "Of course I do. I imagine that you do, too, if only you knew where to look."

"And where is that?"

"Women who have been married to brutes," she suggested, rubbing up against him some more. "Whose viciousness gives the poor women a lasting distaste for men. Some of them turn to their own sex for the love and kindness than men have never shown them."

Jack nodded understandingly. He could forgive women turning to each other as lovers out of desperation or despair. It was a harsh life for some, and everyone was entitled to what little consolation they could find.

"Or even maiden aunts who have never married, but live secluded in the country with their best friend, also a spinster," she went on, with a glint of mischief in her eye. "Society may be foolish enough to pity them for their single state and their barrenness, but I believe that in many a case, society would be quite misguided to do so. Many of these women have made a deliberate choice to live out of society with their loved one — and are quite contented."

Jack thought of one of his own aunts with a sense of great unease, his lust instantly quenched. For as long as he could remember, Aunt Honoria had lived in Gloucestershire with her childhood friend, Lavinia. His mother had told him stories of how Honoria had been a great beauty in her day and had turned down the hand of an Earl, no less, who was madly in love with her. On the death of a distant relative who had left her a modest independence and to her family's great distress, Aunt Honoria had thrown away all her chances at making a good match and retired to the country with Lavinia. The pair had never returned to London, and were well known to discourage visitors. Could his old aunt and her friend be some of these women?

She laughed outright at the expression on his face, evidently able to read his thoughts. "I'm not saying that all aging spinsters are lesbians. Far from it. Many women have other, even better, reasons for staying single. Independence, freedom from the cares of raising a family, power over one's own destiny, or simply a liking for solitude. I was just pointing out that it is a possibility."

"I suppose it is," he said, grudgingly. He really did *not* want to think of his aged aunt and her equally aging friend in such a way.

"You never answered my question, Jack," she reminded him. "Would you like to see such women making love with each other? Would you like to see how they touch each other, what they like to do to each other and have done to them in return, how they pleasure each other?"

He hesitated. Not if they looked anything like his Aunt Honoria. "Who are these women you speak of?"

"Two of the young ladies I am teaching at the moment I am sure have more interest in each other than they will ever have in their husbands," she went on, "and I am of a mind to give them an excuse to explore the delights of each other's bodies. They will never have the courage to do so when they are married, I am sure. I shall tell them both it is just a part of the lesson, to get them used to being touched as they will be when they are married, and I will let them find out of their own accord whether they prefer the touch of a woman to that of a man. Then at the very least," she said with a trace of bitterness in her tone, "they will be better able to console each other when their marriages turn sour."

Two of her current students had tendencies that way? He gave a groan of pain as his cock shot to full attention once again at the mere thought. Two of her young, nubile students wanted to touch each other? That was another matter altogether from his old Aunt Honoria and her friend. All three of her students were young and pretty, even if he didn't want to fuck any of them, not even Clarissa, as much as he wanted to fuck Helen herself.

"It might be good for you, Jack," she went on in a persuasive murmur — as if he needed any more persuading than she had already given him. "It would teach you many things to see two pretty young virgins making love to each other in earnest. You would know just by seeing what they did to each other exactly what a woman wants you to do to her. It could be your most educational lesson yet."

His mouth was dry with anticipation. He moistened his parched lips with his wet tongue before he managed to croak out, "When will this lesson take place, then, that you are inviting me to watch?"

She thought for a moment. "Next week would do, at your next lesson. A sennight from now. That will give me time to prepare the girls."

He did not like the thought of being away from her for a whole week. "I am to have no more lessons until then?"

She flicked him on the nose with the tip of her fingernail. "Don't be greedy, Jack. You will get all the lessons I owe you. Now be off with you. I have work to do. Work that does not include teaching you."

He got up to leave with some regret. He had to while away a whole sennight before the next lesson. A whole sennight to dwell on what Helen had planned for him. Damn her for enticing him with such a wickedly erotic and decidedly naughty delight. It would be her fault if he lost half his wealth on foolhardy speculations these coming few days. He wouldn't be able to concentrate worth a damn on his work for the wildly tantalizing images she had put into his head.

Helen claimed that two of her three students had tendencies that way, he thought to himself, as he walked homewards again. Was his fiancée Clarissa one of those two?

He thought back to the first time he had seen Clarissa and her friend Anna in one of Helen's lessons — the one where she had pretended to be teaching them the right way to address stationery or some such nonsense. He remembered how he had caught a whiff of the odor of a woman from the pair of them, and had wondered briefly at the time whether they could be lovers. He had dismissed the thought, convinced of Clarissa's disinterest in sex.

But was it only *men* that Clarissa was not interested in? Was she one of those women Helen had been referring to—one of those who got excited by other women? Was she another Aunt Honoria in the making?

At any rate, it was high time that he mended fences with Clarissa, he supposed. He had not seen her since she had run from him in the park.

Of course, if she was only interested in kissing and being kissed by other women, it was no wonder she had run from his display of fervor. She must have been deluding herself that their marriage would be mostly platonic, save for a few hurried fumblings after dark under the sheets where she could lie back and open her legs and think of England. The thought that he wanted her to get excited about their lovemaking and respond to him with the passion that she held in check for her best friend Anna must have frightened and repelled her.

Was it possible to change the mind of a woman like her? Was it possible that she would learn to enjoy and respond to his caresses, or would she be forever hankering after the caresses of another woman?

He really didn't like the thought of being shackled to a woman who found him physically unappealing and who would only ever endure having sex with him. He much preferred the thought of a lusty woman who would meet him demand for demand, and heat his bed with as much passion as any man could want.

He had promised to marry Clarissa, though, and he could not easily go back on his word. Still, he was only a man and he had his limits. If she could not respond to him as he wanted and needed any wife of his to respond to him, he could not go through this sham of a marriage.

If Clarissa turned out to be one of those women who preferred other women, he didn't know if it would be possible to change her mind about him. Still, he was honor-bound to try.

He was supposed to be marrying her in just a few weeks. The prospect was getting less appealing the more he found out about his wife-to-be.

Helen lay back on the rug in front of the fire and watched with mixed feelings as Jack adjusted his clothing and disappeared up the staircase, back to his own apartments.

She ought to be glad he was leaving. She knew she ought to be glad, but it was hard for her to feel what she knew she ought to feel. This afternoon had been a foolish mistake, and one that she must not repeat, but still she was sad to see Jack go. She would have liked to ask him to spend the night with her. He had felt so comfortable, so right, curled up next to her on the rug in front of the fire, their bodies twined together like a pair of lovers.

She snorted at her own silly fancies. They were not lovers. He was paying her for her knowledge and she was manipulating him into giving her what she wanted—that was all. The first lesson had gone just as she had planned it to—she had made him hot for her, hotter than he could bear, and then she had forced him to satisfy himself. A few more lessons like that and he would be her slave, and only too willing to give her back the half of her school that he owned just for the promise of a real fuck, of real satisfaction, of finally being able to sink his straining cock into her hot and willing body.

The second lesson had been the mistake. Already physically excited by the first lesson, she had not been able to detach herself from her emotions and desires. In teasing him, she had also teased herself beyond the point of control. Burning with desire to feel his hands on her body, she had let him wield power over her, and she had been unable to hide the effect that his power had on her.

She had been hot and wet for him. So hot and wet that she had been unable to resist the temptation to come in front of him, at his bidding and at his touch. More than that—she had actually begged for him to let her come. And not just once, but twice, she had come for him. Once could be put down to a moment's delirium—but twice? Twice was a disaster. If she could not control her lusts a little better, she would never wield the control over him that she needed to have if she were to wrest control over her life, over her destiny, away from him.

She turned over, nestling her front into the warm fur of the rug. But was giving in to her lust for him such a disaster? Could she not find a way to turn her weakness for him to her advantage?

He desired her badly, that much was certain. Would she not be better off to become his mistress, his willing mistress, rather than simply tricking him into giving her back half her school and being content with that? He was a wealthy man, after all, and could easily afford to shower her with luxuries that were so far beyond her reach that she scarcely bothered to even dream about them. Why should she be content with so little when he could give her so much more?

Even as she considered the idea, she shook her head again, dismissing it.

Was she forgetting the vow she had once made to herself, never to be any man's willing mistress? Was she forgetting her promise to herself that she would use the body that God had given her if and when she must, but only when she had no other choice? Was she forgetting her determination to use her body, and the promise of her body, as a weapon, but never as a tool for love?

She shook her head, annoyed at herself. She had certainly forgotten her determination that afternoon and had let Jack play on her body as if it were a beautiful instrument of pleasure. He had made music on her, and her body had sung for him. He had touched her more deeply than any man had ever touched her before—in pleasuring her body, he had touched her soul.

Pah. Her soul had nothing to do with that afternoon, she told herself firmly. She lusted after him and he lusted after her— and that was all there was to it. They had enjoyed each other's bodies without fear or shame, but that didn't mean she should read anything else into that enjoyment.

She was only a diversion for him. She must not let herself forget that. She must not open her heart to him, or he would be sure to break it.

She was the teacher. He was the pupil. He paid her for her lessons. However much she might secretly wish for it to be otherwise, there was no deeper meaning to their relationship.

She would get her school back under her control and then she could fuck him if she pleased and scratch the itch he had given to her, but that was all. There would be no talk, no thought of any more permanent arrangement. For her own sanity, she had to remember that.

* * * * *

It was with leaden feet and a troubled mind that Jack paid a call on Clarissa the following day.

He was suffering from a guilty conscience, too, after yesterday's sexual adventures with the luscious Helen Fairchild. True, he was not yet married to Clarissa, but they were formally engaged. He doubted very much that Clarissa would be happy if she were to find out that he had allowed himself to be tied up and touched and sucked on by another woman, and had then tied up and touched and sucked on that other woman in his turn, all the time while he was supposed to be preparing for his wedding.

Even if she wasn't attracted to him herself, she might still consider his actions an insult to her. He was being unfaithful to her before they were even married.

The fact that he hadn't actually fucked Helen suddenly seemed scant excuse for his actions. What they had shared was more intimate than any actual lovemaking that he had ever experienced before, even though he had yet to actually thrust his cock into her cunt. Fingers, tongue, balls, even dildo, but not yet his cock.

He groaned aloud as he rapped on Clarissa's door. Thinking about Helen was having the expected effect on him. Thinking about the way she had cried out in pleasure as he had licked her cunt and thrust her baby dildo in and out of her ass was making him desperately hard all over again.

Itching with lust was not the way he wanted to approach Clarissa today. He needed to win her trust—not frighten her away again.

She was in the parlor as usual, sitting upright in her chair with a piece of sewing in her lap. She put it aside when he entered. "Mr. Langton," she said, bowing her head briefly at him. "Pray take a seat."

Was it his imagination or did she seem less composed than usual? He couldn't imagine her ever getting flustered—she was not the getting flustered type—but she seemed less serene than was her wont. A hint of color was present on her pale cheeks and a tendril of hair had escaped from her bun and was curled around her face. Now that she had put her sewing aside, he could see her twisting her fingers nervously around in her lap.

"It's a beautiful day," he began, brushing off her offer of a chair. "I thought we could make use of the fine weather."

She flinched visibly at his suggestion.

"I can have a carriage brought around in moments, if you would like to drive with me in the park," he continued, glad that he hadn't made the mistake of suggesting another walk. Clarissa evidently didn't think much of the idea of being alone with him in the park, even in the complete lack of privacy of a carriage. If he had suggested a walk, she would flat out have refused, he was sure.

As it was, she swallowed nervously and her fingers twisted faster. "A ride in the park?"

"My horses could do with the exercise," he lied smoothly. "As could I." Any reason to get out of the Harlow's depressing house that stank of decay and decrepitude and out into the open air.

He couldn't possibly talk to Clarissa about anything that mattered in that house—not with her father pacing about in his study and her mother sitting in the second parlor, both of them alert for any sound out of the ordinary. He could not kiss her with them on the prowl. He could not even *think* about kissing her, let alone go about seducing her with his newly taught knowledge about how to please a woman, so that she dreamed of him and not of Anna, when she was alone in her bed at night.

He could not even talk to her about sex. For all he knew, her mother was listening at the door to make sure that her daughter was in no danger from her suitor. Heaven knows, he wouldn't be surprised. There were many mothers, he was quite sure, who would stoop far lower than listening at keyholes in exchange for the assurance that their daughters would be well married.

Still she hesitated. "Just a ride in the park?"

"A turn around Hyde Park. Nothing more frightening than that."

With a look of trepidation on her face she went to fetch her bonnet, and climbed up beside him in the open carriage.

He shook the reins and started the horses moving briskly off along the cobbled roads toward Hyde Park.

"I apologize for frightening you the other day," he began, as the horses clomped their way over the cobbles. "When we were out walking."

Even though they were not touching in any way, he could sense Clarissa's body tense up beside him. "You startled me."

"You were not expecting me to woo you with such ardor?" he asked, maneuvering expertly around a cart pulled at a snail's pace by an ancient-looking donkey.

"I did not expect you to be such a physical man," she admitted. "Or so intent on making me a toy for your pleasure."

"You had agreed to be my wife in every way," he reminded her.

"I had, and I am prepared to stick by what I promised you, though I would prefer you to be patient with me." She shuddered. "I did not like you touching me in the park, or saying such things aloud to me. Somehow I did not expect a husband to be so…"

"You did not expect a husband to be so what?" he prompted her.

"So…so intrusive." She gave an uneasy laugh. "It's hard to describe, but I felt as though I had no private space left to me, that you were taking over what belonged to me." She gave a slight shrug. "I did not like it."

"Evidently," he said dryly.

"You startled me." As far as an apology went for running out on him, it wasn't much of one. Still, it was an admission of a kind that she had been in the wrong.

"You are my fiancée now, and you will soon be my wife. You will have to get used to me wanting to make love to you. Once we are married, I intend to intrude on your privacy every night until you have grown quite accustomed to having me there."

He felt her thin body beside him shudder again. "I suppose I will get accustomed to you in time," she said, though her voice was hardly full of conviction.

"No doubt." He was hardly overjoyed in his turn at the thought of a bride who would suffer him in uncomfortable silence until she was accustomed enough to his presence to tolerate him in her life and in her bed.

They made one circuit of Hyde Park in near silence, and then headed for home again.

Both of them were relieved when the horses came to a stop outside the Harlow house and Clarissa climbed out.

She looked back up at him as he sat in the carriage, the reins looped around his wrists. Her pale face was set with a look of unusual determination. "Thank you for the ride, Mr. Langton."

She looked, he rather thought, more thankful to escape his presence than she had been for the ride.

He tipped his hat to her. He could almost be offended by her eagerness to escape his company, but for the fact that he was just as happy to be out of hers. "Goodbye, Clarissa."

He only wished, as he drove away as gloomily as he had arrived, that he was saying goodbye to her forever.

Chapter Seven

Helen stood in front of the class, her nipples tingling already at the thought of what was to come. "We are going to have a new lesson today." She always enjoyed this lesson she gave to the young women she took on as pupils. And the thought of Jack in the next room, watching everything though the peephole she had created for him, gave an extra fillip to her excitement. If the spectacle she planned to put on for his benefit today didn't have him slavering at the mouth like a rabid dog, she had lost her touch. "This lesson is going to be a practical experience in what awaits you as a married woman."

She paused to let her words sink in to the ears of the three young women sitting in front of her. "A practical experience?" one of them queried, shyly.

Helen nodded. "Yes. Today you will learn for yourselves exactly what makes your body feel good. You will learn how to touch yourselves to make yourself feel excited and full of desire, so that you will be able to respond fully and properly to the advances your husband makes to you." She clapped her hands together briskly. "Now then, the first thing that you must learn is how to become comfortable in your own nakedness. Anna, will you please help Clarissa? Clarissa, please help Anna in your turn. And Hermione," she said, beckoning to her third pupil to come toward the front of the room. "Come here and I will assist you."

Hermione stood up, looking like a frightened rabbit. "We are to undress?"

"Yes," Helen replied, matter-of-factly. "We are all to undress. But don't be alarmed," she added, as Hermione went so pale that Helen thought she was about to faint. "The object of this lesson is to show you pleasure, not to make you feel uncomfortable in any way. If it transpires you do not like what I am about to show you, then please voice your feelings, and you may simply sit and watch the lesson until you feel better about joining in."

Hermione swallowed visibly and sidled tentatively up to Helen. "Mama said I must listen and take heed of what you had to teach me, as I would regret it later if I did not," she whispered. "I promised her I would obey you in all things, and I cannot break my promise to my mama. What do you want me to do?"

Helen put gentle hands on her shoulders and swiveled her around until her back was facing her. "Just get undressed," she said kindly. "After you have taken off your clothes, you may be still and listen, for now.

"Every man wants his wife to be willing to couple with him whenever he feels the urge," she continued, as she unfastened the row of tiny pearl buttons down the back of the reluctant Hermione's sprigged muslin gown. "But not many men know enough or care enough, to make their wives feel a similar urge to their own. And then they are put out by their wife's lack of enthusiasm." She sighed. "Men are such contrary creatures there is little point trying to educate them. We women need to take our pleasure in the bedroom into our own hands. We will be the happier for it, and so will your husbands. They will strut and preen themselves and think what clever men they are to have roused your virgin passions to such a pitch. You need never tell them the truth. In fact, I would advise against it."

Hermione, her gown unfastened to her waist, whirled around to face Helen, her hands covering what they could of her bared corset. "You would have me keep a secret from my husband? You would have me tell him a lie?"

Helen smiled at Hermione's gasp of shock. "I am not advocating telling a lie," she clarified. "Just the omission of certain truths that would upset your husband. Every woman needs her secrets. They add a certain mysterious allure to her bearing. A man can never resist a woman who keeps a few secrets from him."

Hermione went still again, her hands still crossed protectively across her corseted breasts, as she thought about it. "Oh," she said in a small voice. "I see."

"You are a smart woman. Come," Helen said, holding out her hand, "step out of your gown and then you may help me with mine."

Hermione gave Helen her hand and stepped tentatively out of her gown, leaving it in a puddle on the floor. Her hands immediately went back to cross over her breasts again, and she was shivering slightly even though, to Helen's senses at least, the room was quite warm.

Helen turned around. "Unfasten my buttons, now, if you please." She felt small hands fumble with the buttons, loosening them off one after the other until she, too, was ready to step out of her gown.

The two other girls had already divested themselves of both gown and shift, and stood quietly, holding hands, waiting for her to continue the lesson. Helen added her gown to the pile on the rug, slipped the straps of her shift over her shoulders, and let that pool at her feet as well. "Your shift?" she said to Hermione.

Hermione gulped and stepped out of her shift as well.

Helen could just imagine how hard Jack's cock was getting at the sight of all four of them, dressed only in their corsets and bloomers, stockings and slippers. She wondered if he was already stroking himself, getting ready to come already, or if he was hanging on, exercising his self-control, waiting until the show really began. Poor Jack. She could almost feel sorry for all the ways in which his self-control had been tested so thoroughly in recent days. This afternoon, though, would surely be the ultimate test.

"Corsets now," she said, twirling Hermione around so that her back was facing her again. "No woman can ever experience pleasure when she is in the grips of an over-tight corset."

Hermione trembled visibly as Helen unpicked the laces of her corset and pushed the heavy garment off her shoulders onto the floor. Helen caught only a glimpse of pale, pink-tipped breasts before Hermione's hands flew up to cover herself again.

She smiled to herself as she turned around for Hermione to unpick the laces of her own corset. She was an expert at turning such modesty around to her own purposes.

In just a few minutes all the laces had been untied and all four of them had removed their corsets and were standing barebreasted in the room.

"Now then, girls, you need to start experiencing for yourself the sort of touch that makes you feel pleasant." Arms by her side, she turned to Hermione with a look of approval on her face. "Look at Hermione, for instance."

Hermione, her hands still pasted to her breasts, her eyes as wide as a frightened rabbit's, gulped nervously at suddenly finding herself the center of attention.

"Hermione has already discovered the joys of touching her own breasts," she said, feeling just a little wicked for poking gentle fun at the poor girl. "Look at how she is touching herself, and try it for yourselves."

Hermione gulped again and her face grew as red as a beet as she dropped her hands by her sides again in haste. "I wasn't...I was just..." she stammered.

Helen curled up her arms and took her own breasts in her hands, not merely holding them to cover them but to caress them. "Take your breasts in your hands just like Hermione did," she instructed the girls. "Weigh them. Feel how heavy they are."

Clarissa and Anna were quick to follow her example. Hermione hesitated for a long moment before she, too, took her breasts into her hands again.

"Experiment with different touches and see what feels good to you," she continued, caressing her own breasts as she spoke. "Squeeze your breasts as roughly as feels good to you, brush your palms over your nipples so you can barely feel the tickle, gently stroke your breasts all around, pinch your nipples between your thumb and forefinger. Just do whatever you like. There are no rules in this game."

The girls began to follow suit, touching their breasts as first tentatively, and then with growing boldness. Helen looked on, mechanically caressing herself as she watched them find out what gave them pleasure.

When she decided the time was ripe to move on, she dropped her hands to her sides again. Hermione instantly dropped her hands to her sides as well. Clarissa and Anna continued to stroke themselves until she began to speak. "There is plenty of pleasure to be found in touching your own breasts, but yet more to be discovered in the touch of another." She beckoned Anna and Clarissa over to her side. "Anna, what makes you feel good when you touch yourself?"

Anna thrust her breasts out and cupped them in her hands, squeezing them gently. "This does."

"And Clarissa?"

Clarissa pinched her nipples roughly enough to leave a mark. "I like it most when the pleasure is mixed with pain," she confided shyly.

Helen thought of Jack in his hiding place, watching her virgins confess what made them excited. The two of them were proving to be just as hot as she had thought they might be. She hoped he was enjoying the show. "Very good, both of you," she said. "Now, Anna, touch Clarissa's breasts, and see if you can duplicate for her the pleasant sensations you felt in yourself. Use your hands to start off with, and then if you feel comfortable, you may want to try using your mouth and tongue as well. Clarissa, you may then take your turn at touching Anna."

Anna's face burned red at the unusual instruction, but Clarissa was there in front of her, mutely encouraging her. With shy hands, Anna tentatively reached out one finger and touched Clarissa's breasts.

Clarissa gave a low moan in the back of her throat and thrust her breasts forward into Anna's hands.

Anna needed no more encouragement than that to start to make love to Clarissa's breasts with all her might.

Helen left the two girls happily engaged with each other and turned to Hermione. "Come, touch me if you like."

Hermione stepped forward, her face a mask of scared determination. She put out one hand and touched Helen's breasts with the tips of her fingers. "Like that?"

Helen murmured in appreciation. "Very nice. Keep going."

There was something to be said for the touch of another woman, Helen thought to herself, as Hermione stroked her gently, and then encouraged by the other two, who were by now sucking and licking at each other with enthusiastic fervor, bent her head to suckle on her nipple. A woman always knew exactly what another woman would like, and was never inconsiderate or too rough. Her cunt was getting nicely wet at Hermione's gentle caresses.

She reached out and touched Hermione's small breasts in her turn. Hermione went still as a statue as she felt Helen's hands on her.

"Does that feel nice?" Helen asked, stroking Hermione's breasts with a featherlight touch.

Hermione gulped at the question, and then nodded. "Please," she forced out, her face burning. "Don't stop. I like it."

The two of them caressed each other for some moments, until, going by Hermione's heaving breathing and flushed face and chest, Helen was reasonably certain that the young girl was ready for the next step. Of Anna and Clarissa's readiness she had no doubts whatsoever. The two of them had hardly stopped for breath.

She stepped back and cleared her throat loudly to get Anna and Clarissa's attention. They broke apart with a guilty start at the noise and stood there, faces flushed and panting audibly.

"Your pantaloons now, ladies," Helen said as soon as every eye was fixed on her. She untied the strings and let her own pantaloons fall to the ground, quickly followed by her slippers and stockings.

This time, not even Hermione hesitated. Moving as one, all three of them similarly divested themselves of their last remaining garments, until they all stood, naked as the day they were born, all their attention focused on their teacher.

"Your breasts are not the only place on your body that can give you pleasure," Helen said quietly, so they had to strain to hear her. She sat down on the floor, her knees bent and legs apart, and touched herself between her legs. "See here? Touch yourself here and you will feel how much better that feels than even your breasts do."

The three girls sat around her in a circle, their knees apart like hers, and tentatively touched themselves between their legs.

"When you have explored yourself," Helen suggested, as she stroked her pussy back and forth with one finger, "explore your partner's body in just the same way. Find out what makes you feel good. Find out what makes her feel good, too. And do not forget that although you are limited to exploring your own body with your hand and fingers, you are not so limited with another's. Do not forget that the touch of a mouth or tongue can be even more delicious here than the touch of a hand."

As soon as she had finished speaking, Anna and Clarissa instantly paired off, their hands and mouths on each other's breasts and pussies, leaving Hermione to scuttle up to Helen and start to stroke her own pussy in the same way.

Helen let her knees fall right apart as she stroked herself, leaving her cunt in full view. "Do you want to touch me now?" she offered. "Do you want to explore another woman's body and see how similar, and yet different, it is to your own?"

Hermione reached one hand over to her and started to stroke Helen's pussy gently, probing in between her cunt lips and teasing her clit with her fingertips.

There was definitely a lot to be said about making love to a woman, Helen thought, relaxing into Hermione's touch. It was just as good as touching herself, but without the hard work involved. She liked it well enough, too, in a half-hearted, undemanding sort of a way. It didn't even begin to compare with the glorious fucking with fingers and mouth and toys that Jack had given her a sennight ago, but it was pleasant enough for all that. "You can lick me too," she suggested. "Explore me with your mouth, and I shall do the same to you."

Hermione, her shyness evaporated, was now as eager a pupil as Helen could ever have hoped for. She lay on her side full length on the ground and began to lap eagerly, if inexpertly, at Helen's cunt.

Helen moved herself around so that they were lying on their sides next to each other, top to tail, cunt to mouth.

Hermione had a sweet, pink cunt covered with soft brown hair—a real young virgin's cunt. Helen gave it a tentative lick and was rewarded with a gasp of delight and redoubled efforts from Hermione.

They settled down into a steady but gentle rhythm, stroking and licking each other with mounting intensity. Finally Hermione gave a cry and exploded into a river of tiny spasms. Helen licked her clit as she came, the sound of Hermione's pleasure pushing her over the edge into a gentle orgasm herself.

They lay there entwined in silence for a moment as their labored breathing slowed and their heartbeats returned to normal.

From where she lay, Helen could see Clarissa and Anna, now lying full-length on the floor and rubbing their bodies up against each other and kissing each other with open mouths and a desperate, passionate intensity. It was just as she suspected— they were desperately attracted to each other. But there was clearly more to their relationship than simple lust—they were more than simply physically attracted to each other. She knew as she watched them make love to each other that they had been in love with each other for a long time, although they had evidently just now taken the step of becoming lovers in deed as well as in their fantasies.

They were both sweet girls and she wished them well in their love affair. If they both had accommodating husbands, there was no reason why they couldn't go on as lovers even after they were married.

In his hiding hole in the next room, his eyes glued to the peephole, not even wanting to take his eyes off the scene in front of him for long enough to blink, Jack was in a state of utter torment.

It had been bad enough for him to bear when the girls were clothed only in their corsets and pantaloons. The sight of the four young women, all looking good enough to eat, in such a state of undress had instantly made his cock stand stiffly to attention.

But then the torment had started for real. Naked breasts, naked thighs, naked bellies, naked cunts, and all four of them kissing and touching and licking and sucking each other until he thought his cock would explode with the delight of watching them.

Though he was near to the bursting point, he resolutely kept his arms crossed in front of him and his hands out of his trousers and off his cock.

Time after time Helen had teased him into pleasuring himself. Time after time she had brought him to the brink and then refused to satisfy him, leaving him with only one option — to satisfy himself as she watched him.

He was not going to play along with her games any longer. He would refuse to give in to the lust that had him in its grip. He would not so much as touch his own cock, in case once he had started stroking himself he was unable to stop and just had to make himself come with a silent splatter on the wainscot. He had self-control. He would show that he had self-control and this time, by God, he was going to thrust his throbbing cock deep into her cunt and fuck her senseless before he let her up again.

As much as he was enjoying the floor show, he was relieved when the action started to slow down at last. First Helen and the young girl she had pleasured, then finally the apparently insatiable Clarissa and her friend Anna, cried out in noisy orgasm and lay still.

He stood motionless, his eyes still glued to the peephole, as one by one they peeled themselves off each other and began to dress.

Helen, he noticed, was so busy lacing the corsets and doing up the buttons on the gowns of the other girls that she only had time to thrown on her shift and her gown, leaving off her corset and pantaloons. All the better for him. He would have fewer clothes to strip off her as soon as the others were gone and the two of them were left alone.

It seemed an age before the three young pupils were all sufficiently tidied to be presentable to the outside world again. Looking very prim and proper, they made their shy farewells to Helen and were gone.

As soon as he heard the front door shut behind them, he strode out of the room he was hiding in and into the classroom. Helen was standing to one side, putting the room to rights again. He took her by the hand and pulled her against his body, holding her close to him so she could feel the strength of his erection through her gown. "I want to fuck you," he growled into her ear. He was sick of lessons. It was time that he taught Helen one of her own.

Helen's eyes were dancing with mischief, but she didn't push him away. "Did you like that? Did you like seeing those two girls making love to one another with such passion? Their husbands will be lucky men if they can keep up with the demands of those two in the bedroom."

"Too damn right I liked it." He ground his pelvis into her belly, needing to feel his cock rubbing against her body. "It's just as well that you've already taught me self-control or I would have come in my pants at the sight of the four of you suckling on each other's breasts and licking each other's pussies until you came."

"You mean you haven't…?"

He grabbed her buttocks and ground himself roughly into her again. "Does this feel like I'm a satisfied man?"

Helen's eyes grew wide at the implication. "I thought you would have pleasured yourself long ago, when we first started licking each other's breasts. At least once, maybe even twice or three times by now."

"I know you thought that, and I was determined to disappoint you. Damn it, Helen, I've waited long enough. I'm going to take you to your bedroom and lay you down on your bed and fuck you now. I want my cock inside your cunt. I want to feel your pussy surrounding me on all sides, and I want to come inside you, where a man was made to come, instead of everywhere else but there."

She tried to pull back. "I only said yes to teaching you. I'm not a whore for you to buy. Fucking you wasn't in our agreement."

"So we'll make a new agreement and you can be my mistress. Just tell me what you want and I'll give it to you gladly. A diamond necklace? Shares in a coal mine? Just name what you want and it will be yours." He took her by the hand and pulled her to the door, too impatient to dally there while she made up her mind. "You can think about it on the way to your bedroom."

Out in the hallway now, she hesitated, pulling back on his hand. "I don't want a diamond necklace."

He was in no mood to wait for her to argue with him. He had to have her—now. He hefted her up over his shoulder and began to carry her down the hallway, pushing open each door in turn as he came to it, in the hunt for her bedroom. "Then tell me what you *do* want," he grated out as he walked.

She wriggled around on his shoulder. "All I want is to run my school the way I want to run it, and to be free of anyone else."

He smacked her sharply on the bottom to stop her wriggling. "You want me to give you the other half of your school back?"

"Yes. That's all that I really want from you that you can give me."

Should he give her back the half of her school? It was worth little enough in monetary terms, but he found himself strangely reluctant to agree. If he were to give her back full ownership, he would no longer have any reason to call on her. She would be free and independent as she wanted to be, but he would have nothing that would hold her to him. "No, not that. Anything but that."

"I don't want anything else. Just that."

Ah, finally a room with a bed in it. He strode in and tossed her on the bed and flung her skirts up around her hips. He couldn't wait even to get her naked before he had her for the first time. "I'll give you a stack of railway shares that are worth double what your school would make in a hundred years," he offered as he unbuttoned his straining fly.

She made no move to cover herself up again or to roll away from him. In fact, she was watching him unbutton himself as if mesmerized by the sight of his hugeness. "I don't like railway shares. I just want my school. I want it to be all mine again."

His cock was free at last. He kicked off his trousers and knelt over her on the bed, his cock poised at the entrance to her cunt. "And I just want to fuck you. I want you to be all mine."

"My school?" One last plea that seemed to come from the bottom of her heart. "My heart's desire in exchange for yours?"

He shook his head. He could not give in to her now or he would lose everything. "Anything but that."

She looked mutinous, as if it was on the tip of her tongue to tell to go fuck himself instead, if he wouldn't give her what she asked for.

He was all ready to give in to her demands, but before he could open his mouth to promise her what she wanted, her body betrayed her. Almost involuntarily her hips jutted up to meet him. She wanted him, too, almost as much as he wanted her. He couldn't wait any longer to make her his.

He reached down and touched her between the legs with one finger to test if she was ready to take him. Her pussy was slick and wet from the pleasure she had already had that afternoon. Her luscious wetness sent him finally out of control.

He drove into her with a tremendous thrust, having no thought for anything but the all-consuming need that was pushing him to take her harder and faster than any other woman could bear. Harder and harder he took her, until his seed shot out of him with blinding force, and he collapsed, momentarily sated, on top of her on the bed.

When he came to a moment later, he was instantly filled with remorse for his selfish and brutal lovemaking. He was hardly proving himself to be a man of the world, a gentle and accommodating lover who treated his mistress with punctilious attention and care. Indeed, he had proven himself to be no better than a beast, falling on her and ravishing her with no thought in his head for anything but his own pleasure. He rolled off her with a curse and raked his hands through his hair in bitter shame. "Damn. I'm sorry, Helen. I was out of control. Did I hurt you?"

She gave a soft shake of her head. "No."

"I have been waiting so long to fuck you that I just lost it." How weak and pathetic his excuse sounded even to his own ears. "But I'll spend the rest of tonight making it up to you, I swear I will. I will make you come a thousand times, and treat you as gently as I know how, in recompense for my unforgivable behavior just now."

She reached out one hand and smoothed the frown off his forehead. "You will?"

"I will."

"A thousand times?" She sighed gustily. "I doubt that even *you* could make me come a thousand times in just one night. But on the other hand," she continued, as she reached over to stroke his temporarily wilted member, "I would be happy to be proven wrong."

Some time during that afternoon or the night that followed they managed to crawl beneath the bedclothes. They snatched a few hours rest, too, in the wee hours of the morning. But every waking moment Jack made good on his promise, taking them both to Heaven and back over and over again.

After one softer and gentler bout of lovemaking as Jack lay back on the pillows catching his breath again, a sudden realization came to him. He could not marry Clarissa now — not now that he had tasted the full sweetness of Helen Fairchild. He had never wanted to marry Clarissa overmuch, and now the thought of it was pure bitterness.

He wanted Helen. Only Helen.

True, he could make her his mistress. In fact, he supposed he already had. But that was no real answer to his need for her. A mistress was not tied to one man — she could leave him whenever she chose or even take another lover if he failed to please her.

He did not want to lose her, and he certainly was not prepared to share her with any other man. He had been jealous enough of the young girl she had pleasured this afternoon, wishing that he had been the one suckling on Helen's breasts and licking at her pussy.

He rolled on to his side, propped himself up on his elbow and stroked her smooth, flat belly with a gentle touch, needing to see her lying there beside him and to feel her skin beneath his fingers.

She gave a sleepy murmur and pulled him down to her.

"I love you, Helen Fairchild," he whispered into her ear. "You are my woman now. Mine forever. And I will never let you go."

Helen lay next to him in a daze, drinking in his words with dizzy happiness. He had refused to give her the other half of her school, true enough, but he had instead given her something of inestimable value, something that she would never had dared to hope for, let alone ask for. She hardly dared believe it. He had given her his heart.

Chapter Eight

"Excuse me, Mrs. Fairchild."

Helen put down the pitcher of water and the basin that she was carrying over to wash the props they had used for that day's lesson and looked up curiously. Like any young woman forced into lessons, her pupils were usually anxious to escape the schoolroom, and did not tend to linger once she had dismissed them. It seemed Miss Harlow would be the exception to this rule tonight. "Yes, Clarissa?"

"I shall not be returning to your class after today. I have decided that I do not want to get married after all, so there is little point in continuing under your tutelage."

Helen looked at the pale, but composed, face of the young woman before her. It wasn't unusual for one of her students to be attacked by a sudden fit of the vapors and to refuse to get married. Marriage was such a big step for a young woman, and many of them were naturally afraid of this leap into the unknown. Most of them placed a naïve reliance on her, as their teacher, to help them in their situation. Exactly what they expected her to do, she never knew. She waited for the request for help from this student, as well, but to her surprise it was not immediately forthcoming.

"This is a sudden decision," she said calmly. "Are you nervous about your impending marriage?" She couldn't really afford for one of her students to take violently against the marriage she was supposed to be preparing her for. Such a disaster would ruin her reputation in the polite world and make it difficult for her to attract well-paying students in the future.

"It is not a sudden decision," came the calm reply, "and no, I was not particularly nervous about my marriage. No more so than any other young woman, I expect. I have simply decided that marriage is not the most appropriate institution for me, or the most conducive to my future happiness. Therefore I intend to cancel my wedding plans."

"Was your wedding to be held soon?" She hoped not. The scandal would be the worse if Clarissa's parents had spent a deal of money on preparations already, and had invited all their friends and family to the happy occasion. The consequent need to uninvite everyone again would entail embarrassing explanations that could well damage the reputation of both her and her school still further.

In addition, Clarissa's parents may well ask for their money back, given that she had so clearly failed to prepare her charge for her upcoming marriage. She did not like to give refunds. They, too, were bad for business.

Clarissa lifted one shoulder in an almost imperceptible shrug. "Quite soon. A fortnight from today."

Helen groaned. It was as bad as it possibly could be. "Have you told your parents?"

Clarissa's calm façade slipped for just a moment so that Helen could see the agitation of her spirits only too clearly. "They will not be very pleased. They had high hopes of my marriage. But they will accept my decision in the end, I am sure."

"Are you being pressured to marry a man you do not want or like?" Maybe if she could persuade Clarissa that her husband was not such an ogre as the young woman evidently feared, all would yet be well. After all, Clarissa had not said that she had tried to back out of her engagement yet, only that she *intended* to.

The composed mask was back on her face again. She stood there calmly, her hands folded in front of her, as if she was the most serenely self-composed young woman in the world. "Nothing of the kind. I agreed quite willingly to the proposal my parents put to me. At the time, I thought it was a sensible decision. But now I have discovered something that I have long suspected, and which has impelled me to change my mind."

So that was what was wrong with her. Her fiancé had a mistress, did he? Trust an idealistic young woman to get so tied up in knots about such a little matter. Every man, married or not, had mistresses. It was not in their nature to be faithful to any one woman for long. "You have discovered something about your fiancé that you do not like?"

Much to Helen's surprise, Clarissa shook her head. "Not at all. He has always been the perfect gentleman in every way." Her face went a little pink, as though she was confessing a secret sin. "On the contrary, I have discovered something about *myself* that I do not think *he* would like. And although I like him well enough as a casual acquaintance, I have decided I would not like to live with him in the state of marriage."

Helen felt a sinking feeling in the pit of her stomach. Had her lesson backfired on her, and made Clarissa determine against men altogether? "And what is that?"

She gave a small, composed smile. "I find that I do not like the thought of a man lying on top of me rutting in me. Nor do I like the thought of having to touch and kiss his nasty, hairy body. Women's bodies are so much cleaner and smoother and more beautiful than male bodies." Her pale eyes grew dreamy, making her look almost beautiful. "Indeed, I am in love with my best friend, Anna, and I have been for as long as I can remember. I do not just love her as my best friend and my companion. I love her with all my heart, and with all my body, too."

It was just as she had suspected when she saw them touching each other so passionately the previous day. "You are in love with Anna?"

"Yes, and she is in love with me, too, in the same way I am in love with her."

"But why so set against marriage? You do not need to love your husband, only to submit to his caresses once in a while.

You will still be free to spend the majority of your days with your best friend."

"But not the nights." Again that dreamy smile that lit up her entire face. "And it is the nights, I find, that really matter."

"So you will refuse marriage and love Anna in secret?" She shook her head, wishing she could make the young woman in front of her see sense. Did she not understand that even for a woman of her persuasion, or especially for a woman of her persuasion, marriage was by far the easiest option? Marriage freed a woman to live the kind of life she pleased, whereas as a spinster, her reputation would always be poised on the edge of a precipice. "You will find that as a married woman you would have a lot more freedom to go as you please and to do as you please."

"Anna has a fortune. Quite a large one, in fact. It was left to her by one of her great-aunts, and is hers to do with as she likes once she reaches the age of twenty-one. She turns twenty-one tomorrow."

"And?" Helen prompted. She could see how Anna's money would make a difference. Two wealthy spinsters would certainly have an easier time of it than two indigent ones would. But to keep up the charade of being friends, and to let no one suspect they were lovers? It would not be an easy task.

"And her fortune is quite large enough for two women to live on in perfect comfort. She will buy a house on the south coast of England, or maybe even over the channel in France, and the two of us will live there together." Clarissa gave the ghost of a grin. "Everyone will think we are a pair of spinsters, unhappy in love, who have retired from the world to seek a life of solitude. Our seclusion will suit us very well, as neither of us have a desperate liking for society. We shall do our best to foster the impression that we have had our hearts broken by rapscallions and are mourning our lost loves in private. We have it all worked out. No one will ever suspect us for what we really are."

Helen groaned inwardly at her decision to introduce the pair of them to making love to each other. They had taken to it like ducks to water. Maybe she should start a new series of lessons for newly married wives. That way she could avoid the scandal of broken engagements for good. "Have you told your parents of your decision?"

"I will tell them in a few days, before I leave. Anna and I have made plans to visit one of her cousins in Dover in a few days. I shall simply not return from my visit, but go on from there to the house that Anna and I will choose together."

"And your fiancé? What of him?"

"I doubt that he will be much aggrieved. He asked me to marry him out of duty to my parents. I accepted him because it was a sound financial decision to do so. He will soon find another woman who is more to his taste."

"Are you sure he does not love you? Men are not always the best at expressing their feelings. He may harbor a desperate passion for you, and your leaving him will break his heart."

Clarissa raised one perfectly arched eyebrow. "You do not rightly understand my situation or you would find such a suggestion as ludicrous as I do. My fiancé, Jack Langton, is a wealthy financier. He spends his whole day making money on the stock exchange. He does not love me, though he wants to make love to me right enough." The last words were said with evident distaste. "I doubt in fact, that he knows what love is, or even has a heart at all. Or if he does, I have never seen any evidence of it."

Helen felt as though she had been hit in the stomach with a battering ram. "Jack is your fiancé? Jack Langton? The speculator?" *Jack* was the unwanted fiancé, the one whose touch made Clarissa shudder, the one whom Clarissa could not bear to have rutting on her in the night? No wonder he had turned to her for the sexual pleasure he would not find in his marriage.

"You know him?"

Helen nodded, her eyes hard with the memory of just how well she knew him, just how much he had used her. "By reputation, mostly. And by sight. We have had some business dealings together." If only Clarissa knew just how much her words encompassed. She knew all of Jack, every part of him. Every part of his body, that is. He had been less than generous in sharing his thoughts or feelings with her.

Jack had somehow neglected to mention when he was lying in her arms last night, crying out with the pleasure that he was both giving to and receiving from her, that he already had a fiancée — and one that he was planning to marry in fourteen days time. He had neglected to mention that his fiancée was taking lessons from his lover on how to please him in the bedroom. He had neglected to mention that this fiancée of his was one of the very women he had watched making love with one another.

Is that why he had been so aroused by the sight of Clarissa and Anna together? Had he been congratulating himself on his choice of bride? Had he been looking forward to being wed to a woman who might be eager to put on a similar show for him in the future? No doubt he had got an extra kick at saving himself, knowing that he would soon have every right to join them in their games.

She meant nothing to him. She was nothing to him except a willing body to slake his lust on. He had been paying her for sex — that was the only relationship they shared. She had thought that part of her life was behind her, all in the past, but he had taught her differently. She was just as much for sale now as she had been when she worked the streets as a starving child, selling her body to strangers, both men and women, for a crust of bread.

Was his forthcoming wedding why he had turned to her with such passion? Was she to be his last fling before he settled down into wedded bliss with his wife, Clarissa? Or did he think to keep her on as his lover, so he could have both respectability and passion, a wife and a mistress? It sickened her to realize that even now, despite her vow not to become any man's plaything and now that she knew the full extent of his double dealings with her, if he asked her to be his mistress, she would not be able to refuse him.

Her heart ached as she turned over his betrayal in her breast. He had told her that he loved her, that he wanted her to be his woman, and all the while he had been engaged to marry another woman in just a few days time. He had not wanted her as his wife—he wanted her only as his toy, his plaything, his sexual slave. His words of love had meant less than nothing, they had been intended to deceive her.

She had intended to be in control, to teach him all she knew about lovemaking until she had him as malleable as clay in her hands, willing to do anything for her. Instead, she had been caught in the trap she had set for him. She was the one who wanted more from him than he was prepared to give. She was the one who wanted to fall on her knees in front of him and beg for him to take her, to possess her, and to make her his. She wanted everything from him. Everything. She would not be content with just his body. She wanted his heart, and his love.

* * * * *

Jack wiped his sweating palms on his trousers, then took off his hat and turned it around and around in his hands. This visit, he knew, would be a difficult one, but one that he had to make. When his heart was disengaged, he had accepted that marriage to Clarissa was a sensible and a proper thing to do. Now that he had fallen in love with Helen, he could not in all honesty marry another woman. He would have to tell her the truth and give her the option to break off their engagement. If she refused to release him, well, then, the situation would become ugly. But one thing he knew for sure—he would not marry Clarissa willingly.

God, how he hoped that she would accept the situation gracefully and release him from his promise. She certainly didn't appear to be much in love with him. She was enough of her father's daughter to have agreed to the match for sound financial reasons, rather than for personal ones. He would make sure that she wasn't the loser financially by her generosity — he was prepared to settle a considerable sum of money on her personally, as well as another sum on her parents, in lieu of marriage. He owed her and her father that much.

If the worse came to the worst and she still insisted on marrying him, he would hold up his end of the bargain. He had never broken his word to a woman yet. But he would make sure she knew the cold, hard facts before she made her decision — that he must renege on his promise of fidelity because he was in love with another woman whom he intended to make his mistress, if he could have her no other way. Mind you, to a cold fish like Clarissa, his lack of ardor for her might even be an advantage.

If she insisted on marriage, he would have to come clean with Helen, explain the reasons that forced him to marry another, and beg her to become his mistress seeing as he could not make her his wife as he wished. God, he would suffer being chained naked in her cellar for a month on end if she would agree to have him as her lover, as her only lover. He would keep her in luxury, and she would never want for anything for as long as he lived. He would make a generous provision for all their children, and make sure she was looked after properly in the event of his death. Nothing would be left to chance.

He only hoped that she would be woman enough to accept his offer.

"Mr. Langton?"

He gave a start. He had been so wrapped up in his thoughts that he had not heard Clarissa entering the room. She was so prim and proper once more that he almost could believe he had dreamed seeing her flushed in the throes of passion in the arms of her lover. "Miss Harlow," he said, sketching a bow in her direction.

She dipped her head in a polite curtsey. "My parents are both out for the evening, and will be sorry to have missed you."

He knew very well they were out, which is why he had resolved not to delay his encounter with Clarissa but to come and see her straight away. Talking to her would be far easier when he could be quite sure that he could not be overheard by a concerned parent in an adjoining room. "I'm sorry to hear it."

"It is, however, timely you came to visit this evening," she went on, after seating herself in an upright chair. "I have something of great importance to discuss with you."

"And I with you." He ran one trembling hand through his hair. Putting off the evil moment wouldn't make it any easier to deal with. He might as well launch right into the speech he had prepared. He took a deep breath to steady his nerves. "I have come to —"

She held up her hand to silence him. "Please, let me speak. Quite possibly what I have to say to you will make your words to me quite unnecessary. You see," she went on after a short pause, her voice a little fluttery. "I have decided that I cannot accept your generous offer of marriage after all."

She wanted to call the marriage off? Before he had said a word of his intentions? He would be free to marry Helen, if she would have him? He could hardly believe his good fortune. "You have changed your mind?"

"I'm sorry if it comes as a shock to you," she said calmly. "I realize now that agreeing to marry you in the beginning was a mistake, but at the time I thought it was all for the best."

He shook his head in disbelief. He was really free of his unwanted engagement? Just like that? "Not a shock. Just a surprise." He didn't want to delve into her reasons too deeply in case she changed her mind again, but he couldn't help wondering the reason for her sudden change of heart. "I am quite happy to accept your decision, but just out of curiosity, can I ask why?"

For the first time ever, he saw a touch of color come and go on her pale face. "I am in love with someone else," she said, her voice as composed as ever.

That *did* take him by surprise, particularly after what he had seen of her just the day before. How could she be in love with another man? "You are? With whom?"

She tilted her chin defiantly, as if daring to criticize her. "With my best friend, Anna Musgrave. I intend to leave my parents' house right away and make a new life with her."

Suddenly her decision made sense to him as it hadn't before. "You are in love with Miss Musgrave? With a woman?" Her coolness toward him, her passionate embracing of Anna, all of it made sense once he realized that she was a true lesbian, loving only women.

Her face still showed traces of pink around the ears. "I find I do not like men as much as women are supposed to, and I am the luckiest woman in the world that Anna feels the same way I do."

How glad he was that he was no longer bound to marry her. Loving women as she did, he never would have had a chance with her. "She loves you, too?"

"She does." Clarissa smiled, her face unexpectedly warm and full of happiness. "So you see, I am quite decided on it. I cannot marry you."

He started to laugh then, a huge laugh born of happiness that filled his chest and burst out of him in a flood.

"You think it is ridiculous that I am in love with a woman?" She sounded not so much offended as hurt that he would react in such a way. "I cannot see what is so amusing about it myself. I am a woman grown, as is she, and we have chosen to spend our lives together. I did not think that you, of all people, would prove so narrow-minded about the choice I have made."

"No, I am not laughing at you," he said in between splutters, his relief making him feel giddy and weak at the knees. Helen would be his. He would insist that she marry him, and he would not take no for an answer. He would make her his wife as soon as he could procure a license. "I am laughing at me. At the whole situation." He forced his laughter back under control with some difficulty. "You see, I was coming to you this evening to tell you that I have fallen in love with someone else, and to ask you to release me from our engagement."

Clarissa, he was glad to see, also saw the funny side of the situation. "You have fallen in love with someone else, too?" she asked, her voice full of merriment.

He nodded. "Deeply. Passionately. With all my heart. While my heart was not engaged, I thought that you and I would do very well together, but now I have tasted her love, I cannot do without her."

A dreamy smile stole over Clarissa's face. "I feel just the same way about Anna. If I had to live without her by my side, my life would not be worth living. I would face down any shame or scandal if she were standing by my side. And she has promised to stand by me as I have promised to stand by her, for the rest of our lives."

"I am glad you have found happiness," he said sincerely. "I hope it lasts you for a lifetime."

"So we are agreed then? You will take my side if my parents are unhappy? You will help me to explain that our decision is mutual — and irrevocable."

The thought of her parents instantly sobered him, tingeing his giddy joy with a twinge of guilt. "You have not told them anything?"

She shrugged one elegant, white shoulder. "Not yet. I hardly want to confess the real reason for my change of mind to my mother. She would have a fit of the vapors. And I suspect that my father would be horrified at the mere thought and disown me for good."

He could think of one way to soften the blow for them both. "I had come prepared to offer you a generous settlement to break our engagement. I am still prepared to settle that sum on you. After all, it was a mere accident that you spoke first."

"You would settle money on me for not marrying you?" She looked surprised at his unlooked-for generosity. "Even though I have refused you, too?"

"Of course. It will salve my conscience, and go some way toward reconciling your parents to your continued single state." He named a sum that made her eyebrows rise and mouth fall open in shock.

"You would settle that much on me? Just for the privilege of not marrying you?"

He shrugged, not wanting to tell her just how badly he had wanted out of their engagement. "I owe your father a good deal."

"So I see." She looked thoughtful for a moment. "I suspect that a true lady would refuse your offer," she confessed, "but I find that I am loath to. Such a sum would mean that I would not have to rely on Anna for everything, but I would be able to go to our new partnership as a true equal. I would not have to be beholden to her for everything." She breathed a gentle sigh. "That means more to me, I'm afraid, than doing the right thing by you and refusing your money. So I shall accept, with gratitude."

That was so like Clarissa, practical to the last, and too sensible to allow her pride to get in the way of a reasonable decision. He would have his freedom and she would have hers, and they would be able to pursue their own brand of happiness.

She *would* have made him a good wife, if circumstances had been different. He rose and put his hat back on his head, supremely satisfied with the evening's work so far. "Goodbye, Clarissa, and may luck always be on your side. I shall deposit the money in your name with my bankers tomorrow morning so you may access it before you leave with Anna."

She gave him her gloved hand to kiss farewell. "You are a fine man, Mr. Langton—much finer than I ever suspected. If I had been otherwise inclined, I would have been proud to marry you and call you husband. As it is, I hope we can at least be good friends."

A picture of Clarissa disporting with her other good friend, Anna, crossed his mind. He knew a momentary pang of regret that he would not be able to join the two of them in the bedroom, fucking first one tender little virgin and then the other as they touched and stroked each other, and licked and sucked on each other in a frenzied abandon of lust. Maybe when they tired of just being with each other and were open to trying some new sensations, he would persuade Helen to invite them over to play one day. "So do I."

Chapter Nine

Helen had thought she was all out of tears years ago, but she had proved herself wrong with a vengeance that day. As soon as Clarissa was safely out of her house, she sank down on to the sofa and burst into a storm of sobbing.

She was ruined. Utterly ruined. The defection of two of her pupils at the same time, both Clarissa and Anna, and the hue and cry that was bound to ensue, was a devastating blow to her business. She could only hope that a full-blown scandal would be averted, and that her school could outface the whisperers of gossip and rumor and limp on until it recovered its reputation. Still, she had faced hard times before and lived through them — she was confident of doing so again in the face of this latest setback.

She was glad that Jack hadn't given her back half her business last night. Having his capital behind her would certainly help to tide her over. As a financier and half-owner in the business, he would be affected in equal measure to her. If things got too tough, she would simply have to make it worth his while to bail her out.

Jack Langton. The thought of him made her burst out crying anew. That was what she was really upset about — not her damned school. How she wished she could afford to fling his money back in his face again, but she knew she could not. She had gone hungry plenty of times in her life before, and she didn't like it any the better now than she had as a child. Memories of that gnawing hunger that gripped her belly when she hadn't eaten for four or five days on end were enough to make her glad to take any man's money, be it the Devil himself who was offering it to her.

Jack Langton. Clarissa was right about him. He had no heart. She had made that age-old error, mistaking a man's lusty nature for evidence of his affection for her. His words of love had born of the moment, not of his feelings for her. He did not care for her, he cared only for the ability to buy her cunt. The language of money was the only language he spoke, or understood. She had lost her heart to a man who used her no better than a whore.

She had promised him one last lesson and one last lesson he would get. But this lesson would be quite different to the ones before. She smiled wryly through her tears. She would teach him that to truly please a woman took not fine words and pretty gifts, but kindness, honesty, and love.

She doubted that he would profit much from her words, but it would at least give her the satisfaction of speaking them to his face.

She had taken herself and her misery early into bed and was just drifting off into a troubled sleep when the heavy pounding on her door startled her into wakefulness again. "Go away and leave me alone," she muttered to herself, but the noise did not stop.

With a heavy sigh she stumbled out of bed and wrapped a heavy robe around her shoulders. She would stop that awful noise, and give whoever it was at her door a proper earful for waking her up.

Making sure the door was chained so it could only be opened a crack, she shot the bolt free and glared out at the figure standing on her doorstep in the dark. "Go away," she said, suddenly too weary to ring a peal over his head as she had intended to. "I don't care why you are knocking on my door. I don't care if my neighbor's house is burning down or if Queen Victoria herself is in the street wanting to talk to me. Just go away and leave me be." And she started to close the door again.

"Helen, It's me. Let me in."

She halted at the sound of Jack's voice, her stomach flipping over at the thought that he was there outside her door, waiting to see her, wanting to be with her. How she hated it that he still had such power over her to make her want him—even against her better judgment. "What do you want?"

"Let me in and I'll tell you." His voice held a world of sultry promise.

With a troubled sigh, she unchained the door and let him in. She had not the heart to refuse him entrance to her house, despite the lateness of the hour and the heaviness of her heart.

He paused only to bolt the door behind him before he took her into his arms and hugged her close to him. "Helen, my love. I missed you today."

She knew his words were empty and without meaning, but she liked to hear them anyway. He needn't think that she was a pushover, though. She had *some* pride still left to her. She held herself stiff and unresisting in his arms. "I should feel special, I suppose, that you even thought of me at all. You must be very busy preparing for your wedding."

He looked as shocked as she had been when she had first discovered that he was engaged to her pupil, Clarissa Harlow. "My wedding?"

"After all, when was it planned?" she went on, ignoring his surprise. "Some fourteen days or so from today? There must be so much to be done I'm surprised you have the energy to come chasing after any other woman."

He hugged her close to him again. "I'm not getting married," he said, his voice full of joy and anticipation as if he was giving her the best gift in the world.

She shrugged. "So I heard already."

He looked confused at her unenthusiastic reaction to his news. "You did? Who told you?"

She took advantage of his confusion to pull away from his embrace. "Clarissa Harlow came to see me today to tell me that she decided against finishing her lessons with me," she said, as she stumbled unhappily in the parlor and flung herself down on the first chair she could find—a long, low sofa near the door. "She no longer wants to get married but has decided to go and live in unwedded bliss with her friend instead."

He sat down beside her on the sofa, took her in his arms and stroked her gently. "Clarissa plans to live with Anna Musgrave, yes. I have settled some money on her so she can do so in comfort."

She refused to be placated by his gentleness. "I knew, of course, that she was engaged—that was the point of her taking lessons with me after all—but until she mentioned the name of her fiancé, I did not know to whom. Imagine my surprise when Clarissa's unwanted fiancé turned out to be Jack Langton the wealthy financier, and part owner of my school." She bit back another rush of tears by sheer willpower. "The same Jack Langton who had spent the previous night in my bed fucking me until he was senseless, and whispering in my ear that he loved me." She snorted. "Some kind of love that must be, when you couldn't even be honest enough to tell me that you were about to be married."

He continued to stroke her hair and shoulders with loving gentleness. "I never loved Clarissa."

She shrugged. What he felt or not about the girl he was supposed to marry was no concern of hers—it still didn't make her feel any better about the way he had treated her as his private plaything. "Does that make a difference?"

"I never felt anything for her. Nothing."

That was supposed to placate her? It only made her madder than before. "And that makes it all right?" she spat at him "To marry a woman you do not love? And fuck the nearest woman who comes to hand when your wife to be doesn't respond to you in the way you like?"

Jack shook his head wearily. "That's not the way of it. I only agreed to marry her because I owed her father a debt of gratitude that I felt honor-bound to repay. Her father had speculated away his fortune and was staring poverty in the face. My marriage to his daughter would have shored up his sinking fortunes with no damage to his pride. Besides, she was young and pretty enough that marriage to her seemed no particular hardship." He paused for a moment to allow time for his words to sink in. "But then I met you."

"You met me and decided to take lessons off me to keep your new wife happy?" She could not keep the bitterness out of her voice. She had thought he had loved her, when all the time he was simply using her for his own ends. "How convenient for you."

His hands had found their way under her nightgown and were engaged in stroking her breasts. "No. I met you and manipulated you into teaching me because I had to find some excuse to be near you. And the more time I spent with you, the more time I wanted to spend with you and the more I got to hate the idea of marrying Clarissa out of gratitude, to pay off a debt."

"You thought you could buy me." She could not keep the bitterness out of her voice. The way he had practically offered to buy sex with her rankled most of all. She had been many things in her time, but she had not ever had to sink that low. Though she had paid for favors in kind before now, she had never directly traded sex for money.

"No." His voice was strong and sure. "I never thought that. I never thought you were for sale."

She tried to shake him off, but he held her too tightly. He would not let her go. "You thought I was yours for the taking. Just throw me a few bones in payment, and you could do what you liked with me."

His hands were on her body now, stroking her stomach and breasts, playing with her nipples just the way she liked. "That is not the truth. I needed an excuse to be near you. Any excuse at all. I would have given you anything just to be near you. Anything. I simply could not keep away from you."

God, it felt so good to have his hands on her again, stroking her breasts and teasing her nipples until they were as hard as little cherry stones. She leaned back into his embrace, and felt his hard cock pressing into her buttocks. He wanted her. Whether or not he was in love with her, he still wanted her, and that was at least a small triumph. She felt her pussy getting wet and hungry as he played with her. "But you didn't call off the engagement," she reminded him. "If Clarissa hadn't discovered the joys of making love with another woman, you would still be planning to marry her in fourteen days time. And then what would you have done with me? Kept me as your mistress in a conveniently located town house in St John's Wood or Shepherd's Bush, where all the other women kept by wealthy men live?" Even as she spoke, the thought of being his mistress excited her even more than it repelled her. For Jack, she would be willing to give up her independence. Only for Jack. He would keep her for him alone, and she would keep him thoroughly satisfied in the bedroom—so satisfied that he had no desire to look elsewhere for his pleasures.

He held her to him, pressing his cock in between her buttocks as he played with her breasts. "I went to Clarissa tonight to beg her to release me from our engagement. If she had insisted on marrying me, I would have held up my end of the bargain. I would not break a solemn promise I had vowed to her. And I would have gone down on my hands and knees to you to beg you to become my mistress rather than to lose you altogether. I would have given you fifty houses, if only you agreed to stay with me."

His words startled her. Was he telling the truth, or was it just another easy lie to try and placate her? She turned around to look at him, to see if she could read the truth of the matter in his eyes. "You broke off your engagement to her? Not the other way around?"

"I didn't get a chance to open my mouth to ask her," he confessed. "Before I had so much as started on my little speech, she had informed me with perfect composure that she had decided against marrying me after all. I was so relieved at her decision that I freely gave her the money I had intended as a bribe to encourage her to break the engagement, and we parted on the best of terms. And I hurried here to throw myself at your feet instead, and to ask if you would have me, to beg you to marry me."

Surely she had not heard him right. Was he really asking her to marry him? "You do not want me as your mistress?"

"If you were my mistress, you would be able to leave me if you tired of me." He gave her a wolfish grin. "Don't get me wrong—I am not intending to let you get tired of me, but I don't want to take the chance. You belong to me. I intend to tie you to me so you can't escape. I don't want you as my mistress. Only marriage will do."

"You really want to marry me?" She had just reconciled herself to the idea of being his mistress, and he was asking her to marry him after all? He was not ashamed of her? He wanted her by his side for all time, not just until he had tired of fucking her?

He put her out of his arms and sank to his knees in front of her. "God, yes. I want to marry you more than I've ever wanted to do anything else in my entire life. Please, tell me you will take me."

He was doing it to her again. One soft look from him and she was putty in his hands. She pouted at this evidence of her own weakness, of her inability to refuse him.

"Come, tell me that you will have me," he said, sliding his hands under her nightrobe and up her thighs. "Tell me quickly that you will have me, or I'll take you down to the cellar and put you in chains until you agree."

She didn't know what to say to his earnest entreaty. Marriage was so…so permanent. Giving up her independence to be a mistress was one thing, but to be his wife? Her life would never be her own again. "I liked the chains."

"I know you did, you hussy," he said, as his questing fingers found her pussy and began to stroke it with long, languorous touches. "Come, tell me that you'll have me." His fingers delved into her cunt, pushing into her wetness with greedy satisfaction. "You know you want me. I can feel how much you want me."

It was true—she did want him. She parted her knees for him so he could delve deeper into her, and let her heavy robe slip off her shoulders, leaving only her thin cotton nightgown to keep her from the cold. "I do want you. I want you now, inside me."

"Now that's what I call an invitation," he said, as he stood up to unbutton his trousers. "You want me to fuck you again, do you? You want me to thrust my cock into your cunt, hard and deep, until you come apart screaming in my arms? And then you want me to do it again?"

"Yes." She could barely breathe with the thought of having him inside her again, of having him in her arms forever. "I want you to fuck me."

He stood immobile in front of her, his trousers unbuttoned. "Say you'll marry me, and I'm all yours."

The glimpse of his proud cock undid her. She would give up her single life, her independence, for Jack. She really had no choice in the matter, because she simply did not want to live without him. "I want you to fuck me now, and every single night for the rest of my life."

"Will you marry me?"

She couldn't hold out any longer. She didn't want to hold out against Jack. She was in love with him and wanted to stay by his side. Forever. "Yes, I will marry you. After all," she added, a wicked gleam in her eyes, "there's still a chest full of toys down in the cellar that we haven't played with yet."

He knelt in front of her, his cock standing up straight and hard, parted her legs and rammed himself home. "This is where I belong."

She grabbed his naked buttocks and helped guide him to the very depths of her being. "And this is where I hope you'll stay for a very, very long time."

About the author:

Leda Swann is a senior executive in a large corporate, the mother of four young children, and partner of a wonderful man. She likes scuba diving, swimming, and any other sport that involves getting cold and wet on a regular basis. She is also the author of outrageously sexy romances, keeps fur-lined handcuffs in her bedside drawers, and fights hard to remember to remove the silk ties off her bed head whenever her parents come to visit.

Leda welcomes mail from readers. You can write to her c/o Ellora's Cave Publishing at 1056 Home Avenue, Akron OH 44310-3502.

Also by Leda Swann:

Sunlit

Seduction of Colette

Claire Thompson

Prologue

"My lord, you can't be serious!"

"Of course I am. She's mine, I can do as I please!" Claude Rousseau shook off the restraining hand of his friend, Andre. It was after midnight at the Court of Versailles in the French countryside, and many of the parties were only just getting started. Rousseau had been drinking hard, as was his habit, and for a while had been winning steadily at Le Poque, as the game of poker was called at Court. The year was 1678, and King Louis the Fourteenth had reached the zenith of his career. All Europe bowed before the nation of France, and the country itself had been brought by skillful tyranny to admire and obey the Sun King as sole sovereign over all.

The splendor of the Court lay in the beautiful palaces constructed at huge expense under the careful direction of the King, as well as in the luxurious furnishings of the apartments, the lavish dress of the courtiers, the sumptuous entertainments, the fame of the men and the beauty of the women drawn there by the magnets of money, reputation and power.

The morals of the Court included discreet but constantly present sexual dalliances, extravagance in dress and gambling, and passionate intrigues for prestige and place, all carried on a rhythm of external refinement, elegant manners and compulsory gaiety. Nobles and their ladies consumed half the income of their estates on clothing, lackeys and equipage; the most modest had to have eleven servants and two coaches, some of the richer dignitaries had seventy-five attendants in their household, and forty horses in their stables.

Gambling at cards was a chief recreation and Louis again gave the lead, bidding for high stakes, urged on by his mistress

Montespan, who herself lost and won four million francs in one night's play. The gambling mania spread through the Court, and Claude Rousseau was no exception. This evening he had consumed several bottles of wine, and his hand now shook as he made what would turn out to be his final bet of the evening. Liquor had colored his ability to judge the skill of his bluff. The pile of coins he had started the evening with had dwindled to nothing, and still he went on. His old friend Andre shrugged, tired of arguing with a man who was about to give away the thing he should have held most dear.

Across the table Philippe de Valon silently surveyed the gentlemen. He noted Rousseau's wig was askew, and rivulets of sweat made little lines down the white powder on his sagging jowls. The man was desperate and drunk, and not in a position to be making the wager he now made. And yet, who was Philippe to stop him? It was a curious wager indeed, and Philippe was not at all uninterested.

Lord Philippe de Valon, master draftsman, shipbuilder, heir to a huge fortune in the northern port of St. Malo, was at present one of the King's favorites. Though he would rather have been home in his own province, tending to his businesses and seeing to his properties, the King had bid Philippe to stay at Court, and continue to design lovely buildings for him. Of course, he was also invited to partake in the elaborate excesses of food, wine and, most especially, women.

Philippe had thought by now he had seen it all. But this latest bid by the Duke of Lyon was extraordinary, even measured against the cynical sophistication of the Court. It must be a bluff, surely.

But again Rousseau said, "As you can see, I am out of coin, but so confident am I in my hand that I am willing to risk the person of my daughter as collateral for my wager. You win, you get her. I win, I get all the gold that has changed hands tonight, as well as two of your horses and a carriage. Fair?"

"More than fair," nodded Philippe, mentally calculating the value of this man's daughter to her father in his own head. It seemed a paltry price to pay for another human being! Especially a lovely young virgin. And did the father have the authority to hand over another human being? Yes, technically he did, as she fell under the estate of Le Duc Rousseau de Lyon. Still a man of some influence in the kingdom, Rousseau's once sizable holdings had been dramatically reduced by the King's taxes and forced "gifts", as well as the duke's own mismanagement and neglect.

The duke's daughter Colette, age eighteen, would surely be considered by most fathers to be a most prized possession. The duke, however, was not a sentimental man, and certainly not a loving one. For him, his three daughters had come down to a matter of gold. Each had a cost, since their father was expected to provide a sizable dowry to get them properly wed. Colette's two older sisters had just been successfully matched, and the cost to the duke had been substantial indeed.

Colette was, at the moment, asleep in her chambers in one of the smaller houses on the King's huge estate at Versailles, blissfully unaware that the course of her life hung in the balance over a game of cards.

"Well, then. Top this, if you can!" With a flourish, Rousseau spread his cards on the table. Philippe studied them carefully, and then slowly, his expression inscrutable, revealed his own cards. Rousseau's hand had been reaching for the pile of gold even while Philippe had been laying down his cards, so sure was he of his bet.

Now Andre, turning pale, shouted, "Claude! You imbecile! You've lost! You do not have the winning hand! Lord de Valon has outwitted you again! And now you've lost Colette! You fool!"

Rousseau spluttered and swore, his hands falling away from the gold as his face reddened, the words of his friend finally penetrating the thick fog of wine in his brain. "No! He cheated! It's impossible! I had the perfect cards! No!" Rousseau stood, pulling and fumbling at the sheath that held his sword. Fashion demanded that every gentleman sport a sword, and this was sometimes a dangerous state of affairs, when tempers were frayed and judgment blurred by alcohol. Philippe also stood, his hand on his sheath, not yet drawing. Several men at the table constrained the old duke, who fell back against his chair, his face now pale and sweating.

"A bet is a bet," intoned one of the men, and they all nodded. Rousseau seemed to age suddenly before their eyes, slumping in his chair and dropping his head into his hands.

Philippe took his own hand from his sword, though he remained standing. He decided to ignore the older man's insult that he had cheated. A duel with the old fellow would certainly lead to Rousseau's death, and Philippe had no desire to kill a man, especially not a drunken old sot like Rousseau.

"Gentlemen," he said, "This has been quite an entertaining evening. Unfortunately, I find myself quite exhausted and would bid you good night. Lord Rousseau, I will be by your chambers in the morning to collect my prize. Good night." Gathering the stack of gold in front of his place, Philippe bowed gracefully to the gentlemen at the table, the plume of his hat grazing the winning cards.

Chapter One

"Wake up! My lady, wake up!" Brigitte, Colette's personal maid, shook her mistress' shoulder. "Your father is here! Hurry!" Colette sat up, pushing her heavy blonde hair from her face, sleep still marking her features, making her look very young indeed.

"Papa!" she said. "Why is he here?" Colette clutched her blanket protectively to her chest. Claude Rousseau had brought his remaining unwed daughter, along with his son Jean Luc, to Court with him.

Colette's mother had died when she was only six, with the birth of Colette's younger brother Jean Luc. Rousseau had not remarried, as he'd gotten the heir he sought, though it cost the life of his wife. Her father had taken no active interest in Colette until recently, when her childish body had begun to fill out, and the responsibility of finding her a husband had begun to loom.

He did find his way sometimes into her bedroom, and slipped into her bed, frightening her each time with his insistent hands probing her, trying to touch her where no one but a husband should. Luckily, he was usually so drunk that he passed out before he did more than fondle her breasts, breathing his foul whiskey fumes over her, making her shudder and bite her bedding to keep from crying out, or worse, striking him.

But mostly he let her be. It was easy to ignore the third daughter of three, when one had a son to teach all the skills needed to run the huge estates, and a busy household of forty servants and several permanent "guests" who found their way into the duke's entourage.

Colette made it her business to be unobtrusive, as she was frightened by her father's drunken rages, which happened more and more frequently as the years passed. She had been beaten more than once in front of the servants, for some imagined infraction, and the shame of those beatings stayed with her long after the welts had healed.

Now Brigitte, who had grown up alongside Colette, serving as playmate and now handmaid, helped her mistress from the high narrow bed where she slept each night at Court in her tiny bedroom, a far cry from the large airy rooms of her father's castle in the south. Hurriedly Brigitte dressed her mistress, putting the heavy brocaded gown on over her soft undergarments, tying the many bows and slipping the buttons through the buttonholes at her back.

"He did not share his errand with me, my lady! But he wants to see you right away!" Brigitte pulled back her mistress' hair, expertly weaving the braids with velvet bands studded with tiny pearls, working as fast as she could to make her young mistress presentable for the duke.

She was just finishing when Rousseau burst into the small room. "Colette! I have something to tell you. What's taking so long?" His own guilt made him brusque. He didn't particularly care about Colette, or any of her sisters for that matter. Women were useful for only one thing—breeding. Now that that bastard de Valon had stripped him of much gold, which was sorely needed, the fellow could take this wench off his hands, and good riddance! Colette would be leaving his household by a rather unconventional route, admittedly, but he was lord of his domain, and it was his prerogative.

Obediently Colette followed her father into the outer chamber. Rousseau sat at her small table, drawing his beefy hand across his face. She noted his color was bad, and his beady eyes were bloodshot. Another drunken night, no doubt, gambling away her dowry.

"I, er, have something to tell you." He paused, looking at her, perhaps for the first time really seeing her—the lovely porcelain skin, the dark red lips, the fringe of dark gold lashes on large gray blue eyes, the little pointed chin. Vague memories, sodden with wine, of her soft body under heavy nightclothes, when he occasionally "accidentally" stumbled into the wrong bed. The budding sweetness of virginal youth. She was a lovely girl, but she was expendable, and he had lost the wager and there was nothing to be done.

He had sent intermediaries first thing in the morning to try and dissuade Philippe de Valon, but de Valon had proclaimed himself very content with the wager, and refused to back down. In all classes of French society, it was *l'honnete homme*, not the honest man, but the honorable man, that was considered the ideal. Now in the sober light of day, Claude Rousseau couldn't possibly risk his honor by backing out of a debt made in front of some of the most influential men in the land.

"Yes, Papa?" Colette said quietly, trying not to betray her nervous confusion as she sat gracefully across from her father at the small table.

"I'm afraid I made a wager last night. That is, I made a promise and now I find I have no recourse but to comply with the terms of the wager." He paused, unsure how to proceed. Little Colette looked across at him, her eyes large, like a frightened little deer. He should have sent that damn Andre in his stead! He was a busy man! Let the man who lived off of his goodwill handle a difficult situation for a change!

Taking a deep breath he said, "I know this will be hard to understand, but I, uh, that is, I lost you to a gentleman last night. You are to move to his entourage this evening. You may take your handmaid. He won you fair and square, and there's no getting out of it. I'm sorry."

Colette stared at her father, a look of incomprehension on her face. Embarrassed and ashamed, Rousseau focused instead on the rising irritation of the situation. "Damn it, girl! Don't stare at me like a stupid cow! You heard what I said. Pack your things. It's a change of household, that's all. And Philippe de Valon is twenty times richer than I'll ever be! So count your blessings, wretched girl!

"And you listen to me." His voice took on an even more ominous tone. "If I find that you have disobeyed Lord de Valon in any respect, I'll have you beaten until you bleed. I'll lock you in my dungeons until you wither and die. Do you understand me? This isn't a choice. What's done is done. Disgrace me, and you besmirch the honor of the House of de Lyon! And I'll never forgive you for that. Daughter or no, you do that, and you can consider yourself dead."

He stood abruptly, knocking the little chair behind him so it fell with a clatter against the stone floor. He swept from the room, his mouth desperately dry for the bottle of wine waiting in his chambers, his daughter sobbing into her arms at the small table.

* * * * *

Colette was led into what were to become her new chambers by a silent young footman. Brigitte was behind her, carrying two large bags that contained some of Colette's clothing and jewels. The rest of her things would be brought later. The young man left them, closing the door behind him before Colette had a chance to question him.

"Oh my, isn't this lovely?" The two rooms to which they had been assigned were nothing like the small little cell Colette and Brigitte had inhabited these past few months at Court. Colette's father did not share the place of favor that Philippe de Valon apparently enjoyed. The outer room contained a large table and chairs and several comfortable couches. There were lovely tapestries on the walls and floor, unlike the bare stone of her prior apartments. The bedroom was equally lavish, with a large canopied bed for Colette, and a smaller bed for her maid. Both had thick feather mattresses and several quilts.

Brigitte ran laughing to the smaller bed. She had never slept on anything other than a small rollup mattress on the floor near her mistress. Collapsing onto her new bed she cried, "Ooo, la la! Isn't this heaven on earth?" Colette sat uncertainly on the higher bed, and couldn't help smiling at her little servant, who rolled like a child among the quilts.

"Brigitte!" she admonished. "How can you care about a feather bed when I've been sold into slavery!" Colette wasn't sure exactly what she had been sold into, but she knew she was no longer part of her father's household, with the status that being the daughter of a duke had afforded her. She was completely confused in fact, as to just what had happened to her, and there was no one to turn to, as far as she could see. Her brother Jean Luc, only eleven, wasn't in a position to come to her aid, and there was no one else to protect or defend her. She was alone, and frightened.

Brigitte sat up, sobered by her mistress' words. "Is that what it is, my lady? Slavery?"

"I don't know, Brigitte. I just know we're stuck here, and I haven't a clue what we're supposed to do!" As if on cue, there was a knock at her door, and a woman entered. She was dressed sumptuously in dark wine velvet, her collar trimmed with lace. From the cut of her gown, it was clear she wasn't a noblewoman, but a servant of some high-ranking dignitary. Her dark hair was pulled back in an elaborate coiffure, and powdered in the style of the day.

"Welcome, my lady. I have been sent by Lord Philippe to greet you. I know the situation is somewhat curious, and he wanted me to allay your fears. My name is Catherine and I serve in Lord Philippe's household. He wants to welcome you, and indeed, would have come himself if he weren't suddenly detained by the King's business. You have the freedom of these chambers, but he has asked that you confine yourself here until he has had a chance to return and introduce himself."

"Please," Colette interrupted, "I'm so confused, Madame! What is my place, that is, my situation, here in Monsieur de Valon's household? I have been told nothing!" Tears spilled now, brimming over her large gray eyes. Colette, only eighteen, had been trying desperately to behave with grace and control, as befitted her noble heritage, but it was so hard!

The older woman's face softened, and she said, "My dear. Please do not cry, as you are safe here. I have not been precisely informed as to your position with us, but I do believe you will be asked to serve as companion to Madame de Valon, Lord Philippe's esteemed aunt. She is getting on in years. She tires easily and, how shall I put this, does not always observe the conventions of polite society." Catherine stopped herself, looking embarrassed, and as if she had said too much.

Colette of course understood the unspoken content of the remark. She, daughter of a duke, was going to be forced to serve as a lady companion to some bitter crotchety old woman! She would never marry, but die an old maid! Papa had destroyed her life with his drinking and gambling! Colette burst into tears, sobbing in earnest now.

"Oh dear!" Catherine exclaimed, realizing she'd made a mess of things. "Please, Mademoiselle! Don't cry. Lord Philippe will return this evening, and he will explain things much better than I have. Trust me, dear, he is a kind man, and you won't be mistreated here." The servant withdrew, after instructing Brigitte to comfort her young mistress. She would send their luncheon, and see that they weren't disturbed.

* * * * *

Philippe knocked quietly on the door, and when there was no response, he opened it anyway and entered. He was used to taking what he wanted, and often flouted such conventions as closed doors. The outer room was empty, and he saw evidence of a repast, with the remains of meats and cheeses, some fruit in a bowl, and two tea cups, one empty, the other full. Stepping forward, he leaned into the smaller bedchamber and encountered a charming sight.

A plump young woman dressed in a servant's simple gown, was nestled on the lower bed, her arms flung over her head, covering her face, fast asleep. In the larger bed lay her mistress, also asleep, her back to the room. This must be the young Colette! Philippe had never seen her, as her father had forbidden her from attending any of the lavish parties of the Court. But he had heard from servants and some of his lady friends, who had met her at the sewing circles and over tea, that Colette was especially lovely.

Philippe, at twenty-six, was devilishly handsome, with dark curling hair that he pulled back in a ponytail and, while at Court, hid beneath the white curled wigs of the day. His face was finely sculpted, with a firm jaw and large dark green eyes that he used to great effect, staring down those who would defy him. He was tall for the times, nearly six feet, and his body was strong and well-muscled, honed by years of horseback riding and fencing. Philippe was well known at Court, especially by the ladies, with whom he was very much in demand.

Unmarried, with no intention of settling down as yet, he enjoyed the intrigues and dangers of wooing and claiming other men's wives, however brief the interludes might be. And as long as he was discreet, the likewise faithless husbands winked at their wives' infidelities.

Nearly every married man who could afford it had a mistress; men plumed themselves on their liaisons almost as much as on their battles, and a woman felt desolate if no man but her husband pursued her. Marriage was a contract of politics and property, and love generally had very little to do with it. As long as one remained discreet, adultery was the accepted order of the day.

The liaisons were generally brief, because Philippe was easily bored, and because he liked a challenge, which was rarely offered by the highly sexed and sophisticated women at the King's Court. This "acquisition" of a young virgin, and a member of the aristocracy at that, was far from usual, and would no doubt be greeted with great interest and probably some resistance at Court.

But Philippe de Valon, an architect and draftsman by training, a shipbuilder by inheritance, enjoyed unusual favor with the King these days, as he had designed an especially lovely little palace for the King's mistress, which had greatly pleased the King. So at least for the time being, Philippe would not be questioned.

He had informed his senior staff that he had acquired the "services" of Colette Rousseau, the daughter of the Duke of Lyon, but he hadn't told them how he had come to such an unusual arrangement, and they of course hadn't asked, knowing never to question the often eccentric ways of their master. He had toyed with the idea of offering her as a companion for his shrew of an aunt, whom he had taken into his household since the death of his uncle two years before, and the loss of his uncle's lands in the skirmish with Spain.

Old Aunt Genevieve was a force to be reckoned with. She ruled his staff with an iron hand and a sour wit, but Philippe loved her just the same. He knew that beneath her bitter exterior was a loving and good woman, but one who had been embittered by the loss of her husband and her wealth, as well as a lifetime of grief hardening around the fact that she was barren, and had never conceived a child.

With Philippe she was as sarcastic and blunt as with anyone, but he, not being subject to her authority, was more amused than insulted by her. And he knew that she loved him as a son, and indeed, he loved her, and admired her grit in the face of her hardships.

Still, many a mature woman at Court had paled at her direct and often insulting discourse, and she was not a popular guest for tea. She was therefore lonely, though it was of her own making. He would have this young lady entertain his poor aunt. She could be a built-in companion; one who didn't have the luxury of excusing herself, as he had "purchased" her.

What an odd situation this was! And yet it amused and intrigued him. Looking at that long slender back, and the burnished gold hair, he now thought perhaps he'd introduce her to his own amorous attentions, if she didn't bore him to death in the process. Surely she'd be good for a tussle in the sheets, if nothing else. Though, knowing the women at Court, she'd probably already lain with more than her fair share!

As he stood there musing, admiring the heavy silk brocade that hid whatever girlish body lay beneath it, he heard a gasp and turned toward its source. Brigitte had jumped up from her small bed, her hands at her mouth, staring in horror at the intruding gentleman. Seeing his fine dress and bearing, she hurriedly dropped to a deep curtsey.

Philippe admired the little woman for a moment. He noted her pleasingly plump figure, with heavy breasts spilling out over her maid's gown, covered in lace that made one think what must lie just beneath it. Philippe bowed gallantly and said, "Excuse me, Mademoiselle. I didn't mean to alarm you, but you were both sleeping so soundly I hated to disturb you. My name is Philippe. Philippe de Valon. I wanted to welcome you to my household."

Colette turned now, and sat up as well, her hands drawn up to her breasts, her face flushed, eyes bright. "My lord!" she said, startled. "Is it your custom to enter a lady's chambers without permission?"

"My lady, pray excuse me. But in fact these are *my* chambers, and you now fall completely under my authority." His voice was stern, but his eyes were sparkling with merriment. She was a feisty one, this Colette!

Colette stood up, smoothing her gown and pushing back a long tendril of blonde hair that had fallen into her face. Her cheeks were flushed, and she looked to Brigitte, perhaps hoping for guidance, but none was forthcoming, as the little maid continued to gape at the tall handsome man standing between them.

Slowly Colette curtseyed, lowering her head and spreading her substantial skirts gracefully about her as she did so. She really was quite lovely! Perhaps he had been premature in deciding to pack her off as Aunt Genevieve's lackey. Perhaps he'd get to know her a little first.

On an impulse he said, "Lady Colette. I know this change in circumstance must be very odd for you, and difficult to absorb. Perhaps you would care to join me for dinner this evening, and we could discuss the situation?"

Colette looked up, still bent in her curtsey. He gestured for her to rise with his hand, and she stood slowly, her face composed but her eyes very large. Obviously it wasn't actually an invitation that she could refuse. She had no recourse to speak of, and was now considered his property to all intents and purposes, though perhaps a real court of law would have disagreed. But as far as the eighteen-year-old girl who had been handed by her father to this man was concerned, she might as well have been branded as his slave and shut in a dungeon for life. There was no one to appeal to, and nowhere to turn.

Trying to put a brave face on it, Colette answered slowly, "It would be my honor, sir, to have dinner with you. Please, could it be here in these lovely rooms you have provided for me?"

Philippe looked at her, wondering what was going on inside that lovely head of hers. Why in the world would she want to eat in this small chamber when he was offering her a chance to dine in his elegant quarters, possibly even to dine with the King for all she knew! Looking at her frightened, innocent expression, he realized, or at least surmised, that she had probably been quite sheltered to this point, and had not had the experience, which admittedly could be a daunting one, of dining in full costumed splendor at one of the larger palaces, with all the Court's eyes on her.

Wishing to spare her for a little longer at least, and also because he found suddenly that he fancied the idea of eating with her alone, and actually getting to talk to her, instead of being distracted by the constant attentions of the nobles and their ladies vying for his attentions, Philippe nodded graciously and said, "But of course. You are no doubt tired from this sudden transition. I shall instruct my servants to bring us dinner in a little while. Until then, I bid you adieu."

After he left, Brigitte turned to Colette and said, "Oh, you were amazing, my lady! I've never seen you so brave and confident! And imagine, eating dinner with Lord de Valon! Unattended! Your father would have a fit if he knew! Oh, I didn't mean…" The poor girl spluttered to a stop, not sure what she meant. The father who was supposedly concerned for Colette's honor had traded her away like a common street whore. For all he knew she was bound and gagged at this moment, on a ship sailing for some foreign land, where all the women lived in harems and never saw the light of day! Brigitte's imagination was very active, aided by stories from servants who had traveled with Colette's father, back when he made voyages across the seas, before Colette's mother had died and he had taken to the bottle.

"I'll be right here attending you, my lady," she now amended, knowing Colette was frightened by the prospect of eating alone with that strange man.

Colette nodded, and tried to smile. "Well, we always said we wished something would happen! All those months cooped up in those drafty little rooms, hoping and praying someone would remember us and invite us to sew or have tea. I guess our wishes came true with a vengeance, eh Brigitte? Our adventures have definitely begun!" Some of the dreadful shock was beginning to wear off. She had met her new "master" and he wasn't an ogre or a boor. In fact, he was quite handsome!

The realization that she might actually be free of the tyranny of her father had begun to pierce the surface of her understanding. Whatever this Lord de Valon was, could he be any worse than the drunken rages, the dreaded nighttime visits and clumsy fumblings with her bedclothes, while she tried to pretend to be asleep, shrinking against the wall, hoping desperately he would pass out before he found his way past the bows and buttons that protected her?

Colette's natural spunk began to rekindle in her blood and she smiled bravely at her little servant. She would make the best of this strange new situation. Forcing herself to sound brave for her little maid, she said brightly, "Now help me to look decent. I have to make up for his seeing me asleep! How humiliating! Let's use the ruby-studded hairnet tonight, shall we?"

* * * * *

Philippe was delighted anew by the lovely Colette when he joined her in her chambers for dinner. The rubies in her golden hair shone deep red, and her eyes sparkled with the reflected light of the overhead candelabra, ablaze with candles.

They were served roast pheasant and an assortment of fruits and cheeses, and of course the finest wines. Philippe was adept with the fork, a relatively new invention, though King Louis himself still preferred his fingers.

Colette had barely touched her food, sitting tongue-tied in front of Lord de Valon, who was lavishly dressed for the evening in silk doublet and satin trousers tied in bows just below the knees. His strong slender calves were encased in silk stockings and his feet were shod in heels in the style of the day, though he secretly hated them and never wore them when away from Court, preferring his sturdy soft leather boots.

Brigitte stood discreetly nearby, not eating of course, but waiting to see if either her lady or the gentleman needed any assistance with their meal. She was silent as a mouse, her eyes huge, staring at the handsome man sitting just feet away from her.

Philippe barely noticed the servant; she could have been part of the furniture. But Colette was another story! He had planned a short visit with the young woman, to make her feel more at ease with the situation, but suddenly found himself in no hurry to get to the usual round of parties, plays, gambling and drinking that awaited him this, as every other, evening at Court.

Colette looked down at her plate, giving Philippe time to study her. He couldn't see her eyes, though he thought he recalled that they were blue. Right now he only saw her lashes, which were a dark golden brown, darker than her honey hair, casting a shadow on her soft cheek, which was still rounded by youth. Her nose was long and rather narrow, but her lips were sweetly full and the color of ripe raspberries. Her blonde hair was pulled back in a pretty French braid, and threaded with red rubies of a color so deep as to be almost purple. Her dress matched the rubies in her hair, cut from dark crimson silk, brocaded in an intricate design.

Philippe was pleased that she didn't wear the heavy powdered wigs that some of the ladies at Court favored. He disliked the style on women, though he himself sported a wig in public at Court, because the King wished it. At home on his own estate in St. Malo, he didn't bother with the hot and dusty head cover, preferring to tie his long hair back with a ribbon and to feel the fresh air and sun upon him, a salty sea breeze blowing.

He hated to sweat underneath the heavy wigs that were so fashionable, even though his was of the finest quality, made from human hair. Those who couldn't afford the human hair had to make do with horse and yak hair, which smelled dreadful when heated under the hot sun of a French summer, and perfumed with the sweat of unwashed noblemen.

Unlike many of his compatriots, Philippe did not believe that frequent bathing was harmful, and had in fact found that it was quite restorative and healthful. Though he couldn't convince his old aunt of the benefits, he had ordered all of his servants to bathe regularly, and found that they were healthier on average than the servants of his peers. Their own initial fears were alleviated when they found they didn't "catch their deaths" by too much water, and found that they didn't suffer nearly as much from the constant heat rashes and lice infestations that were such a part of everyday life.

He also encouraged them to use rags soaked in cold tea to wipe down their teeth after meals. At first he had been mocked, but when he showed his own white smile, and convinced them of how much easier, not to mention less painful, it was when the teeth were sound and not rotting in their heads, they had, again, become convinced.

He would have to make her smile, and judge the quality of her teeth. But for now his eye was drawn to her breasts, uplifted and pressed together by the stiff stays of her gown, as sweet an offering as the apples and pears on the dish in front of her. The fashion of the day exposed much of her creamy dewy skin, and he resisted a sudden ridiculous impulse to lean down and bite her like some luscious fruit.

He wanted to see the rest of those little breasts. He bet the nipples were a pale pink, a virgin pink, as they said in Italy. He was certain no man had ever tasted the sweet flesh of her breasts. Would he be the first? Would he take her maidenhead, just because he could? He felt ashamed suddenly, for thinking of her so callously. He realized he had misjudged her earlier, mistakenly painting her with the brush of brazen Court behavior. He looked at her bowed head, realizing she must be confused and not a little afraid.

"You aren't eating," he said now, his voice gentle.

"Oh, please my lord, excuse me. I can't seem to swallow. I don't know what's come over me."

He smiled. She was clearly nervous, and he wanted to put her at ease. He couldn't remember feeling so excited by a woman in years. And yet, she was barely a girl. He must go slowly, and give her time to adjust. "Perhaps a little pear? Here, I'll slice it for you." Philippe took a rosy pear from the dish of fruit and, taking a small dagger from his sleeve, quickly cut the little fruit into sections and set it on her plate. Colette smiled up at him and took one of the segments.

She bit into it slowly, and the juice ran down her chin. Taking a corner of the tablecloth, she hastily wiped her face, blushing.

"Try this," Philippe said, taking the little square of cloth that had been laid by her plate. "It's called a napkin and is all the rage at Court. Instead of using the tablecloth, each person gets their own personal little cloth, as it were."

Blushing even more, Colette took the napkin and dabbed at a chin now dry.

God, he wanted to have her! He really must control himself.

"Do you wish to return to your father, Colette?" The question was abrupt and so unexpected that Colette didn't know what to say. She thought of her father, his face reddened with wine and whiskey, his heavy hot fingers fumbling at her clothing when he found his drunken way into her bed. She thought of the beatings for misconduct, real and imagined. The last beating had been only last year, and she had been mortified when he'd had her skirts raised, in the public hall of their castle, for all to see, while a servant had switched her petticoated bottom with a thick birch rod until she had cried and begged for mercy. The punishment was meted out for riding a horse in men's garb. Her younger brother had encouraged her, so they could ride together over their vast holdings. The Duke had been away, and she had decided to take the risk, knowing he disapproved of "girls acting like boys".

But he had returned home sooner than expected, and the foreman, a nasty man called Simon, had escorted her father to the scene of the "crime", hoping for just such a beating, as he regarded Colette as impertinent and saucy, and in his estimation, needing to brought down a peg or two.

And brought down she was, as Simon himself administered the beating, which left her poor bottom welted and bruised, despite the covering of her petticoats. Could it be she would never have to see the dreaded Simon again?

Did she want to return to her father? The question echoed in her head, as she thought of his angry tone when he informed her she was to obey Lord de Valon in all things, or be imprisoned like a common criminal in his dungeons until she "withered and died".

No. Not only did she not wish to return to his control, she feared if she were returned, he would make good on his promise, assuming she had disgraced herself with Lord de Valon. There was really no decision.

"No, my lord," she said, her voice small but still a pleasing timbre, lower than that of most girls her age.

Philippe looked at her, seeing the fear in her eyes mingled strangely with something like defiance. He observed the slight tremble of her mouth as she bit her lower lip, trying to contain whatever emotions were roiling inside of her. "You won't miss your papa, Colette? Your family?"

"I will miss my sisters, but they are both gone anyway, having each been married this past year," she answered quietly, tears pooling in those large eyes, which he now saw were more gray than blue. A most unusual color. "And my little brother, Jean Luc. But I cannot return. Papa said so."

"What did he say exactly?"

Colette didn't answer, but ducked her head, looking miserable. The poor girl was afraid to speak more plainly, he could see that. Clearly, she had not been treated in the past in a way that made her feel safe. For all she knew, she had been sold into slavery, and would never see friend or family again.

His heart softened, fantasies of taking her virginity for the moment forgotten. "Please. You may speak freely. I can see that you are afraid. Perhaps you are used to treatment that would make you afraid to respond honestly. You needn't be afraid with me, my dear. You may answer plainly, and indeed, I insist that you do so."

Colette swallowed and looked up at the young lord, seeing his kind face and smiling eyes. Something of the tightly wound grip of fear in her eased somewhat. Taking a deep breath she said, "He told me he, that he, well, he said he lost me to you in a card game! That he bet me as collateral and lost. He gave me away like a horse or a pig! That's how much I am worth to him." Anger blazed suddenly, burning away the fear, and Philippe saw the strong character of the girl peeking through the shy demeanor.

Sitting back, he decided to be honest with her. "It is true, he did gamble you away. He was losing badly and quite drunk at the time. I was curious to see if he would actually go through with it, you know. It isn't legal, of course. You can't give your daughter away, at least not in a card game! He can give your hand in marriage, he can order you to obey him, but he can't physically sell you to me for a bad hand in cards!"

Colette looked at him, not sure what he meant. Was he telling her she was free to go? But where would she go? Papa had made it clear she was no longer welcome at home, as his "honor" superseded her right to remain in a household that she had known all her life!

"What I'm saying," Philippe continued, seeing her confusion, "is that I will not keep you here against your will. You are free to go. And your father's debts are considered fulfilled. A dinner with you is all the payment any gentleman could want." Colette blushed, smiling despite herself. Philippe continued, "I can talk to him, if you like. Explain that all debt is honored and expunged."

"No!" Colette exclaimed.

"No? You don't want to return to your family?"

"I cannot. My father would…" she paused, uncertain how to continue, ashamed of what she had to say.

"What? What would he do? Wouldn't he welcome you back into his arms?"

"I am the daughter of a duke, sir. I have certain duties, and my father has the right to expect me to behave with obedience and grace."

"Oh, stop with the formalities!" Philippe exclaimed, feeling exasperated. "Be honest for a moment, can't you? I can see you are conflicted. Tell me the truth. Forget about your father's expectations and your obligations as the daughter of a duke. Do you want to return to your father?"

"I don't want to go back," she admitted. "Not now that Marie and Jeanette are gone! But for a young boy, my brother, I would be alone. Alone and at his mercy." She blushed and looked away.

"What do you mean, at his mercy? Explain yourself." Philippe did not like what he was hearing, though he wasn't surprised, remembering the old duke, his face reddened with drink, his visage unhealthy from hard living and too much wine. That he would even consider giving his daughter away for a game of cards said enough about the "gentleman" in question.

Colette held her napkin to her face, wishing she could sink into the floor. A daughter, especially the daughter of a duke, must never speak with such disloyalty about her father! She had never done so before, not to anyone, even her sisters. They all knew of his rages, and were no doubt subjected to the same unwelcome nocturnal visits, but it simply wasn't discussed. One bore what was one's duty to bear, and that was the end of it. Lord de Valon would surely be horrified at her dreadful breach of manners.

As it was, this evening was the strangest one she had ever spent! Trying to backtrack she said, "Oh, excuse me. I misspoke. I mean that I would disappoint him if I did not obey the new master of my new household."

Philippe was not so easily put off. "Come, Lady Colette. Let us be frank with each other. I am acquainted with your father. I know something of his ways. Whatever we share tonight will not go beyond this room." He paused, looking meaningfully in Brigitte's direction, knowing how servants gossiped among themselves about every aspect of their masters' and mistresses' lives. "Will it, little maid?" Brigitte flushed and looked down, too stunned at first at having been directly addressed to respond. Slowly she nodded her head, showing that she understood, and he looked back at Colette.

"No," Colette whispered finally. "I cannot return to his household. He would have me k-killed." She began to cry. Philippe gently pulled the story from her, about the threat to imprison her and let her die if she besmirched her father's so-called honor. He was so gentle and easy to talk to that Colette found herself telling this strange man things she would never have dreamed admitting to anyone, even her sisters.

They talked for hours, Philippe having forgotten his plans to attend the new play by Molière that evening, as a guest of Madame de Montespan. As glass after glass of fine red wine was poured, Colette's tongue loosened considerably, and soon she was laughing gaily at the stories Philippe told of various lighter intrigues at Court.

Brigitte accepted her own plate of dinner, and a bottle of wine and a glass. Sitting in the corner, to keep the meeting proper between the Lord and Lady, she listened with ears sharp as a rabbit's, and eyes as big as plates.

The stars were already fading when Philippe finally took his leave. Colette sweetly tried to stifle a yawn as he stood, thanking her for sharing the meal and the conversation. He truly couldn't remember a more enjoyable evening spent. On an impulse, Philippe leaned forward until his face was level with Colette's, and almost touching. She didn't pull back, which he had half expected. The three empty wine bottles on the table might have explained her behavior, but Philippe wanted to believe it was because she fancied him.

Taking a liberty with a girl so young, he kissed those tender lips, slowly, feeling her warmth and her energy seep into him as he did so.

She kissed him back, though her lips did not part. Her eyes fluttered shut and she stayed perfectly still, as if she were dreaming. Brigitte, forgotten in the corner, at once amazed and entranced, emitted such a loud sigh of her own that they pulled apart suddenly, Colette blushing, Philippe grinning. With a graceful bow toward the servant, he bid them adieu and was gone.

Chapter Two

Though she waited the next several evenings for his appearance, it was in vain. In the days following that initial dinner, the charming and handsome Lord Philippe de Valon had not reappeared at her door, and Colette found herself crestfallen. She and Brigitte had discussed ad nauseam every word he had spoken, every nuance of every gesture, every item of his gorgeous wardrobe, every feature of his finely chiseled face.

"Perhaps I displeased him?" Colette fretted for the fiftieth time. "Perhaps he decided that I'm too young and not worth his notice. I may be of noble lineage, but I can't hope to compete with the sophisticated ladies of this Court!" She sighed deeply. "Perhaps it was only the fine wine, not the company that kept him with us for all those hours."

"Please, Lady Colette, don't worry! I was there, don't forget! I watched him when he didn't know I was looking, and he only had eyes for you! If he hasn't been back, it's for a very good reason!"

Almost as if on cue, there was a discreet knock at the door, and Catherine, Lord Philippe's servant, entered. "If it pleases you, Lady Colette, Madame de Valon, Lord Philippe's esteemed aunt, requests the pleasure of your company. Lord Philippe has instructed me to invite you to her chambers for tea this afternoon, and indeed, each afternoon until he should return from the King's business. Tea is at 4:00. Sharp. I shall return to escort you, by your leave." Graciously Colette accepted, though of course there was no real choice in the matter, the pretense of an invitation being in fact a command.

Madame de Valon was Philippe's old aunt, and her formidable reputation was deserved. When Colette had been ushered in to meet her, the old woman eyed Colette with a sour expression and said, "The cut of that gown is obscene. Cover yourself." As Colette had blushed and wrapped the lace shawl Madame had hurled at her around her shoulders, the old woman went on, "Do you have any talents? Or are you as useless as all the other so-called ladies my nephew sends my way?"

Colette was taken aback by her rudeness, but, as she was used to being treated in an abrupt and unkind manner by her father, was less shocked perhaps than someone of gentler upbringing might have been. "If it pleases you, Madame, I can play the harpsichord. I can sew decently, though I cannot turn out the lovely lace my sisters can, as my fingers are not so nimble, and while I can use paints, I wouldn't say that I am an artist. In fact, my artwork is atrocious!" She smiled at the old aunt, and almost thought she saw a ghost of a smile in return.

"Harrumph," grunted the old woman, secretly pleased that the girl was so bold, and also apparently not so taken with herself, as so many of these young noblewomen were. "Well, Nephew has informed me that you will be my companion for the next week while he is traveling to Reims for some business of the King." She grimaced, crooked rotting teeth briefly displayed between rouged cracked lips, in what passed for a smile. "I am old and useless. I cannot walk without this stick, and my stupid hands refuse to obey me. My eyes are as dim as if they were made of glass. Can you read?"

"Yes, Madame." For that Colette was thankful. Though her father was many things she hated, he believed gentlewomen should know how to read, so that they could assist in matters of their estates and not be duped by dishonest foremen and overseers. As a result, a world of imagination had opened for her, and she had read the few books she possessed so many times that the fine heavy paper on which they were printed was frayed and softened at the edges.

"Good. You can read to me. Hopefully you can put some life into the words, not read like some stick of wood, like the last so-called lady Philippe thought would entertain me! But right now you can play me something. Go, sit and play me a tune. Something by Lully, if you know it."

Colette had no idea what to make of this woman. She was truly extraordinary in her blunt rudeness. At least she had asked Colette to do something she felt comfortable doing. Dutifully Colette took her seat at the harpsichord nestled in a corner amidst a clutter of small end tables, couches and loveseats and shelves crammed with knickknacks. The room was crowded and the air was stale, as Madame de Valon did not share her nephew's belief in the benefits of fresh air.

Colette touched the keys hesitantly at first, but her pleasure in the well-made instrument and the fact that it was perfectly tuned, overcame her initial shyness. She was actually quite pleased for the opportunity to play. She had had no chance to make music since being brought to Court, and had missed it greatly, especially playing for her sister Jeanette, who had a voice as lovely as an angel's.

First she played a rather bland harmonic piece by Jean-Baptiste Lully. The old woman nodded slightly, but said nothing. Colette tried something a little more ambitious, a delightful little dance piece by Jean Philippe Rameau. When she was done Madame de Valon said, "You are no virtuoso, but you're tolerable. Sing me something. Do you know anything by Claude Le Jeune perhaps?"

"Oh, really, I couldn't. That is, I don't sing. My sister, Jeanette—"

"I don't want to hear about your sister, or any of your lame excuses, either. Any girl of gentle birth should be able to sing. Let's hear it. I can't abide false modesty."

Nonplussed, Colette breathed deeply, trying not to sigh aloud. This disagreeable old woman was quite demanding! Colette's fingers were beginning to tire, and she was not at all used to singing aloud, except the tuneless little ditties she sang in her bath.

As the old woman glared at her, Colette cleared her throat and began to sing a song from her youth, a little folk song called *Mon Dieu la Belle Entrée*. She accompanied herself on the harpsichord, glad she had the excuse of focusing on her fingers so she needn't look at the old woman. When she was done she dropped her hands and did finally look up. Madame de Valon was grimacing again, and Colette wasn't sure whether she was smiling or angry.

"Well, you weren't exaggerating, I suppose. You sing like a tone-deaf dog, howling in the wind." Colette flushed darkly, at once ashamed and angry. She had told the old bitch she couldn't sing! How dare she! And while she knew she couldn't sing as well as her sisters, she also knew she wasn't tone-deaf, and could carry a tune. She bit her lip to keep from retorting something equally rude to the old woman.

She must behave with grace. After all, Lord Philippe had asked that she keep this old crone company. He had told her how his aunt had lost her husband in battle and most of her possessions as well. She was old, infirm and alone in the world.

Just then the old woman's stomach rumbled loud enough for Colette to hear, even across the room. "Well, don't just sit there, girl. Go call my maid in the next room and order us some tea and cakes."

* * * * *

As the week passed, Colette actually came to look forward to her time with Madame de Valon. While she continued to insult Colette on a regular basis, calling into question her bearing, her manners, her education, her looks, and her choice of clothing, Colette came to realize she did the same to everyone. It was nothing personal. It was her way of dealing with a world that had left her behind.

Madame de Valon had a vast library of books, in both French and Italian. Colette greatly enjoyed reading them aloud to the old woman. When she tired of listening, Colette would play the harpsichord for her, and when Colette tired of that,

Madame de Valon would tell her about the intrigues of Court life, and about her life as a girl in the north of France.

Still no sign of Philippe. Colette did eventually manage to bring the topic around to him, and Madame de Valon was willing to talk about him. She liked to reminisce about his childhood, when he would come to stay with her on her husband's estate. Madame had never been blessed by God with children, she explained, and so the visits by Philippe and his younger brother, Jacques, had been especially treasured. And she was sent to stay with Philippe's family when her husband was on his extended sea voyages, so she got to help raise the lads as if they were her own.

"And Jacques? Where is he now?" This was the wrong question, as Madame de Valon's face darkened, and her dry old eyes actually filled with tears. "Dead!" she cried. "Taken from us when he'd barely become a man. I don't want to talk about it! I'm tired. Call Catherine and leave me be." Colette was careful after that to steer away from the subject of poor Jacques, though her curiosity was piqued. They stayed with the safer subject of Philippe's apparently idyllic childhood.

Madame de Valon showed no interest in Colette's past, and Colette was actually grateful for that, as she had no especially loving memories to share. Her own mother, Anne, had been from the Isle of Britain, and the marriage with her father had been arranged for political reasons. Anne was older by a good ten years than her husband Claude, and Colette did not have many memories of her, even though she had lived until Colette's tenth year.

Anne never truly embraced her new land, not its ways or its language. She dutifully bore Claude children, but then handed them over to a wet nurse and nanny. Indeed, Colette's memories of her nanny, Gigi, were much fonder than any she had for her cold and aloof "maman". Her mother remained in her own rooms, with her two English servants, sewing and writing letters to a family she was never to see again. It must have been an appallingly lonely life, Colette now realized, though at the time she hadn't thought about it in those terms. She only knew as a little girl that Maman was usually unavailable.

Occasionally Colette and her sisters would be dressed up and presented to their mother for tea. She would ask them polite questions in halting French, but their eager and babbling answers had probably not been understood, as she rarely responded with more than an "Oui, oui. Eh, bien." When Colette awoke from some frightening dream in the night, it was not for Maman that she called, but for Gigi, who was never far away, and would always take her little Colette in her arms, and soothe her back to childish slumber.

When a boy at last was born, it was as if Anne finally decided she'd had enough of this earthly existence, as she simply slipped away after what had seemed like a rather routine birth. Her passing was barely mourned except by her servants, who were sent back to England on the first possible ship. Colette had been saddened by her mother's death, but in a vague way, as she had barely felt her presence in life.

No, it was better to hear about Philippe and his little brother, and the wild adventures they routinely got themselves into. It was clear from Madame de Valon's stories that the boys were extravagantly spoiled and wildly loved. Colette found herself caught up in the stories, laughing and clapping her hands with pleasure as Madame cackled over their recalled mischief. Colette was such an attentive and appreciative listener that Madame de Valon was quite mollified and had informed her that, "she would do," —high praise indeed from the formidable old woman.

On the sixth day she announced to Colette, "Have your things packed. We are to return to St. Malo at dawn tomorrow! Ah, to see the water again! I have received a message from Philippe. His business for the King is finally completed, and he has received permission to return to his estate so he can run his affairs. I tell you," she bent forward conspiratorially, in fact committing treason with the words she uttered next, "that damn king has raped the country. His ridiculous taxes to pay for all his stupid wars have bankrupted half the nobility, and he doesn't care a whit! Thank God he's finally letting Philippe get home to oversee his own shipbuilding business! The de Valon fleet is the finest in the kingdom, you know, though if Louis keeps commandeering them for his stupid wars we'll soon be bankrupt!"

Colette's eyes had widened as Madame de Valon spat out her invective against the King. She was aware of the danger of speaking out against Louis in any matter. Even something as seemingly trivial as failure to sit at the King's table in the exact order of one's rank at Court could land you in the dungeons of Versailles, never to see the light of day again. But she barely registered the remarks now, as her brain processed the far more important information—Philippe was done with the King's business!

Willing her voice not to betray her own excitement, she said demurely, "Will we meet him there, Madame?"

"Yes, he will probably be there before we arrive, as it will take some time to pack our entourage, prepare our horses, and secure our carriages for the journey north. Have you ever been to St. Malo? No? Well, it is lovely, my dear. Philippe's castle is right on the water." Her wrinkled old face softened as she saw her beloved home in her mind's eye. Colette had never seen the sea, and asked many questions, all of which Philippe's aunt answered with great enthusiasm, until she suddenly tired and drifted to sleep sitting upright in her chair. Colette tiptoed out, leaving the soft snuffle of an old woman's snore behind her.

* * * * *

Even though they were sitting on cushions, the carriage was bumping and jerking its way along the rutted country roads. The ride out of Versailles had been exciting, as Colette had not been permitted to see much of the grounds during her several month stay there. It was a lovely day in late spring, and the vast expanse of palaces and intricate gardens and fountains of Versailles was breathtaking.

Now they had left it all behind, and instead of the carefully planned and tended gardens and topiaries, wildflowers bloomed along the roads. The entourage was not especially large, as Philippe could not afford to run his estate, and still keep a second household at Versailles. There were twelve traveling in their party, including the four footmen who now commanded the two large carriages that held the women inside. Madame de Valon, Colette and Brigitte were in one carriage, and the female servants were in the second one. Several men on horseback rode in front and behind, keeping their eyes out for the bandits that plagued these country roads.

They had been traveling for about six hours, and Colette was feeling quite nauseated from the bumps and jolts that jerked them around their carriage. She also desperately needed to pee. Madame de Valon, who had been dozing, snoring noisily throughout most of the trip, awoke after a particularly rough jolt and sat upright, her rheumy eyes flying open. "What!" she yelled, and looked around, disconcerted.

After a moment, she recalled where she was. "By God, I'm starving. Brigitte! Pull the bell and tell those imbeciles to stop at once for lunch! Why didn't you wake me, you fools?" Colette and Brigitte had no response, certain that if they had dared to wake her, they would have been severely castigated.

The carriages pulled to a slow halt, as the driver stepped down and pulled open the carriage door. "Yes, Milady?" he said respectfully, holding his plumed hat in his hand.

"We're hungry! Find us a good tree and set out our food at once. And wine! Immediately!"

The servants set up the picnic while the ladies found bushes behind which to discreetly relieve themselves. In short order they were settled under a tree, eating heartily of the cold chicken that had been prepared for their picnic, along with ginger beer, fresh bread, various cheeses and fruits, and of course, wine.

It was such a quiet day. Such a peaceful day that the men, who would normally have stood guard throughout the meal, had relaxed a little too thoroughly. Happy to be going home, none of them really comfortable with the formalities and petty competitions among the servants of the nobles at Versailles, they were perhaps not as careful as they might have been under normal circumstances.

Thus when the two strange men slipped up to the two footmen resting under a tree some distance from the rest of the party, neatly slitting their throats before either knew what had happened to them, none of the rest of the group was the wiser.

And when they slipped up behind the ladies, grabbing the closest person, which turned out to be Brigitte, it took yet another moment before anyone even registered that anything was amiss. Brigitte screamed, but her cry was stifled by a large hand slamming against her mouth.

"Anyone move, and we'll kill her. Don't believe us, look at your friends over there." A wail went up from the women as they saw what had been done to the two footmen. The remaining men reached for their swords, but the bandits shouted, "Touch your scabbards and she dies!" And slowly each man dropped his hand.

Deftly the bandits removed the jewelry and little leather bags of money from the men and women huddled terrified in front of them. All the while the large burly fellow held Brigitte tight under one arm, while she whimpered with fear. They moved very quickly, and then stood back.

"You want one, Albert?" the big fellow snarled to his mate.

"Yeah, Tristan, you bet I do. And I know just the one I want, too. You!" He gestured with his sharp sword toward Colette. "Stand up and come over here! Move it or this one gets it in the throat!" To make his friend's point, Tristan pushed the blade gently against Brigitte's white throat. A small line of red appeared, and the droplets of blood slid down, staining her dress. Quickly Colette stood, terrified beyond conscious thought. Grabbing her arm, Albert pulled her roughly to him, tucking her against his strong sweating body. Together the men backed away from the miserable group, dragging the poor girls along with them.

"Don't try to follow us, you hear! If we see you anywhere near us, we'll kill them. Don't think we won't. Now get yourself away from here! The roads are plagued with bandits, don't you know! Au revoir!" Laughing, they pulled the frightened girls along with them, disappearing into the dark woods of the forest.

* * * * *

Colette found she had actually been dozing, as impossible as that would seem, wedged in the saddle in front of a burly man, her hands tied with coarse rope behind her, his strong arm gripping her tightly about the waist. She no longer had any feeling in her arms, which were smashed uncomfortably between her and the man's leather-vested chest.

The steady clip-clop of the horses' hooves along the old dirt road must have lulled her to sleep for a moment. Now she shot back awake, terror like bile in her throat, her heart pounding. To her left she could see Brigitte, tied as she was, in front of the second man, whose horse cantered along beside hers. There was a third fellow bringing up the rear.

He had been waiting for the others in their hiding place in the woods. As the two men came crashing through the forest, half pulling, half dragging the hapless women along with them, the third man had jumped up from his resting place against the tree. "Ho now!" he shouted. "And what have we here? Gold and jewels not enough for you boys, eh? A little pussy as well. My, my." He grinned widely, a gap-toothed smile. The third man was much older than the other two, who were little more than youths, but his body was still strong and lean, kept so by tough living and adventure. His name was Lucas, and he had stayed behind with the horses while the boys went on their quest for other peoples' gold.

Albert and Tristan laughed, as they thrust the terrified girls toward Lucas. Pushing Colette to her knees, Tristan snarled, "Stay down, bitch! Don't move or talk to your girlfriend or I'll cut your bleedin' head off!" He brandished his sword for effect, as Colette paled and swayed slightly, forced to kneel on the ground, her lavish silk gown spread over the muddy undergrowth. Brigitte knelt nearby, her face streaked with tears, dried blood on her throat and staining the front of her gown.

The two young men began unloading their bulging pockets, dropping their loot on the woolen blanket Lucas had been sitting on. There were bracelets, necklaces and earrings of gold and silver, studded with precious stones, as well as gold sovereigns and several small daggers. They'd left the men their swords, as they had their hands full with the girls. Now Lucas pulled the blanket's edges up and secured the bundle quickly into a saddlebag.

"Make a sound," Albert said to them, "and we'll kill you both. Obey what we tell you, and it'll go much easier on you." In a few moments they were ready to make their escape. The two younger men mounted their horses and held out their arms as Lucas swung each woman up to them like a sack of potatoes.

Now Colette didn't know how many hours had past, but evening was coming on, the sky darkening overhead. She tried to shift slightly, to adjust her arms. "Awake, eh?" The voice, close to her ear, startled Colette and she gasped.

"Don't worry, little one, we're almost there. Well, maybe you should worry, actually." Albert laughed cruelly, and Colette felt a cold shot of fear course through her body, leaving her almost sick with it. She didn't respond, biting her lips to keep from wailing.

At least they were alive! But how had this happened? Why had Philippe's men just stood by and let these monsters take her and her maid! And where were those men now? Why were they not in hot pursuit? If only Philippe had been with them; surely he would have fought them single-handedly.

Ah, Philippe. Colette licked her dry lips, remembering his sweet mouth against them. She had been so taken aback, but secretly so delighted by that kiss! She had thought of it endlessly in the days that passed, hoping he would return to her and do it again. But now she would probably die at the hand of these men, and never see his sparkling green eyes again, or taste those luscious lips that had promised so much.

Her thoughts were interrupted by Lucas' call. "Boys! Here's the place. Turn in here." The three horses swung around, taking a small narrow lane, deeply rutted and overgrown, not noticeable from the public road unless one knew of its existence. They rode several more minutes, the horses slowing to a trot and finally to a walk as the road faded into a field of weeds and wildflowers. Just beyond was a small copse of trees where the men pulled up their tired horses. Lucas dismounted first and took each girl, whose bound hands made them helpless, from their perches.

Behind the trees stood a small house built of old mud bricks with a thatched roof. Lucas opened the small wooden door and the girls were pushed along in front of the men. The inside was one large room, the floor covered in uneven, unpolished wood. There was a hearth with a large iron cauldron hanging from a nail, a table and some chairs, and a large pallet on one side of the room for sleeping.

Colette and Brigitte were dragged to the pallet, their hands still tied behind their backs. Brigitte was whimpering softly, and as they both were pushed none too gently on the straw mattress, Colette felt her maid trembling against her. She leaned into her, whispering, "Courage, dear. Don't let them see our fear!"

The men were busy for the moment, dumping their spoils on the table, as Lucas quickly picked through the items, separating the jewelry and the coins in neat little piles. "You did all right, boys," he said, grinning at them. "But by far your best acquisition is these two lovely ladies! We'll have some fun tonight, won't we? But you know we can't keep them. You have a ship to catch, you know!"

"We could take them with us!" piped up Tristan, who, at only eighteen, was inexperienced both in the ways of the world and the ways of women. "Keep 'em tied up down in the hold! We could sell their little twats to the other sailors!"

"No, don't be stupid. The last thing you need to be saddled with is two unwilling wenches! Not to mention their people will be after us before too long. No, let us use them, and discard them." Lucas wasn't specific as to how precisely the poor girls were to be used or discarded. Brigitte began to wail, and Colette edged closer to her, fear leaving her breathless as she assumed the worst.

"But no reasons you shouldn't enjoy 'em a bit before you leave. You boys want to fuck them first, or eat first?" Both Tristan and Albert, who was only a few years senior to Tristan, laughed roughly and said simultaneously, "Fuck them!"

Lucas smiled indulgently, as if he were watching his children unwrap presents on Christmas morning. But they were women, not packages that were being pulled up, Brigitte crying, Colette pale as death.

Taking a small dagger, Tristan cut the rough cords that bound the girls' wrists. "Don't even think of struggling," Lucas advised them. "These boys will kill you as soon as look at you. Just let them have their way with you, and you'll live to tell the tale." Colette fell forward at his words, a swoon of fear rendering her unconscious.

Unconcerned, Albert knelt next to the girl and slid his dagger neatly down her front, cutting the fine silk and lace of her gown. He pulled it open, revealing her young tender breasts, tipped in dusky virgin pink. Colette stirred as the cold blade touched her skin. Her eyes came open, wide with fear and confusion. "Oh, God!" she cried, fully awake again. "I beg you, please do not do this! My father is a duke. He can pay you in gold many times over. Please don't take our honor!"

Albert laughed cruelly. "Your honor, *Mademoiselle*?" His voice dripped with disdain. "We are vagabonds. We care nothing for honor! We just want to fuck your juicy little cunts! We haven't had any lately, and you're handy! Simple as that. I bet we won't be the first, anyway. You look like a little slut to me!"

Meanwhile Tristan had Brigitte down on the palette. He also used his dagger to cut her clothing, which were less elaborate and confining, from her body. Brigitte's breasts were larger, and the nipples were dark and prominent. He cut away the little undergarments that covered her sex as Brigitte struggled against him, crying in fear. Tristan pulled her wrists roughly over her head and held them there, while he leaned forward, his own long greasy hair falling in her face. He bit and twisted her nipples, making her scream with fear and pain.

Her lush plump little body was made for plundering. Quickly he pulled his own pants open and pressed his erection against Brigitte's thigh. Letting one wrist go, he used his other hand to force her thighs apart. He was so eager to fuck her that he barely pressed the tip of his cock at her virginal opening when he began to spurt his seed against her, hot and sticky into her pubic curls.

Albert was egged on by Brigitte's cries, which had excited him, to pull and cut at Colette's clothing, finally getting the annoying yards of silk away from her, though she tried in vain to cling to it. Colette's fair body was a stark contrast to the dark and none too clean Albert. He also pushed his trousers down and, not even bothering with her pretty little breasts, forced her thighs hard apart and plunged himself, fully erect, into her tight, dry pussy, making her scream with pain.

Putting his mouth down to hers, he forced it open with his tongue, his rotting breath reeking in her nostrils, his spit dripping into her mouth, making her gag and try desperately to turn her head away. Annoyed at her jerking away from him, he bit her lower lip, making her scream again as her blood now mingled with his spittle.

Unperturbed, he held her down and rutted on top of her while she writhed and jerked beneath him, completely captive. Again, youth and lack of opportunity made the young man, mercifully for Colette, come quickly inside of her. He pulled out, dragging a string of semen, mixed with her virginal blood.

Tristan, meanwhile, got his second wind in the way of youth, and forced Brigitte to get up on all fours like a dog. Positioning himself behind her, he forced his way between her ample buttocks, seeking that tight pussy once more. This time he was able to hold himself back longer. Gripping her broad hips, he thrust himself into the poor girl, who screamed and cried out to her god for mercy.

But none was forthcoming. Instead Tristan fucked her, increasing his intensity as he neared his own release. Reaching in front of her, he grabbed her large breasts and kneaded them, dropping his head to her neck, panting heavily, his breath hot and sour in her face.

Brigitte fell forward, her eyes rolling back and Tristan came tumbling down on top of her, just as he shot his second load, this time deep inside the velvet tunnel of the poor wench who had fainted beneath him. "Stupid cow," he muttered, as he rolled off her, annoyed that his orgasm had been interrupted by her fall. He stood, tucking his now flaccid cock back into his pants, and retying the rope belt that held his pants up at the waist.

Albert, himself satisfied with one fuck, was already at the table with Lucas, both of them leering at Tristan, who looked embarrassed but pleased with himself. He joined them at the table.

Colette and Brigitte both lay where they had been plundered. Brigitte had curled over onto her side and was hugging herself, crying, while Colette lay as she had been left, stunned by what had happened to her, beyond absorbing it yet.

As Tristan joined the other two men, Lucas tossed them each a small leather bag filled with coins. "Go on, boys. Go and get yourself some food and drink in the village. It's not far from here. I'll have the rest of this sorted and split between us when you get back. Take the path by the river 'til you come to a road and follow it due north a ways. You'll see the village and the pub. Take your time. I'll see to the girls."

The young men laughed, and Tristan said, "Oh, we know you will! Have fun. We've broken them in for you, haven't we then?" Looking smug and self-satisfied, the two men left Lucas with the disheveled women.

* * * * *

Lucas sat at the table, watching the girls. He tossed each one a blanket and leaned back in his chair, taking his little bag of tobacco from his pocket. He lit his pipe with a stick of kindling from the hearth, sucking gently to light the leaves. He looked over at the two young women shivering in the old blankets he had tossed to them. Their faces were stained with tears and dirt, and the smaller one, the maid, was shivering uncontrollably, though it was hot in the little house.

Leaning back on two legs of his chair, he said, "The worst is over, little ones. They've had their way with you and tonight when they come back they'll be so drunk they wouldn't be able to fuck a fly, much less two lovely robust young girls like yourselves."

Brigitte continued to shiver, rocking slowly back and forth. Colette had her arm around Brigitte's shoulders. She looked at Lucas as he spoke, her eyes dark, almost all pupil. He stared into her eyes and felt old. Taking another drag from his pipe he went on, "Tristan and Albert are dangerous rascals, but my relationship with them is over as of the morning, and good riddance, I say. With this last robbery, they have secured enough to pay their way onto a pirate ship that is setting sail in the morning. They are off to make their fortunes, or lose their heads. I'd put even money on one or the other."

"Please, sir," Colette finally managed, her voice trembling, "Will you let us go, sir? I beg of you—"

But he interrupted with his hand held up toward her. The other hand was resting lightly on the sheath of his formidable sword. "No! Not yet. I will not kill you, girlie, though in not doing so, I'll be taking a risk. But I am tired of killing, and especially for no good reason. I will let you go. But not yet, not yet."

Colette continued to entreat him, but Lucas merely shook his head. "Still that tongue, girl, or I'll gag you; see if I won't. Be glad the boys are gone and you got off as lightly as you did! Now, are you hungry, girls? I have some food and I don't mind sharing." As he spoke, Lucas moved to the cupboard by the hearth and took out some things.

Upon the table he set a large round cheese still sealed in yellow wax and a few small, rather withered apples. A bottle of wine stood at the ready, its cork removed.

Calmly Lucas cut the cheese into wedges, peeled the apples and poured wine into tin cups. "Come on," he said, not unkindly, "join me. I hate to eat alone." The girls didn't dare to disobey. Colette stood, still wrapped in her blanket, and pulled Brigitte to her feet. As the girls sat at the table, Lucas rummaged in a large chest at the foot of the mattress where Brigitte had been raped.

"Here. Put these things on. They should fit all right, and are better at least than those blankets. I'm afraid the boys have destroyed your lovely dresses, though I daresay we can rescue much of that fine fabric for resale. Waste not, want not, I always say."

Gratefully Colette took the offered clothing. They were only rough sewn jerseys and pantaloons made for young men, not aristocratic noblewomen! No undergarments were offered, and the clothing was coarse and rough to the skin. Yet it was preferable to being left naked, and Colette pulled on the clothing, relieved that it smelled of lye soap, and nothing worse.

"Come, Brigitte, pull yourself together, sweetheart," she murmured, as she tried to help Brigitte dress herself. At first Brigitte only sat, staring, but finally she did as Colette urged, pulling up the pants and buttoning the shirt which hung off her, making her look even younger than her twenty years.

Colette managed to eat a little, but Brigitte only sat, hugging herself, trembling. After the little meal, Lucas went behind the house and brought in a bucket of cold water from the stream that ran by the little house. Taking an old rag, he offered it to Colette. She accepted it, washing her face and hands, not daring to wash her private parts in front of this man, though she dearly wished she could. Her sex felt sticky and burned where the brute had ripped her flesh.

She soaked the rag again and handed it to Brigitte, who slowly washed her own face, and then carefully touched the small cut on her throat where the sword had grazed her. She flinched slightly, but dabbed at it until the dried blood was washed away.

"That's better, then, isn't it, girlies? Now, I can't have you escaping in the night, can I? I shall have to tie those lovely little delicate wrists of yours, just to keep you from escaping, or from maybe getting crazy ideas in your heads about using my sword on an old sleeping man!" As he spoke, Lucas cut some thick hemp with a small sharp knife. Ordering the girls to put their hands behind their backs, he tied each girl's wrists behind her, not too tight, but tight enough to prevent them from doing something foolish like opening a door or grabbing a dagger in the night.

Lucas had thrown the old blankets over the straw mattress and now he said, "Go to sleep. I'll keep the boys away from you when they return, if they return! Get yourselves some rest now, as best you can."

Not daring to refuse, the young women lay down together on the blankets. It was awkward to lie down with their wrists tied behind them. The rope was rough and chafed against their tender skin. But at least they were clothed, and the old man did not seem inclined to ravage them as the brutal young savages had done.

They both rested on their sides, Colette behind Brigitte, her face almost touching Brigitte's hair. The little maid was whimpering into the woolen blankets. "Brigitte," Colette whispered, "Brigitte, please, don't fret so. We are safe. We are alive. He is going to set us free! He said so. I believe him. Please. Behave like a member of a duke's house, Brigitte. Remember your place."

At first Brigitte didn't respond. Colette wished she could put her arms around the poor girl, but bound as she was she could only lean closer and whisper comforting words. Finally Brigitte nodded, sniffled, and whispered back, "Yes, my lady. I will be all right. Let me rest here with you, and say my prayers." Colette sighed in relief; Brigitte would be all right in time, though the scars of this horrific event would be with them always. And it wasn't over yet.

How would they escape? Would this Lucas honor his promise and set them free? Even if he did, where were they? How would they find their way out of this forest? How would they return to Philippe's entourage?

At the thought of Philippe, fresh tears filled Colette's eyes and slipped over onto her soft cheeks. The image of his sweet mouth against hers was brutally juxtaposed in her mind with the horrible Albert, holding her down, panting his sour breath into her face as he forced himself against her, into her. Colette shivered and closed her eyes, willing the images away. She pressed her thighs tightly together, as if she could press away the tearing pain of ripped flesh throbbing at her center. Eventually, despite it all, somehow she fell asleep.

The room had darkened as night fell, and Lucas lit only one candle in a tin cup, which he kept near him at the table. The two young women, now still in their slumber, were watched over by the old man who smoked his pipe, his long legs stretched out in front of him, making his own plans on how to get his pleasure from the wenches at his mercy.

Tristan and Albert did eventually stumble into the cottage, reeking of spirits, and Lucas was able to put them to sleep without too much trouble on more old blankets, far from the girls huddled on their pallet.

When dawn put its fingers over the windowsill, Lucas roused the men and gave them biscuits and hot tea. He was eager to have them gone now, and they were eager to go, their pockets stuffed with coins and jewels, their heads filled with dreams of pillaging and making their fortunes in foreign lands. They barely glanced at the poor girls in the corner, as Lucas hurried them out the door, wishing them good luck. He watched, satisfied, as they rode away on their horses to the ship that awaited them.

When he returned the girls were sitting up, and he said, "Come outside and do your business, young ladies. You can wash up at the stream. If you're not back inside of five minutes, I'll hunt you down and slit your throats, so don't be thinkin' about runnin'."

Lucas untied the ropes and each girl rubbed her sore wrists, grateful for the reprieve, even if only temporary. They hurried outside, returning several minutes later, faces reddened from the cold water. Lucas gave them both biscuits and tea, and this time Brigitte ate too, hunger outweighing fear.

"Please, sir," Colette ventured. "When will you let us go? I can get you more money. My father is a duke—"

Again he cut her off. "Listen, little girl. I don't care if your father is the Sun King himself. I'm not interested in your father or your money. What I want is right here. I am not young. I've already seen at least four decades, but I'm hoping for a few more years, if I don't die by the sword. I've had an adventurous life, being a privateer and pirate. I take women when I want them but lately I haven't been looking, to tell you the truth.

"Now that this lovely chance has been dropped into my lap by those reckless boys, I've been doing some thinking. I want to explore some of my fantasies, and take my time with you. I won't hurt you, at least not too much, not if you obey me. But I plan to have my way with you, and the sooner you cooperate, the sooner I'll have my fill and set you free. Do you understand me?"

Neither girl spoke, but Lucas could see that they did, at least to some degree. Brigitte began to tremble again, and to rock back and forth. "Tell me your names, girls. Answer, or I'll use the sword to get a civil response!"

"I am called Colette," Colette offered. "Please, you are terrifying my maid! I beg of you, sir, do not toy with us. Let us go."

"You want to go?"

"Please!"

"Then do as I say! Since your little maid is useless at the moment, we're going to need to calm her down. Let's all have some wine, shall we?" He poured three large cups full, and handed each girl a mug. "Drink it!" he commanded, and not daring to disobey, they did. The wine was strong, more like a brandy, and Lucas knew it was going to their heads, as even he, a seasoned drinker, could feel its robust effect.

Both young women were flushed now, and when Lucas told them to hold out their cups for more, they both did so, and he noted that the little maid's hand was unsteady. He filled the mugs and again commanded them to drink up. "That's it, girlies. That's it. No need to be so bloody terrified of everything. This needn't be a horrible experience for you. Not at all."

"Come." He stood over Brigitte and held out his hand. "Come lie down here a while, and Colette and I will make you comfortable. What's your name, lass?"

"Brigitte, sir," she whispered, her voice slurred with drink.

"Ah, little Brigitte. Let's get you out of these masculine clothes." Lucas pulled open Brigitte's shirt, as he pushed her back against the mattress. Colette blushed and looked away while Lucas stared at Brigitte's mature, round breasts. He reached out and drew one rough, large finger along her flesh, his thumb pressing against a nipple, watching with pleasure as it distended of its own accord. Then Lucas pulled down Brigitte's pants, leaving her completely naked.

Brigitte tried to cover herself, but she was now so drunk she was completely ineffectual, as her hands flopped about. "Now, now, none of that," admonished Lucas. "We want to see your lovely shape, little girl. Look, Colette! Don't be so shy. Your little maid has a lovely round form. Nice and plump, and those tits, sweet Jesus! I could eat them up!"

Colette, also drunk, but not nearly as far gone as Brigitte, blushed beet red and tried to turn away. Grabbing her arm, Lucas said, "Don't look away, wench! I'm going to teach you. Teach you both about the joys of a woman's flesh, and the pleasures of the body! And you'll obey me, because I have the sword, and I'm a big strong man who can take what he wants and plans to do so!" He laughed, and felt the power of wine coursing through his veins, making him feel young again.

Like she was a little rag doll, Lucas flipped Brigitte over and straddled her well-padded bottom. "This," he said, "is called a massage. I doubt you, as a servant girl, have ever had anyone touch you like this, am I right?" Brigitte, caught naked beneath him, didn't answer, but he didn't seem to notice.

"Your job has been to serve, probably since you could barely walk, simply because you were born into to the wrong family, the wrong class." As he spoke, Lucas gently kneaded Brigitte's back and shoulders. She actually sighed with pleasure, the wine having so reduced her inhibitions and motor control that she just lay there, letting the strange man handle her. Colette stood nervously by, wondering what was going to happen, wondering if she could get at his sword, and what she would do with it if she got it.

Noticing her suddenly, Lucas said, "You can do this too, girl. Daughter of a duke, I imagine you've never lifted a bloody finger to do anything for anyone in your life, am I right? No, don't answer. I know the answers. Don't speak. Just take off that top, dear. I want to see your tits. You can leave on your pants for now. Just for now."

Colette stared at him, not moving. Lucas continued to massage Brigitte, who lay beneath him, naked, her dark hair loose around her head, her eyes closed. "Do as I say," he said softly, "or suffer the consequences." There was steel in the voice, and Colette unbuttoned the large wooden buttons of the borrowed shirt with trembling fingers. Slowly she let the shirt fall from her thin shoulders.

Lucas looked up from his work and smiled slowly, eyeing her tender young breasts. He wanted to bite each one, to taste her virgin flesh, savoring the hard little buds at the tips. But for now he contented himself with just looking.

"Now," he informed her, "you will take over. I want you to massage your maid." He scooted back on Brigitte's thighs, gesturing for Colette to come closer. "*You* will serve *her*. That's right. Straddle her nice ass, as I did. Hurry up!"

He pulled the unwilling girl and forced her to sit astride her own maid. Tentatively Colette touched Brigitte's back, trying to copy the kneading motion she had seen him use. "That's it," he said, grinning. "I like the idea of the mistress serving the slave. Keep at it, girl. Don't stop, no matter what I do. Understand?"

As he spoke, Lucas shifted, balancing over Brigitte's sturdy thighs. Leaning his broad chest, clad in its filthy leather vest, against Colette, he reached around and tweaked her lovely little nipples. Colette jumped and twisted away but he held her now with one arm around her waist. Brigitte stirred and moaned beneath them, almost unconscious now from the liquor and Lucas' soothing fingers.

"Be still, girl!" he hissed into Colette's ear, as his arm tightened around her. Colette tried to obey, afraid of the strong man behind her. Again he began to touch and twist her nipples, feeling them respond despite her fear, distending and engorging as they stood at attention. "Keep at your work!" he whispered roughly in her ear, and Colette again began to massage Brigitte's back and shoulders, until an actual little snore was issued.

Lucas laughed softly and stood, saying, "You put her to sleep. Good girl. Well then, it's your turn for some attention. Take off those pants. Let me see you." Though her fingers were trembling, Colette struggled to obey him, watching his hand, which rested idly on the hilt of his ever-present sword.

She stepped out of the rough woolen pants and stood completely naked. There were bruises at her throat and waist, where the brutish Albert had held her as he raped her. Otherwise her skin was fair and soft, tinted with honey gold like some perfect peach.

Lucas' mouth actually watered as he stared at her perfect form. Her long dark blonde hair hung loosely in waves against her shoulders, and her eyes were large with fear. Lucas' cock was rock-hard in his pants, but he knew the time wasn't yet ripe to claim this little aristocrat. No, he would wait for her to beg for it, the little wench. He knew women, and he knew how to make them beg for what they wanted.

Now he said, "Sit down, little one. Don't tremble so; I'm not going to eat you! Well, not exactly, anyway." He laughed at his own little private joke but Colette just stared at him. He pushed on her shoulder and she sat heavily down onto the wooden chair, the wine affecting her balance. Brigitte remained blissfully unconscious on the bed. Lucas took Colette's tin cup and poured another large helping of the strong red wine.

"Drink it," he ordered, and she complied, finding the numbing dizziness preferable to the trembling fear that the wine partially masked.

Lucas knelt before the naked young woman and gently spread her thighs, revealing her luscious little sex, covered in its soft nest of dark golden curls. His hands sought out her little nipples, which he tenderly teased and plucked until they again stood on end, eager little tips that silently begged for his kiss, or so he imagined.

Leaning over, he took a nipple into his mouth and gently sucked, eliciting a gasp from the girl, who had never been touched like this in all her young life. Her father's gropings had always been rough and through many layers of soft fabric.

Despite her obvious fear, Lucas recognized the first hint of lust in her little cry. The wench liked his mouth upon her! Slowly he teased first one and then the other nipple, leaving them dark pink and glistening as he kissed slowly down her belly. When his mouth was quite near her sex he inhaled deeply, loving the musky sweet scent of her.

Colette, whose head had fallen back as he sucked her breasts, sat up suddenly and tried to close her legs. But Lucas had anticipated her coy maneuver, and had his strong hands firmly on either leg, so that she couldn't close those slender thighs, push as she might.

Inexorably, he made his way down to her pussy, and flicked out his long tongue, touching her sex with it, making her jump and squeal with alarm. "Relax, girl. You'll like this. I promise. Give in to it, because I'm not going to stop until I feel like it." Again he dipped his head and tasted her sweet nectar and again she jerked and squealed. He ignored her protests this time, and continued to lick and taste her until she stilled. Despite her fear and confusion at what was happening, he heard her little sigh and grinned to himself. The little wench was just like all women! And he loved women, at least he loved their delicious bodies, and he loved making them moan with pleasure.

Pulling her body toward him, Lucas kissed and suckled her sex, feeling it swell and pulse, tasting her sweet juices as her body readied itself to receive him, though her mind didn't appreciate what was happening. Colette began to whimper, no longer thinking, but only feeling, as pleasure mounted inside of her, coursing through her, creating sensations she had never had, nor even dreamed about.

Unconsciously she grabbed Lucas' head, pulling him against her, holding the lovely pulsing heat of his tongue against her now willing body. He lapped at her, holding her thighs with those big, strong hands, feeling her body tremble, no longer in fear, but with need, need he had created.

She shuddered against him, emitting one high-pitched little cry, her body arching up into him. Still he held her, continuing to kiss and suckle at her sex until she slumped against him, her heart pounding, her breathing ragged.

Lucas sat back, grinning with self-satisfaction. Slowly Colette came to herself and sat up, now permitted to close her legs. Her neck and chest were flushed and her breathing was still labored. Her hair was wild about her face. "Mon Dieu!" she whispered. "What did you do to me? Surely that was a sin! What happened? I feel so strange! I can't explain." Her speech was slurred from the wine, and her head lolled to the side.

Lucas put a finger to her mouth. "Hush, girl. You don't have to explain. I'll explain to you, since obviously you haven't yet discovered this pleasure. There's no sin about it. That's what the body was created for! To take and give pleasure! It's a very natural thing."

Colette stared at him, trying to process what he was saying in her liquor-soaked brain. Though the rape of the night before had brutalized and terrified her, it hadn't surprised her. It fit into the hard world she knew; the world where men took what they wanted and people in power controlled those weaker than themselves.

But this new idea—this idea that women were allowed to experience this physical pleasure—it had never even entered the realm of her conscious thought.

Lucas grinned his gap-toothed leer at her and said, "Thank me for your pleasure, my little slut."

Colette blushed at the vulgarity, but managed to thank him, and it wasn't wholly insincere. Then she fell from the seat, the liquor finally getting the best of her. Lucas caught her easily and laid her next to her gently snoring maid.

Chapter Three

"You heard what I said. Surely you aren't as protected and innocent as your mistress! Surely you've seen a bit more of the world. Don't play coy with me." Lucas stood over a cowering Brigitte. When the girls had finally awakened from their wine-induced naps, Lucas was ready for them. He still hadn't taken his own pleasure, despite having had two lovely young women at his mercy for over twenty-four hours.

Now he stood poised over Brigitte, his cock poking out of his pantaloons, short, but thick and erect, bobbing near her mouth, which was not opening for him. He had forced her to kneel in front of him, still naked, and told her he wanted his cock sucked and to get to it. He liked her ripe little mouth, like a saucy little rosebud, and he wanted to slide his big cock between her lips and feel her small even teeth graze his skin.

Brigitte had gasped with dismay and disbelief when he commanded her, and turned her head resolutely away. Lucas felt himself growing impatient. "Bitch! I could kill you now with one stroke of my sword! Haven't you figured out yet that you have no say in the matter? You'll do as I say or," he paused, an idea suddenly coming to him. He had always resented the aristocracy, with their wealth earned on the backs of virtual slave labor. He himself had bucked the system, refusing to spend his life enslaved by virtue of his low birth to a "master". He had chosen instead this life of the vagabond, taking what he wanted where he found it, and damn the consequences. So now a nasty little idea occurred to him, that would amuse him as well as impress upon these two little bitches just who was in charge.

"Yes, you'll do as I say, or your mistress will get a whipping! In fact, your mistress is going to get a whipping anyway, because you hesitated, and refused me. You will not refuse me, ever, no matter how disgusting you think the demand might be! I am in charge here, little bitch! Not you and certainly not your mistress!"

As he spoke, Lucas tucked his still erect penis back into his pants and strode toward Colette, who was cowering on the pallet where he'd left her, wrapped in a blanket. Jerking her to her feet, he said roughly, "Bet you've never been whipped before, *my lady.*"

In fact she had, a number of times, at her father's cruel command, but she didn't say this to Lucas. She found she couldn't speak at all; she had gone dumb with fear. Lucas pulled the naked girl toward the wall by the hearth. Lifting an iron pot from its hook, he grabbed the rope that had bound their hands before and quickly tied her wrists to the hook, forcing her body against the rough, cold brick of the hearth wall.

"Please! Oh, please, sir! Don't whip my mistress! I beg you, sir! I'll obey! Please!" Brigitte's cries were in vain, as she watched Lucas remove the leather strap that held up his pants.

"Too late, little wench. Next time I tell you to do something, you obey immediately! But for now, Colette has earned a whipping, because of your bad behavior. Let's see what the little bitch can take!" With that he let the leather strap fall with a snapping sound against Colette's bare bottom. Colette found her tongue and screamed.

He smacked that little ass again, enjoying her cries, and the jiggling flesh of those round little globes as he struck her again and again. He would have to whip Brigitte next, as nature had been more generous with her large plump bottom. He did like a big ass on a woman. But still, this little girl was fun to torture, as she writhed and moaned so prettily each time he struck her with the leather strap.

"Gigi, help me," Colette whispered, before he wrenched another cry of pain with his strap. Crazed with fear, Colette had called for her nanny, reverting for the moment to a child. But Gigi could not save her now. Gigi had died just last year, and Colette had been inconsolable. She was buried in the family plot, and even old Claude had shed a tear for the kind old woman. Not a day went by that Colette didn't think of her and wonder if she was at peace in heaven.

Now she was jerked back to the dreadful present by Lucas' rough blows. Her back and ass were stinging from the lash and her breasts and belly were being scratched by the rough brick as she jerked in her ropes. The only thing that saved her from an extended session was Lucas' own pulsing cock. Beating this poor girl had excited him to a frenzy.

Leaving Colette still bound at the wrists, sagging against the wall, her back, ass and thighs crisscrossed with large swaths of red, Lucas turned back to Brigitte. The girl was now crying, still on her knees.

"Now then," he said, the blood roaring in his head at his own power, "Suck my cock. Take it into your mouth. Start slowly. That's it. Just lick it a bit, 'til you get used to it, little one." Brigitte, screwing her eyes tight, tears still flowing for her poor mistress, gingerly stuck out her tongue and made contact with the smooth man flesh. He tasted of acrid old urine and dirt. She felt her gorge rise, but forced herself to go on, for Colette's sake.

A spasm of pleasure shot through him as Lucas felt her soft wet tongue against him. "Yes, lick it, up and down the shaft, yes, just like that." Brigitte, eyes still closed, hands clasped in front of her like a girl in prayer, obeyed the man, afraid of the consequences if she did not.

Lucas let her lick him tentatively for a while, and then, taking her head in his large rough hands, said, "Now, don't move. Just hold your mouth open. Later I'll teach you to suck cock like a whore. But for now, just stay still and don't close your mouth. I'll take my pleasure from you this way."

Slowly he guided his now sizable erection into her little mouth, easing in first just the tip, and then more, gauging what she could handle. Brigitte gagged and tried to pull away, but Lucas' hands were firm on either side of her head and she couldn't move. "Be still!" he ordered. "Didn't I warn you to obey? Shall I whip poor Colette over there some more, or will you cooperate!"

Brigitte tried desperately to obey, though she gagged repeatedly on the hard cock as Lucas drove it relentlessly into her throat. He eased it in and out, slowly, and then, as his own need overtook his self-control, faster and faster, until he was groaning, nearly bursting with pleasure as he fucked this little whore's face. Finally he spurted his seed into her mouth. Brigitte reared back with shock and horror as his semen coated her mouth and throat, its bitter taste mingling with her own vomit.

This time he let her go, wincing in disgust as she retched onto the floor, sobbing and gasping. Satisfied for the moment, Lucas tucked his now flaccid penis into his pants again and moved toward Colette, still bound, her body taut against the wall, her face turned away.

Running his hands down her flanks, he leaned over to her and whispered, "Your turn next, little wench. As soon as I've recovered, for I'm not as young as I used to be, it will be your turn."

* * * * *

They whispered together in their little bed. Lucas had tied their hands again loosely behind them, and thrown the old blankets over them. Now, he seemed to be asleep. He had stretched out in front of the door, blocking any attempt at escape. The single window in the place was too small for a person to fit through, and they knew they were trapped. But at least he had fallen asleep at last!

They had huddled together on the bed. "We have to get out of here! He's going to kill us! I just know he is!" Brigitte whispered, her voice shrill with fear.

"He has said he is going to set us free. He said he just wants 'his way with us' and that he's done with killing. We have to believe him, Brigitte! We have to or we shall go mad! Perhaps if we cooperate as fully as we can, he'll tire more quickly, and let us go."

"Do you think so, my lady?" Brigitte's eyes were pleading, and though she was the older of the two girls, she was clearly relying on Colette's strength to pull her through.

"Yes," Colette said firmly. "Those two ruffians are gone at least, and as horrible as this Lucas is, at least he is better than they were! We have to trust to God to get us through, and perhaps Lord Philippe is even now on our trail, coming to save us."

Brigitte nodded hopefully, comforted, though Colette herself did not believe her own words. No one knew where they were, and they themselves did not know. They were completely at the mercy of this thief and madman, and somehow they had to play along to survive.

* * * * *

When Lucas awoke he sat up slowly and surveyed the two young women. They were sitting together under the blankets, their heads bent close, no doubt conspiring to escape or do him in. He smiled indulgently, knowing they hadn't a chance.

"Get up and come over here, cunts," he ordered, and both girls colored at the vulgar term. They did obey however, the short plump one and the willowy slender one, their arms still tied behind their backs. Lucas stood slowly and cut their bonds. He inspected Colette's ass and back; the welts had faded to pale pink markings. He had barely whipped her after all. He would have to do better with Brigitte.

Now he only said, "Get me my pipe. It's there on the mantle." As Colette brought him the pipe, he said, "Can you cook, girl?" This was directed to Brigitte, since he naturally assumed the useless aristocrat wouldn't know a kettle from her ass, much less what to do with it.

Brigitte nodded and he said, "I have provisions for a decent stew. You'll find what you need in that cupboard there. I'm feeling rather hungry. Quite an appetite you girls are giving me!"

He laughed, and turned to Colette. "While your maid makes us some supper, I think you could use a lesson in how to please a man, eh? Brigitte has some potential, but maybe her mouth is too small. I don't like someone puking after they suck me off, you know? Sort of off-putting." He grinned, his rotting teeth displayed, and Colette turned away.

She knew she had no choice whatsoever at the moment, but just to reiterate her hopeless position, Lucas drew a small sharp knife from its scabbard at his belt. Gesturing with it he said, "Come over here, duchess, and prepare to serve your *king*."

Slowly, Colette stood, her face very pale, her blonde hair hanging loose and disheveled, no trace of the fine complicated braided bun her maid had spent two hours preparing before they left the Court at Versailles.

But that was a lifetime ago. Her entire world had shrunk to these four close walls of rough-hewn wood, to the humiliation and degradation of being held captive by this savage man who held their lives at his sword point.

Lucas pointed at his feet, which were shod in old cracked leather, once brown but now almost white from use and age. Again he opened his leather pantaloons, and pulled out his thick, half-erect penis. Colette knelt, feeling faint and slightly nauseated. She could smell the old urine and musk, and tried not to breathe through her nose.

"Take off your top, girl. I want to see those little tits of yours. That's right. Now, don't tremble so, little wench. I don't want to have to use this knife here." He brandished the little knife, fully aware of its impact on the poor girl. "I plan to use my own personal sword. The sword of love!" He guffawed loudly, fondling his member. He was quite amused at his own wit, which was completely lost on Colette.

"Now, what you must do is open your mouth. Wider. Open your mouth so I can put this sword of love right down your throat." He moved forward, grabbing a handful of Colette's hair, as he guiding his now fully erect penis into her mouth.

She had meant to obey, to acquiesce and get it over with as quickly as possible, but now she bucked and jerked away, horrified by what he was doing. She hadn't seen Brigitte's forced oral homage, having been tied with her face to the wall at the time. But Brigitte had told her what had happened, in sobbing whispers while the man lay sleeping. Now it was Colette's turn, to feel the heavy warmth of his shaft, to taste the salty musky tang of it. She felt her gorge rising and feared she would vomit.

As if reading her mind, Lucas admonished, "Don't you dare puke like that silly little serving girl of yours, or I'll strap you within an inch of your life, see if I won't! It's downright insulting, having you girls act like this is a worse punishment than being horsewhipped! For God's sake, woman. It's just a cock!"

Colette swallowed, closing her eyes, forcing herself to think of something lovely and sweet. Fresh clover in the spring, the scent of new apples just picked, the lavender sachets that were put into her wardrobe to keep her clothing smelling fresh…

"That's it," Lucas said softly, as he pressed his cock past her lips. Colette shuddered, but didn't try to pull away. Lucas grabbed her head, guiding himself into her soft warm mouth.

"Ahhh," he moaned with pleasure. "Yes, that's it, my little whore. Take me deep, all the way into that gilded little throat of yours. Oh, yes." While Lucas impaled poor Colette with his cock, Brigitte tried to make a stew, throwing some wilted vegetables and salted meat she had found into the kettle, and adding water from the pitcher he kept on the table.

She stoked the fire, using a poker that leaned against the mantel. Perhaps a sharp blow to his head, which was lolling back now in pleasure, as he neared his release, would knock the bastard out and they make a run for it!

But what if she missed? Or didn't hit hard enough to knock him out, but only to anger him? Then they would surely die by his sword! Oh dear, she couldn't make these sorts of decisions. Lady Colette would know what to do, but she was kneeling there, her poor body bared like some harlot, his huge *thing* rammed down her throat, just as had been done to her, Brigitte, before.

It was somehow worse to watch this done to the daughter of a duke than to herself, a mere serving girl. She wrung her hands in despair, and then watched in fascinated horror as Lucas withdrew the large glistening member from poor Colette's mouth and his seed gushed forth over her pale white breasts in strings of semen that splashed up onto Colette's cheek.

Colette pulled back, gasping, falling back onto her haunches. Lucas opened his eyes, looked at the lovely young girl covered in his ejaculate and grinned. "Brigitte!" he yelled, though she was only just behind him. "Clean up your mistress; she's a ruddy mess!"

* * * * *

After a stew that wasn't half bad, Lucas, though not yet ready to perform again himself, decided he would like a little entertainment from the ladies. He ordered them to strip, and lie down on the blankets he spread on the floor. "Now, you innocent little poppets, I'm going to introduce you to the pleasures of girl-to-girl loving. I like to watch two wenches go at it.

"Colette, you will begin, since you know what to expect already. I want you to tongue little Brigitte here. Now, don't look so distressed. It's only natural, as I've explained before. You Catholics full of your stupid notions about sin create more problems than you solve, I assure you!

"Now, you lie down, Brigitte, and spread those nice plump legs of yours, so your mistress can get access to that delectable little pussy." Neither girl had moved to cooperate. Lucas stood from the chair and pulled out his large sword, which glittered silver in the candlelight. It was enough to get them moving, and he slowly sheathed it as Brigitte lay back, spreading her ample thighs, revealing her dark patch of pubic hair and the little curved lips beneath it, also covered in soft down.

Colette knelt nervously between her legs. His hand still on his hilt, Lucas commanded, "Do what I did to you, girl, though I daresay you won't have the skill I do, because for me it's a labor of love!" He laughed and continued, "Just lick her little cunt, girl. I want to watch you lick that pussy, and do it right! I want to see her come, just like you did, you little slut."

Colette blushed, remembering his strange kisses and the pleasure he had ripped from her against her will. At least she wasn't being asked to hurt Brigitte, though she was mortified at what she *was* being commanded to do, and knew that Brigitte was terrified.

"I'm sorry," she whispered to her little maid. Then, gently placing her hands on either thigh, Colette leaned forward and delicately touched the folds of Brigitte's sex with her tongue.

Since her mind could not process what her body was doing, it conveniently shut down for the moment, leaving her blank and almost peaceful as she submitted to the madman's will, having no choice in the matter. She felt Brigitte's body trembling beneath her hands, and gently stroked her, wishing she could take her in her arms and soothe the poor frightened girl. But she dared not. Instead, she licked again at the little folds of sweet spicy flesh, feeling their heat, and not finding it entirely unpleasant.

It was better, at any rate, than having Lucas thrust his huge salty erection down her throat! At least here, she could control the pace, and it was, after all, only Brigitte, her maid. They'd bathed naked together as children, and even now Brigitte saw Colette's bare or partially clothed body as she helped her with her toilette.

"That's it," Lucas encouraged. "Why, you look almost as if you like it, you little slut! Spread the lips a bit. Get at that little tip in the center. That's what drives a woman wild, see? I want you to make her shudder and moan with pleasure. If you don't, I'll cut her little cunt with a blade, to remind her how your tongue failed!"

Colette looked up at him in horror! Was he saying he'd cut Brigitte's sex if she didn't please him by her performance? The man was a fiend! She started to protest, but he silenced her with a raised hand and said, "Please her, girl. That's all you have to do. Then she will be spared."

Bending again toward her task, Colette, now also trembling, began to lick and suckle her little maid, trying desperately to remember what he'd done to her when the wine had so befuddled her that she'd sat willing in her chair, legs lewdly splayed as he kissed and licked her to some secret, dangerous paradise.

Slowly she licked up and down Brigitte's vulva, pausing to kiss and play with the little nubbin that seemed to actually be growing and swelling under her tongue. Brigitte moaned, very quietly, and Colette worried for a moment that she had hurt her. She pulled back, but Brigitte, to her surprise, actually arched forward slightly, as if her sex was seeking the hot wet tongue that was suddenly removed.

Colette realized then that the moan was one of pleasure. She must be doing something right. She almost smiled, and knelt back to her task, spreading Brigitte's thighs wider for better access. They made a pretty picture, the two naked girls, one crouched over, head bent in concentration, blonde hair spilling out over soft spread thighs, as she tongued the other to orgasm.

Brigitte was moaning steadily now, and Colette felt the girl's pussy swollen and hot beneath her mouth. She knew they were sinning, but it could not be helped and surely God would forgive them both.

At the same time, somewhere deep in her psyche, she felt a curious sort of pleasure, not sexual pleasure exactly, but a sort of rush of power, that she was causing this woman to experience what she knew was an indescribable sensation that welled from somewhere deep inside, to overwhelm and engulf the receiver.

A few more licks, placed just so over the tip of that nubbin, and Brigitte began to buck and cry out in little mewling gasps. Colette held on, as Lucas had held on to her, riding out Brigitte's climax, her tongue still tickling Brigitte's sex, until the little maid fell back, limp, her body bathed in a sheen of sweat.

Colette could feel Brigitte's heart pounding, the little pulse of it in her pussy. Slowly she sat back, wiping her mouth with the back of her hand, hoping she had pleased Lucas and he would continue to spare their lives, and not hurt her maid with his knife. She dared to look around at him, and saw to her horror that he was holding his own member in his hand, and it looked huge and purple as he pumped it.

"Pull off those pants, wench. I need to fuck you! Lie down and get those pants off before I kill you!" Quickly Colette obliged, her heart hammering in her chest, her mouth dry from terror. The pain of the rape was fresh in her mind, and her body still hadn't healed from the onslaught. And now he was going to do what that horrid young man had done! God, take me now, she begged silently.

The large man lay heavily across her. Brigitte had recovered, and was cowering nearby, crying, helpless to save her mistress. Colette squeezed her eyes shut, trying to ready herself for the onslaught. But instead of his thick cock forcing its way past her entrance, she felt his fingers, which he had wet with his own spittle.

A single finger pressed at her opening, gently probing, as he grunted on top of her. Lucas was a strange man; at once taking what he wanted, but possessed of a curious compassion that was at odds with his persona as robber and scoundrel.

He had no compunction about raping this poor woman, or keeping the two women captive for as long as he liked, and subjecting them to his perverted will, but at the same time, he didn't want to hurt them. At least not with his cock, not like this, though he did enjoy a good strapping, and saw no contradiction.

So now he probed, carefully, opening her slowly, moving that finger up to her clit, trying to arouse her, or at least ease some of her terror, so that he wouldn't rip her flesh and have to fuck a dry cunt. After a few minutes he felt some of the rigidity of her body beneath him ease.

"That's right, love," he murmured. "If you relax it's so much better, don't you see? Just relax, because it's going to happen anyway, and you might even like it, if you can just give yourself over to it. This is, after all, a woman's duty to please a man." He rubbed slowly, feeling the clench of her muscles give way slightly. Impatient with desire, he let his cock head touch her entrance, and then he gently pushed, easing just the tip inside of her.

Colette cried out and clenched herself against him, fear winning out over her attempts to relax. She believed him that it would hurt less if she could relax, and she believed him that he would do this anyway, whether she was relaxed or as taut as a board, but her poor body wouldn't cooperate, and her muscles were again rigid with fear, the imprint of Albert's brutal rape still fresh upon her.

Lucas didn't press further for the moment. He stayed still, exercising self-control as he allowed her to adjust to just the tip of his cock head nestled at the entrance of her sex.

Lifting himself onto his elbows, he smoothed back the wild blonde hair that half obscured her face. He could feel her heart pounding against her narrow chest, and he almost felt sorry for her. But his need for what she offered, naked and helpless beneath him, was too great for sympathy.

He pressed slightly more, easing the head past the clench of muscle, settling himself fully inside of her. Again he stilled, savoring for the moment the deliciously tight velvet grip of her involuntary muscles clamped around his cock. Oh, this was surely heaven. This was the way to die, nestled to the hilt inside a lovely tight pussy.

He began to move, slowly at first, then with more abandon. His pleasure was almost painful, it was so intense, and he knew it was going to end too soon, too soon.

What was this? Was he in love? Because he felt his very heart pounding as if it would burst. The pleasure that had coursed through his veins, firing his blood, now seemed overtaken by this pain in his heart. Surely he was too old to love;

too cynical certainly. A sharp pain overcame him, like a stabbing of hot iron inside his chest, accompanied by a pain through his shoulder, down his arm.

He groaned loudly, thrusting hard into Colette, hurting her now, as he fell hard against her, calling out something incomprehensible as he smashed down, pinning her to the floor. Then he was still.

Deathly still.

Colette was breathing hard beneath him, her heart pounding so hard she could feel it against his dead weight, which had knocked the very air out of her as he fell against her. She braced herself, waiting for the next onslaught.

But he did not move. He barely even seemed to be breathing. With a dawning realization, Colette dared to push against the still man who lay so heavily against her, his cock still embedded inside of her.

"Mon Dieu!" she cried now. "Brigitte! Where are you! Help me! Help me! Oh God, help me!"

* * * * *

"We have to wait until morning. The roads are not safe at night!" They were dressed again in their peasant boy clothing, huddled together at the table, heads almost touching. Lucas hadn't moved, and lay sprawled as he had fallen, a blanket thrown over him by the girls once Colette had managed to get herself out from underneath the dead man with Brigitte's help.

Brigitte was urging that they leave at once. She was terrified at the idea of staying even another minute in a cottage with a dead man. "His ghost will haunt us, my lady! It's bad luck to sleep with the dead, if they aren't properly blessed! Everyone knows this! We must go now!"

The time they had spent together as captives, and the extraordinary things they had been forced to do to one another and in front of one another had altered their relationship. Though Brigitte still used the formal terms of mistress and lady, theirs was now more a bond of sisterhood. The kind of bond forged in war that lasts a lifetime. Thus Colette, who in the past would have been shocked to have a servant argue with her, barely noticed.

"Well, it will be worse luck to run out unprepared in the night and be accosted by the first band of drunken thieves to cross our paths. At least in the daylight we have a chance! Look, Brigitte, he's doing us far less harm just lying there like a sack of potatoes than he was doing when he was alive! I believe *we* have been blessed, even if he hasn't! The Lord smote him down for his barbaric and perverted ways! And now you and I have been given a second chance. Let's collect ourselves, pack some provisions and decide what to do!"

"We don't even have any idea where we are! We're helpless, miles from anything or anyone we know! We might as well be dead ourselves!" Brigitte began to cry, and Colette reached out a hand to comfort her, when suddenly a thought came to her.

Unbidden it came, as she wasn't even aware that she had been paying attention to Lucas' words as she lay in the grip of pain and fear following the first rape. But now the words came back to her, as if the man now lying dead was actually speaking to her. She could hear his gravelly voice in her mind, saying to the two men as they prepared to leave that evening: "*Take the path by the river 'til you come to a road and follow it due north a ways. You'll see the village and the pub.*"

"Oh my God! Brigitte! I know what we must do! I remember the old man's directions! We are to take the path that runs along the river, and follow it until we come to a road. We're to go north until we get to the village! It can't be that far. They came back after several hours!"

They embraced, tears of joy and nervous energy spilling down their cheeks. They were too keyed up to sleep, but still they lay down together on the pallet one last time, their arms wrapped around each other.

The room was pitch dark now, and not even a sliver of moon shone through the little window. In the silence Colette turned to Brigitte. "Are you awake?"

"Hmm?" Brigitte said sleepily.

"Well, I don't know how to say this. But I, well, those sinful things I was forced to do to you. You know I had no choice!"

"Oh please!" Brigitte whispered back, embarrassment palpable in her voice. "I do know that, my lady! I am so sorry you were forced into such an awkward and dreadful position. We were only doing what we had to in order to stay alive! Let us keep it a secret between us, and cast it away with all of this hideous nightmare!"

"You are wise," Colette said, and turned away, trying to sleep at least a little before a journey that would take them she knew not where.

Brigitte turned away as well, so that their backs were lightly touching. She pressed her thighs together, vaguely confused by the slight pulse between her legs as she recalled, against her will, Colette's hot tongue licking against her most secret place.

When dawn came, pale and cold, the two young women loaded the pockets of their strange clothing with what apples and cheese remained, as well as the jewels and coins that Lucas had intended to keep as his own. Among the items was Colette's own gold bracelet, which Brigitte clasped again onto the arm of its rightful owner. She had lost her earrings and rings, but it hardly seemed important now, as they were alive and free, if lost.

Brigitte made them some hot tea and they set out for the river path, leaving the blanket-covered corpse, a smile still on its gray face, behind them.

Outside the cottage door, Lucas' old horse whinnied when she saw them. She was hungry, surely! "Why, we can take this mare, Brigitte! It'll be easy to ride in our breeches! Here, let's get her fed and watered first."

Brigitte found the old water pail, and Colette provided of few of their dry little apples to supplement the grass the old horse had been grazing upon. But when they went to place the saddle upon her, she reared back and snorted.

"Come on, girl! Relax!" Colette tried again, not exactly certain what she was doing, as she was rarely allowed near the stables at home, and had certainly not saddled a horse before. Brigitte tried to help, and between them they only succeeded in irritating and frightening the poor animal, who whinnied nervously and kicked at them, almost striking Brigitte in the head.

"Oh! This is hopeless," Colette cried, dropping the heavy saddle in frustration. "She's so frightened now we'd never be able mount her, even if we did get the stupid saddle on her! We'll just have to let her go and be on our way ourselves, on foot."

Together they untied the knots that tethered the old horse to the tree. With a baleful glare in their direction, she trotted away along the river path, leaving them to fend for themselves.

The first problem came when they realized they didn't know which direction to take along the path, as it extended in either direction from behind the cottage. After some examination, they decided the path looked more worn to the west, and so they headed that way, walking slowly in their ladies' shoes, which, with their peasant pantaloons and long hair flowing, created an odd picture indeed.

They had walked only about twenty minutes when Colette saw the road. Hurriedly they ran the last few feet through the grass and brush and found themselves on a public road such as now crisscrossed all of the King's France. Using the sun, they determined a northern course and set out that way.

Luck was with them that morning, after so many dark and dreadful days, when they heard the sound of horses pulling a cart behind them. Gesturing and waving excitedly, they tried to get the driver's attention.

At first he cursed them, yelling to get out of his way, assuming that they were just village boys making a ruckus. But when he got close enough to see their features, especially the fair Colette, whose hair fell in wavy tresses to her waist, he did a double-take and pulled his horses to. "Whoa!" he said, patting their flanks as their hooves kicked up a cloud of dark red dust that made the girls cough and turn their heads. "What have we here? Do my eyes deceive me, or are you two women dressed as men? My curiosity has got the best of me, I do confess. Speak, and explain yourselves!" His clothing and accent were rough, but his eyes were kind.

Colette drew herself up to her aristocratic best and said with her perfect diction, "Kind sir. We are two ladies who have been waylaid from our entourage and kidnapped. We have escaped and now seek to return to our home. I have means to pay you if you will be so gracious as to offer your aid."

The man looked highly skeptical, and it took much explaining until they finally persuaded the fellow as to the truth of their claims. The man's eyebrows had risen higher and higher as the terrible story unfolded.

Finally Colette reached into the little leather bag and pulled out a single gold coin, which she held up to the man. Now completely convinced, at least of their ability to pay him, the man jumped down from his perch and bowed low before the two young women. "Michel Alphonse, at your service, my lady! Where might I take you?"

For a moment Colette was stymied. She was a woman without a home now; her father had traded her away like a sack of grain, and yet she barely knew the man whose hospitality she would claim. But what choice had she? Remembering Madame de Valon's fond and eager talk of their destination, she said, "How far is St. Malo, sir? If you please?"

"Ah, St. Malo. That is a day's ride from my village, which is only an hour or so from here. Your people are there, Madame? I am familiar with the great houses there; I don't recall two young women…" There was a question in his voice, though he didn't dare inquire directly just who they were or what their business was. It wouldn't do to offend obviously refined young women bearing gold coins! Even if the two young women were dressed like peasant boys, except for their fancy shoes and silk stockings.

But Colette supplied the wanted information. "I am Colette Rousseau, of the house of Lyon. This is my companion. We are guests of Lord Philippe de Valon. Do you know of him?"

The man was clearly impressed and more certain now of his fortune this day than ever. "Only by reputation, Madame, but that reputation is a fine one indeed. His ships are known all over France, and his palace is the finest in the north. Here, let me help you." He lifted first Colette and then Brigitte up and over the side of his little wooden cart, which was filled with hay and a few ducks in a slatted wooden cage.

"I apologize for the accommodations, gentle ladies," he said, nodding toward them, trying not to grin as he surveyed them in their boys' clothing and fine high-heeled shoes. "But I'll get you to the village and there we will secure you a proper carriage. Uh, providing you have more of these sovereigns to cover the cost. Will that suit, Madame?"

"It will indeed," Colette nodded, her heart soaring. The worst was over, and they were on their way to St. Malo!

Chapter Four

"Hurry, hurry! A carriage is approaching!" Little Marguerite, the kitchen maid, had been dumping the dirty dishwater in the back when she saw the carriage come lurching round the bend toward the de Valon castle, which was really more of a large house, made from pink and gray granite, solid as time itself.

When guests were expected, the entire household would ready itself for weeks, cleaning, cooking, airing out the guest rooms, making sure everything was in tiptop shape to honor their Lord Philippe and his formidable aunt, Madame de Valon. But today no guest had been expected. The household was still in mourning from the loss of Valentine and Gérard, the two young footmen who were brutally murdered in the highway robbery several days before.

Madame de Valon had arrived in hysterics, crying about the two girls who had been in her charge and were now lost, surely murdered or worse! (Innocent Marguerite wondered but didn't dare ask what could be worse than murder.) It had taken some time to get the complete story, as all the members of the traveling party were stunned and in shock, but it was clear that the two footmen were never coming home, and two young women were probably lost as well, sold into slavery, or murdered.

Cook came out in the yard to see what little Marguerite was going on about. "Get Charles! Hurry! Send him to the front gate to meet this stranger. I'll summon Madame." The little kitchen maid hurried away to get the head footman as the carriage pulled up to the large gate and the driver dismounted.

It took several minutes and much explaining, but at last Colette and Brigitte were admitted to the castle, and the carriage driver, well paid by Colette, rode away. Madame de Valon came running into the front hall, still in her lounging robes, her wig slightly askew. Gone was the formal grande dame, as she squealed and slapped her chest with both hands. "Mon Dieu!" she cried. "Colette, chère! You are alive! You are risen from the dead! Saints preserve us, you are alive!"

They ran toward each other, and embraced. "Charles! Have tea brought in the salon. Come Colette, you too, Brigitte. You must tell me how you escaped the kidnappers and lived to tell the tale! And what are these strange clothing you are wearing? You look absolutely ridiculous! You are hungry? Yes, you look hungry to me! And filthy! First some food, then a nice hot bath, and your own lovely clothes. We have all your things, your trunks, your baggage."

Colette and Brigitte followed the old woman, stunned to silence by her effusive outpouring. It was hard to believe this was the formidable and disapproving Madame de Valon who had seemed to barely tolerate their presence before! She seemed not only relieved but genuinely delighted to see them.

Between bites of hot fresh buttered croissants and sips of sweet tea, the girls explained how they had been taken to the cottage. They both blushed deeply and turned away when Madame de Valon probed as to what had happened to them there. Their painful blushes and stammers were enough for her to draw her own conclusions, and she wisely didn't press them.

Instead she ordered water boiled for their baths, and led them herself to their chambers. Catherine and another servant helped the girls out of the filthy clothing, which Madame de Valon ordered to be burned at once.

Finally Colette dared to ask, "And Lord Philippe? Is he here, Madame?"

"Please, call me Aunt Genevieve. I feel as if you are my kin now. When we thought we lost you, I cannot tell you my grief! Philippe was outraged at the loss, and being a man of action, he was determined to do something about it! As to your question, my nephew is out even now with a party of men, searching for you! He has many connections in the surrounding area and, though to tell you the truth we had no real hope, he was going to do what he could! I wish we could call him back now! The poor man was beside himself with guilt that this had happened to you, his guest!"

Only guilt? No pain to his heart? Silently, of course, Colette asked this question of no one. Who was she, anyway, but some brief acquaintance? The hours of sweet conversation, and that kiss, oh that kiss. Surely it had only been the foolish dream of a lovesick girl! She was an idiot to ever assign it any importance. The dashing Lord Philippe probably kissed hundreds of girls far more lovely than she!

But at least she would see him again! She allowed a serving girl to help her into her bath, and to wash her heavy mane of hair. It felt so wonderful to wash away the grime of the last few dark days. She dismissed the servant and scrubbed her own body, trying to wash away all traces of the horrible things that had been done to her at the hands of the kidnappers.

Unbidden and certainly unwelcome, the image of the graying visage of Lucas, his face frozen in a death grin, floated into her mind. Colette shook her head, shuddering, willing the image away. The water was cold now, and she called to the servant to dry her.

* * * * *

Dressed again, properly clothed in her own lovely clothes, Colette felt very much better. Brigitte was also dressed in her own things, her face scrubbed clean, her dark hair pulled neatly back as befitted her station. Colette had told her to go and rest, but Brigitte wanted to stay by her side and Colette acquiesced.

They were waiting in the sitting room that had been set aside for them, which opened onto what would be Colette's bedroom. Brigitte had her own small room just off Colette's. The room was finer than what Colette was used to at her father's castle, and far finer than the austere quarters to which she'd been assigned at the Court at Versailles.

Brigitte was sewing and Colette was fiddling with a lace fan, turning it this way and that, thinking thoughts of her own.

After a decent interval Madame de Valon, or Aunt Genevieve, as she now insisted upon, came to the door and lightly knocked, sailing in before Colette could invite her. She was dressed as well now, in all her silk and lace finery, her fine white wig piled high on her head as befitted a woman of her standing and stature. "My dears, you look a thousand times improved! We thought we lost four, but we have only lost two. Very tragic, of course, but the Lord is mysterious. And of course, we lost all our fine jewelry and gold. Not that that matters; it can all be replaced. They are only things, after all."

She sighed heavily and continued, "Though my dear mother's brooch, which had been passed from eldest daughter to eldest daughter until it came to me, has been lost forever, I fear. No doubt it's on a ship to foreign lands, for resale at some distant court. I suppose it's my fault, for never having been blessed with a daughter of my own..." The old woman trailed off, staring into the middle distance, a tear actually trickling through the heavy rice powder on her wrinkled cheek.

"A brooch, did you say, Madame?" Brigitte piped up, dropping her sewing in her lap, sitting up very straight.

"Yes, a simple piece really. It had opals set like the petals of a flower, with rubies between each petal and for the center. It was laid in gold, with little gold leaves at the bottom. How I will miss it."

Colette and Brigitte grinned at each other, and with a nod from Colette, Brigitte ran from the room and returned with the grimy leather sack they had taken from the cottage, stuffed still with coins and jewelry. In all the excitement and relief of the escape and arrival at the estate, they'd completely forgotten it!

Madame de Valon looked on, thoroughly confused, as they dumped the contents onto the little table in front of her. And there, in the center of the treasure, lay her little brooch, like a spring flower waiting to be plucked. "Oh!" Madame de Valon cried, grabbing the little piece and clutching it to her heart. "What a day this has been! So many things restored to us!"

After Brigitte had helped pin the brooch on Aunt Genevieve's gown, they examined the remaining contents, determining what belonged to whom. They were still at it when a servant knocked lightly at the open door and exclaimed, "Pardon, Madame, but Lord Philippe has returned!"

* * * * *

Philippe came striding in a moment later, having left his tired horse to be taken care of by others. The servants had breathlessly told him the news of the girls' safe return, and his relief was palpable, his joy unexplored.

Bursting into Colette's sitting room he exclaimed, "By all that is holy! You are safe and returned to us! I had despaired of ever seeing you again!" Colette and Brigitte had both stood abruptly at his entrance. They were still guests, after all, in the castle of this important man. Brigitte had dropped into a deep curtsey, and Colette had bowed her head submissively.

"Are you safe? Unharmed? The brutes! The cowards! To kill men as they sat at rest, and take our women! What happened! You must tell me everything!"

"The girls are fine," Madame de Valon interrupted, aware of the dangerous ground of indiscretion upon which Philippe was treading. "Catherine!" she called to the servant, who was waiting quietly at the door, "Bring refreshments for Lord Philippe at once. We will remain here." She waved an imperious hand and Catherine retreated.

"Now sit, Philippe, and tell us of your efforts. Obviously you didn't find the girls, since they cleverly made their way here all by themselves!" Colette smiled shyly and Philippe raised his eyebrows in surprise. There was even more to this girl than he knew!

"Well," he said, taking the seat offered by his old aunt. "I took ten men to search with me, and we scoured the area near where the girls were taken. We were able to follow the trail through the forest, but lost it once they took to the public road. This morning we found a horse that one of the footmen believed might have been ridden by one of the kidnappers, but it was unsaddled and looked to have escaped or been set free."

"We set it free!" Colette interjected. "It belonged to Lucas. The old man. We let it go when we escaped, because we couldn't saddle it and didn't want it to starve." She stopped suddenly, blushing, realizing she had spoken without being invited to do so.

But Philippe was leaning toward her, his face alight with interest. "This is so extraordinary! You must begin at the beginning. Tell me what happened, and how you managed to escape!"

Now Colette colored a dark red, looking pained, and turned her face. Again Madame de Valon was forced to intervene. "Philippe! The girls have only just returned themselves. You look exhausted, and you're filthy! Take some tea, wash and rest, and we will talk more of this later. Suffice it now to say that the two vagabonds left with their shares of the stolen valuables, off on a pirate ship to seek their fortunes, and the older, er, gentleman, why, his heart failed and he died! God's intervention as sure as I'm alive!"

"He died! But first he held you for several days against your will! I must know—" Again Madame de Valon interrupted him, the tone in her voice making it clear she was pulling rank as his aunt, and he had better obey her or face the consequences.

"Philippe! Please, use your head for once, instead of your heart, and hold your tongue! Off with you!"

Philippe stopped, looking from his aunt to Colette, whose face was now turned away, and belatedly he understood the delicacy of his questioning. Looking sheepish, he bowed to the ladies, and took his leave.

Later that evening they all sat together at dinner, Philippe, Aunt Genevieve and Colette. Brigitte was of course with the other servants, taking her meal in the kitchen. Catherine had taken her under her wing, and Brigitte seemed content to part from her mistress for the time being.

Over dinner Philippe was careful to avoid asking anything of too personal a nature to the young woman at his table, though he burned with curiosity and concern. Aunt Genevieve made idle conversation, filled with her usual barbs and insults toward those of whom she disapproved, which was most everyone.

The old woman left to retire to her chambers after the meal, as was her habit. Philippe and Colette remained at the table, watching as a servant set out a thick crystal decanter of fine port, and two crystal goblets, along with some soft cheeses and fresh fruit. Philippe nodded his dismissal with a small smile and took the decanter, pouring first for the young lady and then himself. Colette was silent, sipping delicately at the sweet wine. Her expression was pensive, almost brooding.

Philippe dared, "My lady, I know you have been through hell. I am so grateful to find you returned to us! But I know, as one who has been to battle, that not talking about the wounds sustained there, the horrors witnessed, leaves these events to fester in your bosom like a poisoned barb. I am not asking that you share what happened with me. But you must find someone in whom to confide. Perhaps my aunt?"

Colette looked up at him and smiled slightly. "Please, my lord, you can't be serious." She flushed slightly, but as he grinned, she continued, "Your aunt would rather die than hear what happened. Her delicate sensibilities would be so compromised by my words that she would expire on the spot!" Now Colette blushed full out, realizing what her remarks revealed, not only as to her regard for his aunt, but as to the nature of what had occurred in the little cabin.

Philippe laughed, hoping to put her at ease, realizing she was perfectly correct. His aunt would indeed rather die than have to hear about sins of the body. And no doubt, adhering to the double standards of the day, Colette would be held guilty in some way for whatever was done to her. But what was done to her? He had to know. He wanted to know, and then somehow to repair it for her, to make it right. To take away that sad and haunted look on her face, which was so new, engraved there no doubt by whatever those horrible men had done to her.

But not now. He could wait. He would be patient with the young girl and give her time to come to trust him. "Come," he said. "You are tired. Let me escort you to your rooms."

"No!" she said, suddenly. He looked at her, surprised. "That is," she stammered, embarrassed, "I don't want to be alone. Not yet. I'm not yet ready to sleep. If you would stay with me a while longer?"

"I should like nothing better, my lady," answered Philippe. Standing, he held out his arm, and together they moved to Philippe's favorite room, a small den paneled in dark honey colored wood, lined with bookshelves and paintings that had caught Philippe's eye over the years. He led Colette to a divan, and sat next to her. A small fire was burning in the fireplace, not enough to throw off heat, but just enough to make the room cozy.

They sat quietly for a time, sipping their port. Colette was staring into the fire, allowing Philippe the chance to admire her profile. Her hair was pulled back in a pretty chignon at her neck, which was long and slender. She was so different from the young women at Court, who were always vying for his attention, their chatter gay and constant, as they fluttered their fans and their eyelashes at him. They reminded him of parrots, garishly colored, talking endlessly but saying very little.

Colette was quiet, though her silence tonight was no doubt from whatever hideous ordeal she had had to endure at the hands of those savages. What he wouldn't give to find them and have them hanged! Colette's free hand was resting on her lap, and Philippe dared to reach out and touch it gently with his fingertips. Colette startled, but didn't pull away. Slowly she looked at him, her eyes large and sad.

"Speak to me, Colette. Tell me what happened. It's over. You mustn't hold onto it. Let it go. Give it over to me, if you like."

"Oh, Philippe," she whispered, her eyes pooling with tears. "You can't possibly be serious. You wouldn't want to hear! You wouldn't want me in your house if you knew!"

"Don't be ridiculous!" Philippe interjected. "How can you think for one moment that anyone holds you at all accountable for what happened! Whatever happened, you were overpowered. How could that possibly be your fault?"

"I could have resisted more. I could have died instead of letting him do the things he did. Letting him make me do the things I did…" She stopped, her voice catching, biting her lips, shame etched in all her features.

"You could have died? You mean let yourself be killed rather than submit? Well, thank God you didn't do such a foolish thing! Are you saying that rather than sully your virtue, you should have fallen upon their swords? Which do you think is the greater crime in God's eyes? To submit to something in order to stay alive or to take your own life?"

Colette didn't answer, but she looked at Philippe, with something like gratitude in her face. He continued, "Please, Colette. Whatever happened to you, it is over. You did the right thing. You saved yourself and your maid. And you managed to escape! What an adventure you have had! Tell me at least of that, of how you managed to get out of that hut and all the way to my castle all on your own! It's quite astonishing!"

Colette did tell him, actually smiling as she recounted the expression on the man's face when he realized the two boys who had stopped him were actually women! She even laughed as she described their fight with the poor horse, as they tried to saddle it and finally gave up.

They talked late into the night, and Philippe was so relieved to see her smile that he didn't press again for any of the more troubling details of her capture. There was time; all the time in the world.

* * * * *

Days passed and Colette and Brigitte settled into Philippe's household quite comfortably. Aside from the trauma of the kidnap, it was the happiest time Colette could remember, though she did miss her sisters and her little brother. Perhaps one day she would be able to invite them to see her.

The odd thing was, she didn't really understand her place in this household. She wasn't Philippe's lover, certainly, nor was she a servant. A family friend? Not really, as she hadn't known these people until her father had given her away like a bolt of silk or a barrel of wine.

No one else seemed particularly perturbed. Aunt Genevieve clearly enjoyed her company, and now that she had somehow proved her mettle with the old woman, she no longer spewed her invective in Colette's direction, to Colette's relief. Colette found she quite enjoyed the old woman's tales and reminiscences about her life before she was widowed and about Philippe and his brother when they were small.

Together they continued to explore the many books in Aunt Genevieve's library, and Colette played for her each day, exhausting her repertoire. She began to work on new pieces of music that she had discovered, to her delight, inside of the little harpsichord bench.

Philippe was gone during each day, but always returned for dinner, which he took with the two women. Afterwards, after bidding Aunt Genevieve goodnight, it had become their habit to retire to his den, where they talked easily of whatever came to mind, though always carefully avoiding the subject still very close to the surface for Colette.

Philippe liked to entertain Colette with stories of Court life. But as he described what had once seemed so exciting and wild, when viewed through the lens of her perception, he came to realize how much of that life was shallow and false. Colette was stunned by the descriptions of married noblemen and women at Court, constantly seeking to cuckold each other's spouses, just for the sport of it.

When Philippe told her of a particular costume party, where everyone wore elaborate masks constructed to look like animals, she was especially shocked. So much champagne was consumed, and people had felt especially free because their faces were covered, allowing them to behave incognito. The event had degenerated into a kind of frenzied free-for-all, with half-dressed women, disguised as cats and rabbits, being pursued by men with the faces of bears and snakes.

When he told her of one very high-placed marquise, wearing the mask of a bird, who had been debauched right on the ballroom floor by a very drunken King disguised as a lion, she was horrified.

"But my lord, are these not adults? Are these not the rulers of our nation? Surely they have better things to do than run about like children creating a ruckus and behaving like fools!"

What had seemed very gay and daring at the time, took on a new light when seen through her innocent eyes. And Philippe found himself agreeing. He did not miss those heady but childish days. How many nights had he himself wasted in idle pursuit of women who meant less than nothing to him? He felt something close to shame as he pondered her words, and thought to himself that she was wise beyond her years.

Occasionally they would touch on what had happened to Colette and Brigitte at the hands of her captors. Philippe continued to try and draw her out, but she was like a skittish mare or wild rabbit. If he moved too suddenly, she was gone. Colette would usually fall silent at that point, and Philippe would leave her to stare into the fire, lost in her own thoughts.

Colette tried not to dwell on what had happened, but it was always there, demanding attention in her mind, pushing its way to the forefront of her thoughts. Though Philippe continued to gently probe, she found that she couldn't yet talk about it with him. She was mortally ashamed, even though she was aware she was not at fault.

Not only had she been abused and raped, but she had been forced to behave unnaturally with her maid, with Brigitte. Neither of them had spoken of it, but she noted that Brigitte sometimes seemed shy around her now, and something had changed between them. The easiness of a relationship built from years spent together had been altered irrevocably by the events of those few horrible days.

But worse, much worse, were the nightmares. The brute Albert would be on her, forcing her legs apart, pressing his huge member into her. Only it wouldn't be a man's penis at all, but a sword, sharp and tearing, ripping at her flesh, making her blood gush, covering her in her own blood, suffocating her as it filled her nostrils and mouth with a stench of death. She would wake, screaming, sweating, her heart pounding, until Brigitte would rush to her side, soothing her mistress, pushing her hair from her face, murmuring that everything was all right; she was safe now and no one could harm her ever again.

Other nights it was Brigitte who would toss and turn, prey to her own feverish dreams, and Colette would comfort her in kind, even though she was nobility and Brigitte a mere serving girl. Their connection now as sisters in a kind of war was forever forged, and Colette no longer regarded Brigitte as simply her maid, but as a friend. It saddened her that a rift seemed to remain between them, but she didn't know what to do to address it. She hadn't the courage to broach the subject of their forced encounter.

One night Colette awoke to a tap on her shoulder, and Brigitte leaned over her and whispered, "Please, my lady, I know it's very forward of me, but do you think I could slip into bed with you? I keep having the most horrible nightmares and I can't seem to stop shivering."

Colette took pity on her maid, and pulled back the soft covers, inviting her in. Brigitte snuggled gratefully against her and Colette wrapped her arms around the young woman.

Unbidden into her mind's eye came the image of herself, crouched between Brigitte's naked legs. She remembered the spicy taste of Brigitte's sex and the way it swelled and heated as Colette's tongue found its mark. It had been a strange and peculiar thing she had been forced to do to Brigitte, and yet she knew, from her own submission at the mouth of Lucas, that what she had done had been pleasurable to Brigitte.

She wondered now if Brigitte remembered it, or if the terror of the whole ordeal had wiped it from her mind. She felt her own sex stir as she recalled the sweet sensations that had been wrested from her by that horrible old man. It didn't make sense, that she could derive pleasure even in the middle of fear so great she had felt her heart might burst from it.

And what of Brigitte, being forced to endure such humiliation at the hand of her own mistress? Colette had never dared to apologize, though she'd held entire conversations in her head about it, over and over. Now, in the easy darkness, she dared to murmur, "Brigitte, about what I did to you. You know, with my tongue. I'm sorry. You know I had no choice."

Brigitte was silent, but Colette could feel her stiffen next to her, and was certain she had heard her. At length Brigitte said, "My lady. I have thought of it often. As I said that very night, I don't blame you at all!" She was silent a moment longer and then said, her voice lowered, "But here is the odd thing, my lady. I think there's something terribly wrong with me. I think the sin of it has unhinged my poor brain! I'm so afraid!"

Brigitte began to cry, little muffled sobs. "Why, Brigitte! Whatever do you mean? What happened was in no way your fault! We were at the mercy of those men! If we hadn't obeyed, we would have been killed! Would that have been preferable?" All of Philippe's persuasive arguments came back to Colette now, and she knew he was right.

"I don't know," Brigitte cried, "I don't know! I've been defiled by those horrid men. That was bad enough. But when you did, that is, when you did the thing you did…" Brigitte stopped, seemingly at a loss for words. But after a moment she went on, "I have to say this, as it's been burning a hole in my mind. I have to say this, to tell someone or I shall go insane! My lady, I will confess, I liked what you did! It felt good! I must be insane, or perhaps the Devil himself has got into me! But I can't stop thinking about it! The way your tongue felt against my secret place! Like a bit of satin heaven. That's what I keep thinking. I didn't hate it; I loved it! I've never felt such pleasure. There! Now I've told you! Now you can dismiss me, or have me jailed or hung for my depravity!" She burst into fresh tears, crying bitterly into Colette's pillow.

Colette propped herself on one elbow, stunned by her little maid's admission. And yet, if she were honest, she too had taken pleasure, even through the fear, from Lucas' skilled ministrations. And who was to say what was "depraved" and what wasn't? Philippe talked often during their conversations about what was "sin" and what was "virtue", arguing that much of what was deemed "virtue" was in fact the aristocracy's and the church's way of keeping people in line!

At first his remarks had shocked Colette, but she was a bright woman, capable of thinking for herself and in time his ideas had come to make sense to her. And if it were the case socially and politically, why not also in matters of the body?

Why was pleasure wrong, and who was to say where it must be found? And if she were even more honest with herself, a secret little part of her thrilled to the fact that she had given Brigitte such pleasure; that her tongue and fingers had given the young woman such an experience! Knowing it would be useless to try and explain any of this to Brigitte, she simply said, "Brigitte, dear. Please don't cry. What you are experiencing can only be natural! God gave us these bodies, and the feelings that are created in them! If you took pleasure from what I did to you, how can it be evil, or a sin? Not only that, you had no choice in the matter; nor did I. We did what we had to do to stay alive, and by God, we got out!"

Brigitte continued to cry for a while, but eventually her sobs subsided and she slept, her tearstained face next to Colette's on the pillow. Sleep didn't come so easily to Colette. Images kept swirling through her mind. The memory of her plump naked little maid, her legs spread. The smell of her sex, sweet but spicy, hard to describe. Tentatively, checking first that Brigitte was truly asleep, Colette put her hand inside her night clothing. She felt her own pussy, the delicate folds, and the little entrance below. She pressed a finger inside of herself and withdrew it, bringing it up to her face. Holding it to her nose, she inhaled, and it was similar to the musky scent Brigitte had exuded. This, then, was a woman's scent.

She slipped her hand back beneath the nightgown, and this time her fingers slid up higher. To the place where Lucas had licked her, creating that curious but admittedly lovely tension that resulted in exploding relief. Did it take a man's tongue? Would fingers work as well?

She rubbed herself for a moment, but found it was irritating. Remembering his wet tongue, she licked her own fingers, wetting them, and slid them back to her sex. Ah, much better. She touched herself lightly, enjoying the sensation, somewhere between a tickle and massage.

As the pleasure seemed to mount, she found herself rubbing harder. It felt good! It wasn't the same as when Lucas had done it, because now there was no overlay of fear. Curiously, the sensations weren't as heightened. Had she experienced such sexual pleasure because of the fear? Surely not!

Even now, she saw the old man's gray lifeless face, his eyes bugging out at her, his cock still buried inside of her! And her fingers stopped their sweet little dance. Her mind was taken over for the moment by the horrors of the abduction. Now she saw Albert, leering over her, ripping her tender flesh, pressing that huge penis into her small, tight opening. Even now she could feel that pain, and she cried out a little in remembered fear and dismay.

Brigitte stirred slightly and moaned, very softly. Colette leaned toward her and covered her gently with the sheets. She lay back against her pillows, wondering if she and Brigitte would ever be spared these horrible memories and dreams. Hopefully, they would fade over time, and be replaced by happier things.

Such as Philippe. Dear, patient Philippe. She wanted to be carefree with him. Not to trouble him with her sorrows or fears. A man would grow tired of a woman always atremble, afraid to be touched, or kissed.

Ah, his kiss! She remembered it now, so sweet and so insistent. What would happen if he were to kiss her again? Would she be able to receive it without her foolish mind confusing it for the abductors?

Now she focused, intent on bringing him to life in her imagination. Those broad shoulders and long strong legs. Lord Philippe was a strikingly handsome man. How was it that he had not married? Ah, but men were lucky in those things. They did not require a wife to function in society. They only needed one when they were ready to produce an heir. But we women, she thought, we wait, sitting in our father's house, waiting to be selected as someone's wife, someone's property. And who will want me now?

Stop! Colette admonished herself to stop this fruitless and endless line of thought. She was alive; she was safe in the castle of a wonderful man. She was free, not only from her abductors, but from a father who had treated her as chattel, as property or as a recalcitrant child.

She must behave with grace and please this Lord Philippe, so that he should not send her away; send her back to her father, to his nocturnal gropings which she now understood could have led to much worse than they did!

No, she was here, safe, in Philippe's house. And perhaps one day she could find her way into his heart. Her fingers crept back, and she touched that little spot again. She rubbed it a bit, and let her fingers fall to the entrance. Now it was moist, and the moisture was more effective than her spittle to keep her feeling supple and lubricated as she rubbed, harder now.

Her breath came in little gasps, and she had to stifle the sound, aware of the still sleeping girl next to her. What was she doing? She'd think about it later, because for now, it just felt so good. Mercifully, all thoughts finally drifted out of her head. She was sensation now, pure sensation, as the sweet buildup of pleasure made her moan into her pillow.

All at once, it caught her unaware. She felt a rushing tension centered at her sex, and her heart started to pound, in just the way it had when Lucas' foul but effective mouth had been upon her. Her fingers whirled across her clit until the shudders slowly subsided. Colette found she was bathed in a light sheen of sweat, as if she'd been exercising. Her heart thudded in her chest, and her breathing was fast and deep. Slowly her blood cooled, and she lay still, spent.

Brigitte, mercifully, still lay in deep slumber beside her. Colette found herself drifting, a feeling of sweet peace stealing over her. She fell asleep, and for the first time since the abduction, no dreams tormented her.

* * * * *

When Colette awoke the next morning, her maid was long gone, down in the kitchen helping with household duties. Brigitte seemed to fit so well into the de Valon household, as if she'd always been here.

"Let's go on a picnic!" Philippe said at breakfast that morning. "It's a lovely day. We can go down by the shore. You haven't had a proper look at the sea. And I'll show you my shipping yard! We've almost completed a warship for his majesty's naval fleet. Would you like that?"

"Oh, yes!" Colette said, her eyes shining. Aunt Genevieve was invited, but declined, saying her old bones couldn't tolerate the sea wind today. Colette was secretly delighted that they wouldn't have the old woman hovering over them, listening to their every word and making scathing comments about every subject. She would be alone with Philippe! Well, there would be servants about, but they would keep to a discreet distance, she was sure.

Colette was transfixed by the sea, its rushing, breaking waves of pearl gray and green breaking in frothy foam against the white sands. She and Philippe sat together on heavy blankets set out by the servants, with a tarp stretched over them to protect Colette's delicate skin from the sun. They ate cold chicken and drank white wine, talking about this and that. Philippe sat very close to Colette, and at length he ventured to put his arm around her, as she sat staring out at the sea.

Instead of pulling away, as he half expected, Colette dipped her head so that it rested against his shoulder. Philippe stayed very still, not wanting to frighten her with any sudden movement. To his own surprise, his heart was pounding as if he were a youth! He, who had bedded half the women at the Court at Versailles, was actually nervous with this young lady that once he would have eaten for breakfast and never thought about again.

The wind was blowing harder now. Leaning forward, he brushed back a tendril of her hair which had escaped. He ached to kiss her. Those lips were so ripe and lush. He leaned down and gently touched her lips with his. She did not pull away. Carefully his lips sought out hers, and she sat, still as stone, receiving without returning his offering. Turning toward her, he brought his arms slowly around her, encircling her slight frame in his powerful embrace. She fell back against him, closing her eyes, still offering up her little face.

Emboldened, he pressed her lips with his tongue, offering a lover's kiss. She parted her lips slightly, but when his tongue met hers, with a little cry Colette pulled away, as if his mouth had burned hers. Turning her head, she jumped up and said she wanted to go back to the castle. She offered no explanation, but her eyes were imploring.

Philippe sighed, and cursed himself for rushing her. More roughly than he had meant, he shouted to his servants to pack their things at once and take the Lady Colette home. He himself strode off in the opposite direction, disappearing along the shoreline as Colette was driven away alone.

* * * * *

How she cursed herself for rebuffing his kiss! She hadn't meant to, but as his tongue touched her mouth, the image of Albert, heavy and sweating on top of her, forcing her mouth open to his fetid tongue and rotting teeth, had flashed across her mind's eye so vividly she had smelled his stink for a moment, tasted the bile of her own fear and loathing.

For the thousandth time she relived the rape, the brutal crushing of her sex with his heavy turgid organ, invading her most private self, wrenching screams from her at the pain of the onslaught. She bit her knuckle and shook her head, desperate to cast these images from her brain. And dear Philippe! The one man whom she so admired and adored — she had rejected him! She had seen the anger in the tightness of his shoulders as he ordered her carriage and sent her away alone.

What had she done? And yet, what choice had she? Against her will, his kiss had somehow transmuted into the rapist's bite. She felt powerless against a memory that was still stronger than the possibility of a lover's kiss. She was ruined! She was no longer fit for any man; she would spend her days alone, bitter and without hope.

Brigitte found her mistress crying in her bed, though it was only afternoon. "Please, my lady, don't cry. What is the matter? You can tell me." She poured a cup of cool water from the pitcher at Colette's bedside. Helping her mistress to sit up, she offered her the cup, and a scented handkerchief to dry her eyes.

At length Colette confided in her maid, how Philippe had tried to kiss her, and she had spurned his advances. Brigitte nodded and sighed. "There's no hope for us, I'm afraid," the little maid offered fatalistically. "We're fallen women, my lady. No man will want us now."

Colette stared at her maid. Was this really true? Were they doomed because of one horrible event to never marry, never have children? Surely not. Brigitte's certainty of their shared doom irritated Colette, drawing her out of her own funk in a way no cajoling or pity could have.

"Don't be ridiculous," she shot back. "We haven't fallen anywhere! We've done nothing wrong! I didn't rebuff him because I felt unworthy. It was just a reaction, an instinct. My imagination got the better of me for a moment and I forgot where I was, and who it was whose lips touched mine. You really need to stop all this negative talk of doom, girl! It's quite getting on my nerves! You may consider yourself ruined and a whore, but I am most certainly not!"

She had spoken more sharply than she intended, and Brigitte blushed and bowed her head, jumping from the bed and falling into a deep curtsey. "Begging your pardon, I'm sure, my lady," she whispered, her face scarlet. Backing from the room, she continued to apologize, leaving Colette to feel ashamed.

Poor Brigitte had been through the same ordeal, and had fewer resources to call upon than Colette. She had been unkind and even rude with her last remarks. She would have to make it up to the poor girl. But for now she let her be. She was too tired to go in pursuit and offer comfort.

Sighing deeply, she let her head fall back against the soft pillows and fell into a restless sleep. She began to dream...

In the dream, she and Philippe were sitting again at the shore, watching the waves roll in. Philippe reached over, as he had that afternoon, and kissed her. Instead of resisting, she had let him, and opened her own mouth, entwining her tongue with his, sighing with pleasure, tasting his sweetness.

His mouth moved down from hers, to kiss her neck and her breasts. She was naked suddenly, but not cold, and not at all embarrassed in front of her lover. For lover he surely was, as he suckled a nipple, biting lightly as Lucas had done, wrenching a sweet little moan from her lips. Down her belly he moved; she could feel his mouth, soft and lovely against her flesh, but she kept her eyes closed, reveling in the warm sun that shone down on her.

They were alone. No servants were hovering helpfully nearby. They were completely alone. His mouth found her sex, and she let her thighs fall open, feeling the velvet lick, like a large cat lapping at her secret place, making her swell with pleasure and need. At length, desire coursing through her like liquid fire, she opened her eyes, looking down to see her lover's head.

But it wasn't Philippe at all! It was Brigitte lapping and suckling at her mistress' sex! In horror Colette cried out and tried to push the other woman away. But she held Colette's thighs tightly, gripping her with nails that cut into her flesh, drawing blood. Raising herself over Colette, Brigitte leaned down, pressing her hard body against her, her breath fetid and hot against Colette's cheek.

For Brigitte was no longer Brigitte, but had become Lucas, who grinned his gap-toothed grimace and pressed his cock into her pussy. She struggled, trying to scream, but she had no voice.

Lucas morphed into Albert, who thrust hard into her, splitting her body in two, cleaving her in half, spilling her life's blood. She was dying, and prayed it would come soon. When she woke, she was bathed in sweat and real tears were wet on her face.

* * * * *

Later that evening Colette managed to apologize to Brigitte, who tried to say it was nothing, but they both knew better. Colette decided that Brigitte needed a young man herself. Someone kind and gentle to distract her from their ordeal. Delicately, she tried to find out if there was anyone in Philippe's household who had caught Brigitte's fancy.

"Oh, there's a certain lad," Brigitte confided, smiling shyly. Colette realized she hadn't seen Brigitte smile in quite some time, and it gladdened her heart to see it.

"Go on," she urged, grinning back conspiratorially.

"His name is Adrian," she admitted. "He works in the gardens. He is first assistant to the head gardener, and has great prospect to one day take over the gardens himself! At dinnertime I try to sit next to him, but there's this girl." Her expression clouded. "Bernadette. She is always rushing over to him, bringing him extra little treats from the kitchen, simpering and batting her eyes at him, hanging on his every word. It's enough to make your stomach curdle, it is!" Brigitte's dark eyes flashed, and she tossed her head, looking quite beautiful herself in her anger.

"And this Adrian, does he return her attentions?"

"I can't be sure. He doesn't seem to be especially taken with her, but perhaps that's only my own wishful thinking."

"Well, we must come up with a plan so that he notices *you*! Surely this Bernadette cannot be as lovely as you, with your dark curls and fine skin." Brigitte blushed as Colette continued. "We need to devise a plan. The best way to a man's heart is through his work. If you can take an interest in his work, in gardening, that could be a way to get him to notice you. Then, of course, it will be up to you!" Giggling, they put their heads close together, conspiring good-naturedly.

A few words with Catherine, and Colette was able to give Brigitte the happy news that she would be working in the gardens for the next few days at least. She was to select the flowers for the house vases, a job that Catherine normally did, but was only too happy to hand over to the new girl, though Catherine would still make the floral arrangements, of course. Brigitte was to work directly with Adrian, the junior gardener. What she did with that opportunity would be up to her!

* * * * *

They had just finished afternoon tea, and Aunt Genevieve had retired for her nap. As it was Sunday, Philippe was taking the day off, and so had joined them for tea. Now he and Colette strolled together in the lovely gardens, his arm lightly touching her elbow. She held a little parasol in her other hand, to shade her face from the sun. The little train of her long gown trailed behind her becomingly, its satin and lace pale and lovely against the finely swept walkways between the flowerbeds.

Colette seemed to be lost in a daze, though Philippe had been trying to engage her in conversation for several minutes. He would remark upon something, and she would respond, and then fall silent, not taking up the social cue to offer something new. He looked at her now, her features closed, her eyes not seeing the beautiful foliage all around them. He felt his heart ache for her.

"Come!" he said suddenly. "I have an idea! Let's take a ride, just you and me, to my favorite little stream near the mouth of the River Rance. It's a lovely secret place. My brother and I used to hide there when we needed some peace, or when we were up to mischief!" He smiled a roguish smile, and Colette found herself smiling back despite her melancholy mood.

First she had to change out of her finery, with all its many skirts and layers, which would have been crushed and ruined in the saddle. With Brigitte's help, she put on something less elaborate and went to find Philippe, who was waiting for her in the front hall. Together they made their way to the stables, where Philippe himself helped to hoist Lady Colette onto a docile mare. Then he leapt astride his own horse and they cantered together along a shady wooded path.

Colette loved the freedom of being on a horse, though she was constrained by her clothing and her sex, being force to ride with her legs dangling on one side of the horse. At home she had sometimes donned a man's pantaloons and ridden in secret with her brother, but when caught she had been beaten by a father who didn't believe girls should be on horses at all, and indeed, this was the prevailing sentiment.

Now she rode alongside Philippe, feeling her spirits rise despite herself. When at last he stopped she gasped with pleasure. They had come to a little clearing in the wood. The sound of a waterfall rushing and tumbling over rocks smooth and shiny met her ears. She saw the little falls, splashing and frothing into a large round pool. High weeds and wild flowers grew all around it. The effect was enchanting. "Oh, we're in the middle of a fairy story!" she said, clasping her hands in front of her.

Philippe smiled, pleased that she liked his secret place. He would come here alone sometimes to think, or to sketch out new ideas and building plans on a large pad with a stick of charcoal. He had never brought another person here since his brother had died, and had never expected to. But somehow it had seemed right to bring Colette. The place was soothing, and perhaps it would give her some solace; solace that he didn't seem able to provide.

Leaping from his horse, he helped her down, and then tied the horses loosely to a tree, near to the water so they could take their fill if they wished. They stood in sweet grasses and Colette's mare lowered her long neck gracefully and took a little bite.

Philippe spread out a large blanket and placed the basket his servant had packed for them. Inside were sweetmeats and little cakes, and the ever-present bottles of wine. "I shall turn into a huge fat thing here! It seems we do nothing but eat!" Colette exclaimed. Philippe laughed, and they sat together on the blanket.

"I haven't been here in a long time," Philippe remarked quietly, gazing at the little rushing falls. "Jacques and I used to come all the time when we were lads."

"Tell me about him? That is, if it isn't too painful," Colette stopped, worried now she had overstepped.

But Philippe seemed glad of the chance to talk about his little brother. He told of how they would slip away, tired of the constant training and lessons, tired of the Latin and mathematics, the fencing and riding lessons, just wanting to be little boys and take a swim in the little pool, without servants or instructors critiquing their every move. "We would escape. They never found out where we went, either, because we were careful. This was our secret place, just for us, and when he died," Philippe stopped, and bit his lip. He never spoke of Jacques, had been certain he'd put it all behind him, but now felt himself vulnerable and sad. How he missed his brother!

"What happened to him, Philippe? Tell me." Colette's voice was tender, and she touched his arm, her eyes entreating him to relieve the burden of his obvious suffering.

He looked at her, at the warmth and compassion in her face, and said, "He was captain of our finest ship. He had always loved the sea, and everything to do with the water and with adventures on the seas. At last he had his own command at the young age of twenty-two, and I, a year older, was very proud of him."

"You didn't share his love of the sea?"

"No, not in the same way. Much to our father's disgust, I would rather design buildings, and draw pictures than build ships and sail in them. He saw no point in what I did, and never appreciated the beauty of line and space, unless it had to do with ships, same as my brother. It's in the de Valon blood, I suppose. I just missed that particular passion somehow. I do my duty by the shipyard, now that they are both gone, but that's all it is, a duty."

He sighed, and Colette said, "But Jacques. He loved the sea?"

"Yes, and this was his first voyage as full captain. He was on a trade mission for the King, and they were returning from a successful trip abroad when the ship was lost."

"Lost?"

"Lost at sea. There was a terrible storm, and the ship never returned. I still dream sometimes at night that he has come back. That they were shipwrecked somewhere on an island, and had managed to make their way back at last. I see him climbing out of the sea, my little brother, and coming home. But it's been three years, and never a word. My hope diminishes a little each day." He stopped speaking, staring into the pool, as if his brother would somehow appear there. There were tears in his eyes and he sighed.

Brushing a hand across his brow he tried to smile at Colette. "Well!" he said, a little too brightly. "See what you've done! I never discuss that with anyone. Let the living get on with it, I always say!" He was quiet a few moments, busying himself with pouring more wine for each of them.

Turning to Colette he now said, "I must tell you, my lady. I feel as if a burden's been lifted! Just in sharing it with you. Saying it out loud, somehow it's relieved the pain a bit. I never admitted to anyone that a part of me still waits for him. I know it's silly."

"Not at all!" Colette assured him.

"Now you see, dear," he ventured. "What I've been telling you is true. When you share your burdens, they are lessened. You must confide in me, or in someone. And since there seems to be no one else, let it be me. You can trust me, Colette. Unburden your heart and then put it to rest. Don't let those vagabonds keep a hold on you. Send them away, I beg of you."

Colette sighed. But she realized she did want to talk about it. Anything to send away the nightmares that came relentlessly, night after night. And Philippe was so kind and easy to talk to. Haltingly she began to tell him what had happened. She told him about the abduction, and the journey by horseback with her hands tied. She told him about the brutal rape, and how Lucas had kept them captive and forced himself upon them, keeping them tied up when he wasn't having his way with them. She told him how Lucas had died, collapsing on her like some horrid animal, his member still buried inside of her.

What she didn't admit, found herself too shy and humiliated to confess, was what he had forced her to do to Brigitte, and, what she barely admitted to herself, that she had in some ways enjoyed. She didn't tell him about Lucas' mouth upon her sex, and the feelings he wrested from her, or her own kisses on her maid's sex, and the response she in turn had elicited. These were not things she could share, not with anyone.

As she spoke, haltingly at first, and then in a rush, Philippe took her head in his lap. He released the many pins that held her hair and stroked her face gently, saying nothing, but just offering his silent support. The words tumbled out of her, and sometimes she cried while she spoke, but he would only soothe her, and tell her to go on, to get it all out and be done with it.

And when finally she stopped, the sun was at a lower angle, and she was lying down, completely at rest, almost asleep. Slowly Philippe bent down and lightly kissed her lips. He pulled back, not wanting to startle her, though the sight of her, her long blonde hair spread about her on his lap, her long-lashed eyes closed against soft pale cheeks, made him desire her keenly. Instead he sat, staring out at the pond, letting the poor girl take what rest she could. He would make it better somehow, that he promised to himself.

* * * * *

Philippe had to leave for a few days on business, and Colette found that she didn't want him to go. He had been right, to finally talk about the horrible events of the kidnapping had released something that had been tightly wound inside of her, and she felt giddy, released somehow. They spent every possible minute together, and even Aunt Genevieve had commented. "I must say, my dear, I've never seen our Philippe so taken with a lady! He isn't one to waste too much time on any one girl, you see. Though probably this is just a phase, and he'll soon tire of you, as he does of all the rest."

Colette tried to ignore the old woman's callous words, but secretly was afraid that they were true. Her worst fears were confirmed the next morning when she overheard Philippe and his aunt in her drawing room. He had come to say goodbye, just as Colette was coming in for her morning visit with the old woman. She stopped outside the door, pausing as she heard her own name.

"I tell you, Philippe, what you are doing is not right. Leading on a young girl who has no prospect any longer of finding a man who will take her. Not one who knows what happened to her, at any rate. For God's sake, she's damaged goods! No, I know it wasn't her fault, but she is no longer pure and can never hope to be a nobleman's wife. Your keeping her here, spending all that time with her, taking her for walks and picnics, is keeping her ridiculous hopes up. I know women, and she is smitten with you, mark my words. Do the noble thing, and send her home to papa. You'll soon be back at Court anyway, and you know you won't have the time of day for her then. The latest marquise or princess will turn your fickle head and you'll be off and running."

Colette herself had turned then and run, not waiting to hear Philippe's response, too terrified to have him confirm what his aunt had so brutally laid out. Hiding in her room, she cried bitterly, refusing Brigitte's attempts to calm her. "Tell them I'm sick. I don't want to come to luncheon. Tell them to eat without me."

She had calmed down later that day. After all, what Aunt Genevieve had said was nothing she herself hadn't been saying to herself for weeks now. She was "damaged goods" and he knew all about it! A lord such as himself would never want a girl like her, even if she did come from nobility. Not that he'd said a word about anything like some kind of liaison! Why, he'd never even said he'd loved her, though sometimes she thought she saw something in his face…

But that was ridiculous. She had no dowry, no prospects, she was a "fallen woman" though not by her own design, and Philippe was one of the most sought after men in the kingdom. To even entertain for a moment that he might want her, it was absurd! And yet, if he didn't, what was she doing here? Aunt Genevieve was right!

How long did he plan to keep her here? She was going to be nineteen soon, and it was high time she were married, if that were in the cards. And please, let it be, or she would be doomed to be this old woman's companion until she was past the age when a man would want her!

She had always been a rather docile girl, obeying her father, even to the point of leaving her own home when he "lost" her in cards. She had obeyed Philippe in coming to stay at his household. Perhaps enduring the horrors she had at the hands of the villains had somehow given her courage. Now it was going on a month that she'd been here, and she simply had to stand up for herself, or at least to gain an understanding of his intentions. She would ask to be released, to return to her father's castle. At least there, her father could arrange some kind of marriage, so that she could have her own home, and perhaps a family.

When he returned, she would speak to him! She felt resolute, confident, determined! But a moment later, inexplicably, she burst into tears.

She had bided her time, waiting for the next opportunity when they could be alone together. Philippe had been busy for several nights, entertaining men from his shipping business. While Colette had been included at the meals, she was not invited to join them afterwards as they discussed matters of import that did not concern her.

Finally tonight they were alone again. After another excellent meal, Aunt Genevieve had slowly lumbered to her rooms, and Philippe had offered his arm to Colette, escorting her to his den for a little brandy and conversation.

They chatted idly for a while, as Colette gathered her courage to make her request. Her demand. She could not go on as some undefined presence in his home, some vague companion with no prospects and no idea as to her future. She would ask to be released from his care, and returned to her own home. Whether or not her father would accept her was another matter, but she would deal with that later.

"My lord," she said now, sitting up very straight, unaware of the regal tilt of her chin as she screwed up her courage.

"My lady," he smiled back at her, noting her serious demeanor, her high color, her hands clenching, white knuckled, on the armrests of her chair. She clearly had something important to say, and he mustn't make light of it, though he found her utterly charming and difficult at this moment to take seriously.

"Forgive me, sir, for being so bold. But I cannot go on as we are any longer."

He waited. What was the girl getting at? Wasn't she happy here?

"My lord, I will be nineteen in just a few weeks. I am no longer a child. I am the daughter of the duke, and as such feel it my duty to take my place as a married woman and begin a family of my own."

Good Lord! Was the girl asking him to marry her? Was there ever anything so ridiculous? Surely she was teasing. He smiled and began to speak, but Colette cut him off, not aware of his amusement, as her eyes were staring fixedly at a painting on the wall across from her, so as not to lose her courage.

"Please do not misunderstand me. I appreciate all you have done for me. And I have greatly enjoyed my time with you, sir. You have behaved most graciously in all regards, and my servant and I are most grateful indeed for all you have done. But it is time I returned to my home, and took up my responsibilities, whatever my father may think.

"To be perfectly blunt, I am asking for your release from my father's promise. I am asking that you send me home." Her eyes were blazing and tears brimmed now, unspilled. As bravely as she had spoken, her heart was cleaving in two as she realized she was asking to never see this darling man again; to be sent hundreds of miles away from him, and back to the mercy of a father who had made it clear she was no longer welcome.

How she would miss Philippe! And yet, Aunt Genevieve was surely right. He would never marry her, not in a thousand years. He would choose someone unsullied to be his bride, and have his children. Not she; her destiny lay elsewhere.

"Colette! But why? Have we offended you in some way; have I?"

"Please, my lord, don't make this more difficult than it has to be. I know how you feel about me. I know I am 'damaged goods'. I know you are soon to return to Court, and the last thing you need is a young woman hanging about your neck. And yet, I will not be left here with your old aunt to wither and languish. I pray you do not take offense at my words, but I am still young, sir, however sullied in your eyes and the eyes of the world, and I mean to take my place in society, if I can."

Philippe sat stunned, slowly absorbing what she had said. "And what is all this talk of being 'sullied' and 'damaged goods'? When did I ever, for a second, give you the impression that was what I thought?"

"You are too kind to be so blunt about your true feelings, but I overheard you and Aunt Genevieve. I know your true feelings, so please save us both the humiliation of denying them."

"You speak with a bold tongue, my lady," Philippe said, his face darkening. "But before you decide you know my *true feelings*, perhaps it would behoove you to ask me. Think back, if you will, to when you eavesdropped on the conversation to which you must be referring." Colette colored and looked away, but still sat erect and determined.

His voice was hard, almost angry. "If you'll recall, my lady, you did not hear me utter a word against you. Perhaps you did not hear the second part of the conversation, and so I shall I repeat it for you now. I told my dear aunt in no uncertain terms that I liked having you here, and had no intention of packing you off to your father. Furthermore, I have no plans to return to Court, unless the King demands it. I believe that part of my life is played now; I've lost the desire to attend endless rounds of parties, to play cards until dawn, to drink until I pass out and find myself in someone else's wife's bedchamber. No. What I want is right here. I have my work, and the shipyard, and my gardens, and most importantly," he paused, and almost whispered, "you."

Colette said nothing, but stared at him with eyes wide and round, the pupils dilated. A spot of color appeared high on each cheekbone. "I don't understand."

"I have come to enjoy your company. I had hoped you felt the same way. Indeed, I can't quite imagine what life was like before you stumbled into mine, due to your father's foolish wagers and misplaced honor. I know it is selfish of me, but I don't want to let you go." Something clarified inside Philippe's heart as he spoke, and though he hadn't planned to say this next thing, he realized as he said it that it was what he wanted more than anything in the world.

Standing slowly, he knelt in front of the confused girl and took one of her slender hands in his. "Lady Colette, if you would have me, I am asking for your hand. I want you to be my wife."

Chapter Five

The world seemed to slow down suddenly. Colette found she couldn't seem to catch her breath. She saw Philippe's kind face, now smiling gently at her, and she believed he was in earnest. But how could it be? He couldn't possibly want her, as she was no longer a virgin, and he more than anyone alive, other than Brigitte, knew the gory details.

"I don't understand," she said again, her own voice distant in her ears. She really felt most odd! As if she would faint. If only she could catch her breath, fill her lungs, clear her head.

Still kneeling, her small hand in his, he said softly, "I love you, Colette. I didn't realize quite how much until you faced me with that extraordinary proposition to be sent away! You really are quite remarkable."

"How can you want me?" Her voice was small, like a child's. "You know what happened. You know what I am! Or more precisely, what I am not!"

He laughed gently, and said, "Your concern stems from the fact you are no longer a virgin? Please, my darling, you must believe me that that means less than nothing to me! You were perhaps the last virgin left at Court, dear lady! Please, I don't take stock in such absurdities! I love you because of what and who you are, not because I harbor some fantasy that you have never lain with a man!

"Please, I know, it was not of your choice, but even if it had been, it means nothing to me. Why should men be permitted to have sex with whomever they please, but women be expected to stay as innocent as little girls? It doesn't even make sense!

"Not only that," he went on, perhaps hoping further to persuade her. "In your heart you are still a virgin, as far as I can see. It isn't just the claiming of a woman's body by a man; it must involve her spirit, her soul. What you gave to those rapists wasn't given freely. They stole it. They violated your body and your trust. It had nothing to do with your soul, which remains intact. It is your soul and your heart that I hope to reach. I love you, Colette. And I will make up to you what those men wrested from you. At least, I would try, if you would have me. I would try with all my heart."

Colette sat silent, her face pensive. She looked so young; so vulnerable, that Philippe knew he was rushing her. He had to rein in his own ridiculous desires. She was still a girl. Taking a deep breath, speaking softly and gently, Philippe said, "Just tell me this, and speak honestly. I will respect your decision and not try to sway you, if your heart is set on leaving. But first answer me this. Do you return my feelings in any way?"

Now it was he who looked young and vulnerable, waiting for this girl to render her verdict. "Oh, Philippe," she whispered. "If you had any idea." She bit her lip, as if afraid to speak. Philippe squeezed her hands gently and urged her with his eyes to continue. Gathering her courage, Colette continued, "I have loved you from the moment you first kissed me, in what seems a lifetime ago, when we were still at Court. If only I still possessed the easy innocence I had then; the joy of living that I seem to have lost…"

"Oh, Colette!" Philippe interjected, and then paused, trying to think how best to phrase what he had to say to reach this girl, without offending her. "This may sound odd, but in fact, I must tell you, though you were a charming and lovely young girl, I doubt if you could have captured my heart so thoroughly if you had never been through the torments that you have. I know this sounds strange, but somehow they seem to have forged something stronger in you. To have improved your mettle. Instead of breaking, as many would have, you are stronger and as a result, all the more desirable to me. Please believe me. If you become my wife, I will help you to wipe away the sadness, and the memories, and we will forge new memories together."

Colette did not answer, but closed her eyes, leaning her face close to his, a silent offering. This time when he dared to touch her lips with his, she didn't pull away. At first she sat still, like a stone goddess, and let him touch those soft lips. He kissed her chastely, though his own heat was rising as her feminine scent aroused him. Still, they stayed this way for many moments, bodies touching only at the lips. Philippe put a hand on her silky hair, his fingers gentle on her head, as if he were taming a wild mare.

She didn't pull away, but stayed still, her eyes closed, her head tilted up toward his, but the offering was unclear. Knowing he was taking a risk, he kissed her more ardently, pressing against her mouth, forcing her to part her lips, just a little, yearning for her yielding.

He had been more than half afraid of another rebuff, but, to his surprise and delight, she did yield, receiving his tongue with her own, letting her head fall back slightly, but not resisting when his mouth followed hers. She was leaning back against the silk cushions, and as he pressed forward she had nowhere to move. He waited for her to sidle out from beneath him, and he would have made no move to stop her. He had vowed he would earn her trust, the trust that had been so brutally destroyed by the kidnappers, and he would stand by that vow, however long it took.

But she only sighed slightly, and kept her eyes closed, and her body still, as if pretending that nothing was happening. Well, he supposed, it was better than an all-out resistance, and he wanted her, whatever he could have of her at this moment. And so he leaned forward as she fell back, and he felt her breasts, firm and sweet, pressed against his chest. His cock responded by expanding in his breeches, and he shifted, moving so that it met with her thigh.

Colette opened her eyes then, no doubt aware of the rock-hard erection poking against her leg. He pulled back, again afraid he was rushing her, but she reached out to him with her slender arms, and drew him back into the kiss.

"Colette, my love," he murmured, the fever of his desire urging him on. Now he took her into his arms and kissed her mouth, her throat, the curve of her delicate collarbone. He wanted her so fiercely he was suddenly afraid he was going to lose his reason and take her as those wretched men had done, without her permission or consent.

And so he pulled away, abruptly. Colette's eyes opened again and her expression was questioning. She clearly wanted the kiss to continue. "I'm sorry, my lady," Philippe said, his voice hoarse with the effort of control. "I cannot continue in this vein and promise you protection from my desire. I want you too much."

"Oh, Philippe!" Colette cried, her voice small and sad. "I want you too! But I too am afraid..." She trailed off, and he stood, breathing deeply, smoothing his shirt down and passing his hand over his face. She had not said yes, but she had not said no.

"Colette, you must take all the time you need. I have never wanted another woman as I desire you. I will wait a thousand years for you, my love. And now, you must sleep. The hour is late and we have tarried longer than we meant. Sleep, and in the morning perhaps things will seem brighter."

She looked as if she would protest, but then fell silent, and he left her, not looking back, closing the door softly but firmly behind him.

* * * * *

In his own bed, he mused at how this girl had captured his heart. He had been infatuated before, many times. And as with many men, he knew that the hunt was sometimes more what he sought than the actual prize. Most women at Court had eagerly spread their legs for him, and he was delighted to accommodate, taking the cheap thrill they offered, but never for a moment fooling himself that they meant anything.

His hand dropped down now to his cock, rising again as he remembered Colette's sweet breasts pressed briefly against him.

He recalled another girl, a shy girl also of tender years, named Yvette. She was married to a much older man; the marriage was a political alliance, and they had no interest in one another at all. The husband was no longer sexually active, and had not even consummated the marriage. It was rumored that even when the blood had run young in his veins, it was boys not girls that he sought for his pleasure.

So the husband had turned a blind eye when Philippe had flirted with his young wife at parties, and Philippe had enjoyed making the sweet young thing smile and blush at his attentions.

For many weeks she would let him kiss her, but never anything more. Instead, she would run from him, laughing, to the safety of her women friends and servants, leaving him frustrated but not surprised, night after night. There were many other women waiting to comfort him in their sympathetic arms, and he was not then one to suffer alone.

He hadn't intended to take it any further, but opportunity and desire had combined to present him with the chance to deflower the shy little virgin, and, cad that he was at the time (he was twenty-two and still quite full of himself as newfound favorite of the King), he had seized the chance.

Yvette was waiting in her quarters, having sent a perfumed note hidden in a fan to her paramour. Most of the Court was attending a huge outdoor party under tents that the King had had erected to celebrate some new victory in his constant warring. Philippe had begged off, pretending illness, and had stolen away to meet with little Yvette.

For the first time she was alone, having sent all her servants and companions to the party. She was ready at last to succumb to Philippe's often offered charms. He still remembered her soft flesh, and her small hard breasts. She hadn't dared to undress fully, as that would acquire assistance, both in the disrobing and redressing afterwards. All the layers of fabric, the bone stays and ribbons were daunting to a young man, and he had contented himself with pulling her little breasts from their low-cut covering, and lifting her wide skirts to find the sweetness hidden beneath them.

Her face had been obscured by her finery, but Philippe didn't care. He wasn't interested in her face. He ignored her weak protestations as his fingers found and pulled at her underclothing, his fingers trembling with haste lest someone return from the party and find them thus.

It was as much the thrill of taking the forbidden, as the fact that it was Yvette lying now beneath him that spurred him on. He would have her; he must have her! If her husband could not do the job, he would do it for him, by God.

At first he had been careful, not wanting to hurt her. Normally he avoided virgins, as they were uncooperative and could be messy. He didn't like to spill their blood, even if that were the natural course of things. It frightened him to hurt a woman.

And yet, as she lay there, so pale and willing, with her finery spread around her, her bare sex offered up like some kind of sacrifice, he was moved by a compulsion he didn't entirely understand. It was lust at work, pure and simple. Love had never even entered the equation, and wouldn't have occurred to either of them.

He had been careful, but insistent, as he pressed past her hymen and claimed her in the most primal of ways. Yvette had been passive, barely moving underneath him, only emitting a little cry of pain as he entered her. He had pushed aside the garments then, seeking out her face, trying to kiss her, hoping to elicit more of a response, but she lay still and quiet, averting her face, as if instead of pleasure, she was suffering.

Her reaction had deflated him, and he withdrew from her, not having ejaculated. He wasn't used to a woman who didn't respond, and her passivity wilted his manhood. He pulled out of her, and pulled up his breeches. Still she lay like some broken doll, her clothing framing her nakedness.

Gently he pulled up her stockings, and smoothed down her many layered skirts. She sat up, confused, but did not seem distressed. Perhaps she, in her innocence, assumed that it was over and that was that. He didn't disabuse her of this notion.

Instead he smoothed her hair, and told her she was lovely. She smiled at this, but her eyes were flat, as if somehow she had vacated the premises.

Philippe, wishing he were gone, had instead stayed for a while, and talked quietly to her, realizing that suddenly he felt no more than brotherly feelings for her. Was it only the hunt that he had craved? For once he had got her, he had realized there was little there, little between them to sustain further passion or even interest. Yvette was lovely certainly, but statues and works of art were also lovely.

Philippe had found to his own dawning surprise that he wanted something more with a woman. A more tangible connection. Something that lasted beyond the stolen embraces and secret kisses that he had thought, until then, the height of adventure. And yet his work, and his own succumbing to the constant temptations of Court, had made him forget that desire for a connection, or at least put it aside. Until now.

It had taken a simple girl from the country to remind him of what was worth having in this world. She had slipped into his heart and awakened his higher sensibilities. Now he wished to claim her, in all respects. And yet, there lingered a little fear.

If and when she finally came to his bed, would his interest flicker and die, a fickle flame of desire snuffed out by the very spark that had initiated it? Surely not.

Colette was different. She was no cynical sophisticate, but neither was she an innocent and bland naïf. She had her own thoughts and ideas. She was willful and independent.

She had been brutally abducted and raped, and had not only survived, but escaped and found her way to him unscathed! At only eighteen, she had more life and vitality than any woman at Court he could compare her to. She was open to new ideas and receptive and eager to discuss them, without just mimicking his opinions back to him.

In other words, he wasn't just attracted to her obvious beauty. And he didn't only love her. He actually liked her! As a friend and an equal. This was something so new to him that he realized he had never expected to find such a thing with a woman. He had been raised to believe that women could not think as men could, and would always have to be shielded and led. Yet this woman had been through a more difficult ordeal than most men would be called upon to handle, and she was still full of fire and life!

And yet she didn't act like a man. Far from it. She was as feminine as any beauty at the Court. Her skin was as soft as the finest silk, and her hair was thick and lustrous, glowing with honey highlights in the summer sun. Her form was long and slender, but her breasts curved in an alluring offering, like ripe exotic fruit. How he longed for her!

What would make her feel safe? How could he possess her, and know he would never lose her? But perhaps theirs was a universal condition, only brought into sharper relief by the fact of her abduction. No man could make a woman feel totally safe, or protect her from all danger, or be assured that her love for him would never stray. Just a glance around the Court at Versailles would convince anyone of that.

Yet he could try. He could behave with honor and not betray her love, as so many of the men and women did in fashionable society, without it meaning a thing to any of those involved. He felt shame for the first time at how wild he had run among the eager and willing ladies at Court. But now things would be different.

If she would have him.

If Lady Colette Rousseau of the House of Lyon would accept his offer, he would immediately ready a messenger for the Duke Rousseau. For he would still have to grant his permission as her father, and certain legal and economic arrangements would have to be made. Philippe had a feeling

Claire Thompson

that when the messenger came, not only with the request of her hand, but with assurances that no dowry was required, and also with attendant lavish gifts of horses and bolts of fine silks and precious jewels, the good Duke could easily be persuaded to part legally with that which he had been so eager to wager away over a game of cards.

Still, he didn't want her unless she herself was a willing bride. Not daring to feel hopeful, Philippe drank a large goblet of strong wine and willed himself to fall asleep and suffer no dreams.

Colette was not at breakfast that morning, and Philippe passed an anxious hour with his aunt, not hearing her constant prattle, and not tasting the food that was presented before him. As soon as he could politely depart, he hastened to Colette's outer chamber and knocked on the door. It was opened by Brigitte, who curtseyed deeply and bid him good morning.

"Yes, yes," he said impatiently. "And where is your mistress this morning? Is she ill? We missed her at breakfast."

"Yes, sir, she is ill," Brigitte answered, as Colette had instructed her in the event she was missed. "I had her tea brought up, sir, as she is feeling poorly."

"Hmm," Philippe grunted, annoyed that he was being prevented from seeing her; from demanding a response to his proposal. Normally a patient man, he found himself desperately on edge. He had to know, whether it was yes or no, he needed an answer. And yet, how could he demand anything from his guest, who claimed to be indisposed? She had put him in a frustrating situation, damn her! He was not used to being kept waiting by a woman. His voice was rougher than he intended as he finally said, "Well, give her my regards. Tell her if she is not better by dinner I shall call in the doctor to apply leeches. Probably needs her blood thinned."

As he left, shutting the door just softly enough not to be considered a slam, Colette peeked out from her bedroom. Her hair was still down, rolling in thick waves of gold over her shoulders, but her face was pale, and there were smudges of worry and fatigue under her eyes. She'd spent a restless night, tossing and turning, and finally waking Brigitte to discuss the situation.

Now she asked, "Is he gone?" As Brigitte nodded, Colette said, "Good. I know I can't avoid him forever, but I don't know what to do!"

"Begging your pardon, my lady, but to me it's clear as day! Knowing how you feel about him, why hesitate? I should be beside myself with delight if a fancy lord like Lord Philippe wanted me! Even if he were an old toad, anyone would consider it a fortunate match! But he's not! He's young and handsome, and he's smart too! Look at those fine buildings he's designed. And the King himself thinks highly of him! And he's rich! His title may not be as important as your father's, but I'd wager his coffers are a good deal fuller! Begging your pardon, my lady."

Brigitte blushed, knowing she had overstepped her station, even if they had an altered relationship due to their shared plight. What she didn't add, but was on the edge of her ardent speech in favor of the proposed marriage, was her own budding relationship with the junior gardener, Adrian. Colette's little plot to place Brigitte in the way of the young man had worked beautifully, and he had asked her to dance three times in a row at the little village summer's eve celebration several nights before. And because Brigitte was essentially Colette's indentured servant, with no means to support herself or find other employ, it was understood that she would be leaving St. Malo along with Colette, should that come to pass. Thus her interest in her mistress' well-being was not entirely altruistic.

"I wish it were so simple, Brigitte. But I am afraid Philippe is only acting out of frustrated desire at the moment. He is used to having his way with women, you see. And I suppose I have confounded him by resisting, though my resistance is not born of a desire to be the coquette, but because I am truly afraid. I want to receive his kiss, but the horrible leer of that old man intervenes, poisoning my pleasure. I want to feel his sweet hand touching me, and yet the rough paw of that monster, that Albert, still weighs heavily on me, turning Philippe from someone kind and loving to something dangerous and evil, only by virtue of his sex.

"So he is confronted with a woman who resists him. How do I know that he won't tire of me the moment he 'gets' me? I don't only want a liaison with a 'proper husband', though that is important to me. I have come to love Philippe, and the thought of him having to 'settle' for me, once the bloom is off the rose, as it were, once he 'claims' me with his body and his rights as a husband, why that would break my heart clean in two."

Brigitte did not respond, not knowing what to say. She had her own demons to wrestle with, and Adrian had yet to kiss her. But she was a simple girl, less given to introspection. She hadn't the luxury of refusal that Colette had. If Adrian were to ask for her hand, he would have it in a heartbeat, whatever her secret misgivings might be. Of course she voiced nothing of this. Instead she poured a cup of hot tea for her mistress, and straightened her pillows for her. "Come and rest a bit, my lady. Perhaps this will sort itself out, and you won't have to decide. For now, put it aside and take some rest. We don't want that old leech being sent in! Ugh!"

Colette smiled wanly and let herself be led back to bed.

She did join Philippe and his aunt for dinner. They were also joined by several of Philippe's business associates, and there was no opportunity for the two to see each other alone that evening, for which Colette was grateful. She managed to escape to bed without having to speak a word directly to Philippe, though if eyes could burn, his would have burned holes right through her.

* * * * *

Things were not so grim for little Brigitte. With less imagination and less of a penchant for brooding than Colette, good-natured Brigitte was recovering more quickly than her mistress. Her own dire predictions about their being "fallen women" with no hopes of finding mates had been fading steadily as she became more and more enamored of young master Adrian. Perhaps she would never have to tell him? She buried the niggling worry; she was too busy to think about it now!

And tonight, he had invited her for a walk! It didn't necessarily mean anything more than that, a friendly walk. Still, she hadn't forgotten his hand upon hers as they had shared a dance. Adrian was not a tall man, nothing like the towering Philippe. He was more in line with Brigitte, stocky and solidly built. She'd wager he could lift the Lord Philippe and hurl him a ways! The image made her smile—the little junior gardener tossing the fine lord like he was a bale of hay!

Catherine was aware of Brigitte's crush. She approved, as she believed married servants made better servants, as they weren't wasting all that energy on courting and breaking each other's hearts. And it was time Adrian settled down. She smiled, thinking of him. Ever since he'd appeared, a bedraggled little serf with no parents and nothing to his name, Catherine had had a special place in her heart for the boy. And he was an excellent gardener. He could coax flowers out of rocks.

Catherine had been scandalized and horrified by the casual dalliances at Court, not the least of which were conducted by her master, Lord Philippe. But, she reasoned to herself, those of noble lineage had naught in common with us peasant folk.

We are the backbone of the world, she told herself, and rightly so. We don't have the luxury of bedding every dandy or wench who catches our fancy. Catherine herself was a widow, but before her husband had died, he had given her two fine daughters and a son. If they hadn't been precisely in love, they had been good partners for one another, and she missed him every day of her life.

She found she quite liked little Brigitte, a spunky but well-mannered girl. She even had a talent with those flowers, and Catherine had begun to show her how to make artful arrangements. Brigitte had a good eye, and learned quickly.

So Catherine was happy to help Brigitte make herself especially attractive for her "walk" with Adrian. He was a good lad, and between Catherine and the wall, she was just as glad he hadn't been swayed by the sassy Bernadette. Young Bernadette needed a tougher man than Adrian to take her in hand. And she was young, not yet sixteen. Her time would come.

Now Catherine, several pins in her mouth, was pulling and braiding Brigitte's pretty dark hair this way and that. She'd been at a while and Brigitte was growing impatient. She wasn't used to anyone else spending time on her! That was her job with the lovely Colette. Brigitte enjoyed playing with Colette's lustrous gold hair, so different from her own curly black hair. She was always telling Colette, "Please, my lady. Just a little longer. If you could just sit still!" Now she shook her own head with impatience and said, "Please, isn't it done yet? He'll be all finished with the walk and I won't have even got there!"

Catherine laughed and stood back. "Very well, my dear. Here, have a look in this glass and tell me what you think?"

Brigitte took the little mirror and held it out. "Oh my," she breathed. She barely recognized herself. Instead of the girl with the unruly curls, here was a young woman, her hair elaborately styled in the fashion of the day, and piled high upon her head. "It's lovely! Thank you! But I shall be afraid to move!"

"Oh don't worry. I put so many pins in there we'll be lucky to get them all out in time for breakfast tomorrow! Now turn around, let me see your gown and make sure everything is in place."

Brigitte slowly pirouetted, feeling very glamorous in the new gown Philippe had had made for her, in honor of their safe return. It was a dark crimson velvet, the color of which reflected onto her cheeks and contrasted prettily with her dark hair and eyes.

Adrian seemed very pleased to see her, though they had only just seen each other earlier in the day, in the gardens. Then he'd been dressed in his leather work clothes. Now he was outfitted in soft dark pantaloons, his Sunday best, and his hair was combed back and looked to be recently washed.

"Don't you look that lovely," he said, and Brigitte blushed, very pleased. He smiled shyly and handed her a little sprig of flowers. She took them, smiling shyly back at him in turn, and they set off on their little spin around the grounds.

The evening was warm and pleasant, and stars were just poking through the darkening fabric of a new night's sky. At first they just walked side by side, but eventually Adrian dared to take Brigitte's hand. He led her to a secluded spot, where a little gazebo had been erected. Little red and white flowers were growing up along the trestles, and their scent was light and sweet.

He led her up the steps and together they sat, side by side, on the little bench there. "I love to come here," he told her, and Brigitte could see why. It was a lovely little spot, surrounded by expanses of velvet green and little plots of flowers, probably planted by Adrian himself.

They sat in silence for a while and at length Adrian said, "Brigitte. It's been wonderful getting to know you. I feel as if we've been friends forever. But I have to know. There's been talk, you know, among the other servants."

Oh Lord, she thought. Here it comes. He's going to ask me about the kidnapping, the rape! And I can either lie, and trick him into being with me, or tell the truth, and lose him for sure. She bit her lip, turning from him so he wouldn't see her expression of fear and anxiety.

"Well, they say you might be leaving us soon. Going back to your home. To your mistress' home. I would hate for that to happen, Brigitte. I've grown so fond of you." For a moment Brigitte sat still. Surely she had misunderstood him? But no, he was worried she was leaving!

Brigitte laughed aloud, relief awash over her features. "Why no! At least I don't think so! My lady hasn't said a word of this to me."

"Oh, good!" Adrian smiled happily back at her. "Because to tell you the truth, I can't help falling in love, even if you were to leave tomorrow."

Falling in love! Brigitte looked at the earnest young man. She realized that she, too, was falling in love. Closing her eyes, she leaned her face very close to his, a clear invitation for a kiss. His warm lips met hers, and he took her into his arms.

* * * * *

Surprisingly, it was Madame de Valon who got through to Colette. They were visiting as usual one morning after breakfast. Madame de Valon had asked Colette to play a tune for her. When Colette was done, Madame said, "Now, come over here, dear. We need to talk. Or more precisely, you need to listen."

Colette went to sit near the old woman, having no idea the turn the conversation was going to take. Madame de Valon, direct as usual, said bluntly, "Now what's this nonsense I hear about you refusing my nephew? I knew you were blockheaded, as all young people are, but frankly, I had no idea you were so stupid as well!"

Colette gasped and her hand came to her mouth. Before she even realized she was speaking aloud she retorted, "Well! And what do you know about it?" She flushed as she realized how impertinent her remark was, but Madame de Valon seemed unperturbed.

She snorted back, "I know plenty! My nephew has confided in me since he was a wee lad. He didn't have to tell me something was wrong; the way you two have been moping about the past few days is enough to make anyone want to slap you both to your senses! Well, I asked him outright. Philippe, I said, I'm your aunt, your last living relative. I've taken care of you since before you could toddle. Something's wrong, and I have a horrible feeling it has to do with that girl we've been keeping here. Now, out with it! Is it time we sent her away, I asked. Now, don't go looking at me like that; I'm telling you plainly what I said. As pleasant a companion as you've been for me, I'll not have my boy unhappy!

"At first he tried to lie to me, but I can see right through him. I almost fell out of my chair when he said he'd asked for your hand in marriage! Not that the alliance wouldn't be a good one, mind you, and you are of noble lineage. But you, a fallen woman!" Colette's cheeks darkened to a deep pink, and her eyes were flashing now, her mouth pressed shut with unspoken retorts. Madame de Valon sailed on, indifferent to the effect she was having on the young girl, or perhaps not.

"That's right. A whore! Nothing but a whore, no doubt subjected to all sorts of debauchery and shame. A broken vessel. A used piece of property. What man in his right mind would want someone who has been exposed to God knows what indecencies? Who has perhaps developed a taste for being raped at sword point! In a word, a slut! And not only that, Philippe, I said, but you know yourself. You always think you want some woman, want her desperately, until you get her! Think back, boy, I told him. You like the conquest, the game. You're not any more ready to settle down than the randy stallions we keep in the stables!"

"That's enough!" Colette could no longer hold her tongue. Her face had gone from dark pink to pale, with two spots of red, one on each cheek. Her eyes were preternaturally bright, as if she suffered from a fever. She spoke quietly, but gone was the tremulous obedience of youth that usually marked her tone when speaking to the grand Madame de Valon.

"How *dare* you speak of me, daughter of a duke, as if I were a common tramp! How *dare* you! How dare you imply that I wanted what happened to me! If you knew the nightmares, the unspeakable shame and sorrow I've felt over what's happened. It had nothing to do with me! If you're going to blame someone, blame yourself for not providing me with better protection!"

Colette's voice was raised now, as her rising anger gave her courage, "And Philippe! What do you know of him, either! What we have shared is far sweeter than a simple conquest! We have spent hours just talking about things dear to our hearts. He had no ulterior motive, and has only treated me with the utmost deference and respect! He has assured me again and again that he regards me as pure, no matter what dreadful things were visited upon me. He understands I had no choice, not even death! I was taken against my will, and Philippe says if anything, it's made me stronger! He says he admires my courage in the face of danger, and my willingness to go on when other women might have taken their own lives!

"So what do you have to say to that, you — you old crone!" Realizing what she had said, Colette's hands flew up to her mouth, and she burst into tears. Madame de Valon, far from being outraged and horrified, only smiled. She had accomplished just exactly what she intended. Silly Colette had finally let go of her own fears and self-loathing. Times, Madame de Valon mused to herself, were changing. And if her boy wanted this girl, then by God, he would have her!

Heaving herself slowly to her feet, the old woman shuffled over to Colette and put her arms around her. "There, there," she whispered. "Now everything will fine."

Chapter Six

"Brigitte! Can this be true?" Colette was still in her bedclothes, feeling very lazy in fact, lolling in her bed despite the late morning hour. Brigitte had something important to tell her, but kept hemming and hawing until Colette lost patience and demanded that she just come out with it!

Brigitte had blurted, "It's Adrian, my lady! He's asked me to marry him! And, with your permission of course, I'd like to say yes!"

Colette stared at her little maid. At little Brigitte, who had been her playmate and helpmeet since they were children. If Brigitte were to marry and Colette to return to Lyon, of course she could not now expect Brigitte to return with her. Unless of course Adrian too wanted to return. But what would they be returning to? It wouldn't be fair of her to drag them into exile.

"Oh, Brigitte. Of course you have my permission! And my blessings! How wonderful for you. He seems like such a nice young man. But Brigitte—" she leaned forward, dropping her voice. "Did you tell him? I mean, does he know?"

"Well, he certainly knows about the kidnapping, my lady! I mean, they all know that, of course. And I'm sure he's surmised that we weren't offered tea and cakes for the duration of our stay!" Brigitte bit her lip at her own impertinence and amended, "Begging your pardon, my lady. But, no. I haven't actually talked about the, um, details."

"And he hasn't asked?"

"He's hinted around the edges a bit, but no, not specifically."

"And if he does?"

"Well, I've been doing a lot of thinking, Lady Colette. I've decided to be open with him. Honest. Adrian's an orphan, you know. He understands that life can knock you about a bit. Lord Philippe found him when he was just a little lad. His parents had both died suddenly of the fever, and poor little Adrian was sitting in the dirt outside their hut. They were farmers on a little plot of land that belonged to Lord Philippe's father, and now to Lord Philippe of course. Young Philippe wasn't much older than Adrian. He was out riding when he saw the boy and stopped, thinking it odd that he was alone in the yard with no one around. Usually the peasants always come out to greet the nobility, same as at home.

"When he questioned Adrian, the boy began to cry, saying his maman and papa were dead. Lord Philippe brought him back to the castle and he's worked and lived here ever since!"

"That's quite a story," Colette agreed. "I wish you all the best. But I shall miss you so!"

"But why? Well, granted, I won't be sleeping in your outer chamber anymore, but of course I will tend you, my lady! Adrian will stay as gardener, and I will help dear Catherine, to whom I've grown quite attached! It will be lovely; you shall see."

Colette looked sad, but smiled a little smile. "Yes, it does sound lovely." If she stayed. Colette changed her mind still a hundred times a day. To go or to stay. It was true, she was leaning toward staying, after old Aunt Genevieve had gotten her dander up with her impossibly rude remarks!

And Philippe continued to be kind and attentive, taking her for picnics, and teaching her about some of his work, which she found fascinating. He still stole a kiss from time to time, but did not press her further. Perhaps because of that, she was feeling a little safer to show her own affection.

She liked to watch him when he was working, when he was drawing up building plans in his study. She would sit nearby, pretending to read from his wonderful library, but in fact she was memorizing the perfect planes of his face. The way his nose curved down at the end, the way his lashes touched his cheeks when he was bent over in concentration. His long slender fingers that held the quill or charcoal he used on the lovely thick parchment he worked with.

When she'd told him about Brigitte and Adrian, he'd been delighted. "She is welcome in my household for as long as she lives," he said graciously.

"As are you," he added quietly.

Colette did not respond.

* * * * *

As they were now officially engaged, Brigitte agreed to come to Adrian's hut. He actually had his own little place, on the grounds. He could have lived in the castle itself, in the servants quarters, as most of the unmarried servants did, but Adrian was a solitary sort of fellow, and Philippe hadn't minded at all when he had asked to use extra pieces of lumber and brick to build his own place. In fact, Philippe had helped him work out some of the design, so that the place would hold up well, but still have some pleasing features, like windows placed to catch the sunrise and sunset.

Brigitte and Adrian sat now at his little table, each with a cup of hot sweet tea. Brigitte had brought some fresh tarts from the kitchen and Adrian was happily helping himself to a few of them.

She had been tossing and turning for several nights now, feeling that she must confide in her husband-to-be, *before* they were wed. Saying it aloud to Lady Colette had solidified her position in her own mind. She would not trick Adrian into marriage with someone he *thought* he was getting. He would go in with eyes open, or not at all.

Screwing her courage to the sticking point, Brigitte said, "Adrian. I have something I must tell you."

Adrian, finishing the last of the tarts and licking his fingers, mumbled, his mouth full of pastry and sweet cream, "What is it, Brigitte, my love?"

Brigitte smiled, feeling very nervous indeed, as if she were poised to jump into a cold pond on the first day of spring. But it must be done. Now or never, and so she squeezed her eyes shut and jumped. "When we were kidnapped, Lady Colette and myself, we were raped. I am no virgin." There! She'd said it, the first thing at least.

Adrian smiled gently and put his hand on hers. Brigitte opened one eye, squinting at Adrian to see his reaction. When she saw his kind smile she opened both eyes, though her expression was still tense as she waited for his judgment.

"Well, I figured that, my love. And I'm so very sorry that horrible thing was done to you. You have seemed so brave and sure, that I can't help but admire you all the more, for all you've been through. A lesser woman might have fallen apart, but not my Brigitte!"

"Well, thank you, Adrian. I do appreciate your attitude. But there's, well," she hesitated, now truly nervous, but determined to go on, to tell him the things he hadn't surmised, "there's more."

"More?"

"Yes. I want to tell you everything. I want to share it now, before you are locked in forever with someone who may not be what you thought she was." Adrian stared at her, his face now concerned, confused.

She plunged on, "Certain unnatural things were done to me, and I was forced to do them in return."

"Unnatural? Did they hurt you? Mark you in some permanent way? Is that what you're trying to tell me?"

"No, no. I am not marked. There's no permanent damage as far as I know, except perhaps to my heart, or my soul. No. I will tell you, though I am sore embarrassed to say such things to any person, much less a man! And my betrothed. But I will not have you under false pretenses."

She took a deep breath and continued, certain now that her life hung in the balance. Either he would accept her, or reject her, and the moment of reckoning was at hand. "You see, my lady was forced… Oh, this is so difficult."

"Go on, love. And let me offer you comfort. Please know there is nothing you could say to me that would dissuade me from wishing you for my wife. I am no stranger to bandits and to their cruel ways. You are not the first women to be abducted, if that is of any comfort to you. And you are very, very lucky to be alive."

Brigitte continued, "Well, my lady was forced to put her mouth upon my," her voice sank to a whisper. Adrian had to lean forward to hear her. "Upon my sex, my private place. She was forced to lick and caress me there!" Brigitte could not meet Adrian's eyes, and her skin was suffused with the blood of embarrassment and shame.

Adrian touched her arm, squeezed her consolingly, as Brigitte continued, "And that is not all. I was forced to put my mouth on the organ, the manhood, of one of the men. I was forced to take it into my throat, until its invasion made me retch. There! Now you know it all! You see, such vile things have been done that I may be ruined for proper relations with a man, with a loving husband!"

"Oh, Brigitte. I hope I don't shock you too much to say I have heard of these things and they are not so unusual! You should hear some of the things that are done in Paris and at Versailles! The debaucheries there would rival the ancient Roman tales that Catherine used to read to me from her book of myths!

"And to tell you the truth, I don't even think they have to be horrible. Between two loving and consenting partners, perhaps the kissing and touching of any part of our bodies is blessed? Why should it not be so? I have watched animals licking and nuzzling one another as a sign of affection. Why should humans be restricted only to those things which get us babies? Why would a god in heaven create our bodies to give and receive pleasure, and then brand the taking and giving of that pleasure as a sin?"

Why indeed? Brigitte stared at Adrian with new respect and awe. He was so intelligent! And with no formal schooling! He smiled reassuringly at her and continued, his voice now sober and subdued. "But what happened to you and the dear Lady Colette is unconscionable. I don't believe it is the acts themselves that are unnatural, but that they were forced upon you. That you were made to do things that were not of your own free will, and with someone you feared and despised.

"Please, Brigitte. I would that you never thought another second about the awful things that were done to you. But I know that isn't possible. So the next best thing is to let me spend the rest of our lives making it up to you. Let me kiss away the fears; let me show you the joy that our love can bring to each other. Say that you will, my love, and I will be the happiest man in France."

"Oh, Adrian! And I shall be the happiest woman!"

* * * * *

Adrian and Brigitte were married a fortnight later. Lord Philippe, as lord of the estate, performed the brief ceremony, and then any and all who cared to attend were at the huge party held in the gardens of Philippe's estate. The wine flowed freely and there was much dancing and merrymaking until dawn.

Instead of going to bed in her little room in Colette's chambers that night, Brigitte went with Adrian to his little house, dressed in the pretty bridal gown that Catherine had lent her. The party was still going on outside their door, but all sound fell away when they were alone at last.

Brigitte was nervous now, with new bride jitters. Her brief but terrifying experience with sex had not prepared her for a loving relationship. On the other hand, many brides knew nothing at all of what was waiting for them, so in that regard, perhaps she was lucky.

Adrian, keenly aware of her fears, and desperately determined not to reawaken them, was gentle and patient. Once they were lying together in their new bed, he held his bride and kissed her hair. She was so soft and supple in his arms. He longed to take her now. To claim her as a husband had a right to do, but he feared that if he rushed her, she would shut down. He could take her by force, of course, as was his right, but he wanted her willingly. He wanted her heart as well as her body.

Adrian himself had lain with women before. He was discreet, but he was, after all, twenty years old and not bad looking. Not all girls were as worried as Brigitte seemed to be about presenting themselves to their new husbands as virgins! And to his credit, Adrian had not been lying when he said it didn't matter to him. It truly didn't.

In fact, he hadn't admitted as much to Brigitte, because he didn't want to alarm her or make her think the worse of him, but he was intrigued by her tales of "unnatural acts". It didn't seem so unnatural to him; it seemed kind of sexy! Not, of course, under duress with someone you found abhorrent. But with your own husband or wife, why not?

He loved women's bodies, and had never had the chance to properly savor them. What sex he had had was quick and tumbled, with girls as inexperienced as he. Now, at last, he had his own lovely girl, and all the time in the world to taste the pleasures of their marriage bed.

For now, he would content himself with holding her. Feeling her sweet, full breasts pressed against his chest, her lovely arms entwined in his. He kissed her neck, and she sighed, snuggling against him. He kissed her mouth, and she responded, kissing him back. She opened her mouth, offering her little tongue, and they tasted each other.

Adrian could feel his cock rising, hard and stiff between their two bodies. Oh, to take this lovely girl now! He rubbed against her thigh, and she didn't pull away, though she must have been aware of what that hard rod against her was.

"I want you," Brigitte's new husband whispered, and to his delight, she answered back in kind. For Colette was not alone in her nocturnal explorations of her own body. For better or worse, the rapists, or more accurately, Lucas, had awakened something in each of the women. Something sexual and primal. And, despite the horrible way he had done it, each girl had been brought to orgasm at the hand, or mouth, of another. Having once experienced that sexual rush, they had sought it out for themselves, both for solace and for pleasure, alone in the dark.

Now Adrian dared to reach his hand under Brigitte's little gown. She was naked underneath, and her skin felt soft as satin to his rough workman's hand. She trembled at his touch, and sighed sweetly. He felt her ripe full breasts, his fingers lingering over the round nipples, making them harden into sweet points.

Brigitte did not pull away, and so he took courage, and moved his hand down, over the soft curve of her belly. His hand stopped on her pubic thatch, and Brigitte seemed to stiffen and hold her breath.

Adrian moved closer to her, his hand still on her mons, and whispered, "Be calm, my love. It is only your Adrian. Your true love. I will not take you by force. Not now or ever. We will move forward by your leave, when you are ready."

Brigitte's taut body relaxed, and she whispered, "How did I ever get so lucky? What star was I born under to find a man like you?" He kissed her, deeply, and she spread her legs a little, so that his hand slipped lower.

"Touch me there, my husband. Take what is yours. Just please, be gentle."

"Is that what you want?" Oh God, it was what *he* wanted so badly he could barely constrain himself. But gallantly he went on, "Because we can wait. We don't have to do this tonight. It's nobody's business but our own what we do here, despite all their ribbing and joking."

"I want it," Brigitte whispered. "I do."

Adrian dropped his hand lower, and touched her gently. To his pleasant surprise he found that she was wet and ready to receive him. Carefully he positioned himself over her and whispered, "It might hurt a little. Even though you've done this before, you are barely used, and I might hurt you. But after the first little pain, it will be lovely, I can promise you."

Brigitte squeezed her eyes shut, trying not to cry out with fear. Now that it had come down to it, she was terrified that he would rip her flesh and hurt her, as that horrid brute had done. And yet, she wasn't lying. She *did* want it! If letting Adrian enter her, use her in this way, was what it took to secure his love, she wanted it. And pain be damned! She could take it, and more, for her man.

She pulled Adrian down, so that he wouldn't see her face, or her fear. As she had hoped, he took this for a sign of her desire, and she felt the press of his cock head at her sex. He kissed her mouth, slowly and sweetly, and then dropped down to her nipples, taking first one, then the other, into his mouth. He savored the large dark cherries, lightly pulling and tugging at them, as Brigitte moaned with pleasure.

"Does it hurt?"

"Oh no, it's lovely. I love whatever you are doing! My breasts are so sensitive, and your mouth feels like a bit of heaven!"

"Oh, well, I'm glad you like that. They are glorious! But that isn't what I meant. I meant, down there. Am I hurting you?"

"Well, no. I mean, not yet. Please, just do it. Take me." Get it over with, she almost blurted.

Adrian said, confusion in his voice, "But, Brigitte. I already have. I'm inside your lovely sweet sex as we speak! I slipped right in, and now I'm trying like hell not to finish, because it feels so incredibly good, I know just one thrust and it's all over!"

"What?" Brigitte's eyes flew open and she stared at Adrian still perched over her. She had felt no pain! No searing burn as flesh was ripped and taut muscles jarred. He had so distracted her with his kisses and attentions that she had missed the most important moment, when he claimed her with his body!

Brigitte started to laugh, and, after a moment, Adrian laughed too. They laughed until tears spilled down their cheeks, and then they hugged each other tightly. As Adrian rocked in Brigitte's arms, he began to moan, and now she felt the sweet fullness of his manhood inside her. But still there was no pain, only pleasure and her own rising desire.

They would not sleep that night, taking pleasure in each other until rosy dawn filled the eastward window, and at last they fell, exhausted but still entwined.

Chapter Seven

Philippe and Colette were again strolling in the gardens. The air was turning cooler, as autumn whispered its arrival. They stopped a moment, watching Adrian pulling up some flowers, as his wife, Brigitte, pointed and gestured what she wanted. She was now entirely responsible for the floral arrangements, and very proud indeed of the charge.

As Adrian handed her a bunch of flowers, their heads dipped together for a moment, and then they broke away, laughing. Philippe turned to Colette and said, "They are so easy together. So right for one another."

Colette nodded, taking real pleasure in how happy her little maid was now. Would she find such happiness herself? Almost as if she'd spoken aloud, Philippe said now, as if in response, "We could have that. You and I. If you could but find it in your heart to trust me. To trust yourself."

* * * * *

Philippe was tired of waiting. He had told her, yes, that he would wait a thousand years, and he would. But he was tired. Why did she resist him, when Brigitte, who had suffered the same indignities, had been able to move on with her life? To find a happy union with a man? Perhaps it was more than that. Perhaps Colette sought to spare his feelings. To hide behind the excuse of the abduction and thus keep him permanently at bay.

Once this idea had slipped into his head, Philippe began to obsess about it. Colette did not love him, had never loved him. She did seem to enjoy his company, but in her eyes, he was no more than a kind older brother.

If he were more honest still, he had not tried to even kiss her in quite a while. What was the point? It only agitated him all the more, because he could have nothing beyond those sweet lips. Why put himself through the torment of arousal and then rejection, again and again?

And yet, was that fair to her? Perhaps, for both their sakes, he must force the matter once and for all. As much as he admired and loved the foolish and willful Colette, he could not tarry for a lifetime. He did, after all, have some obligation to the de Valon name, to produce an heir. And now at twenty-six, he wasn't getting any younger!

He decided on a plan. He would employ the wiles of his days at Court. He would take Colette away to his little country home along the shore. They would bring the requisite servants, of course, but he would send them away, and she would not know. He would steal into her rooms and seduce her, and that would be that!

There was no honor in it, but he was, frankly, at his wits end. He simply had to have this woman. Whether by accident or design, she was the first woman in a long line to finally get under the skin and into the heart of the once avowed ladies' man, Lord Philippe de Valon!

* * * * *

Colette happily agreed to their little country outing. She was intrigued by the sea, and looked forward to taking long idle walks along its shores with Philippe. They went by carriage, along with three servants to take care of them, and she was given a cozy little bedroom to herself.

The first day did pass as she'd imagined, with long walks and a pleasant lingering dinner. As much as she liked Aunt Genevieve, it was refreshing to be alone, just the two of them. Neither of them felt the need to make the constant conversation that Aunt Genevieve seemed so to enjoy over meals.

They sat in comfortable companionship, watching the waves crash in and roll away again, as the sun set in wild oranges and purples, and for a just a second over the horizon, in a flash of green.

Colette didn't notice that the servants had seemed to vanish. She took servants for granted, having always been taken care of by them. Since Brigitte no longer slept near her at night, she found she had become used to retiring alone, and in some ways preferred it.

Philippe at first bided his time, pondering in his head which night he would choose to seduce the young woman. But he realized that his heart was not in it. He knew that while he might even succeed in his "conquest", if it was not freely and lovingly given, it would be an empty victory, or worse, a betrayal.

Unaware of Philippe's plans, and his own foiling of them, Colette had kissed him sweetly good night and gone alone to her bed. It had been many nights since a nightmare had visited her, and Colette was jerked suddenly from her sleep by her own muted cries of help, as she struggled in her dreams to escape the savage monsters who pursued her.

At once Philippe was at her side, cradling her in his arms, urgently whispering that everything was all right. She was safe here, with Philippe, and her dreams were nothing more than wisps of bad memory, to be brushed away like old cobwebs.

Colette didn't want to return to her little bed, and so they went together into the larger room of the little house, and Philippe made a small fire to frighten away her lingering demons. They sipped brandy from large crystal goblets and Colette nestled close to Philippe.

"You know, Philippe, you have become the dearest friend in the world to me. I can't imagine my life without you there. If only…"

"What? Continue your train of thought, my lady. If only what? If only things were different, and you felt a romantic love for me, instead of just a sisterly kindredness?"

"What? Why, no! Heavens no!" Colette blushed prettily and turned her head away. How could he not know her ardent, even passionate feelings for him? What she had been about to say, what she did go on to say, feeling she owed him that was, "Oh, my lord. You misunderstand me. I was going to say, if only I could come to you as pure and chaste as you deserve."

"Colette! What, please tell me, can I do to convince you that is absurd! How long will you cling to this illusion that I want some blank tablet of a girl, someone with no life experience so I can write her a personality as if she were made of clay? Damn it, it's you I want! You with all your fears, with your stupid dolt of a father, with your loss of a mother, even with your memories of those horrible days at the hands of criminals! It's you I want! Not another. You!"

A stunned Colette watched as the great and valiant Lord Philippe began to cry. Not all-out sobbing; he just put his head in his hand and was still, save for the shaking of his shoulders.

Colette began to cry as well, in sympathy and shame, hurrying to kneel beside him and console him. "My lord! You stun me! And yet you speak with such conviction and grace that I can't help but believe you at last! By some miracle, you want me! Broken and fearful, and yet you want me still! Forgive me, Philippe. If you will still have me, I would love nothing better in this world than to be your wife."

* * * * *

The wedding ceremony was glorious, and the bride, of course, was radiant.

It had taken several weeks for word to make its way to and from the House of Lyon, but as Philippe had predicted, Rousseau was only too happy to give his permission for the union. Ill health had prevented his attendance, as a fall from a horse had resulted in a broken shoulder that didn't seem inclined to heal, and would eventually be his death.

Preparations had taken another month, including sending out the word over the countryside to nobles far and wide that would want to attend the wedding of such an important figure at Court as Lord Philippe de Valon. The Sun King himself had sent congratulations and an elaborate gift, though he was not able to attend.

Madame de Valon seemed to grow younger with each day of the preparations, flying to and from the kitchen with elaborate instructions, overseeing the decorations and barking orders everywhere she went. She was also directing the sewing of Colette's wedding gown, which was an elaborate construction of much satin and lace, adorned throughout with tiny seed pearls, so that in the light it shimmered as if aglow. Colette's hair was pulled back in an elegant twist of braids, embroidered with hundreds of the tiny pearls. On her ears hung large natural pearls which Philippe's mother had worn at her own wedding, many years before.

At her breast was pinned the lovely floral brooch that Aunt Genevieve had recovered from the kidnapping. "Please, Colette. I want you to wear it on your wedding day, and keep it safe always." Aunt Genevieve had insisted, when Colette had protested. "I am old, dear, and my time on earth is almost over. No, no! Don't waste your breath denying it. Don't forget with whom you are speaking! I always speak my mind as I see it, as well you know. Even about myself."

She went on, rather enjoying the drama of her speech. "No, darling Colette. This lovely flower will make the perfect adornment for your wedding gown. And you can pass it on to your daughter when that lovely day arrives."

Colette's sisters Jeanette and Marie were in attendance. Jeanette's husband was there as well, though Marie's could not attend, as his business kept him too occupied. Jeanette brought her baby daughter, Isabelle, to everyone's extreme delight. Sadly, Colette's little brother, Jacques, had not been able to attend, staying instead by the side of his dying father, who had always doted on the boy to the exclusion of his sisters. While not happy that her father had been hurt, Colette was secretly relieved he was not there to find fault with her, and with her prospective husband.

There was feasting for two full days, with the actual ceremony nestled somewhere in between. Three pigs, two cows and three sheep had been slaughtered and carefully prepared for the occasion in any manner of cutlets and pies. There were also mounds of fresh vegetables and fruits, cheeses and pies, cakes and puddings to rival any sumptuous excess at Court. All of it had the stamp of Madame de Valon, as neither Colette nor Philippe cared a whit for the details.

Philippe was not big on formal church occasions, and the ceremony itself was mercifully brief. As he placed a heavy gold ring with the crest of his house on Colette's finger, a tear slipped over onto his cheek, and his smile of pure joy made Colette herself laugh aloud with happiness and pleasure. Few people in their positions married for love, but none who attended that day had any doubt about these two.

* * * * *

The party was still going on in full swing, with champagne and wine freely flowing. Colette's head was almost drooping on her chest, when Philippe gestured to his new bride that they could gracefully exit at last. With much cheering and teasing about Philippe's ability or lack thereof to consummate the marriage, and much blushing on Colette's part, they were at last permitted to retire to their chambers upstairs.

Brigitte accompanied her mistress, looking very sleepy herself. She brought Catherine with her, and between them they carefully removed the many layers of satin and lace that had created Colette's bridal gown. Brigitte laid out the soft simple silk dressing gown in which Colette would be led to her new husband. Philippe had been sent to his bedroom while this was going on, and now Colette knocked gently against the door, her heart beginning to beat a little too hard.

Fatigue and the effects of the champagne seemed to fall away as she heard him call out softly, "Come." Slowly Colette pushed open the door, as her two servants slipped away. She stood for a moment in the doorway, her hand gripping the brass knob. This was the first time Philippe had seen her without the benefit of many layers of fabric, bone stays and the requisite corset that were the style of the day. Now there was nothing between her bare body and his vision than the sheer silk of her gown clinging alluringly to her curves. Her nipples rose against the satiny fabric and the outline of her round breasts was compelling. Self-consciously she hugged herself, as if she could hide her lovely body with her slender arms.

"Come in, my love," Philippe said again, his voice soft. "Close the door." Slowly Colette entered, and closed the door, shutting out the sounds of revelry downstairs in the great banquet hall.

Colette looked slowly around the room. This was her first time to view her husband's bedchambers. Chambers that, if she wished, would also be hers. Many couples of their wealth and lineage had completely separate quarters, and met only at meals and for public affairs, but those couples were the ones who married for convenience and political connection.

Still, Philippe knew that Colette was deeply shy at this point, and might need time to wish to share his bed. Now she stood looking at it—mounds of feather mattresses were piled high on a wooden frame, so high a little ladder was necessary to climb up. The frame was curtained with gauzy lace netting, creating a little canopy to keep out the mosquitoes during spring and summer, as Philippe favored the fresh night air.

The room was lit by hundreds of candles set in little china saucers, creating a lovely warm effect, like something in a dream. Philippe himself was not in the bed, but sitting on a divan nearby. He had removed his wedding jacket, but still wore his silk shirt, tucked into fine satin breeches. He had taken off the ceremonial white wig and she saw that he looked tired. It had been a very long day indeed.

Colette came and knelt next to her new husband, resting her head on his knee. He stroked her hair and whispered, "You were so beautiful today. I will never forget how lovely you looked in that bridal gown. No woman could hold a candle to you, Colette. I want to have your portrait painted in that gown, once things settle down." He stroked her hair a little more and then asked, "Are you happy, darling?"

Colette nodded, smiling up at him. Her heart was pounding and she found her palms were sweating. All the champagne that had made her feel so giddy and gay now made her feel woozy and sick. She wanted nothing so much as to go to her own familiar chambers and climb into bed.

But she knew what was expected of her, and was determined not to make a fool of herself. Even if she had been a total innocent, all the leering comments and good-natured jibes Philippe had had to endure all evening would have spelled it out for her. They wouldn't be considered truly married until they consummated the union by coupling.

While she desired Philippe, she found that now that it had come down to it, she was frightened. These past weeks and months had been idyllic. They had spent a great deal of time really getting to know one another, and Colette was certain Philippe was the right man for her. He never pressed her, only taking a sweet kiss when offered. She had come to feel safe with him, and certain that he wouldn't try to take advantage of her in any way.

But now that was all changed. Now she belonged to him, in every possible way. Legally all her rights and property reverted to him, and he had full control over all her actions. It was his right now to "take her" however he wished. Indeed, it was considered his duty to consummate the marriage by claiming her body with his.

She wanted to obey; she wanted to be his wife in all ways. But now that it came down to it, she was terrified. What if his mouth turned into Lucas', as it had so often in her nightmares? What if his penis ripped and tore at her, as Albert's had, leaving her bleeding and sobbing?

He would feel rejected, and rightly so! He would hate her! What was she thinking, to have agreed to marry this perfect man, when she herself was broken? Oh, they couldn't see it; they all thought she was fine and completely recovered, but she wasn't, no, most surely not.

She would humiliate herself and anger her new husband. How had it come this? Her own foolish pride had brought her this far! Now she must get through this, or lose the man she claimed to love. She looked up at Philippe again, and tried again to smile, but instead, ridiculously, burst into tears.

At once he pulled her into his arms, cradling her gently in his lap. "Please, my darling. Please don't cry. I know how tired you are, and what a strain these two days have been, indeed, these past weeks of endless preparation! Our lives have been turned upside down! But now it's done! In the eyes of the King and the eyes of God, we are man and wife."

Colette continued to cry, and Philippe held her, making soothing sounds, and stroking her soft hair. Finally she stilled, and they stayed together in a sweet embrace. At last he shifted, sitting forward, and saw that his young bride was asleep, the tears still wet on her cheeks.

Carefully Philippe stood and laid the sleeping girl on the high bed. Her body was so lithe and inviting. He longed to caress her, to feel the soft undercurve of her breast, to taste the sweet little nipples, to feel the welcoming wetness of her velvet embrace. But he would not touch her thus. Not tonight. Let them all assume what they will; he would wait until his bride was ready.

Kissing her lightly on the forehead, he turned away from her, afraid that if he held her, he might lose control and take her with force, something he'd promised himself he would never do. She would come to him of her own free will, or not at all.

Finally feeling himself to be under control, Philippe carried the sleeping girl to her own familiar chambers. He would not have her in his bed until she came willingly.

Once back in his own room, alone, he allowed his valet, Georges, to help remove his elegant clothes. The valet wisely refrained from commenting on the lack of a bride in the bridal bed. Philippe knew that Georges was completely discreet, and would not make this obvious aberration the source of gossip around the servants' breakfast table.

Thanking and dismissing him, Philippe took up the little ceramic candle snuffer. One by one, he put out all the little candles, leaving the room to be lit only by the moon, which was already setting in the late night sky.

* * * * *

The days passed sweetly. Colette was enormously grateful to Philippe that he had not forced the consummation of their marriage. She herself suggested that perhaps it would be more seemly if she slept in his chambers, now that they were married, but she didn't protest too much when he demurred. Secretly she was greatly relieved.

At first she had tried to tell him how thankful she was, and to promise that it wouldn't last forever, but he silenced her on the subject whenever she brought it up. "Colette, I will say this only once, so you will understand. I've said it before, but you must realize now that I mean it. I told you once that I would wait a thousand years for you, and that is what I intend to do. You've been through what no woman should have to bear, and you need time to heal. You need trust and understanding. I'm in no hurry, darling. You know my history. I have no urgent need to discover the sweetness of women. I'm sure there are many who would say I've had enough of them to last a lifetime!" He grinned, somewhat ruefully, and continued, "It is you and you alone I desire, and I will wait for you, my love. Please, take all the time you need. And now, let us say no more about it."

Philippe and Colette spent much time together. This particular late summer afternoon found them sitting on a blanket in their secret hideaway by the creek. Colette's head was resting in Philippe's lap. Leaning down, he kissed her on the cheek, but she moved her head, so that his mouth landed upon hers.

They stayed this way for a few moments, as if testing the waters. Colette parted her lips and brought her arms up around Philippe's neck, pulling him down to kiss her properly. He responded, carefully at first, and then more ardently. They had shared such kisses before, but it had never gone past that, even now, weeks into their marriage.

Her skin was so soft and supple. Philippe drew a finger down her throat, and further, to her soft breast, displayed so alluringly over the top of her gown. Instead of pulling away, or trying to cover herself, Colette stayed as she was, even arching up slightly, as if offering herself to his hand.

Philippe touched the soft tops of her breasts, and pressed down against the fabric a little, causing one breast to spring free of its sheath, exposing the tender bud of her nipple to the warm summer air. Colette kept her mouth locked upon Philippe's, and her eyes tightly closed, but she didn't pull away.

Slowly, Philippe let his finger trail down her breast, to stop at the nipple, which he touched and teased lightly, watching with pleasure as it distended. Colette moaned slightly against his mouth, but did not open her eyes or move away. Gathering courage from her silent cues, Philippe dared to press the fabric further, so that her second breast was also revealed. Now he gently disengaged from their kiss, and lowered his head to one succulent breast.

His tongue flicked across the nipple, and he felt it stiffen further. Daring to put his lips fully around the nipple, he gently sucked and pulled the sweet little marble until it hardened and engorged in his mouth. Colette sighed sweetly, and did not move away. Philippe had to shift now, as his cock was pressing painfully against his breeches. "Darling," he whispered, his voice hoarse. "Do you want me to stop?"

Colette still did not open her eyes, but she shook her head slightly, and cradled the back of his head with her hand, as if willing him to bend over her again, and again kiss and suckle her breasts. This he eagerly did, now crouched on his knees over the inert girl. He fondled and kneaded her breasts, bending forward to kiss and lightly bite her nipples until they glistened and shone dark red.

After a while he sat back, surveying the still woman, wondering what was going through her mind right now. Gently he touched her chest, and found that her heart was pounding like a little drum against her delicate bones. "Colette," he whispered, and then again, when she didn't respond, "Colette! Sit up. Open your eyes." As he spoke, he lifted the fabric of her gown up and over her luscious breasts, covering her.

Slowly Colette opened her eyes and sat up. "What is it, my husband? Have I displeased you?"

"No, no. It isn't that. But your heart is pounding so, and I can see by your face, and the way you lie so still, that you are still afraid. I don't want you this way. I only want you when you're ready. Completely ready to submit to my will as your husband, not through fear and obligation, but because it is truly what you want to do. Until you are ready for that, let us content ourselves with kisses."

Colette looked at him, pursing her lips in what could only be described as a pout. Then she said, "Very well, my lord. If you do not want me now—"

"Oh, no, you little vixen! Do not twist my words. You know I want you. But I want you on my terms, not because you feel a sense of duty or obligation. If and when that day comes, we will both know it. It is not today." So saying, he held out his hand to help her up, and Colette took it.

Since that day when he had been the one to stop things, something changed for Colette. Not only had her husband promised not to press, but now he himself seemed to stand in the way of their moving forward. This had the perverse (and probably intended) effect of making Colette want to move forward more quickly! She found occasion to get him alone as often as possible, and when she did, she would encircle his neck with her arms and pull him down for many a sweet kiss.

"Please, Philippe," she dared to whisper one morning just after breakfast, when they stood alone together in the hall. "I want more."

"More what? I have kissed you so much my lips are turning raw."

Playfully she slapped him. "No, you silly! More! I want more than kisses! I need more! I am your wife!"

"Yes. So? You are my wife. This is not news to me, Colette. Please tell me exactly what you are saying."

"Oh, Philippe! Stop teasing me! You know what I am saying! I want you! I want us to be man and wife! To truly be man and wife. In all things. Please. Don't make this harder for me than it is already."

"If it is hard, then you are not ready, my love. Now go and visit my dear crabby old aunt. I have business to attend to. I shan't be back until very late this evening, so do not wait up. Go on, there's a good girl." And with an infuriating little pat on her bottom, Philippe sent a very frustrated little wife away. Luckily she didn't turn back, or she would have seen the broad grin on his face.

* * * * *

Two nights later Philippe was awakened by a scuffling sound. He came awake in an instant, his instincts of protecting his household rising to the fore. "Georges! Is that you? Who goes there?"

"Philippe," came Colette's small voice. "It is I." Colette entered his bedroom, dressed in the same cream colored silk gown she had worn on their wedding night. She stood now silhouetted against a window. Tonight the moon was full, and high in the sky, so that she appeared illuminated, like some kind of goddess sent down in a dream to this mere mortal.

"Oh, my wife. You are so beautiful. Why are you here?" Philippe sat up in bed, fully awake. He was completely naked under the soft quilts, and his erection was visible beneath the sheets.

"I'm here to, that is," Colette faltered to a stop, taking a step toward him and then standing still, her eyes now on the erection lifting the sheets like a little tent pole.

"Yes. What is it? Did you have a bad dream? Why do you wake me?" His voice was gentle, but not the voice of a lover.

"Oh, Philippe! Why do you make this so difficult?"

"My love," he said, "I make it difficult for precisely the reason that you find it so hard! If this is so hard to you, you are not ready. When you are ready, you will know it, darling. You will come to me of your own accord. Until that time, it will seem insurmountably difficult to you, and that is not of my making."

"I will come to you?"

"Yes, of your own free will."

Colette slipped a strap of her gown down past one white shoulder. Philippe watched her, drawing in his breath, saying nothing. She slipped down the other strap, so that the gown fell slightly, partially revealing her high breasts. "I will come to you, offering myself in complete submission, as your bride and now most prized possession?" Colette spoke in a low voice, a voice he hadn't heard before. It was very sexy, as was her behavior, as she now shimmied slightly, allowing the silky fabric to fall in a little cascade that settled at her slender waist.

She stood in front of her husband, bare to the hips, her body gleaming in the moonlight. Philippe blew out his breath, realizing he had been holding it for quite some time. He found to his surprise he couldn't quite draw another; his heart seemed constricted somehow.

Taking her gown now on either side of her body, Colette pushed it down, revealing herself completely naked for her husband. She stood still, smiling slightly, her eyes very wide, her lips parted. He stared at her perfection, at the full sweet breasts, tipped with rosy erect nipples, at the feminine curve of her belly, at the lush blonde pubic curls covering her delicate sex. Philippe groaned slightly, his desire now a fierce ache in his loins.

"Come to me," he said, his voice husky with urgency. Colette walked slowly forward, her arms at her sides, her eyes glued to his face. When she was close enough for him to touch her, he pressed her shoulder, forcing her to kneel next to the bed.

"Colette, listen to me. You are lovely beyond my wildest dreams. I want you more than I ever thought it possible to want a woman. But I have to know; is this what you want? Even now, it's not too late. You can change your mind. You can go back to your rooms and go to sleep, and we can leave this as a lovely dream, as a promise of things to come."

"No! Please, my lord. I beg of you, don't send me away! I want it. I have thought of nothing else these past days. I want you, Philippe. I long for you. Please, accept me and let me fulfill my duty at last as your wife."

Philippe opened his arms then, beckoning to the lovely young girl kneeling naked beside him. Slowly she stood, gracefully sliding into his arms. He could smell the sweet warm scent of her, like fresh bread and something spicy, something sexual.

As he kissed her, he pulled her close against him, knowing she could feel his nakedness against her, could feel his erect cock pressing now against her belly. It was enough for this moment just to kiss her and hold her close, but he knew soon, soon, he would have to take her, or he would die.

Carefully he slid his hands between her thighs, and they willingly fell open. Gingerly he touched the sweet little folds of her sex, and she shuddered but did not try to move away. He kissed her some more, and suckled and teased her nipples, hoping to relax her and make her ready to receive him.

Again he dared to reach down and touch that little pussy, but it didn't seem wet enough. He was used to the wanton women at Court, who could accommodate a man like him, known to be well-endowed, without blinking an eye. But this girl, this angel of a girl who was his wife! She was no virgin, granted, but she had been used only a little, and it was some time ago. He would have to be careful; he didn't want to hurt her, and to undo the careful weeks and months of gaining her trust. And so he withdrew his hand, and kissed her some more.

When he touched her a third time, this time she grabbed his hand and held it there. "What is it?" she whispered urgently. "Please! Why do you not take me?"

In response Philippe took her hand and placed it over his erect manhood. She gasped slightly, but didn't pull away. It was huge! Old Lucas' penis, the only one she'd been exposed to, other than Albert's brief and brutal rape, was small by comparison, and not nearly as hard. "Oh dear, Philippe!" she cried, dismayed. "What will we do?"

He laughed a little, this being a reaction he had never received from any lady before. "I will be very careful, my love. We will take our time."

Colette nodded, though her expression was fearful. Had his head been clearer, Philippe would have stopped things at that moment. But his head was full of dreams, and his penis was engorged and dripping at the tip. He needed nothing so much as to plunge himself into this perfect flower, to claim her completely.

Carefully he positioned himself above the young woman and lowered himself slowly until his cock was touching the entrance to her pussy. He pressed slightly and she squirmed but tried to stay still and open for him. He pressed again, harder this time, and Colette squealed.

Philippe sighed, and pulled away. This was impossible. No, surely not impossible. She was just acting like a virgin, was all. But she wasn't a virgin, was she? She'd experienced this before! Couldn't she take it, for her own husband? His own desperate need now clouded his judgment, making him selfish in a blinding moment of desire. He lowered himself again and thrust against her. Colette cried out and jerked away.

"Ouch! Oh, it hurts! It hurts! I'm sorry, Philippe. I can't! I'm afraid!"

Philippe, now deflated by her cries, rolled away, angry and frustrated. He was embarrassed to have forced her like that. And after all this time of being so careful, so sensitive. He had just wasted weeks of precious coaxing, hoping to finally put her at ease. Tears of frustration actually pricked at his eyelids.

After a silence, it was Colette who turned back toward her husband. "Please, if you're willing, my lord, I have an idea."

Philippe didn't turn back toward her, but he did say, "I'm listening."

"Well, you might possibly, no, you will surely, think this is very strange indeed. But it actually might make things much easier. That is, if you weren't offended by the proposition. That is, I don't know if this is something that's normally done, but—"

"Colette! I don't have a clue what you're trying to say! Please speak plainly!"

"Well," she whispered, scrunching up close so she could whisper in his ear, "You could kiss my, um, that is, if you kiss me a little down there, it might be easier?" She stopped, sighing deeply, blushing from the roots of her hair all the way down to her chest.

Philippe rolled over slowly to look at her. What was this? How did this girl even know of such a thing? Well, of course. It must have been done to her, and yet she had never said so.

"Colette. How do you know of this? I have heard of it, of course, as anything goes at Court, you know, even things you've never dreamed about, I can guarantee. But did they do that to you? I mean, it seems surprising. Not something your typical rapist would do to his victim!"

Now it was Colette who turned away. But she'd gone too far to deny it. "It was very strange, Philippe, and I feel ashamed to admit it, but it was quite pleasurable. The old man did it to me. He licked and kissed my, uh, private parts, until something very bizarre happened."

"Do tell," Philippe interjected, beyond intrigued. What else was he feeling? Jealousy? Surely not! That was absurd.

"Well, this sort of heat seemed to build up in me. Not heat exactly. Sort of like butter melting, maybe? I don't know how to describe it, but it was lovely, and also tickly, and it made me want more until suddenly I couldn't bear it any longer, and then I wanted him to stop. And it made my heart pound, and I couldn't catch my breath. And then I felt very sleepy. Isn't that bizarre? I thought at first it was the strong wine he made me drink, but he did it again, when I'd had no wine, and when I did it to Brigitte—"

"What?" Philippe sat straight up in bed, not realizing he had shouted. This was too much! His blushing tender bride had done this thing to her maid! Surely she was forced, but nonetheless, it wasn't natural!

Colette's eyes opened wide now, and she too sat up, pulling the sheets up to her chin, looking thoroughly miserable, biting her lip and twisting the sheets between her fingers. Philippe looked over at her, and despite himself, he grinned. This was a surprise, but wasn't it actually a good thing? The girl admitted that she had taken sexual pleasure from being kissed "down there". Surely that was an excellent sign that she could be taught to love all aspects of lovemaking.

And though he himself had never kissed a woman's sex, he had certainly allowed them to kiss his! Why was it so different to pleasure a woman in this way? The women he had laid with had always assured him they weren't interested in reciprocation, and he had never pressed the matter, not even thinking about it. He had generally been too eager to dip his stick into their lovely honey pots to give the matter another thought.

Now here was his wife, a girl of tender years, asking him to kiss her "down there". All shock and anger evaporated, and he laughed aloud. Colette was amazing; there were no two ways about it. She looked back at him, confusion and relief showing in equal parts in her face.

"You, Lady Colette, are, quite simply, the most amazing and confounding woman I have ever met! Inviting me to kiss your secret places! Well, spread your legs, my lovely wife. And get rid of this blanket." As he spoke, Philippe ripped the sheets from Colette's naked body. He pressed her thighs apart.

Colette covered her face, pulling a soft feather pillow over her head. "Oh, Philippe, I am so embarrassed! I can't believe I said that out loud! What you must think of me now!" And yet, despite her protestations, she didn't try to close her legs as her naked husband scooted down between her slender thighs.

He knelt, placing a large hand on either of her legs, forgetting at once how soft her skin was when he inhaled the musky sweet scent of her sex, now spread before him. The labia were sweetly folded, delicate shades of coral, fading into pinks and reds at the core, like some rare and precious seashell. Slowly he lowered his head and touched the outer labia with his tongue.

Colette jumped slightly and gasped into her pillow. She was clutching at the edges of the pillow as if hanging onto the edge of a precipice. But her thighs were still open; her sex bared for her husband's view and touch. He licked again, this time a long, slow lick from the entrance of her canal, up to the top, pressing between the soft folds, making her squirm and sigh.

Colette, the pillow still over her head, was suspended for the moment in a state of disbelief. Not only had she dared to voice her suggestion, and not only had her husband not rejected her as depraved, but now his sweet velvet tongue was upon her, his warm breath tickling her, his nose and mouth against her secret folds! This had happened so many times in her dreams, but they invariably ended with the old gap-toothed man, his rotting gums dripping with slime pressed against her, making her retch and vomit her disgust.

But this was no rapist. It was her own darling husband, now licking and kissing her sex, and it was heavenly. The young woman's tight grip against the pillows slowly released, her fingers now resting limply. She sighed again, this time with pure pleasure, as Philippe found his stride. He licked and teased around the little nubbin at the center of her. When he flicked his tongue over it, she jumped and moaned, making his cock even harder, if that was possible, than it already was.

He found the power of arousing a woman like this, solely with his mouth, intoxicating. All his other sexual experience involved taking his own pleasure, and leaving the women he had lain with to derive what pleasure they would. He had never even considered the matter. But now, this was something so new! To feel her writhe against him, causing him to tighten his grip against her spread thighs; to feel her sex engorge and heat; to taste the sweet nectar of her sex! Philippe, the supposed experienced man at Court, who had bedded dozens of wenches, found himself actually dizzy with desire and sheer need.

Would she receive him now? Cautiously he pressed a finger against her entrance, and found it impossibly, deliciously wet. He savored the sweet torment of denying himself just a little longer, as he licked and suckled her, his tongue directly against her little clit. Colette was yelping now, a little steady staccato of pleasure that indicated her impending release. Philippe's cock was throbbing, mashed between his thigh and the bed as he continued to lick and tease his darling girl until she bucked, hard, and thrust up against his mouth, crying out his name as she came.

Before her trembling shudders had subsided, Philippe lifted himself and quickly put his cock against her slick entrance. Slowly, holding his breath, praying she wouldn't resist, he slid the tip into her, half expecting a cry of pain. But Colette grabbed his hips, wanton now in her abandon, and pulled him against her, into her, pressing his entire length up into her hot, impossibly tight perfection.

Now it was Philippe who shuddered and moaned, his pleasure so acute he thought he might pass out. Slowly he withdrew from her velvet embrace, and she pulled him back again, murmuring his name over and over like a little prayer. He eased himself back, and then again pulled away, stringing out his own delicious torment, until he could control himself no longer. He plunged into her, hard, in one perfect thrust and Colette screamed. But there was no fear in the cry, no resistance. It was lust, pure and simple, that was guiding her now.

At last the gates of fear and damage that had been wrought at the hands of her brutal assaulters were broken open like so many sticks of kindling, burned away in the fire of her passion and trust. She was open at last, in every sense, to the loving and passionate onslaught of her husband. He used her hard and furious, riding her like some wild mare beneath him, his sweat mingling with hers, the smell of their sex ripe in the air until at last he jerked forward, crying her name, and released his precious seed deep into her womb.

Falling against her, he rolled to his side, pulling her with him so that his cock remained nestled inside her as it softened. He wanted to stay this way forever, or until his cock hardened again, and then he would do it again. He would kiss her sweet sex, and then enter her, over and over, until they were both raw from it. But for now he just held her, feeling both of their hearts beating together in a sweet rhythm which slowed, slower and slower, until they were both asleep, still locked in a lovers' embrace.

Philippe was awakened by something unfamiliar but not unknown. This had happened to him before, at Court, but it had been done without love, and strictly to "get him ready" as he recalled. This felt lovely, and it took him a minute or two to realize he wasn't dreaming.

Colette wasn't next to him in the bed any longer, but was now down between his legs, and he could feel his cock rising in her warm mouth. He had never dreamed that his innocent and shy little flower would want to take his cock into her mouth! He opened his eyes and looked around. This wasn't a dream. There was his familiar room, and the large bay window that he loved, that he had designed himself. The sun was just barely peaking over the horizon, and the dawn sky was a lush gold, tinged with dark pink.

His eyes shut again, and he forgot the beauty of the sunrise as Colette's tongue slid up and down his rapidly hardening shaft. He moaned his pleasure and dropped a hand to her head, silently bidding her to go on. He was afraid to acknowledge what was happening in any more direct sense, as she might somehow come out of whatever lustful dream she must be in, and stop.

Philippe felt he would die if she stopped. But she didn't stop. Her velvet hot mouth slid up and down his erection, and she knelt up now, so as to take the whole shaft down into her throat.

Gently she cupped his balls in one soft hand, as her other hand slid up and down his cock, following the path of her mouth, heightening the sensations he was feeling until he felt he would faint with pleasure. Oh, God! How he wanted her. He had to have her now.

As lovely as that perfect mouth was, he needed her pussy now, its sweet heat surrounding him in a tight embrace. Reaching down, he pulled up the young girl, dragging her up so that her face was level with his, and her lithe body was warm on top of his.

He kissed her mouth, smelling his own sex on her. His cock was rock-hard, sticking straight up. Slowly he pressed her into a sitting position and whispered, "Sit back, my love. Let me take you thus." As he spoke, he lifted her up and then settled her carefully over his erect penis.

She was wet and open for him, as he held her up and then slowly lowered her body onto his own, sinking his cock deep into her. Colette was flushed and her eyes were bright, fevered with passion.

Slowly she began to lift her body up and down, his cock all the time in her tight hot embrace. Her eyes shut, and her cheeks were flushed as she let her head fall back. A sweet moan issued from her mouth, and her tongue flicked out, licking her full lips, tasting him on them.

"Philippe," she moaned. "Take me! Do it! I need it! I love you!" She moved like a snake charmer over him, and Philippe felt his pleasure explode inside of this amazing woman. But she wasn't done yet. Now that the floodgates were open, it seemed she was insatiable with lust! She bounced and moved on top of her husband, her hair flying, her breasts bouncing, crying his name as she shuddered and came herself, pulling his sweet seed further into her.

At last she fell against his hard chest, and he wrapped his arms around her, feeling her heart thudding against his. He barely had the strength to pull the silken sheets up over them before sleep dropped its net.

When Georges entered his master's chambers to assist with his toilette, he took in the scene, and discreetly vanished, a smile on his face.

Lord Philippe de Valon, confidant to a King, heir to a fortune he'd tripled since he'd come into his inheritance, lover of some of the most beautiful and influential women at Court, had succumbed at last. A young girl of noble but obscure lineage, sheltered and innocent, had completely shattered the wall of careful indifference he'd cultivated over the years. As surely as he'd claimed her for his own, so she too, had claimed him. At last, they were truly man and wife.

About the author:

Claire Thompson has written numerous novels and short stories, all exploring aspects of Dominance & submission. Ms. Thompson's gentler novels seek not only to tell a story, but to come to grips with, and ultimately exalt in the true beauty and spirituality of a loving exchange of power. Her darker works press the envelope of what is erotic and what can be a sometimes dangerous slide into the world of sadomasochism. She writes about the timeless themes of sexuality and romance, with twists and curves to examine the 'darker' side of the human psyche. Ultimately Claire's work deals with the human condition, and our constant search for love and intensity of experience.

Claire welcomes mail from readers. You can write to her c/o Ellora's Cave Publishing at 1056 Home Avenue, Akron OH 44310-3502.

Also by Claire Thompson:

Enjoy this excerpt from
Sunlit
© Copyright Leda Swann, 2004

All Rights Reserved, Ellora's Cave Publishing, Inc.

He came to her again that night, as he had done each night that week. In her dream she saw him, in the silky, deep-brown garb of a huge bull seal. He swam alongside her small rowboat, keeping time with her clumsy attempts at rowing with the occasional easy flick of his powerful tail. He was born for the water, making swimming look as effortless as breathing—his sleek body more fluid and graceful than any human she could imagine.

In her dream, she tucked her long dress up out of the way as she waded through the shallow water of the rocky islet and hauled the small boat up on to the sheltered beach, out of the way of the waves. All the time the seal watched her with an unblinking stare.

The rocks were warm on her skin as she eased open the laces of her too-tight bodice and lay facedown on the shore to rest.

As she dozed in the sun, she became aware of a presence beside her. The bull seal that had followed her rowboat to the island had clambered on to the rocks beside her and was looking at her with the deepest brown eyes she could imagine.

She gazed back at him, not at all frightened despite his size and bulk. She could read his soul through his eyes and knew instinctively he would not hurt her.

Then, as she watched, he began to change. His round seal head became longer and narrow, his shoulders broadened, his small front flippers lengthened into arms, his torso slimmed out into the shape of a man's body, and his tail divided into legs. When the transformation was complete, a young man, as naked as the day he was born, his hair as soft and brown as the seal's fur and his skin tanned a golden brown, lay beside her in the seal's place.

Soothing her with gentle words, he began to stroke her. As he stroked her, her clothes began to disappear, until she, too, was as naked as he was. His hands were fondling her breasts, and stroking her buttocks, and his fingers exploring the mound of hair and the cleft that lay between her legs.

And as he stroked he whispered to her. She could make out the words now. "Come to me," he urged her over and over again with gentle insistence. "Come to me."

Then his voice faded and she was left alone on her rock. "Where are you?" she called into the misty dreamscape around her. As the mist swirled around her, cutting off the sunlight and muffling the sounds of the sea, she became more insistent in her distress. "Where are you?"

There was no answer but the harsh cry of a sea bird in the distance and the lap of the waves against the beach. He was gone.

She gave a cry of despair and threw herself down off the rocks into the sea in search of him. The sensation of falling overtook her. She fell and fell for what seemed like an eternity...

Shannon woke up in her own bed bathed in sweat, her heart pounding and an insistent ache in her loins. For seven nights now, her phantom seal lover had come to her in her dreams, and each night he had left her panting and unfulfilled until she was desperate for his touch on her naked body, desperate for his kisses on her open mouth, desperate for him to make love to her as a man makes love to a woman.

Her old nurse had warned her about the seductive powers of the seal men and about the danger of falling under their spell, but the old woman's fearsome stories had fallen far short of the truth. The seal man was calling to her in her dreams, and she had lost the willpower to resist him. Her need for him was burning so strongly it was greater than any fear of danger, greater even than her need for food or drink.

She wanted, nay she needed him to make love to her. If he would not come to her except in her dreams, she would go to him as he asked, whatever the danger.

Why an electronic book?

We live in the Information Age—an exciting time in the history of human civilization in which technology rules supreme and continues to progress in leaps and bounds every minute of every hour of every day. For a multitude of reasons, more and more avid literary fans are opting to purchase e-books instead of paperbacks. The question to those not yet initiated to the world of electronic reading is simply: *why?*

1. *Price.* An electronic title at Ellora's Cave Publishing and Cerridwen Press runs anywhere from 40-75% less than the cover price of the <u>exact same title</u> in paperback format. Why? Cold mathematics. It is less expensive to publish an e-book than it is to publish a paperback, so the savings are passed along to the consumer.

2. *Space.* Running out of room to house your paperback books? That is one worry you will never have with electronic novels. For a low one-time cost, you can purchase a handheld computer designed specifically for e-reading purposes. Many e-readers are larger than the average handheld, giving you plenty of screen room. Better yet, hundreds of titles can be stored within your new library—a single microchip. (Please note that Ellora's Cave and Cerridwen Press does not endorse any specific brands. You can check our website at www.ellorascave.com or

www.cerridwenpress.com for customer recommendations we make available to new consumers.)

3. *Mobility.* Because your new library now consists of only a microchip, your entire cache of books can be taken with you wherever you go.

4. *Personal preferences are accounted for.* Are the words you are currently reading too small? Too large? Too...**ANNOYING**? Paperback books cannot be modified according to personal preferences, but e-books can.

5. *Instant gratification.* Is it the middle of the night and all the bookstores are closed? Are you tired of waiting days—sometimes weeks—for online and offline bookstores to ship the novels you bought? Ellora's Cave Publishing sells instantaneous downloads 24 hours a day, 7 days a week, 365 days a year. Our e-book delivery system is 100% automated, meaning your order is filled as soon as you pay for it.

Those are a few of the top reasons why electronic novels are displacing paperbacks for many an avid reader. As always, Ellora's Cave and Cerridwen Press welcomes your questions and comments. We invite you to email us at service@ellorascave.com, service@cerridwenpress.com or write to us directly at: 1056 Home Ave. Akron OH 44310-3502.

THE
☥ ELLORA'S CAVE ☥
LIBRARY

Stay up to date with Ellora's Cave Titles in
Print with our Quarterly Catalog.

TO RECIEVE A CATALOG,
SEND AN EMAIL WITH YOUR NAME
AND MAILING ADDRESS TO:

CATALOG@ELLORASCAVE.COM

OR SEND A LETTER OR POSTCARD
WITH YOUR MAILING ADDRESS TO:

CATALOG REQUEST
C/O ELLORA'S CAVE PUBLISHING, INC.
1056 HOME AVENUE
AKRON, OHIO 44310-3502

ELLORA'S
CAVEMEN
LEGENDARY TAILS

Try an e-book for your immediate
reading pleasure or order these titles in print from

WWW.ELLORASCAVE.COM

ELLORA'S CAVE
THE BEST IN TODAY'S ROMANTICA™

erridwen, the Celtic Goddess of wisdom, was the muse who brought inspiration to storytellers and those in the creative arts. Cerridwen Press encompasses the best and most innovative stories in all genres of today's fiction. Visit our site and discover the newest titles by talented authors who still get inspired - much like the ancient storytellers did, once upon a time.

CERRIDWEN PRESS

www.cerridwenpress.com

Discover for yourself why readers can't get enough of
the multiple award-winning publisher
Ellora's Cave.
Whether you prefer e-books or paperbacks,
be sure to visit EC on the web at
www.ellorascave.com
for an erotic reading experience that will leave you
breathless.

www.ellorascave.com